Praise for her novels

"[An] emotionally compelling, subtly nuanced tale of revenge, redemption, and romance . . . This flawlessly written book is worth every tear." —*Chicago Tribune*

"Romance, passion, and thrilling adventure fill the pages of this unforgettable saga that sweeps the reader from England to the Old West." —Rosemary Rogers, *New York Times* bestselling author

"A romance you won't soon forget." —Sara Donati, bestselling author

"Draws readers into the romance and often unvarnished reality of life in nineteenth-century America." —*Library Journal*

"Kaki Warner's warm, witty, and lovable characters shine." —*USA Today*

"Filled with passion, adventure, heartbreak, and humor." —The Romance Dish

"Halfway between Penelope Williamson's and Jodi Thomas's gritty, powerful novels and LaVyrle Spencer's small-town stories lie Warner's realistic, atmospheric romances." —*RT Book Reviews*

"This book is just fabulous." —Smexy Books

"Bring[s] the Old West to sprawling and vivid life." —BookLoons

"This is Western historical romance at its best." —The Romance Reader

Home by Morning

KAKI WARNER

BERKLEY SENSATION, NEW YORK

BERKLEY
SENSATION

An imprint of Penguin Random House LLC
375 Hudson Street, New York, New York 10014

HOME BY MORNING

A Berkley Sensation Book / published by arrangement with the author

ISBN: 978-0-425-26328-0

PUBLISHING HISTORY
Berkley Sensation mass-market edition / July 2015

PRINTED IN THE UNITED STATES OF AMERICA

10 9 8 7 6 5 4 3 2 1

Cover art by Judy York.
Cover design by Lesley Worrell.

Penguin
Random
House

*To my family for their continued love,
support, and understanding.*

My thanks . . .

To all the readers who have taken the characters
of Heartbreak Creek into their hearts. I
appreciate your kind letters and emails,
and hope this final chapter in the saga of
this crusty little town meets your
expectations.

To my editor, Wendy McCurdy, for her patience
and gentle guidance.

To my agent, Nancy Coffey, for her weather
reports and encouraging words.

To all those artists, copyeditors, salespeople,
publicists, and editorial assistants at Berkley
who have worked so hard to help make my
books the best they can be.

To Jodi Thomas, queen of the genre and an
amazingly talented lady who has so
generously given of her support and
expertise throughout the last five years, from
my debut with *Pieces of Sky* in 2010 to this
story of Thomas and Pru. You're a very
special lady.

To all the doctors, veterinarians, horse trainers,
friends, neighbors, family members, and
strangers who have patiently answered my
questions. You know who you are. With
special thanks to Karen Atkerson for her

invaluable help with research—Stephanie
Tucker, beta reader extraordinaire—and
Cyndi Thomson, a great friend, listener, and
crybaby.

I love you all.

Part One

What is life?
It is the flash of a firefly in the night.
It is the breath of a buffalo in the wintertime.
It is the little shadow which runs across the grass
    and loses itself in the sunset.

—Crowfoot, Blackfoot warrior
and orator, 1830–1890

Prologue

In an eagle is all the wisdom in the world.

—Native American proverb

Squinting against bright morning sunlight, Prudence Lincoln stood at the library window of the Friends School for The Betterment of People of Color and studied the letter in her hand.

"*. . . rise from your dreams, Voaxaa'e, and together we will fly away.*"

What did that mean? She knew *Voaxaa'e* was the Cheyenne word for eagle, a fanciful name Thomas had given her months ago. But *fly away* where? Back to Heartbreak Creek?

Their last meeting had been horrid. When she had told him she still had work to do here at the school and needed to stay longer in Schuler, he had allowed his anger and frustration to show. It was the first time Thomas had ever raised his voice to her, and it had frightened her, awakened old memories she still fought hard to keep buried. She had reacted without thinking. When he had seen her cowering before him, arms raised in defense, he had been stunned. Then hurt. And without allowing her to explain, he had walked out the door and had never come back.

Pru's half sister had written from Heartbreak Creek that he

had gone to Britain with Ash and Maddie Wallace to purchase thoroughbreds. But she hadn't heard a word from Thomas.

Terrified that she would never see him again, she had written to him in England, trying to explain her fears.

And now, months later, he responded with this? Bemused, she read again the words written in the familiar bold script she had taught him back in the one-room schoolhouse in Heartbreak Creek, Colorado Territory.

"Look for me, Prudence Lincoln. When the wind blows cold and the Long Night's Moon rides in the sky, I will come to you. Listen for my voice in the shadows. Then rise from your dreams, Voaxaa'e, *and together we will fly away."*

She didn't know whether to laugh or cry.

"Are you ready?" a voice said behind her.

Turning, she saw Cyrus Marsh standing in the doorway beside her valise, one gloved hand on his hip, holding back his overcoat, the other gripping the brim of the hat he tapped impatiently against his leg.

"I can't go, Mr. Marsh." As she spoke, she slipped the letter into her coat pocket, not sure why she didn't want him to see it. She disliked Mr. Marsh, and had from the moment they had met. Despite his practiced smiles and polite words, she sensed an undercurrent of coldness within him.

"Oh?" His blond brows rose in arcs above eyes of such a pale hazel they seemed yellow against his sallow skin. "I'm sorry to hear that, Miss Lincoln. We've gone to a great deal of trouble to make arrangements for you to join us on this trip. May I ask why, at the moment of our departure, you feel you can't go?"

"I'm expecting a visitor. He's coming a long way, and I wouldn't want to miss him."

"Your Indian friend." His voice carried no emotion, but she saw the slight curl in his thin lips. "A woman as beautiful as you, Miss Lincoln, shouldn't waste herself on an ignorant savage."

Pru's chin came up. "Mr. Redstone is neither ignorant nor savage." Most of the time, anyway.

The hat tapped harder, faster.

Behind him, a small figure moved silently through the hall.

Lillie. Eavesdropping again. Pru would have to speak to the girl. Not that it would help. The child had little enough to keep her insatiable curiosity and bright mind occupied, and listening in on the lives of others was her dearest pastime. At least the girl was honorable enough not to repeat the things she heard.

"When do you expect him?" Mr. Marsh asked.

"When the wind blows cold and the Long Night's Moon rides in the sky."

"Mid-December," she guessed. "I'm not sure of the exact date." Possibly around the twenty-first, since that would be the longest night of the year. Thomas's colorful speech was often difficult to decipher.

"Perhaps you could write back and ask him to delay the visit."

"I wouldn't know where to reach him." Pru realized she was rubbing her fingers over the scars on her right wrist and made herself stop. Confrontations made her nervous. Bad enough that Mr. Marsh ordered Brother Sampson around as if he were still a slave, but to have him interfering in her life was intolerable. She had never been a slave, despite her mixed blood, and was unaccustomed to such treatment. Still, as trustee of the school that employed her, he deserved at least a show of respect. "He's traveling from England, you see."

At least that's what Maddie's latest letter had said. The freighter carrying the thoroughbreds, Thomas, and the Wallaces' wrangler, Rayford Jessup, was scheduled to arrive in Boston near the middle of this month. From there, they would travel by rail to Colorado, with stops along the way to rest the horses, which would drag out the journey for several weeks or more. Maddie had concluded by saying she assumed Thomas would stop to visit her on his way through Indiana, and for Pru to expect some changes.

Changes? In Thomas? He was solid as a rock. He certainly had no need to make changes.

"If he's not due until mid-December," Mr. Marsh said, regaining her attention, "that would still leave us ample time to accomplish our purposes in the capitol. I see no problem." Looking pleased, he set his hat on his head. "I'll instruct the school administrator to send word if your Indian arrives before we get back. But should he do so, you can leave a note, telling him you'll return shortly. Schuler is only a six-hour train ride from Indianapolis."

"But things could have gone more smoothly than anticipated," Pru argued. "He might arrive any day. I would like to be here if he does." Being Thomas, if he did arrive and found her gone, he might simply leave. He had a habit of disappearing when things weren't to his liking.

"Miss Lincoln." Marsh paused as if struggling with words—or his temper. Marsh hated to be contradicted, especially by a woman. "You know how important this trip is. Not only for Brother Sampson, but for your education initiative, as well."

"Yes, but—"

"And with backing from important key people in Indianapolis," he went on, ignoring her protest, "the two of you can advance equality and education for blacks more than the Quakers have ever done."

"I understand that, and I—"

"Our efforts could reach all the way to Washington. Isn't that what you want? What we all want?"

"Certainly, but—"

"For God's sake, then why are you defying me? Do you think I'll allow you to ruin everything because of a damned Indian?"

Pru shrank back, old fears flooding her mind.

"Christ." Dropping his hands to his hips, Marsh let go a deep breath.

Moments passed. Tension weighted the air while Pru stood locked in fear, waiting to see what he would do next. *Breathe. Show no fear.*

When he finally spoke again, his voice was as cold as the glint in his near-colorless eyes. "I didn't want to have to resort to threats."

Threats?

Tipping his head to the side, he said in an almost conversational tone, "I know what you've been up to, Miss Lincoln."

Fear ballooned into an almost overwhelming urge to flee. How could he know? How did he find out? "I-I don't know what you're talking about."

"Don't you?" His smile showed small, pointed teeth. A predator's smile. "I know the Underground Railroad has started up again. Only this time, it's not to aid runaway slaves seeking freedom, but to help black felons and agitators escape into

Canada. The misguided fools helping them could go to jail. Or worse. I know you're involved, so don't bother to deny it."

She didn't. "They only want to live free, Mr. Marsh. Instead of being brutalized in the name of Southern Reconstruction."

He waved a hand in dismissal. "Save your speeches. If I could, I would turn the lot of you over to the authorities today."

Perspiration gathered under her arms. "Why do you care if a few desperate colored people seek a better life?"

"I don't. But I do care about Brother Sampson and your education initiative." He leaned toward her, that icy gaze eroding her courage. "The more people who flock to hear him preach, the more exposure your cause will get, and the more opportunities will come my way. A grand future awaits us all . . . as long as there are no scandals. No untoward attention. Nothing to raise questions or generate doubt. Voters can be so fickle."

The hairs on the back of her neck lifted. This was about votes?

"You're an intelligent woman, Miss Lincoln, especially for one of your race. Surely you're aware that you and Brother are my stepping-stones to the real power in Washington. I've invested a great deal of time and effort toward that goal, and I will not allow *anything* to jeopardize those plans."

He moved closer, his yellow eyes burning with the fervor of a fanatic. "So be warned, Miss Lincoln. Behave. Stop this foolish business with the railroad, because if you persist, I will exact a terrible price, if not from you, then from someone dear to you. One of your students, perhaps. Or your Indian. Maybe even Brother Sampson. But rest assured, someone will pay. Do you understand?"

Pru fought to drag air into her lungs. *He's insane. Evil, like Satan is evil.* Just being near him made her feel unclean.

Another step. "Have I made myself clear, Miss Lincoln?"

Pru nodded.

He studied her for a moment, then stepped back, his smile once more in place. "Then we'll speak no more of it." Bending, he picked up her valise. "While I put this in the carriage, you write that note to your Indian. When I return, I'll take it to the administrator, along with my instructions to wire us if Mr. Redstone arrives before we return. And do hurry, Miss Lincoln.

Brother Sampson is waiting, and you know how the cold aggravates his hands."

Light-headed and shaking, Pru watched him leave the room. Terror careened through her mind, muddled her thinking. But one thought kept surfacing. After she finished this last rescue through the railroad, she would tell Brother Sampson about Marsh's motives. Perhaps together they could find a way to stop him. But for now, and for his own safety, she had to send Thomas away.

And there was only one way to do that.

The pain of it almost doubled her over.

On leaden legs, tears streaming, she went to the desk by the window and extracted a piece of paper from the drawer. Struggling to keep her hand steady, she wrote . . .

Dear Thomas,

I fear you misunderstood my last letter to you. I am not seeking a reunion. Our last visit made it clear to me that despite the deep feelings I have for you, we come from such different worlds we could never build a solid future together. I am sorry. Please give everyone my regards when you return to Heartbreak Creek.

I will always remember you fondly.
Prudence Lincoln

One

With an unaccustomed twinge of nervousness, Thomas Redstone paused at the gate in front of a large brick building on the outskirts of Schuler, Indiana. He studied the words on the sign planted in the front yard. With the help of Rayford Jessup, his reading had improved, but it was still troublesome, and he wanted to be certain the sign had not changed since his last visit. It had many words.

The Friends School for the Betterment of People of Color. It was the same.

From inside the building came the distant voices of children chanting their numbers. He pictured Prudence Lincoln standing before them, smiling as she had once smiled at him, her oldest pupil.

Had she received his letter? Would she welcome him? Or would she choose these strangers over him once again, and send him away with more excuses? If so, it would be the last time. He could not spend the rest of his life waiting for her to accept him. If she turned him away this time, he would not come back.

He did not want to think of how empty his days would be if that happened.

Pushing the thought aside, he brushed back his shoulder-length hair and tugged the collar away from his neck so he could breathe. As he walked toward the front porch, he looked around.

The yard was bare but for a leafless willow tree. There was no snow on the ground, and few clouds hung in the sky. Even though it was early morning, the breeze off the Ohio was so gentle it felt like a cool hand against his cheek. Much warmer than in Colorado. For a moment, the horizon beckoned, and the call to return home was strong in his mind. He had been gone many months and had traveled far. He wanted to go back to his snowy mountains.

But first, he must see Prudence Lincoln.

When he started up the steps, he saw a black-skinned girl-child sitting in a chair on the far end of the porch, staring in his direction. She looked small and thin beneath her worn coat, and probably had less than a dozen years. She was darker than Prudence Lincoln, and tiny ribbon-tied braids sprouted from her head like raven feathers from a war bonnet. He wondered why she was not at her lessons with the other children.

"Mornin'," she called. "My name Lillie. It really Lillian, but ev'rybody only call me Lillie."

He nodded without speaking. Setting down the leather pouch holding his extra clothes, he stared at the closed door, that uneasiness rising in him again. He did not like it. Did not like the feeling of doubt that came with it. Irritated at such weakness, he smoothed a hand down the front of his jacket. He did not like these fancy clothes the Scotsman had bought for him, either. Or the boots he had to wear instead of his moccasins. He missed his topknot and eagle feather.

But to honor his white grandfather—and Prudence Lincoln, who was half white—this was the path he had chosen. For now. But once he returned to his mountains, he would cast aside these foolish trappings and become Cheyenne once again.

"Ain't you gonna knock?" the girl called.

He scowled at her for interrupting his thoughts.

She seemed not to notice and continued to stare, her head cocked to one side.

He took a deep breath, let it out, then lifted his fist and pounded on the door.

He stepped back and waited.

Footsteps approached. He stood stiffly as the door opened and a stern-faced old woman in a plain brown dress looked out at him. He did not recognize her from before, when he had left Prudence Lincoln in anger and sailed across the wide water to buy horses.

"How may I help thee?" she asked.

A Quaker. He remembered the strange way they spoke. "You will take me to Prudence Lincoln." Seeing the woman's mouth tighten, he added, "Please."

"Miss Lincoln is not here." The woman tried to close the door.

Thomas stopped it with his hand. "Where is she?"

She blinked round, dark eyes, reminding Thomas of a tiny brown wren. "I was told they went to the capitol."

They? And what was this capitol?

This time, she shut the door before Thomas could stop her. "*Noxa'e!* Wait!"

The footsteps faded into silence.

Muttering, he turned to find the girl rising from her chair.

"I knows you." She reached out to touch the porch rail. "You her Indian, ain't you? Thomas Redstone." She walked closer, one hand on the railing, the other pointed his way. "You a Cheyenne Dog Soldier."

He saw nothing familiar in the girl's face, or in the odd way she looked toward him, but not *at* him. She spoke like other black skins he knew who had been slaves. Not like Prudence Lincoln. She had never been a slave, and her white father had raised her to speak in the white way. *The proper way,* she called it.

Thinking this girl—proper or not—might be more help than the Quaker woman, he put on a smile. "I did not see you when I came here before."

"I not see you, neither," she said and giggled.

Then he understood. Her careful gait. That blank stare. The intent way she listened, her head tilted to one side to catch every sound. "You cannot see."

"Scarlet fever. Three years back when I eight. You sounds tall."

"If you cannot see me, how do you know who I am?"

She continued toward him. When the fingertips of her outstretched hand brushed his coat, she stopped and let her arm fall back to her side. "You talk different from the Friends. Or

Miss Pru. Or anybody." She smiled at his chest. "Can I feel you face?"

He drew back. "Why?"

"That how I learn what you look like."

Forcing down his natural wariness around those marked by the Great Spirit, Thomas bent to within reach of her hands.

Her touch was as soft as a moth's wings. And ticklish. But he stood motionless while she felt everything, even his ears and lips and eyes. When she finally took her hands away, he straightened, glad the ordeal was over. He was not comfortable with such touching, except with Prudence Lincoln. He liked to keep people far enough away that he could see all of them at once and know if a threat was coming. "What did you learn?" he asked.

Another giggle, showing a gap where a front tooth had been. "You gots a big nose and you eyebrows very stern. What color you eyes?"

"Dark, and my nose is not big. What is this capitol the Quaker woman spoke of?"

"Indianapolis. I go there 'fore I blind. It a big place, sho' 'nuff. What color you hair?"

"Black. Why did Prudence Lincoln go there?"

"To raise money for Reverend Brother Sampson and talk 'bout schoolin' fo' black folk." A spark lit the blankness in her brown eyes. "You fetchin' her? She 'posed come back long time ago, but she ain't showed."

Thomas stared past her, plans already forming. If he fetched Prudence Lincoln, it would not be to bring her back here.

"Oh. Well." A deep sigh. "They not let you take her, anyways."

He glared down at her dark head. "Who would stop me?"

"Mistuh Marsh. He say Reverend Brother Sampson need her."

"Tell me of these men."

Leaning over the rail, she groped until her hand brushed a shrub planted beside the porch. Plucking a withered blossom, she sniffed it, then slipped it into her coat pocket before moving down the rail to another plant. "Reverend Brother Sampson a preaching man. He a slave in Kentucky 'fore he come here on the Underground Railroad. Now he preach the Holy Gospel in a big tent. He nice. Always bring me peppermints."

"And the other man?"

She plucked another dead blossom, sniffed, then put it in the pocket with the first. "Mistuh Marsh. He white." Her voice changed. Held a trace of . . . fear? "He take Reverend Brother Sampson 'round so he can preach. This time, he take him to Indianapolis. Miss Pru say folks there maybe send him all the way to Washington to talk to the President."

Thomas knew what a talk with the White Father in Washington meant. More treaties, more broken promises, more trouble for the People. "Why do they need Prudence Lincoln to do this?"

"'Cause she smart. Mistuh Marsh say with her by his side, folks maybe like Reverend Brother Sampson 'nuff to make him a leg-a-slater. I ain't sure what that is. Nobody tell me nothin' 'round here. They think 'cause I blind, I stupid, too."

Thomas frowned. "And Prudence Lincoln? Does she like Reverend Brother Sampson, too?"

"'Course. Everybody do. Even the Friends."

A coldness gripped him. Did that mean she had chosen this man over him? He did not want to believe that. Prudence Lincoln was his heart-mate. But why, then—after he wrote to her that he was coming—was she not here? What was he to do now? Wait for her until he grew old and his days ran out?

He could not do that. He would not live his life that way. Better to walk away now than to be sent away later.

Fury burned away the chill. But it also awakened that part of him too stubborn to give up . . . not even when he hung in agony from the ropes during the Sun Dance ceremony . . . or when he saw his chief killed and the People driven from their lands onto government reservations . . . or when he searched tirelessly, despite his wounds, to find Prudence after the Arapaho renegade took her.

He would not walk away this time. He would go to this other place—this Indianapolis. He would find Prudence Lincoln and tell her what was in his heart. Then he would go back to his mountains. If she chose to stay here, that would be the end of it. He would put her from his life forever.

If he could.

He looked down at the girl staring blankly across the yard, her thin fingers tugging at a loose thread on her worn cuff. "Where is this place called Indianapolis?"

She looked up.

Her eyes might be blank, but he sensed a sharp intelligence hidden behind them. This girl was not stupid.

"You go after her? 'Cause I tell you how to get there. I even get you a map." She leaned closer to whisper at his jacket. "But you gots to take me with you. Miss Pru need both us to get her away from Mistuh Marsh."

Thomas almost smiled, amused that she thought he needed help from a blind girl who probably weighed little more than his bag of extra clothes. "I cannot take you with me."

Chin jutting, she crossed her arms over her chest. "Then I ain't helpin'."

"Goodbye, Lillian." He picked up his leather bag.

"Where you goin'?"

He started down the steps into the yard.

"You cain't jist leave me!" She stumbled forward, hands clutching at air. "A po' blind black girl who ain't got nobody to look out for her, not even a dog to lick away her tears!"

"Go inside, Lillian," he called over his shoulder.

"Don't go!" She flung herself toward him.

With a curse, he dropped the bag and caught her before she flew headfirst down the steps. "You foolish *ka'eskone*," he scolded, setting her back on her feet. "You could have hurt yourself!"

Behind him, the door swung open. A man in a dark collarless coat over a plain white shirt stepped onto the porch. "What's going on out here? Lillie, what mischief have thee gotten into this time?"

When she tucked her head without answering, the Quaker turned his attention to Thomas. "I am Friend Matthews," the older man said. "Administrator of the school. Who might thee be?"

"Thomas Redstone."

"The man seeking Miss Lincoln?"

Thomas nodded.

"Weren't you told she was in Indianapolis?"

"Yes, but I was not told when she will come back."

"We don't know when she'll be back."

Thomas thought for a moment. "She knew I would come. She left no message for me?"

"None that I am aware of. I am sorry, friend." Turning to the girl, he held out his hand. "Come along, child."

"No." The girl fumbled until she found Thomas's hand. Taking it in both of hers, she grinned at the Quaker's stomach. "I'm going with Daddy."

Ten minutes later, Thomas walked back toward the Schuler train station, this time with two bags of clothes and a beaming little black girl by his side.

"I know'd you catch me 'fore I fall down the steps," the girl said, clinging to his arm as they walked along the road. "You a good daddy. Gots any other chilrin 'sides me?"

"No. And I am not your father." He had spoken those words many times . . . to her, the Quaker, and to anyone else who would listen before they were gently, but firmly, herded out the door. The people at the school seemed eager to send the girl away with him. He could guess why.

"I knows you ain't."

"Then why did you tell them I was?"

"'Cause I need a daddy and they wouldn't let me go with you if you wasn't. Slow down. I'm just a po' little blind girl, 'member?"

More like *heavoheso*—a devil—in pigtails. Reining in his temper, Thomas slowed his pace. He did not know what to do with this strange child. He was not a nursemaid. "Where are your parents?"

"You mean 'sides you?"

"I am not your father."

"Don't know where my other daddy is. He sold off 'fore I born. Mama gone to Jesus. Drowned. Up and walk out the field one day, straight into the river. Overseer find her floatin' in the weeds. You know skin turn white and come off you stay in the water too long?"

Thomas kept walking, not sure what to say. The girl had lied about him being her father. Maybe she lied about this, as well. He hoped so.

"Mama always want to be white. Guess she got her wish. She make a pretty white lady, sho' 'nuff. Miss Pru pretty?"

"Yes."

"That probably 'cause she half white."

Thomas smirked at the notion. "It is not the color of her skin that makes her pretty. It is the goodness in her heart." And her smile. And the way she looked at him when he touched her. Would he ever hold her against him again?

"After your mother died, who took care of you, Lillian?"

"Whoever around. When the fightin' stop, Friends come and bring us to freedom lan'. Been here since. They nice, even if they talk funny."

They talk funny? Thomas wondered what Prudence Lincoln thought about the way this girl spoke. He remembered how she had sat beside him, pointing out the letters in her book and teaching him to speak in the proper way. He had not been a good student. It was hard to think about words when she sat so close.

"Hey," the girl said, giving his hand a yank to get his attention. "Since I be your little girl, my name Lillie Redstone now?"

Thomas did not answer.

After a while, they turned onto a side road that ran along the railroad tracks. Up ahead, the depot squatted like a beetle beside a spindly water tower balanced on eight skinny wooden legs. A beetle and a hungry spider. He felt caught in a web, too. He still was not sure what to do when the train came. He could not leave the girl by the tracks. And he could not take her back to the school. Maybe when he found Prudence Lincoln . . .

"She not fo'get."

He looked down at her. "What?"

"Miss Pru. She not fo'get you comin'. She leave you a note, but Mistuh Marsh not give it to Friend Matthews like he say he do."

Thomas smiled. She had remembered.

"And he mean to Miss Pru. Take her to Indianapolis when she want to wait for you. Say she better behave. He a mean one, make Miss Pru cry like that."

Cry? Thomas's steps slowed. *Eho'nehevehohtse* rarely cried. Not even after he freed her from Lone Tree. Or when she tended him after he was shot, and he heard her awake from night terrors. Who was this man and why did he warn her to behave? Prudence Lincoln always behaved. When Thomas was with her, that was his hardest task—to convince her *not* to behave.

But maybe the girl was lying about this, too.

He stopped and looked down at her bent head. "How do you know this?"

"I listen. A shadow on the wall, that me. And I hear Miss Pru say, 'Here the note.' And he say, 'I take it to Friend Matthews right now.' 'Cept he don't. And he don't tell him you comin', neither. Mistuh Marsh, he a damn liar."

"Like you, *okom*?"

"No, I better'n him." She frowned. "What *okom* mean?"

"Coyote."

Lost in thought, Thomas resumed walking, the girl close at his side, her hand on his arm. If Prudence was in trouble, he would help her. But if he had to take this strange child with him, she must obey him so he could keep her safe.

Stopping again, he hunkered onto his heels and gripped her thin shoulders. "Listen well, *Katse'e*."

"Cat see what?"

"*Kat-se'-e*. It is the Cheyenne word for 'little girl.'"

"So I not *okom* no more?" She frowned, her gaze fixed on a distant horizon her eyes could not see. "Cats sneaky. Dogs nicer. And horses. Chickens, they—"

"Never mind that," he said, more harshly than he should have. "Heed my words. From this day, there will be no more lies. You will speak only the truth to me, or I will send you back to the school."

"They not take me."

"Then I will leave you by the tracks with your bag of clothes."

"Fo' true?"

"For true," he lied. "Do you understand?"

"I 'pose." A sniff. "But you not a very nice Daddy."

The quaver in her voice left him unmoved. And unconvinced. "Now you will make your promise to me. You will tell no more lies."

She huffed out a deep breath. "All right. No more lies."

"And you will do what I say."

"That two promises."

"And you will do what I say," he repeated through gritted teeth.

"All right! But we ain't got time for no more promises, Daddy. I hears the train comin'."

Behind him, a locomotive whistle blew. With a sigh, Thomas

rose. If Prudence Lincoln sent him away again, he would leave this devil-child with her. It would serve them both right.

Several hours later, as the sun began to slip behind the trees, their train rolled into Indianapolis. The girl had been talking when Thomas dozed off, and was still talking when he awoke. She had strong lungs.

And she was right. Indianapolis was a big place. Not as big as the city where the English queen lived and people spoke with a strange accent. But bigger than Schuler. With the girl anchored in one hand, and their bags of clothes gripped in the other, Thomas stepped outside the depot and looked around.

People rushed along the street as if they had someplace important to be. Many stared at them as they went by. Thomas wished he had brought his war axe instead of sending it on to Heartbreak Creek with Rayford Jessup. But he had his long knife under his jacket, tucked into his belt at his back. That would be enough if danger came.

"We just stand here all day?" the girl complained.

She was probably hungry after so much talking.

"I will find food," he announced, and led her in the direction most of the people were headed. Before they had walked far, they came to a place that had a strong smell of cooking meat. He led the girl inside.

A worried-looking woman with fox-red hair rushed to meet them. "Coloreds ain't allowed," she whispered, looking around at the other tables and the white people sitting there.

"Allowed to do what?" he asked.

"Eat here. Roy, you better come."

A big man with hair on his face and angry eyes came from behind a counter where a brass money box sat. "Look here, mister—"

"Don't hurt him!" Lillian shrieked, pressing against Thomas's arm. "He only tryin' to find my mama 'cause I a po' little blind girl and cain't find my way! He mean no harm!"

The man called Roy looked at her in surprise. Thomas did, too. The white people watching from the tables muttered to one another.

"We leavin'," Lillian cried, almost yanking Thomas off

balance and into the branches of a plant in a pot beside the door. "Please don't hurt us, mistuh. We just hungry, is all. Don't mean no harm."

"Roy, let me take them around back," the woman whispered. "Cook can give them something and send them on their way." When the man hesitated, she gave his arm a shake. "For heaven's sake, Roy, the child is blind, and people are looking."

"I will pay," Thomas said.

A few minutes later, he was carrying the girl with her box of food across the tracks toward a grassy field. "You promised no more lies," he reminded her.

"Somebody gotta do somethin'. You jist stand there like a big lump while my belly scream for food."

Setting her down beside a stump, he dropped the clothes bags and looked around. In the distance, a big white tipi stood in the middle of a grassy meadow. People went inside. Others hurried to follow. Along the edge of the field, food carts lined up along the street. Soon the smell of cooking hung in the air.

Perched on the stump, the girl dug through the box of food. "'Sides, it not a lie. We lookin' for my mama, sho 'nuff."

"You said your mother was dead."

"That my other mama. You hungry?" She pulled a chicken leg out of the box, sniffed it, then took a bite. "Tasty. Got biscuits in here, too. Want some?"

Taking a share of the food, Thomas settled beside the stump. While he ate, he watched people go into the big tipi. None came out.

The girl finished eating and wiped her hands on the stump. "Where we sleep? Not outside. Chilrin ain't 'posed sleep outside. 'Pecially blind ones." She suddenly stiffened and cocked her head. "That gospel singin'? There a church nearby?"

Thomas was surprised he had not heard it, but she was right. From inside the tent came the sound of many voices singing a tune he recognized as one he had heard coming from the Come All You Sinners Church of Heartbreak Creek. "Yes, there is singing."

"Maybe it the tent meetin'."

Thomas took a bite of chicken.

"You Injuns not talk much." She pulled her coat tight around her thin body. "How long we sit here, Daddy? I gots to pee. And I liable freeze dead we don't find Miss Pru soon."

Thomas tossed his chicken bone into the brush. "We just did."

Two

Prudence Lincoln studied the eager faces singing with such fervor the glorious sound of it filled the tent. There were even a few whites in attendance—other than Marsh, the devil in the shadows—and more came every night. Latecomers stood three deep along the canvas walls, and come spring, assuming they made a return trip to Indianapolis, Brother Sampson would have to hold his gospel meetings outdoors to make room for the ever-increasing converts that flocked to hear him preach the Lord's Word.

They wanted so badly to believe things would get better.

Seeing the joy in their faces brought a catch to her throat. Their hope raised hers, lifting her spirits from the fog of anxiety that had plagued her ever since they'd come to the capitol almost three weeks ago.

Had Thomas arrived in Schuler yet? Had Friend Matthews given him her note? Would he leave, as she hoped, or try to come here? He was a stubborn man.

As much as she wanted to see him, she hoped he would go on to Heartbreak Creek. If he came here and Marsh acted on his threats . . .

With effort, she pushed that unbearable thought away. Nothing would happen to Thomas. More likely something would befall Marsh should the Cheyenne warrior learn of his threats. Thomas was very protective. And lethal.

"Thank you for coming," Brother Sampson called as the last notes of the closing hymn faded away. "May the Lord shelter and protect you. Bless you all."

Rising from her chair behind the lectern, she came forward to join him in greeting the people filing past the small platform that served as a stage. Despite his twisted fingers, the good preacher took the time to shake every hand offered, and his smile never faltered, no matter how weary he was.

When the crowd finally began to thin, she turned to him with a smile.

Then froze. A tall, solemn figure stood by the tent opening, his gaze locked on her face.

Thomas.

She stared, one hand pressed to her throat, her heart beating like a wild thing. Tears burned in her eyes, but she quickly blinked them away, not wanting to lose sight of the face that drifted through her dreams every night.

People shifted, obstructed her view. She started forward, searching frantically until a gap widened and she saw him again.

He looked different with his glossy black hair reaching barely to his shoulders. Gone were the topknot and eagle feather. If he still wore temple braids, they were tucked behind his ears. Instead of his war shirt and leggings and tall, fringed moccasins, he wore a fine suit of clothes and sturdy boots.

But he was still her Cheyenne warrior. No matter how he dressed, he would always be that.

Had he gotten her note? If so, why was he here?

On trembling legs, she hurried down the open space between the rows of crude benches. People blocked her way as they shuffled toward the exit. Straining to see past them, terrified he would disappear before she could reach him, she pushed through them as best she could.

When finally the way cleared and she saw him again, she could only stare through tear-blurred eyes, still not believing he was there. He didn't give her that startling smile that turned heads, but she saw the quirk at the corner of his wide mouth and the warmth in his dark eyes. Suddenly everything else was forgotten—Marsh and his threats—her fears—even the work she was so desperate to finish.

"You're here," she said and reached out with a trembling hand.

"Me, too!" A small figure darted from behind him, arms outstretched.

Startled, Pru drew back, her hand hanging in the air. She blinked down at the round face beaming up at her with the familiar gap-toothed grin. "Lillie?"

"It me!" Giggling, the child clasped Pru's waist in a tight hug. "Praise the Lawd we find you!"

"Wh-What are you doing here?"

"Me and Daddy come fetch you home."

Daddy? Pru looked at Thomas. His face told her nothing, yet his eyes showed amusement. Dark, deep-set eyes the color of strong, black coffee. She could drown in them. "Why does she think you're her father?"

He shrugged, as spare with words as he was with his smiles. Pulling Lillie's arms from around her waist, Pru looked down into the child's face. "What is this about, Lillie?"

"We worried."

"About what?"

"Mistuh Marsh. He close?"

Pru looked around and saw him speaking to Brother Sampson and one of the patrons who had paid for their travel expenses to Indianapolis and their rooms at the colored hotel. "No. He can't hear us."

The girl motioned for Pru to bend closer. "He not give you note to Friend Matthews," she whispered. "And he not tell him Daddy on his way."

So Thomas hadn't read her note. Pru straightened, a jittery feeling of panic battling a sense of relief. He was here. For now that was all that mattered.

"Did he threaten you, *Eho'nehevehohtse*?"—One Who Walks in Wolf Tracks—another fanciful name Thomas had given her, this one referring to someone as smart as a wolf, and able to outwit humans.

She forced a smile. "He's all bluster," she lied. "Nothing to worry about." Being truthful to his core, Thomas often didn't see dishonesty in those he trusted. But she dare not let him know the danger Marsh posed. The Cheyenne was capable of great violence when necessary or if someone he cared about was threatened. She loved that about him—and feared the consequences of it.

Noticing Lillie rubbing her eyes, Pru gratefully sought a change in subject. "Lillie looks tired. Have you found a place to stay?"

"We stay with you," the girl said, yawning. "I not sleep outside."

"Of course not." Seeing Marsh shake hands with the patron and fearing he might head their way, Pru motioned Thomas toward the exit behind him. "If you don't mind staying at a colored hotel," she said, as they stepped outside, "I'm sure they have room. The Beckworth Arms, two blocks south of the depot on Third. Do you have money?"

Thomas nodded. "The Scotsman pays well."

"I'm in room two eleven. I'll leave the door unlocked. Go now. I'd rather Mr. Marsh not know you're here."

"Do you fear him?"

"Of course not, but—"

"Come on, Daddy," Lillie cut in, saving Pru from further explanation. "It cold and I still gots to pee."

"We'll talk later, Thomas, I promise." On impulse, Pru reached out and put her hand on his arm. Feeling the solid strength beneath the sleeve of his jacket reassured her. Gave her courage. "I'm so glad you're here." And she meant it. Despite her worries over Marsh, she was relieved her note hadn't reached Thomas. Knowing she wasn't alone and that he was nearby was a great comfort.

Thomas studied her in that silent, probing way he had. She could almost feel him searching her mind, seeking answers to questions he hadn't voiced. Then, with a nod, he turned and led Lillie into the fading light.

It was late. And still no Thomas. Had something happened? Or was he not as anxious to see her as she was to see him?

Rising from the worn chair flanking the bed, Pru paced her small hotel room. After a few laps, she stopped at the window and looked out at the deserted street, her mind spinning with possibilities.

Could Marsh have waylaid him? She thrust that frightening thought away. Perhaps Thomas hadn't been able to get a room. Many places barred Indians. Or maybe Lillie was proving difficult and he didn't want to leave her until she was asleep. But how could he leave her, anyway—a blind child in a strange place? What if she woke up and found herself alone?

She should check with the desk, find out what room they were in—or if they were even at the hotel—then go to him. Resolved, she turned from the window and almost slammed into a tall form standing directly behind her.

She stumbled back, then felt his hand on her arm, steadying her. "Thomas? I didn't hear you come in."

"Then you were not listening."

Relief thundered through her. "Oh, Thomas," she choked out, throwing her arms around him. Now that he was here, all thought of sending him away fled her mind. Later, she would find another way to keep him safe. But for now, all she wanted was the comfort of his arms. "I was so afraid you wouldn't come."

"You doubt me, *Eho'nehevehohtse*?"

"No. I would never doubt you. It's just that . . ." She took a deep breath, drawing in the earthy scent that was his own. It seemed that no matter how many months or miles separated them, the moment she saw him again, it felt as if they had never been apart. "I've missed you so much."

"I have missed you, too, Prudence."

But he didn't pull her closer as he usually did. And even though she was close enough to feel the warmth of his breath against the top of her head, she sensed a space between them.

Leaning back, she looked up into his face. "Aren't you glad to see me?"

"Always, *Eho'nehevehohtse*."

Yet he didn't stop her when she pulled away. "You don't show it."

"No?" Taking her hand, he placed it on his chest. "Can you not feel how you stir my heart?"

"Then why do you act as if you're afraid to touch me?"

"Because I am. I do not want to frighten you like I did when last we were together."

She sagged with relief. "You didn't frighten me. What happened before . . . it wasn't you, Thomas. You could never frighten me."

"Then why did you cower before me?"

"I was startled. You were angry, and for a moment . . ."

He finished when she couldn't. "You thought of the Arapaho."

She made an offhand gesture. "It's nothing." And why were they even talking about this now?

"A fear that makes you shrink from me is 'nothing'?" Taking her face in both hands, he looked into her eyes. "You will banish him from your thoughts, Prudence. He can never hurt you again."

She felt walls come up in her mind. To distract herself—and him—she turned her face into his hand and kissed his callused palm. "I don't want to talk about Lone Tree right now."

"You will have to someday, *Eho'nehevehohtse*."

She drew back. "I know." Terrors she had long suppressed skittered through her mind and sent her moving restlessly about the room. Aware of his gaze following her, she battled a momentary resentment. Thomas would never let fear rule him. He would dance a reel around danger and smile the whole time.

She paused to straighten a book on her night table, making sure it aligned precisely with the edge, then continued pacing, touching this and that. "It's just that sometimes, something happens that makes me remember, and I overreact." And Lone Tree would rise up in her mind, ready to pounce. "But I'm doing better."

"He was Indian. I am Indian. But we are not the same."

"Of course not. I'm sorry. I'll try harder. Do we have to talk about this now?"

"Prudence."

Just that. Only her name. Said in the low, husky voice of a man who spoke seldom, and not at all to her for the last several months. She pressed the heel of her hand against her brow to stop a sudden sting of tears. She didn't want to show weakness before this strong man.

Yet, somehow, he knew. He always knew.

Moving toward her, he pulled her into his arms. "Do not be afraid to weep, *Eho'nehevehohtse*," he whispered against her hair. "It will free your mind of sorrowful thoughts."

She didn't want to cry. Didn't want their first meeting after so long an absence to be filled with sorrow. But with the release of tension, tears broke in a flood. Knowing that he was here and hadn't given up on her, and that for a while, at least, she could let down her guard and rest in his arms, filled her with a raw, instinctual wanting that stripped her bare.

"I am here with you, Prudence. I will keep you safe. You know this."

She nodded, unable to speak, pushing to the back of her mind the awareness that Lone Tree wasn't the only barrier between them.

Rocking her gently in his arms, he held her for a long time.

This man was life to her. Hope. He had found her broken with despair and had put her back together again. He was her way out of the past and into a safe and loving future . . . once they got beyond the threat of Marsh, and *if* they could overcome the obstacles before them.

But not tonight. Tonight she only wanted to hold him, and love him, and lose herself in his strength. Pulling out of his arms, she laced her fingers through his, and led him over to sit beside her on the edge of the bed. His hand felt rough and big against hers. Familiar, yet alien. That single contact of flesh against flesh made her body tremble with awareness.

"Why is Lillie with you, Thomas?"

"The school believed her when she said I was her father. They seemed glad to send her with me." She saw the smile in his beautiful, dark eyes.

"What are you going to do with her?"

He shrugged, his shoulder rubbing against hers. "She chose me to be her father. She needs someone to take care of her. So that is what I will do."

Pru knew the loss of his wife and son years ago haunted him still. Was taking on Lillie his way to atone for that? "She can be a difficult child."

This time his smile included a flash of white teeth. "This I know. But I admire her spirit."

"Will you take her back to Heartbreak Creek?"

He studied her for a long time, his gaze boring into her in that knowing way that reached so deep inside her mind she felt stripped bare. "You say 'you' instead of 'we.' Does that mean you are still not ready to come home, Prudence?"

Dread moved through her. She knew that was the question he had come to ask—the same question he had asked on his last visit, and the visit before that: When would she give up this dream of helping every ex-slave who crossed her path and come back to him?

And do what?

There was some truth in the note she had written him. Their differences were vast. She couldn't live in a tipi any more than Thomas could live in a city. She needed people around her, not a life of isolation in the mountains. And she needed to do something for all the poor, lost freed men and women who had never been given the advantages she had. Guilt at what they had suffered while she'd lived an easy life rode like a demon on her back. She couldn't simply walk away from people so desperate for help.

But she couldn't walk away from Thomas, either.

"Just give me a little more time. Please, Thomas." Once she had her education initiative going, and she felt she could turn over her part in the Underground Railroad, she would be able to leave.

She saw his chest rise and fall on a deep sigh and knew she had disappointed him again. She had a sense of him slipping away and tightened her grip on his hand. Maddie had been right. He had changed. Not just that he had cut his hair and put away his Indian attire. There was something fundamentally different. It frightened her, made her wonder what other changes had come about while he was in England. "Can't you wait just a little longer? I'll be done soon."

For a long time, he didn't speak. "You weaken me, *hem-e'oone*—sweetheart. When I am with you, I think only of how much I want you."

"Is that a bad thing?"

When he didn't answer, she looked over and saw the frown on his face.

"I do not know, *Eho'nehevehohtse*. Being apart from you leaves an ache inside me I cannot find. It is a wound that will not heal. But when I look on your face, it hurts a little less." Lifting his other hand, he reached over and gently brushed aside a curl that had escaped her pins. She felt the slight tremble in his fingers and wanted to weep.

But this wasn't the time for sadness. She didn't want to ruin their time together with fears about the past or the future.

"I'm sorry." Tipping her head against his shoulder, she blocked her doubts and let his familiar scent flood her senses—earth, sunshine, strong healthy male. "I've missed you, Thomas."

"Have you?"

Confused by the question, she drew back to study his face. His expression told her nothing, but she sensed that change again. "What's wrong?"

"I am troubled."

"By what?"

He made a vague gesture with his free hand. "This. You and me." His dark eyes carried an unfamiliar hint of sadness, which brought an ache to her heart. "A space grows between us, Prudence. I understand that you seek things beyond the mountains and Heartbreak Creek. Beyond me."

When she started to interrupt, he held up his hand. She thought she saw that tremble again in the long, blunt-tipped fingers, but decided she must have imagined it. Nothing ever rattled Thomas.

"I feel you drifting away, *Eho'nehevehohtse*," he continued in that same strained voice. "I have tried to accept that. But I cannot. You are like a second heart beating inside me. But if it is not to be, and I must pluck you from my life, I will try one last time to understand why."

She should stop this now. He had opened the door. All she had to do was say the words that would send him away and keep him safe from Marsh. Save them both from future heartache.

But how could she do that to the man she loved with all her heart?

Loving Thomas was such a bittersweet thing. She didn't know where this odd, mismatched relationship was headed or how it would end, and she liked to have the pieces of her life neatly arranged, each in its own place. But she couldn't do that with him. She didn't know where to put this man who held her heart in such a gentle grip. She didn't know if his vision of the future would ever meld with hers. But sending him away would be like casting aside all hope of a better life.

"So now I ask you, Prudence. What is it you want?"

Time. A different world.

She looked up into his dark, fathomless eyes . . . eyes that had seen all her scars and imperfections and loved her still. She didn't understand it. Or this bond that went deeper than thought or emotion or physical need. It was as if he had tethered her soul to his in a way that could never be broken. Heartmates, he had called them. Perhaps he was right.

"I want you, Thomas."

"For how long?"

"For as long as you will stay with me."

She could see it wasn't the answer he wanted. "You will not come back with me to the mountains?"

"I can't. Not yet."

"Then when? How long must I wait and hope you will return to me?"

"I will always return to you, Thomas. I just need to finish this first."

Even though he didn't move, she felt that distance between them widen a little more. "I am past my first youth, *Eho'nehevehohtse*. I cannot wait forever."

"It won't be long."

He snorted. "Only until another thing comes between us, and you ask for more time again. I cannot live on promises of *later*, Prudence."

Panic clutched at her throat. "Don't go. Please."

He studied her, then he let out a long exhale. It sounded like defeat. "I will stay until I know you are safe from this man named Marsh. Then I will go. If you do not come with me, I will know you have chosen a different path."

The tears of gratitude overflowed, spilling down her face in hot streaks. "Thank you, Thomas."

He stood. "Enough talk. You will undress now."

She smiled even as she blotted the tears from her cheeks. His arrogance always amused her. "Will I?"

He smiled, that spark flaring behind his eyes. "You will."

An answering heat spread through her body. "What about Lillie?"

"She sleeps."

"And if she wakes up?"

"She knows where I am and will wait for my return. Do not worry so much." Putting his big hands around her waist, he stood her on her feet in front of him. "She is only next door. I will hear if she needs me." Head bent, he worked at the buttons down the front of her dress. "And I left her my knife."

Pru's head flew up, bumping against his chin. "Your knife?"

Pushing the fabric aside, he leaned down to kiss her neck.

"She's blind, Thomas! And a child! She could hurt herself."

Another kiss on her jaw. "She is a child who has lived a hundred years." He continued to loosen the buttons on her dress so he could lick the hollow at the base of her neck. "Little *okom* is blind, not helpless." With his tongue, he traced the scars across her shoulder

It was hard to breathe and think when he did that. "Still—"

He straightened, a frown bunching between his dark brows. "Why do you waste our time with arguments, *Eho'nehevehohtse*? You know I cannot stay with you for long."

He was right. He couldn't be away from Lillie much longer. Besides, with Thomas's acute hearing, he would hear if Lillie called out to him. These walls were woefully thin.

Resolved, she leaned into him and let her worries slip away. Simply having him so close made her tremble with want. Her breath grew shallow. A shimmery, itchy feeling made her desperate to cast off her clothing and press her shivering body against his.

He skimmed his knuckles across the fabric over her breast. "I grow impatient. You will finish undressing now, Prudence."

Three

A warm rush of anticipation fluttered in her belly. With fumbling fingers, Pru did as she was told, aware of his gaze tracking every movement. When she pulled the dress down her arms, he trailed his fingers gently over the pattern of pale scars spreading across her shoulder and one side of her chest.

Those same scars had enraged Lone Tree, driven him into a kicking fury. Perhaps he'd feared they were the mark of the devil, as her father's wife had called them. Or he was angry that she didn't cry out as the blows had rained down. Or maybe he had beaten her for fun. The man was less than an animal, from the rankness of his unwashed body and the venom that spewed from his mouth, to the wild, inhuman glitter in his eyes.

But that was over a year ago. She was safe now, and with a shuddering breath, she blocked the image and sent the Arapaho scuttling back into the darkest corner of her mind. Now was the time for loving, not remembering.

She kicked off her shoes and let the dress fall around her ankles. Then, untying the tabs on her petticoats, she let them slide down to pool over the dress.

And still he watched, his face taut.

It awakened that pulse low in her body and made her limbs weak.

With her hand braced on his sturdy shoulder for balance,

she lifted one knee, then the other, to roll down her garters and serviceable black stockings. After she unlaced her corset and stepped out of her drawers, she stood before him, wearing only her mended cotton chemise and a nervous smile.

He studied the garments piled on the floor. "White people wear too many clothes."

"I'm only half white."

He looked up. She saw desire . . . and laughter . . . in his eyes. "So you wear only half too many?" Before she could answer, he gave the strap of her chemise a tug. "You will finish now." He slipped off his jacket and hung it over the back of the chair, then sat on the edge of the bed to pull off his boots.

Pru lifted the chemise over her head and tossed it aside. Steeling herself, she watched his gaze move over her in that intimate, possessive way. When his eyes finally met hers, she saw only love reflected there. And hunger.

It made her whole body clench.

"Where is your nightdress?"

She pulled her flannel gown from beneath her pillow.

"Put it on."

"Now?"

He nodded. Once she'd slipped it over her head, he rose and pulled back the covers on the bed. "Lie down."

She did, scooting over to make room for him beside her. She was trembling now, her skin prickly with desire, her nerves humming. It was always that way with Thomas. With a glance, a touch, a few words, or only a smile, he could break through all her fears to find that passionate woman beneath.

But instead of undressing, he pulled the covers over her, then stretched out atop them. Feet crossed, his shoulder against hers, he leaned his back against the headboard.

Confused, she rose up on one elbow and frowned at him. "What are you doing? We're not . . . You don't want me?"

A crooked smile showed the edge of his strong white teeth and the dimple in his cheek. He gestured to the bulge in his trousers. "Do I not?"

His interest was apparent. And gratifying. "I don't understand."

He brushed a hand over her hair. "As much as I would like

to join with you, Prudence, I will not risk making a child until
you decide if you will stay with me."

Pregnancy might not be much of a risk. Lone Tree's vicious
kicks had left her bleeding for days, and her courses had been
irregular ever since. And in the previous few times she and
Thomas had come together, she hadn't conceived. Perhaps she
was barren. The thought left a hollow place in her heart.

"If I bear a child, we'll raise it together," she told him.

"In Heartbreak Creek?"

"Yes."

He was silent for a time. "And how will I know, Prudence,"
he finally said, "whether you came to me because of the child,
or because being with me was what you wanted?" He gave a
small, sad smile. "No, *heme'oone*. This is best. Come. Lie beside
me and tell me what has kept you apart from me for so long."

With a sigh of frustration, she curled against him, her cheek
resting on the arm he slid beneath her neck. "I would rather
hear about England, and Maddie's confinement, and Rayford
Jessup's new wife." She cuddled closer, lulled by his warmth,
his scent, and the steady thrum of his heart beneath her ear.
"And you."

"What do you want to know, *Eho'nehevehohtse*?"

"To start with . . . why did you cut your hair?"

Thomas thought for a moment, not sure of the right words.
Some things did not move well from Cheyenne to English. "To
look more white," he finally said.

She tipped her head back and looked at him in surprise.
"You don't want to be Cheyenne anymore?"

He smirked at the notion. "I will always be Cheyenne, Prudence. But there is a part of me that is also white." His smile
faded. "I also did it for you."

"For me? Why?"

"So I would be more acceptable to you." When she started
to protest, he shook his head, sending a fall of dark, glossy
hair over his brow. He shoved it back with his thin temple
braids, annoyed that his shorter hair would not stay behind his
ears like his long hair had. He should cut it even shorter, or let

it grow. "I know there are times, Prudence, when my Indian ways confuse and trouble you."

"Only because I don't understand them. Not because I don't like them."

"I am glad." Lost in thought, he trailed his fingertips along her arm. "I also did it to honor my grandfather. The People believe that to know a man, you must walk for a time in his moccasins. So now I walk in my grandfather's tracks and hope that he will give me the wisdom to understand the pale skins who have overrun our land."

He noted her stillness and wondered what she was thinking. She, too, carried mixed blood. He knew the evidence of his own white blood showed in his height and paler skin. But he did not know if she liked that or not.

"Tell me about him," she said.

It took him a moment to work the words out in his mind. Patting her head back onto his chest, he pulled the covers over her shoulder to keep her warm, then began. "He was a trapper. He visited our camp many times, trading for furs. One day he saw a young girl and was so taken with her beauty he wanted her for his own. But she was too young to take a mate, so he waited. Whenever he came to our village, he brought gifts for her family and stayed longer each time. He began to learn our ways and often went hunting with the men. When the girl was old enough, they married. Later, they had a daughter, who was to become my mother."

"Did he stay with your tribe after that?"

"Sometimes." She stroked his chest, making it hard for him to concentrate. "He was an old man when I knew him, but the tribal elders held him in much esteem. He understood the changes ahead and tried to warn us. More whites would cross the prairie in their long wagon trains. Bluecoats would treat our land as if it belonged to them. Forts and trading posts would rise along every river.

"But few listened. The young warriors thought only of war and driving the invaders away. It was a difficult time for us. My grandfather counseled the old ones to make peace before it was too late. Many resisted. In the end, they were defeated and the whites took everything, even the sacred land where our ancestors rest."

"And yet you cut your hair so you would become more like them."

He looked down at the slim fingers sliding between the buttons on his shirt. The feel of her skin against his sent a shock of arousal all through his body. "Not to *become* like them, Prudence. Only to look like them." Determined to stop her explorations while he still could, he rested his hand over hers. "Do not do that."

"Do what?"

"You know what. And if I am to be part of the white man's world," he went on, seeking to distract them both, "then I must look less threatening."

Laughing, she pulled her hand from beneath his and patted his cheek. "Silly man. It's not the length of your hair that makes you appear threatening. Or your scars. Or the words you speak. It's the way you say them. Without equivocation or doubt. That unshakable confidence shows in everything you do—in the way you move, what you say, how you observe the world around you. Some," she added with a knowing smile, "might call it arrogance."

"This troubles you?"

She stretched up to kiss his strong jaw, than settled once more against his side. "I envy you. You're so comfortable within yourself you don't need the attention of others. Yet you get it anyway by simply walking into the room."

"You want such attention?" Did she not know that men watched her with hunger in their eyes, and women coveted her beauty?

"Heavens no. I much prefer being in the background. But I do envy your confidence and your willingness to meet the world's challenges head-on."

"That is the big difference between us, Prudence. I want to challenge the world and you want to change it."

"Can't we do both?"

"I do not know. We each will do what we must to find our place in this white world." Dipping his head down, he pressed his lips to hers.

It was a quick, hard kiss that made her hunger for more. But when she tried to pull him down again, he slid his arm from beneath her head and rose from the bed. "You sorely tempt me, *heme'oone*—sweetheart," he said with that crooked smile. "But it is best if I go back to *Katse'e* before she wakes and finds me gone."

Folding her arms atop the blanket, Pru leaned against the headboard as he retrieved his boots, then sat beside her on the edge of the bed to pull them on. She watched muscles bunch and stretch beneath his shirt while his comment circled in her mind. Did he think her drive to teach ex-slaves was because she wanted to fit into the white world? Didn't he know that no matter what either of them did, they would always be on the outside of that chosen circle?

As if reading her thoughts, he turned and rested his hand on her hip. A gesture of possession. That connection again. "I know you want to help the blacks who were slaves, Prudence. That is a good thing. A thing I want to do, too, for the People."

"How?"

His chin came up in that stubborn way he had whenever he felt challenged. Taking his hand away, he bent to slide his trouser cuffs over the tops of his boots, keeping his head down so she couldn't read his expression. "I wrote a book."

The answer was so unexpected it took her mind a moment to accept it. She sat up, too stunned to hide her surprise. She had taught Thomas his letters and numbers at the school in Heartbreak Creek, but she didn't think him advanced enough to write an entire book. "A book about what?"

"Chief Black Kettle." Seeing her confusion, he explained. "Before his death at Sand Creek, he told me to go out into the world and learn the white ways so we would know how to defeat them. But when I returned, after my wife and son were taken from me, it was too late. The People were already being herded onto reservations. I stayed behind, thinking I could use my white blood to help them. But there was little I could do."

He frowned down at the clenched fists resting on his thighs, battling the frustration that never seemed to leave his mind. "The time for war is past, so now I will fight with words. Rayford Jessup helped me write them down. We finished when we sailed over the big water, and he sent the papers we wrote to a man in England who will put them into a book."

When her shock prevented her from responding right away, he looked over at her, his expression daring her to mock him.

Instead, she threw her arms around him. "I'm so proud of you, Thomas! An entire book! That must have been very difficult to do."

He shrugged, but she saw the quirk of a pleased smile at the corner of his mouth.

"Will you write another? If so, perhaps I can help you."

"You will be too busy."

"Doing what?"

Laughing, he whipped around in one of those lightning moves that seemed impossible for a man his size and pinned her on her back. "Doing this," he said, and kissed her. One kiss led to another, then another, until they were both breathless and she had forgotten what they had been talking about.

"We have been apart too long." Pushing the covers aside, he kissed her breast through the thin fabric of her gown. "We have much to make up for."

She arched to his touch, all her pent-up desire rising again in a warm rush. "Stay with me," she said breathlessly. "Just for tonight."

His mouth stilled. With a sigh, he straightened, covered her breast, then rose. "I cannot. But I will keep you safe from the man you call Marsh."

A chill swept her. "What makes you think he's a threat to me?"

He looked down at her, his face set in implacable lines. All warrior now. "Why does he warn you to behave?"

She blinked in surprise, wondering how he knew, then remembered the small figure in the hallway the day they had left for Indianapolis. "Lillie told you."

His dark brows drew low over his deep-set eyes. "Did you think you could keep it from me, Prudence? That I would not see the fear in your eyes?" Muttering in Cheyenne, he lifted his jacket from the chair. He walked to the door, then stopped. Without facing her, he said, "Tomorrow you will tell me of this man. And of the one who speaks in the big tipi. Then I will decide what to do."

"You'll do nothing!" Fear sent her scrambling off the bed. "Just leave it be."

He turned, the jacket hanging in his grip. "You defend this man?"

"No!" She made a dismissive gesture. "Marsh is nothing. A nobody. He shouldn't even concern you."

"Did he not threaten you, *Eho'nehevehohtse*?" he asked in a tight voice.

She stared mutely at him. Thomas might be lethal, but he was also honorable. He would be no match for the deviousness of a man like Cyrus Marsh.

When she didn't answer, he nodded. "So he does concern me."

Desperate to stop him before something terrible happened, she gentled her tone. "He's my employer, Thomas. I don't want any trouble. Please."

Grim-faced, he turned toward the door.

"Promise me you won't start anything," she pleaded.

He hesitated, one hand on the door latch. "I will not start anything." He looked back at her, and the malice in his smile almost drove the air from her lungs. "But I will finish what he has begun. That is what I will promise to you."

Thomas awoke to a scream, a knee in his belly, and someone crawling over his chest. Fearing a knife would come next, he grabbed the flailing arms and struggled to catch his breath. "Lillian, be still."

"Daddy? That you?"

He saw no knife, and slumped back. "Yes. *To'estse*—get up."

She plopped beside him. "Lawdy. I thought you Cooter Brown."

"Who is Cooter Brown?"

"Old drunk boogeyman who not fight. What you doing on the floor?"

"Sleeping. Why would he not fight?" The idea was alien to Thomas.

"'Fraid, I 'pose. You not sleep in bed?"

"Not if someone else is already in it." Unless that someone was Prudence Lincoln. He smiled, remembering how she had trembled beneath his hands and the little sounds she had made when he'd kissed her hours ago. He liked making her forget all her proper ways. He liked making her cry out his name.

"When we eat? My stomach howling."

Images of a warm, soft body faded on a sigh. He rolled onto his feet. "Put on your clothes and we will go."

Several minutes later, they walked downstairs to the room called a lobby, where they found Prudence Lincoln sitting with the man who had spoken in the big white tipi the previous night. Thomas saw no sign of the other man, Marsh.

Smiling, Prudence rose. The man rose, too, but hung back when Prudence came to meet them. Thomas studied him.

He was broad rather than tall, with a round face and no hair on his head. His skin was the color of the rich, brown earth along a slow-moving river. His hands were damaged, as if they had been broken in the past and left to heal wrong. The fingers were as bent as twisted twigs. He had the eyes of a man who had seen much, and suffered more.

Prudence stopped before him and *Katse'e*. "What happened to your braids, Lillie?"

"Daddy hands too big to make 'em."

Thomas had done his best, but the girl's wiry hair poked out in all directions. Whenever he tried to flatten it down, it sprang back up.

Prudence eyed the temple braids tucked behind his ears. "Who did yours?"

"The man who cut my hair. He did not want to put in the braids." Thomas gave a tight smile. "But I convinced him it would be a good thing to do."

"When we eat?" Lillian cut in. "I so hungry my belly cavin' in."

"Ladies don't talk about their bellies," Prudence reminded her as she led them to the waiting black man. "The hotel has a lovely tearoom here. After we say hello to Brother Sampson I'll get you a muffin."

"Jist one?"

The man smiled in welcome, but Thomas saw sadness in his dark eyes.

"Thomas, please meet Reverend Brother Sampson. Brother, this is Thomas Redstone, the Cheyenne Dog Soldier I told you about."

The man's smile broadened. "Delighted, Mr. Redstone." He offered a hand.

Thomas accepted it, taking care not to grip too hard.

"You gots peppermint?" Lillian asked, bouncing on her toes.

"I'm not sure."

"Check you pocket."

"Mind your manners, Lillie," Prudence murmured.

"I jist helpin' case he forget."

"I wouldn't dare." Laughing, the man pulled a hard candy from his pocket and put it in Lillian's outstretched hand. That kept the girl quiet, and after a few comments about the weather, they followed Prudence into the small eating room and asked for food to be brought.

Thomas ate in watchful silence. Although Reverend Brother Sampson moved like an old man, he was probably not much older than Thomas—maybe thirty-five winters. Yet he showed only a fatherly interest in Prudence Lincoln, which surprised Thomas. Even the men in Heartbreak Creek looked at *Eho'nehevehohtse* with admiration, although none would dare act on it. Maybe this man was like the Catholic priests who had come to the Cheyenne village when Thomas was young. Maybe he was not allowed to have a woman. That would account for the sadness in his eyes.

While they ate, the reverend spoke often about his Christian god. Thomas remembered similar words from the book the missionaries had used to teach the Cheyenne children their letters. When he saw the interest in Prudence Lincoln's eyes, he wished he had paid better attention to those early lessons.

Smiling, the black man turned to Thomas. "Are you a Christian, Mr. Redstone?"

"I am Cheyenne."

"Does that mean you don't believe in our Savior?"

Thomas glanced at *Eho'nehevehohtse*. Even though they seldom spoke of such things, he could see that his lack of an answer disappointed her. "The Shawnee have a saying," he said to the reverend. "'We are all one child spinning through Mother Sky.' That is what I believe."

"Black people, too?"

Thomas nodded. "Even white ones."

The reverend threw back his head and laughed, showing many white teeth. "True equality. I like that, Mr. Redstone. And I pray that someday it will be true."

Thomas shrugged. "In death we are all equal."

They continued eating. Thomas tried to curb his impatience. He had not been outside since waking. He needed to breathe. Feel the breeze on his face and the earth under his feet. Staying inside too long made him restless.

"Do you live in Colorado Territory, too?" the reverend asked after a while.

"Yes. In the mountains." Thomas glanced at Prudence. "Unless I have a reason to stay in town."

"You owns two houses?" Lillian grinned, smears of berry jam stuck to her cheeks. "We rich!"

"I have little use for money and own no houses, except for a *xamaa-vee'e*—a tipi made of buffalo hide and wood that I put up when I need shelter."

Lillian's spoon clattered to her plate. "You ain't gots no house? None at all? Where I 'posed to sleep?"

Thomas looked at the faces staring back at him, showing surprise, shock, and, from Prudence Lincoln, a small, troubled smile. And in that moment, like a rockslide roaring toward him down a hillside, the truth slammed into him. Cutting his hair and wearing *ve'ho'e* clothing was not enough to look white. He would have to go to their church, too. Speak like they did. Earn money to buy the things white people thought they needed. He would have to give up his tipi, too, and live in a dwelling made of wood and stone and mud. The thought of locking himself inside four walls every night made his chest so tight it was hard to take a breath. But if that was what he must do to keep Prudence Lincoln by his side . . .

"If I need a house, I will build a house," he said, ending the discussion.

"Good. 'Cause I ain't sleepin' outside, no ma'am, not me."

The meal was almost over and they were laughing about something Lillian had said when Thomas saw Prudence Lincoln tense and look across the room. Turning, he saw the man called Marsh standing in the doorway.

Sitting back, his hands resting on his thighs within easy reach of the knife under his coat, Thomas watched him walk toward them. Unlike Reverend Brother Sampson, this man showed no warmth in his smile or his odd, pale eyes. Thomas had seen eyes that same yellow color on *ma'ęhóóhe*—a fox—its muzzle red with blood as it calmly tore apart a screaming rabbit.

Except now, Prudence Lincoln was the rabbit.

The reverend rose as Marsh approached. Thomas didn't, and when Prudence Lincoln started to stand, he murmured, "He does not deserve your respect, *Voaxaa'e*."

She stood anyway. Always proper, his Prudence.

On his other side, Lillian stopped picking at her muffin. "Who here?" she whispered, her eyes round and anxious. "Mistuh Marsh?"

Thomas patted her arm. "You are safe, *Katse'e*. I am here."

Some of the worry left her face. But not all of it.

The preacher introduced Marsh. Thomas nodded without speaking. As the others returned to their seats, Marsh took the chair beside Lillian. "Aren't you from the Friends school, girl?"

Lillian nodded and stuffed the muffin in her mouth.

"What is she doing here?" he asked the others.

"I brought her," Thomas said.

"Did you? Why?"

Seeing Prudence tense, Thomas did not respond.

"How did your meeting with the senator go?" she asked in a nervous voice.

"Very well. He wants to host a fund-raiser for the reverend next week. He expects you to attend, too. It would be an excellent opportunity to put your education initiative before key donors." He turned to Thomas with a smile that was more of a sneer. "And by all means, bring your friend along."

A hot surge moved through Thomas. Crossing his arms over his chest, he met the smile with a glare. "And if I do not behave, will you threaten me, too?"

Shock. Then a false laugh. "Threaten you?" Marsh looked innocently at Prudence Lincoln and Reverend Brother Sampson. "What's he talking about?"

Thomas held out his hand. "You will give me the letter now."

Marsh frowned at him. "What letter?"

"The one Miss Pru write," Lillian piped in, bouncing with glee. "The one you 'posed give Friend Matthews, 'cept you didn't."

Seeing the look Marsh gave the girl told Thomas he now had two to guard.

Prudence rushed into the sudden silence. "You probably

forgot, with the rush to leave and all. No matter. Thomas is here now."

"Yes." Thomas gave Marsh a thin smile. "I am here now."

Bolting to her feet, Prudence grabbed Lillian's hand with such vigor she almost pulled the girl from her chair. "If you'll excuse us, Mr. Marsh, we'll leave you and Brother to discuss the fund-raiser. Thomas, I need you to show me where you put Lillie's hair ribbons."

It was more of an order than a request for help, but seeing the worry in her eyes, Thomas rose. With a nod to the black man and a long, level look at Marsh, he followed Prudence and Lillian from the room.

"I asked you not to start anything," Prudence murmured as they went down the hall toward their rooms.

"I remember."

"Yet you were baiting him."

"What 'baitin'' mean?" Lillian asked.

"Why, Thomas? What do you hope to gain by making him your enemy?"

"Who him?"

"He, Lillie," Prudence said in exasperation. "Who *is he*?"

"That what I ask."

Reaching past Lillian, Thomas stroked a hand down Prudence Lincoln's tense back. "You worry too much, *Eho'nehevehohtse*. And he is already my enemy because he frightened you. I only wanted him to know I will be watching him."

"You talkin' 'bout Mistuh Marsh, ain't you?"

"*Aren't you*, and this doesn't concern you, Lillie."

"'Course not. I jist a po' no 'count blind black girl. Don't mind me."

"That, *Katse'e*," Thomas said, giving the girl's shoulder a thump, "is baiting."

Four

They spent the rest of the morning shopping. Although she and Thomas hadn't discussed what to do about Lillie—whether to take her back to Schuler or on to Heartbreak Creek—Pru could see the child needed a warm winter coat to replace her castoff from one of the older children at the Friends school. She also wanted to use shopping as an excuse to stay away from the hotel so there would be no repeat of the breakfast confrontation between Marsh and Thomas.

She knew the Cheyenne only wanted to shield her from harm. Even as they walked, he kept turning his head to look behind them, as if expecting to see March leap out of an alley. Having lost his wife and son years ago in a senseless act of violence, he had become overly protective of the people he now considered his "tribe"—his friends in Heartbreak Creek, her, and now, apparently, Lillie, too. The bond between the solemn warrior and the blind child was already strong, and Pru doubted Thomas would leave the girl behind when he returned to Colorado. She hoped not. They probably needed Lillie as much as she needed them.

"While we're out, there's a bookstore I would like to visit," she said, trying to ignore the way women looked at Thomas as they walked by. The man had a way about him that made heads turn. And he knew it, judging by that devilish grin he sent her over Lillie's head.

Pretending indifference, she feigned admiration for the Christmas items already on display in storefront windows and the wreaths and garlands hanging on shopkeepers' doors. In truth, the colorful decorations soured her mood, bringing to mind unpleasant memories of Christmases back at Rose Hill Plantation in Louisiana.

Her white father, Charles Whitney, always tried to include her and her slave-born mother, Ester, in the yuletide celebrations. But Pricilla Whitney, his wife and the mother of Pru's half sister, Edwina, ruined the festivities with her erratic behavior and daily tantrums. It all came to a head on the Christmas Eve when Pru was seven and Edwina six. Thrown into a rage over a pitcher of spilled milk, Mrs. Whitney had begun to shriek and beat her daughter so hard the switch left bloody marks across the back of Edwina's dress. When Pru tried to intervene, a pot of scalding water had spilled over her, leaving her with the scars she bore today. They never knew if it was an accident or a deliberate act, but thereafter, Christmases were barely marked at Rose Hill.

But she wouldn't let those sad memories ruin Lillie's Christmas, or her own fun in finding the perfect gifts for the child and Thomas. She had already begun teaching Lillie the embossed alphabet of the Braille six-dot method of reading and writing, and with the recent French invention of the Braille keyboard printer, she was hoping to find a book Lillie could read . . . a more appropriate form of entertainment than eavesdropping.

They stopped by the dry goods store first, where they picked out a coat, mittens, a soft woolen scarf, and a sturdy pair of shoes for Lillie. Thomas paid for it: apparently Ash had paid him very well. They gave Lillie those purchases in the store— much to her squealing delight—but Pru also purchased warm stockings, a new dress, and a thick sweater to give the child on Christmas Day.

They exited the store thirty minutes later, Lillie clinging to their hands and skipping along between them, beaming with pride. "I never gots no new store-bought clothes before. Not of my very own."

"I never *received any* store-bought clothes," Pru gently corrected.

Lillie grinned up at her. "Don't worry. Daddy get you some. Maybe a new Christmas dress, right, Daddy?"

"Maybe." Thomas's dark gaze met Pru's over Lillie's bobbing head. His smile told her he was remembering last night when he had watched her undress for him. "Something without so many buttons and laces."

Heat rushed over her. Hiking her chin, she looked away to hide her blush. The man could do the most amazing things to her without lifting a finger.

When they reached the bookstore, Pru stopped and turned to Thomas. With elaborate gestures and mouthed words, so Lillie wouldn't hear, she suggested that Thomas take Lillie on to the candy shop several stores down and get her a peppermint while Pru looked through the bookstore for a Braille book.

He waited calmly until she finished, then told Lillie to cover her ears. "Use words, *Eho'nehevehohtse*. You are not that good at sign."

Pru repeated her instructions.

"You will not leave the bookstore until I return," he ordered, and, taking Lillie's hand, went down the street.

Pru was delighted to find a primer in Braille for Lillie, and for Thomas, a book about the Corps of Discovery Expedition by Lewis and Clark. She had just paid for her purchases and was heading toward the door when a figure moved up behind her. With a start, she turned to find a man looming over her—Chester Hogan, a black man she had met through Levi Coffin, a staunch activist and supporter of the Underground Railroad.

"Sorry I scare you, Miss Lincoln." He looked furtively around to make sure they wouldn't be overheard. "It time," he went on in a low voice. "You meet with us at the old machine works behind the depot?"

"When?"

"Tonight. We knows you helping at the gospel meetings in the big tent down a ways. Machine shop not far from it. Just past the depot, in the 'bandoned rail yard. Maybe come during the meeting? Say, seven thirty?"

"I'll be there."

Pru walked with him to the door. "Is it the man you told me about? The one from New Jersey?"

"Mose Solomon. He a good man, Miss Lincoln. Didn't

hardly do nothing, but they needs someone to blame for them Patenburg railroad riots, and he easy pickin's. Been hiding out, but gots to get moving soon." He opened the door.

"Then let's do what we can." Pru stepped outside, then lurched back as a figure lunged past her. Before she could catch her breath, Thomas had Chester pinned against the wall, a forearm across his throat.

"Why do you follow us?"

Chester gagged and clutched at the arm pressing against his neck.

"Stop!" Pru tried to pull Thomas back.

He didn't budge. "Did he hurt you, *Eho'nehevehohtse*?"

"No! He's a friend."

Thomas looked at her, savagery still showing in his eyes. "A friend?"

"Yes. He came to give me a message, that's all. Let him go."

Reluctantly, Thomas lowered his arm and stepped back.

Chester sagged, gasping and coughing and rubbing his throat.

"He dyin'?" Lillie asked, white showing around her blank eyes.

"Of course not." Pru patted the injured man's back as he struggled to catch his breath. "Are you all right, Chester?"

Slowly the man straightened, his frightened gaze locked on Thomas. "Who he? Why he do that?"

"He protectin' us, that why," Lillie burst out. "He a Cheyenne Dog Soldier and he my daddy. You come after us, he come after you, and kill you dead like a mangy three-legged hound dog. Ain't that right, Daddy?"

"Lillie, please be quiet." Pru put on a strained smile to reassure the passersby gawking at them. "Chester, this is my . . . friend, Thomas Redstone, from Colorado."

Thomas gave her an odd look.

"He watches over Lillie and me," she quickly added, but knew that wasn't what he wanted to hear, either. But how could she explain her relationship with Thomas when she wasn't sure herself what it was?

Chester didn't seem to care one way or the other. He just wanted to get away. Which he did, as quickly as he could.

Thomas watched him scurry off, speculation in his gaze. "If he is a friend, why did he track us like a hungry wolf?"

"He didn't want to be seen speaking with me."

"He was ashamed?"

"No, it's not that. But it's all rather complicated." She glanced meaningfully down at Lillie, who stood at his side, rubbing her new mittens against her cheeks. "We'll discuss it later."

"Yes, *Eho'nehevehohtse*. We will."

They were able to avoid Marsh for the rest of the afternoon, and when they went into the tearoom for an early supper, Pru was grateful that only the reverend was there. As they walked over to join him, Pru warned Lillie not to mention the scene outside the bookstore.

"We don't want him to think badly of Thomas, do we?"

"He only protectin' us."

"Nonetheless, you're not to bring it up. Understood?"

"I a mouse in the cupboard." Leaning toward Thomas, she added, "They talk less than you, Daddy."

"Good evening, Brother," Pru said, stopping beside the reverend's table. "May we join you?"

"By all means."

After they had ordered and were waiting for their food to arrive, Lillie prattled on about her new coat and gloves and scarf. She would have worn them throughout the meal if Pru hadn't insisted she remove them when the server brought their plates. It was heartwarming—and a little sad—that the girl was so ecstatic over something as mundane as a new winter coat.

"Will you be coming to the meeting tonight?" Brother Sampson asked, his smile including Thomas.

"We look forward to it," Pru said when Thomas didn't answer.

"I hope you gots singin'," Lillie said through a mouthful of carrots.

Pru gently reminded her not to speak with her mouth full.

"I jist loves gospel singin'. I good at it, too. Ev'rybody say so."

"The Friends don't sing much, do they?" Brother Sampson asked her in a gentle voice.

"No, but I 'member songs my other mama used to sing."

"Other mama?"

"The one gone to Jesus. Now I huntin' a new one." She waved her spoon at her dark mane of untamed hair. "Daddies not so good at making braids."

Pru could see the reverend was confused. "Lillian has decided that Thomas is her father."

"My first one sold off long time ago." Using her left hand to corral peas on her plate, Lillie pushed them onto her spoon, then carefully lifted the spoon to her mouth. Pru was pleased to see only a few escaped to roll across the floor. "Maybe you him. You gots chilrin, Reverend Brother Sampson?"

A wistful smile crossed the black man's face. "I'm sorry to say I don't. But if I did, I think I'd like one very much like you."

Lillie grinned, peas showing in the gaps in her teeth.

The meal was a short one. As soon as Brother Sampson cleaned his plate, he excused himself to prepare for the tent meeting that evening. Pru insisted Lillie rest, too, and when they finished eating, she and Thomas took her upstairs.

"Will you go with us to the meeting?" Pru asked as they moved down the hall toward their rooms.

"Yes. I do not want you to walk there alone."

Pru didn't argue. She didn't want him out of her sight, either. No telling what mischief he might get himself into.

When they reached 211, Thomas announced that from now on Lillian would sleep here, in Prudence Lincoln's room.

Pru knew he was right. It was inappropriate for him to share a room with a young girl not of his family. Yet knowing he was not usually one to bother with the rules of deportment, she wondered if there might be another reason for his decision. Was he putting distance between them to make a later parting easier? Or did he plan to disappear on a scouting foray—perhaps to confront Marsh?

The idea pressed like a hand against her throat.

"You not want me no more?" Lillie asked him, her face crumpling.

Pru could see Thomas was unsure how to respond, so she answered for him. "It's lonely in here all by myself. I would feel better if you were with me. And I can braid better than Mr. Redstone."

Lillie gave that some thought. "You won't sneak off and leave me?" she said to Thomas's belt.

Pru almost snorted.

"I do not sneak, *Katse'e*. If I must leave, I will tell you."

"Can I still have you knife?"

"No. You will not need it with Prudence Lincoln there."
His gaze flicked up to meet Pru's. A smile teased his mouth.
"When I was hurt, she watched over me and kept me safe. And
warm. She will do the same for you."

"But I—"

"*Katse'e.*" He put his hand on Lillie's shoulder. "Have you
forgotten your promise to me? Did you not say that you would
do what I tell you?"

A dramatic sigh. "All right. But you better not run off, Daddy."

This time, Pru gave him a knowing look. The child knew
him too well.

"I will not. Now take your nap, while I talk to Prudence
Lincoln about the man who followed us."

"Nap?" Lillie huffed indignantly. "I not a baby. I 'most
'leven, you know."

"You're ten," Pru reminded her. "But she's right, Thomas.
I think it's important that she's aware of what's going on so she
won't be confused or frightened. And she'll be discreet. Won't
you, Lillie?"

"What that mean?"

"It means you won't repeat what we say."

"Make her promise," Thomas muttered.

"I promise," the girl said. "But first I gots to go to the necessary room." Turning, she whispered to Thomas's arm, "That
mean I gots to pee, Daddy. Miss Pru make me say I goin' to the
necessary room instead. Do Indians do they business in necessary rooms?"

"Lillie!" Pru scolded.

"Indians do everything everybody else does, *Katse'e.* But
better. Now go with Prudence Lincoln."

Thomas stood at the single window, waiting for them to return,
his face lifted to the sunlight streaming through the dust-
streaked panes. Even two floors above the busy street, the sound
of so many people and wagons seeped through the glass. The
constant noise buzzed in his head like angry bees, adding to his
restlessness. He felt trapped in a rabbit warren and wondered
how people—white or black—could live this way.

The need for quiet solitude rose in him, but he forced it

back down. Soon he would be back in his mountains. He would find harmony there, and this sense of being off-balance would leave him.

Several minutes later, the two females returned. Prudence settled on the edge of the bed and told Lillian to sit on the floor between her feet so she could braid her hair. Thomas continued to stand at the window, arms crossed over his chest, waiting for *Eho'nehevehohtse* to explain about the man at the bookstore.

"Have you ever heard of the Underground Railroad?" she finally asked.

Thomas shook his head.

"I has," Lillian said. "The Friends bring us to freedom lan' on it. But it not a real railroad."

"No, it's not," Prudence agreed. "Nor is it underground, but more of a network of secret pathways Negroes used to escape slavery and travel to places where they could be free. Like Indiana."

"If it is not a railroad, why do they call it that?" Thomas asked.

"Because it was all very secret, and to avoid suspicion, the people who ran it used railroad terms as code names for different aspects of the organization."

"White people complicate everything," Thomas muttered.

"Perhaps. But many blacks helped on the railroad as well. Harriet Tubman, an ex-slave, was famous for it. Do you remember the stories you learned at school about Harriet?" she asked Lillie.

"The one who change her name from Minty?"

"Araminta Ross. Yes, that's the one. I'm proud you remembered." In addition to her work with the Underground Railroad, Harriet had also aided the abolitionist John Brown before his disastrous raid at Harper's Ferry. Even now, Mrs. Tubman continued to further the Negro cause, and though they had never met, Pru felt a strong connection to the courageous black woman.

"Anyway," Pru went on, "'stations' or 'depots' were safe resting places along the secret routes, and 'conductors' were people who helped move the runaways from place to place. I've heard that over a hundred thousand slaves escaped to freedom on the Underground Railroad, many through Indiana. But that was before the War of the Rebellion."

Thomas watched *Eho'nehevehohtse*'s long, slim fingers work the braid and remembered those same fingers sliding through the gaps in his shirt the previous night. She liked to touch him. He liked it, as well. And it pleased him that beneath her shy smile was a ferocious passion awakened only by him.

"Hold this, dear." Prudence put Lillian's fingers on the end of the braid so she could tie a ribbon around it.

Thomas noted the girl's hair was not as smooth and shiny as *Eho'nehevehohtse*'s, and it took many small braids to tame it. Like *Katse'e*, it seemed to have a mind of its own.

"For several years after the war ended," Prudence went on as she started another braid, "there wasn't much need for escape routes. But lately, with increasing unrest because of Reconstruction, many Negroes feel their only hope of a better life is to escape into Canada . . . although I've been hearing things can be difficult up there, too."

"If there is no more slavery, why do they not go there on their own?" Thomas asked. "Why do they need the secret railroad?"

"Because there are those who have gotten into trouble and need help."

"Lawbreakers."

"Some. But not all laws are just. Or enforced equally."

"You do not need to tell a Cheyenne that." Moving from the window, he sprawled in the worn chair beside the bed. "The man today is a lawbreaker who needs your help?" Thomas would not have thought the frightened black man had the courage to break laws.

"Chester Hogan? No. He's more of a 'conductor.' There, Lillie. All finished. You look quite grand."

Thomas thought she still looked like she had sprouted raven feathers.

Grinning, the girl climbed back onto the bed and began humming to herself as she wrapped her new scarf around her thin neck.

"Chester's not in trouble," Prudence explained. "But he's helping someone who is."

"And he needs you to do this?"

"I'm just a step along the way."

Thomas did not like this. Many of the white man's laws might be foolish, but their lawmen were quick to punish those who broke them. When he was Declan Brodie's deputy in Heartbreak Creek, he had locked several men away for breaking the rules. He had even been in jail himself. Once in Heartbreak Creek, and for a short time in a faraway place named Liverpool. "Is this why Marsh threatened you? He does not want you to do this?"

A look of disdain marred the beauty of her face. "He's afraid if we're caught it might cause a scandal and ruin his chances of getting to Washington. The man's evil and corrupt. He puts his own wants and ambitions above those in need."

"As you put those in need above your own wants." Thomas did not want Prudence Lincoln to be trapped by the white man's laws. He did not want her to know the fear of being caged in a jail like an animal. "You will not help him, *Eho'nehevehohtse*."

Her chin came up.

On the bed, Lillian quit twisting her scarf and listened intently.

Ho. It seemed he would have battle on two fronts. "If Chester Hogan needs help, Prudence," he said calmly, "I will do it. I do not want you in danger. You will tell me what to do, and I will do it."

"I don't know yet what Chester wants me to do," she said with impatience. "When I see him during the tent meeting tonight I'll find out."

"I will meet with him instead."

"After you almost choked him to death today? He's liable to run as soon as he sees you. I need to go."

"Then you can come with me."

"Me, too," Lillian said. "I ain't staying here by myself."

Thomas looked at her. "No, *Katse'e*, you will not be by yourself. The reverend will need you to help him with the singing."

A grin replaced the scowl. "Fo' true?"

"For true."

Prudence narrowed her eyes at him.

He pretended not to notice. He had made his point and had no more to say.

"I jist loves to sing. Wanna hear?"

Thomas winced, imagining what noise would come out of that mouth.

Prudence gave him a look. "Save it for the meeting, why don't you, Lillie dear? Then it will be a grand surprise for everybody. Now put on your coat and gloves. It's late, and we don't want the meeting to start without us."

Thomas rose from the chair and straightened the knife under his coat. He wondered if he should change his clothing. He could move more quietly in his moccasins, and the war shirt didn't pull across his shoulders the way this coat did. But after thinking it through, he decided against it. Chester Hogan had been frightened enough for one day.

Five

People were already streaming into the tent when they arrived. Every day more came, and every evening more vendors' carts crowded the street beside the meadow. The sound of happy voices blended with the smell of roasting sausages, creating a fair-like atmosphere despite the chill in the evening air. Pru hoped people were coming for the worship, not the food.

"Wait here," she told Thomas and Lillie when they reached the tent's entrance. "I'll be right back after I speak to Brother about leaving Lillie."

Thomas didn't respond, his gaze fixed on something inside the tent toward the small raised stage at the front. Turning, Pru saw Marsh speaking with the reverend.

Drat. She had hoped he wouldn't attend tonight. Now it would be more difficult to leave to meet Chester. She was debating what to do when she saw a familiar face huffing and puffing across the field toward them, a bulky contraption under her arm.

"Bessie Prescott," she called. "You're just the person I was hoping to see."

"Evenin'." Bessie waved her free hand, setting off jiggles of motion in the ample breasts swaying beneath her dress. "A glorious day for the Lord's Word."

"It certainly is." Smiling, Pru brought Lillie forward to meet the elderly black woman, who served as the choir director, joyfully leading the hymns on her ancient, wheezy accordion. "Might I ask a favor?"

"Sho' you can, child." Panting for breath, Bessie shifted the accordion to her other arm. "What you need?"

Pru introduced Lillie, explaining about her blindness, and that she needed someone to keep an eye on the girl while she ran an errand. "I won't be long and she'll be no trouble at all. Will you, Lillie?"

"A fly on the windowpane, that me. Singin' praises to the Lawd."

Pru heard a snort behind her.

Bessie beamed down at the grinning scamp. "Ain't she the cutest thing? I happy to watch her. Come along, child. You sit up front with me." Hefting the accordion higher on her hip, Bessie took Lillie's hand and started down the aisle between the rows of rapidly filling benches.

"I'll be back as soon as I can," Pru called to her retreating back.

"Take you time. We be fine."

Pru shoved Thomas away from the opening. "Hurry, before Marsh sees us." Although, judging by the prickle between her shoulder blades, he might have already spotted them. She didn't turn around to find out, but ushered Thomas through the crowds gathered around the carts.

"Do you fear he will follow us?"

"I don't want to find out."

As they passed a vendor's cart, he looked with interest at a rack of dripping sausages. "Those smell good."

"We don't have time for that. After that supper you ate, I don't know how you could still be hungry, anyway."

"That was a long time ago."

"All of two hours. Keep moving."

A few minutes later, they arrived at the abandoned machine shop and rail yard on the far side of the depot. Pru was glad Thomas had come with her. It was quite dark, although he didn't seem to have any trouble making his way through the discarded railroad equipment, crates, and bent rails.

"I hope this is the right place," she murmured.

"When do you meet him?"

"Not for a while yet," she whispered. "Seven thirty."

"Then why are you whispering?"

She refrained from punching his shoulder and clung to his arm instead. "I can't see a thing. Can you?"

"Of course. I am Cheyenne."

It was exhilarating and a little frightening to be lurking about in the dark. It reminded her of the haunting games she and Edwina had played as children, tiptoeing around the raised vaults in the resting place at Rose Hill—until they frightened themselves so badly they had run shrieking back to the slave cabins and the safety of Pru's mother's arms. "Can you hear anything?"

"Not with you talking."

"What if we're in the wrong place?"

"Then we will miss him."

"But what if—"

"You worry too much, *heme'oone*. Now be silent so I can hear."

For a long time he stood motionless, his face turned into the slight breeze that rustled through the weeds growing along the tracks. Pru moved closer, seeking his warmth. She listened, too, but heard nothing.

After a few minutes, Thomas said in a low voice, "He comes."

Surprised, Pru glanced around. "He does? Where?"

"You will wait here. I will be nearby. When I am sure he is alone, I will return to you." Looping an arm around her shoulders, he pulled her hard against his strong body and kissed her. "Do not be afraid, *Eho'nehevehohtse*," he whispered against her lips. "I will let nothing harm you." Another hard, quick kiss that left her mouth tingling, then he released her and faded soundlessly into the shadows.

"Don't scare him, Thomas," she whispered in warning.

Low laughter sounded on the right. No, the left. Behind her? She looked around, but saw nothing move. The man was a ghost. Shivering, she thrust her gloved hands into her coat pockets. She spied a long crate nearby and went over to it. She tested it for soundness, then, satisfied it would hold her weight, she sat, shoulders hunched against the cold.

The night was so still she could hear the faint sound of singing coming from the direction of the tent. The call to worship. The meeting had begun, which meant it was a little past seven thirty. Where was Chester?

She tugged her collar higher, wishing Thomas were still there to keep her warm. She also wished he would relent about keeping her at arm's length. Having him close kept her body humming with frustration. Doubtless, that was his plan all along. He knew that when she was around him she couldn't think. When they were apart, reason told her this odd, mismatched relationship would never work, but as soon as he came near, all she wanted was to do was lose herself in his arms.

She sighed. But he was right about one thing—even if she was barren, it was still unwise to be intimate until they had made the decision to continue on together. But was there truly a decision to make? The idea of not having Thomas in her life was unthinkable. He was the one constant she could depend on. The strength she'd never had. Yet she was loath to give up her dream of advancing education for Negroes. Was there no way she could have both?

Moments dragged by. She was beginning to think Thomas was wrong and Chester wasn't coming when she heard the scuff of a shoe on gravel to her right. She rose, poised to flee, when a familiar voice called out.

"Miss Lincoln? You here?"

She let out a shaky breath. "Yes, Chester. Over here."

"I can't see nothing."

A figure stepped out of the shadows. "I will help you."

"Christamighty!"

"Thomas, don't hurt him!"

Heavy breathing, scrabbling noises, and muttered words, then Chester stumbled up beside her, Thomas gripping his shoulder. "He came alone, Prudence."

Even in the faraway light from the lanterns by the tent, Pru could see the fear in Chester's eyes. "Oh, for heaven's sake, Thomas! Stop frightening the poor man. Chester, it's all right. He won't hurt you."

Thomas took his hand away, but continued to stand at Chester's side.

Fearing the man's legs might give out from the fright Thomas had given him, Pru gestured to the crate. "Perhaps you should sit down, Chester."

He sat, and Prudence sat next to him. Thomas stood in front of them, arms crossed over his chest.

"Now tell me about the man who needs our help. Mose, is it?"

"Y-yes, ma'am. Mose Solomon."

It was a dismal story. Pru had read about it in a newspaper left in the hotel lobby. But since the article had been written by a white man, she suspected a bias against the blacks involved. The whole affair was shameful—not only because of the four lives lost, but because of the apathy on the part of those who were supposed to uphold the law.

That indifference to suffering awakened memories of what had happened to her in the Indian camp, bringing up such a well of bitterness it almost clogged her throat. How could people witness such brutality and do nothing?

"I read about the massacre, Chester," she said in a tight voice. "Was Mose a part of that?"

"He only protectin' what was his, ma'am. They was wrong on both sides. But the Irish got the best of it. And they start it."

"This happened in Patenburg, New Jersey?"

Chester nodded. "On Mulhockaway Creek in Hunterdon County. The railroad hire Irish and colored gangs to dig a tunnel through Musconetcong Mountain. Pay's good, but it hard work, I hear."

"You'd best begin at the beginning."

Chester settled more comfortably, hands tucked against the chill. "It all start on payday, when the Irish boys set on some blacks after a night of drinkin'. 'Fore long they shooting at each other. Then the Irish break into the colored shanties, steal they wages, and set everything on fire. An Irishman named Colls got shot, but it warn't the coloreds what did it. The whites got to fightin' amongst theyselves and they the ones did him in, but they tell everybody the black boys do it. By the time the smoke clear, Colls and three blacks all dead."

Memories of her own helplessness surged into Pru's mind. "Did no one do anything? The sheriff? Somebody?"

"Oh, yessum, the sheriff do something." Chester's voice shook with pent-up anger. "He round up three coloreds right off and start huntin' more. Governor Parker even offer a reward. He and the sheriff afraid to go against the Irish, so they blame everything on the black boys. Most of the coloreds run off, hidin' wherever they can. But Mose, he big like a house and bald as a cannonball. He hard to hide."

"Where is he now?"

"Tumbledown barn north of town. But he need to get away pretty quick." Chester heaved a great sigh and shook his head. "It not right. None of it. Mose didn't kill nobody, Miss Lincoln. I swear it."

"He wants to go to Canada?"

"Yes, ma'am. He got family escaped up there 'fore the war."

"Then we'll make arrangements to get him started." Pru pushed herself to her feet. "Meanwhile, does Mose have food and water and a way to stay warm?"

Chester nodded as he rose. "He fine fo' now."

"Then bring him here tomorrow night. I'll find out where the next station is and tell you then."

"Thank you, ma'am, and God bless."

After Chester disappeared into the night, Pru turned to Thomas, who had remained silent throughout Chester's recitation. "What do you think?"

"I think it is a sad story. One I have heard around many campfires. Whites, whether they are Irish or English or American, are not to be trusted."

"We both have white blood."

He didn't respond.

"My sister is white. We have white friends in Heartbreak Creek."

He still didn't respond.

"It wasn't a white man who beat me." Bitterness rose inside. "Nor white people who watched and did nothing. Am I to hate all Indians now?" She realized her hands were shaking and thrust them into the pockets of her coat. "I would have, I think, if I hadn't known you."

He pulled her hard against his chest. "It is not the same, *Eho'nehevehohtse*. I am not the one who hurt you."

"No, Thomas, you're not. For that reason, I don't blame all Indians because of what Lone Tree did. There is too much hate and injustice and brutality as it is."

He leaned back to study her in the dim light. "Do you try to civilize me, Prudence?" He asked it in a chiding way, but she heard the serious intent behind the words. "I am as *Ma'heo'o* made me. Even if I wear city clothes, and cut off my topknot, and write books in English, I will still be what the whites call a savage."

"Only the whites who don't know you."

The tension left his big body. Dipping his head, he kissed her forehead. "We must return to Lillian now. But later, after she sleeps, you will come to my room. You have never told me what Lone Tree did to you. Tonight you will, and together, we will banish him from your mind."

She shivered, reluctant to dredge up all those horrid memories. But Thomas would press her until she did, and perhaps he was right. Maybe the telling of it would close that distance between them. At least for a while.

They returned later than Pru had anticipated, and the meeting was breaking up when they arrived back at the tent. Stepping past those crowding around the exit, she made her way toward the front, where Bessie Prescott spoke to the two ladies who sang in the small choir.

"I apologize for taking so long," she said, joining them. "Did Lillie behave?"

"Like an angel," Bessie said.

"She a sweet little thing," one of the ladies added.

"And that voice," the other put in with a hearty laugh. "Mercy sakes."

Thomas stepped forward. "Where is she?"

At his harsh tone, Pru felt a prickle of alarm. She turned and scanned the empty benches, but didn't see Lillie.

"She go to the carts out front," Bessie said. "Mistuh Marsh think she deserve a treat for being so good."

Thomas began shoving his way through the line of people filing out of the tent, Pru right behind him.

"I'm sure she all right," Bessie called after them. "Mr. Marsh say he take good care of her."

Alarm building, Pru rushed toward the carts at the edge of the field. *If he hurts her, I . . . I'll . . .* She couldn't think of a punishment dire enough.

Thomas pulled her to a stop. "Calm your fear, Prudence. *Katse'e* is safe."

"How do you know that?" She looked fearfully at the crowd gathered around the vendors' carts. "He could have—"

"Why would he hurt her when people know she is with him?" His eyes narrowed in speculation. "And why are you so afraid, Prudence? Has he said he would hurt her?"

She should have told him about Marsh's threats. But she had seen what Thomas had done to the man who had tried to hurt Brin, her niece through her sister's marriage to Declan Brodie. She was there when he went after Lone Tree with his bare hands. And she remembered the spent bullet he once carried in a pouch around his neck, and his vow to shove the piece of metal into the beating heart of the trapper who had killed his wife and son. She knew if he was aware of Marsh's threats, he wouldn't allow them to go unchallenged. He would act in some violent, lethal way that would bring ruin down on all of them. This wasn't the mountains where he could strike, then disappear like mist through the trees. Here, they would hunt him down and cage him like the savage they thought him to be.

She couldn't tell him and put him at such risk.

And yet . . . what if her silence brought harm to Lillie?

Terror building, she hurried toward the carts.

Thomas fell into step beside her. "I know you do not like to cause trouble, Prudence. But sometimes it is not enough to endure. Sometimes you must fight—if not for yourself, then for those you love. And I will not let you fight alone."

"I am not a coward," she said stiffly.

"No, you are not. You would not be part of this Underground Railroad if you were. But you have a gentle heart, which can blind you to the truth. And the truth, *Eho'nehevehohtse*, is that Marsh means to frighten you, not Lillian."

She stopped and blinked at him. "Me?"

"To make you behave and do as he says. You must show him he has failed."

"And if that pushes him to do something worse to get my attention?"

"Then I will take care of it." He smiled with such malice she almost flinched.

She knew he blamed himself for her abduction by Lone Tree, and this drive to protect her was probably a reaction to that. But if he put himself in danger on her account . . . "Thomas, please . . ."

"Please, what, Prudence? Let this man bring harm to you and Lillian?"

"What if Marsh provokes you into doing something that lands you in jail? How will you help us then?"

"I will keep you safe," he said stubbornly. He started to say more, then his gaze focused on something behind her. Sudden tension stiffened his shoulders.

"You see her?" Pru spun around, searching faces, but there were too many people milling about. "Is she all right?"

"She is safe. Now hide your fear."

She tried, but almost cried out in relief when she saw Marsh strolling toward them, holding Lillie's hand.

He was smiling.

Lillie wasn't, even though she clutched a greasy bag of popped corn in her free hand.

"There you are," Marsh said amiably. "We missed you at the service. Had something more important to do?"

"An errand," Pru said distractedly, searching Lillie for signs of harm.

At the sound of Pru's voice, Lillie's face brightened. "You back!" Jerking free of Marsh's grip, she stumbled forward, her free hand grabbing at air. "Daddy here, too?"

Marsh frowned. "Daddy?"

Thomas went down on one knee, catching Lillie before she fell. "I am here, *Katse'e*."

She clung to him, the desperation on her face sending a chill through Pru. What had Marsh said or done to put such fear into the child's eyes?

"I thought you gone fo'ever," Lillie whispered against Thomas's neck.

"I will always come back to you, Lillian. You know this." He patted her back, then rose, bits of popped corn trickling down the front of his jacket. Taking her small hand in his, he looked levelly at Marsh in a way that made the other man step back a pace.

With a strained smile, Pru broke the tense silence. "Thank you for keeping an eye on her, Mr. Marsh. But we should go now. I can see she's tired."

"All that singing, no doubt. Our Lillian made a big

impression on Senator Brooks." Marsh gave Lillie's head a pat, despite her attempts to duck out from under his hand. "He's quite an advocate for orphaned Negro children, you know. On the board of the Riverbend School for the Disabled. An asylum, really, but they have several fine programs for the blind. And luckily they accept Negro children." A not-so-friendly tug on one of Lillie's braids, then he looked at Pru, his reptilian eyes cold and unblinking. "He'll be at the tent meeting tomorrow night. Be sure to bring Lillian along so the senator can meet her."

Pru couldn't seem to draw in enough breath to form an answer. *He's using the child to get at me.* Her stomach rolled. Bile rose up the back of her throat.

When she didn't—couldn't—answer, Marsh's pale blond brows rose in twin arcs. "You are coming, aren't you? It will be our final gathering, after all."

Pru nodded, scarcely able to think.

Thomas moved up beside her, menace rolling off of him like sweat.

Panicked, she reached down and squeezed his arm in warning, terrified of what he might do.

She had to think. Come up with a plan. Keep him safe, protect Lillie, find out where the next station was, then send Chester and Mose Solomon on their way.

But how?

Run? Or stay?

By morning, they could be on the first train headed to Colorado. But was she ready to leave her work unfinished? Perhaps she should send Thomas and Lillie on to Heartbreak Creek without her. Yet, she sensed that if she sent Thomas away again . . .

Marsh's voice cut through the terror buzzing in her ears. "Then there's the fund-raiser on Monday, which the senator will also attend. Perhaps after the gospel service tomorrow evening, you can discuss with the reverend how best to present your initiative."

Tomorrow evening, she would be meeting with Chester again. "Y-yes," Pru choked out, her mind reeling. "I-I'll talk to him tomorrow."

"Excellent. Well then, I bid you good night." A tip of his hat, then he turned and sauntered back toward town.

"Oh, God." Releasing Thomas's arm, Pru bent, a hand over her mouth, her heart pounding so hard she felt light-headed. Somehow, Marsh had guessed why she had met Chester earlier. He knew about Mose. And he was using threats of sending Lillie to an asylum to make her stop.

Dimly, she felt Thomas's hand on her shoulder. "Prudence?"

With effort, she straightened. "He knows."

"Knows what?"

"I not like Mr. Marsh. He mean." Lillie stuffed a handful of popped corn into her mouth, then cocked her head. "What an asylum?"

Pru couldn't fathom how Marsh had found out about her work with the Underground Railroad in the first place. Or why he suspected she was still involved. But somehow, he knew. *How could he lock Lillie away?* What had a blind orphan ever done to him?

The impulse to flee shattered as rage exploded inside her. Arcs of heat shot through her body with such force she began to shake.

No! Not again!

This time she wouldn't simply endure. She wouldn't run away to Heartbreak Creek or hide behind her sister or Thomas or fears of making a scene. This time she would stay and fight back.

"What is wrong, *Eho'nehevehohtse*?"

She saw the strength and concern in Thomas's dark eyes, and everything settled into place. She knew what she had to do. If Marsh wanted a fight, she would give him one . . . using the deadliest weapon she had.

Filled with cold resolve, she took Lillie's hand. "Let's go."

As they moved past the carts and into the street behind the depot, she glanced at the man walking silently at Lillie's other side, his expression stony, his lips drawn into a tight line.

She hated pulling him deeper into danger, but she couldn't do this alone. And the best way she knew to keep Thomas safe was to arm him with the truth.

"Thomas, we need to talk."

Six

An hour later, Pru slipped into Thomas's room. "She's finally asleep. But I don't want to be away long in case she wakes up with night terrors."

Thomas whirled from the window, his expression thunderous. "He hurt her?"

"No. But he scares her. Being blind, she's sensitive to the emotions around her. Especially those of a threatening nature." With a sigh, Pru sank down into the chair beside the bed. The earlier rush of fury had subsided, leaving her feeling drained and weary.

"*Katse'e* is wise for one so young. The People see it often in those touched by the Great Spirit." He walked over and sat on the bed beside her chair, feet planted, arms folded over his chest. A stubborn pose. One that told her he was ready to act, not wait. "You will explain this school Marsh spoke of."

Brushing a hand over her brow, she struggled to gather her thoughts. "They call them schools, but many are little more than asylums . . . places where they lock away people who are different or disabled or insane."

"Marsh would cage Lillian because she is blind?"

"Not if I can help it."

"How will you stop him?"

"Not me. You."

He let his hands fall to his thighs and smiled. It wasn't a pleasant smile.

She had come up with the perfect plan—one that got Thomas away before he killed Marsh and still left her free to concentrate on this latest threat to Lillie. The hardest part would be to convince Thomas to agree.

"What do you want me to do?" he asked.

"Meet with Chester tomorrow night and take Mose Solomon on to the next station."

He studied her for a moment, then shook his head. "No. I will kill Marsh instead."

This was what she had been afraid of. She sighed, wondering what she could say to steer him away from violence. "If you do that, Thomas, you'll bring every lawman within a hundred miles down on our heads. You think people haven't noticed the bad blood between the two of you? If something happens to Marsh, they'll know it was you."

He shrugged.

She wanted to strike him.

"I was once a lawman, too, Prudence. And when we searched our canyon for the murderer in Heartbreak Creek last year, Brodie explained to me that without a body, there is no way to know if a law has been broken. It is called proof. Another of the white man rules. So if they never find Marsh's body, they will have no proof that he is dead, and can make no arrests."

Were they truly having this conversation?

"It doesn't always work that way, Thomas." The stubbornness that had amused Pru earlier now infuriated her. Jumping to her feet, she paced the room, trying to find the right words. "And while they hunt for Marsh's body, where do you think you'll be? In jail. Me, too, probably."

"Why would they put you in jail?"

"Because of my association with you. Because I'm colored. Because I'm a woman. What does it matter? If they want to put someone in jail, they'll invent a reason to do so."

Thomas shook his head. "You are wrong, Prudence. Declan Brodie taught me much about the white laws. They cannot lock a person away without a strong belief that they have broken the law. He called it 'just cause.'"

Pru almost snorted. How he could be so naive? Didn't he know that Indians and blacks were the first people whites looked to blame if something went wrong?

Quelling her bitterness, Pru stopped pacing and looked at him. Declan Brodie might be an honorable man, but many lawmen weren't, especially if politics was involved. "Marsh is a powerful man, Thomas. The law wouldn't take his disappearance lightly. And since neither of us would have enough money for bail, we'd be stuck in jail for weeks while they searched for Marsh. Months, even. And what would become of Lillie then?"

He shrugged as if it didn't matter, although she knew the thoughts of hurting Lillie or of being caged in a cell were intolerable to him. "If you will not let me kill Marsh, then leave with me now, Prudence. Come home to Heartbreak Creek. Put this man and his threats behind you forever."

The fight went out of her. "I thought of that." Wearily, she sank back into the chair. "But I can't do it, Thomas. I won't." Reaching out, she lifted his hand from his thigh and held it between both of hers. It was so different from hers, with the raised tendons and ropy veins along the back, the knobby knuckles and callused palm. Warm and big and capable. Strong enough to rescue her from Lone Tree. Capable enough to pull her from this quagmire and save her from Marsh and all the dangers surrounding them.

But she was tired of being saved. Of running away, or of simply enduring. She had to take a stand someday. And with Thomas beside her, she had the courage to do it. "I can't leave yet, Thomas. I won't let Marsh chase me away from doing what I must. And the Underground Railroad still needs me for this final mission."

In a furious gesture, he yanked his hand from hers and slammed his fist against his chest. "*I* need you, *Eho'nehevehohtse*! Lillian needs you! You seek someone to teach? Teach her! Someone to save? Save me! Are we less to you than these strangers?"

"No!" She drew back, shocked by his vehemence. Thomas needed no one. He was the most self-reliant person she knew. "But they need me more, Thomas. Just this one last time."

Muttering in Cheyenne, he rose and stalked to the window, his shoulders stiff, his hands fisted at his sides.

"Give me until Monday night," she said to his back. "Until

after the fund-raiser. By then, you will have taken Mose to safety, I will have put the education initiative before people who can see it through, and Marsh will no longer be a threat. Just two more days. Three, at the most."

"I grow tired of hearing 'one more day.'"

"Please, Thomas."

He turned to face her, anger radiating from his rigid body. "Time does not last forever, Prudence. Patience is not boundless."

"I know." She looked away, hating that she was doing this to him again. But she saw no other way out of this mess she had gotten them into. "This will be the last time I ask this of you."

"Yes, Prudence. It will."

She looked up, hope rising. "You'll do it?"

He studied her for a moment, then let out a deep breath. "I will take the black skin to safety."

"Thank y—"

"Then I will take Lillian home to Heartbreak Creek."

Without me? She realized she was twisting her hands, and forced herself to stop. She would worry about all that tomorrow. The important thing right now was to put Thomas and Lillie out of danger, and get through the next two days. "I'll find out tomorrow where the safe house is."

He turned back to the window.

Realizing he would say no more, she rose from the chair, her legs shaking beneath her. The distance between them seemed wider than ever. Unbridgeable.

A panicky feeling pressed against the walls of her chest. "Thomas . . ."

"Go, Prudence. Before *Katse'e* wakes and finds you gone."

Things were still cool between them the next morning when they went downstairs to the dining room for breakfast. Thomas had reverted to his silent self, his face expressionless, his mouth a hard seam in his stern face. Even Lillie seemed subdued. Luckily neither the reverend nor Marsh was in the dining room.

After a quiet meal, Pru suggested they take a walk through town.

"I gets a peppermint stick?" Lillie asked.

Pru glanced at Thomas, but he avoided her eyes. "We'll see. Come along. Let's get our coats."

The day was brisk, but sunny, and the breeze was gentle. With Lillie between them, Pru steered them toward Main Street and the shop where she had met Chester the previous day.

It was through the bookstore that messages were exchanged between workers on the Underground Railroad. She had been there several times, but as far as she knew, had never met her contact.

On an earlier trip to Indianapolis, after she had given a talk at a local church about her education initiative, a woman, who introduced herself as Wisteria Price, had stayed behind. They had spoken for some time, then, apparently feeling Pru was trustworthy, Wisteria had asked her if she wanted to help with the Underground Railroad.

Delighted, Pru had quickly agreed. After explaining how Pru would be contacted through the bookstore, she left and Pru never saw her again. Since then, the only way she had communicated with anyone in the organization was through notes hidden inside one of the store's more obscure books— *The History and Art of Phoenician Blown Glass During the Roman Period*.

When they neared the shop, Pru turned to Thomas. "Will you mind taking Lillie to the Sweet Shoppe while I look for a book I saw earlier?"

He pointed to a bench in front of a store two doors down. "We will wait there." The first full sentence he had spoken to her since the previous night.

Pru nodded and stepped into the bookstore. With a smile to the proprietor—an older, bespectacled white man with a kind smile and the largest ears she had ever seen—she wandered idly along the narrow aisles between the tall bookcases at the back of the store. After leafing through several dusty tomes—happily finding one featuring watercolors of First Nation Indian tribes—she slipped her note into the glassworks history, then carried her art book up front.

The proprietor smiled when she set it on the counter. "George Winter. One of our local artists, and very talented. A Christmas gift?"

Pru nodded as she counted out her coins.

"Then I'll wrap it in colored paper." He dug beneath the counter, then straightened with a sigh. "I'll have to get more paper from the back. It might take a few minutes. Or, if you'd prefer, you can come back for the book later."

"Later will be fine. We still have shopping to do."

"Say, in about an hour?"

"An hour it is, then."

As she stepped outside, Pru looked around, wondering if her contact was watching. Perhaps the kindly proprietor was her contact. Or perhaps he didn't even know his store was being used by the Underground Railroad. The people in the organization were all quite secretive . . . which was probably why they had been successful for so long.

Thomas and Lillie were waiting on the bench. Thomas, eyes closed, his head tipped back to the warm sunshine— Lillie, licking the last smear of peppermint from her glove. Pru walked toward them.

"I'll have to come back in an hour for my purchase," she said, stopping before them. "It's a gift, so I'm having it wrapped."

Lillie stopped licking. "A present? Fo' me?"

"Not this time." Pru glanced at Thomas, but he was studying the road behind them. Smiling down into the child's sticky face, she said, "But I hear they have a collection of musical snuff boxes at the Clockworks Store. Would you like to go listen to them?"

Lillie bounced off the bench. "Oh, yes! I hear one once. It sound like angels playin' they harps."

It did sound like angels. And was apparently just as rare: the owner of the store hovered nervously nearby as Lillie listened to each music box twice, her face the picture of awed delight. Pru didn't know what worried the poor man more— the idea that the blind child would knock one of the precious boxes from the counter, or having Thomas staring at him.

From the Clockworks Store, they went on to the General Merchandize Emporium. Leaving Thomas studying the knives and guns in a glass-faced cabinet by the front counter, Pru and Lillie went to the small selection of toys at the back of the store. She knew she was spoiling the girl, but the minute Lillie's hand fell on a yarn-haired rag doll, Pru had to buy it for her.

"Daddy," the girl shouted, waving the doll overhead as they returned to the front. "A doll! Of my very own. I think I call her Miss Minty. That a good name?"

"*Epeva'e.* It is good."

"Yes, a very good name." Pru hoped the child was naming the doll for Araminta—Minty—Ross, later called Harriet Tubman—rather than a peppermint stick.

When they stepped back onto the street, Lillie grinning and clutching her new doll tightly to her chest, Pru checked the watch pinned on the inside of her coat. Over an hour had passed, so her package should be ready. If all had gone well, she would find an answer to her note waiting for her, too.

This time all three of them went into the bookstore. Leaving Thomas and Lillie at the front, Pru went to the cases in back. There, in the history book, she found scribbled directions to the barn of a Quaker family on the outskirts of Westfield, a town twenty-five miles north of Indianapolis. With lawmen hunting Mose, taking the real train would be out of the question, so two horses would be waiting at the previous night's meeting place. *"Nine o'clock,"* the note read. *"A fresh horse will be supplied for the return trip. Go thee with God."*

As instructed previously, Pru dropped the shredded note into the coal stove by the rear wall before going back to the front. After picking up her book and thanking the shopkeeper, she and Thomas and Lillie headed back to the Beckworth Arms.

While Lillie kept up a running monologue with Miss Minty, Pru relayed to Thomas what was in the note. "How long will it take?" A fifty-mile round trip seemed a huge distance on horseback.

"The horses will need water and rest along the way. One day. Maybe more."

"Assuming there are no problems."

"There will be no problems."

"If you don't leave until nine tonight, that means you might miss the fund-raiser tomorrow night."

He shrugged.

Considering the tension between Thomas and Marsh, that was probably a good thing. And hopefully, by the time he returned, it would all be over, and the next morning they would be on their way to Heartbreak Creek.

One more day. Then everything would be fine.

"Come along then," she said, hurrying their pace. "We can have an early supper at the hotel before we leave for our last gospel meeting."

Thomas chewed thoughtfully, his gaze drawn to the people and wagons moving past the dining room window. The noise they made filled his head, drowning out everything else. Closing his eyes for a moment, he tried to remember the trill of birdsong, the whisper of wind over buffalo grass, the burble of water in a cold mountain stream. Instead, he heard only the rattle of wheels, people calling to one another, the clatter of plates and glasses. The music of his mountains was distant now, and that worried him.

Laughter broke into his thoughts. He opened his eyes and saw Prudence cutting meat into tiny bites for Lillian. As he watched them, another troubling thought arose. Like the people rushing past outside, *Eho'nehevehohtse* had a purpose. Something to do. Somewhere to be. Reasons to keep putting him off.

But what was *his* purpose?

Forking up another bite of stew, he thought about that.

Throughout his youth, his purpose had been to become a warrior and bring honor to his tribe. When his chief sent him away, his task had been to learn the ways of the whites so he would know how to defeat them. But after his tribe was herded into the government camps, his only duty had been to protect his wife and son. But he had failed at that, too. And in the dark time after he sang their death songs, vengeance had been his purpose and alcohol had fed his rage . . . until Declan Brodie locked him in a cell. After the demons left his spirit, he put aside his Indian ways. He took work as a deputy sheriff and lived among the whites. He sought peace, not war, and he learned that not all whites were without honor.

But he still did not belong.

Then Prudence Lincoln came. He knew from the moment he saw her sitting in Declan Brodie's wagon that she would be the one to give him new purpose and bring joy back into his heart. She taught him letters and numbers and words. She showed him how to fill the darkness of his spirit with books. And for the first time in many years, he had felt he had a place in this troubling world.

But now she was leaving him, too. She had not said it yet, but he knew.

Panic filled his chest. An unfamiliar feeling. One that left him confused and off balance. Yet he could find no other word for what he felt: fear. He could already sense he was spiraling back into the dark despair of a man who had no sons to follow in his steps, no tribe. No purpose.

He did not want to go back to that place. He did not know if he could crawl out of it again. Or if he would want to without Prudence Lincoln.

"May we join you?"

Startled, Thomas looked up to see the preaching man and Marsh standing beside the table. He sat back, surprised that he had not heard them approach, but comforted by the feel of his knife resting against the small of his back.

"Of course." Prudence smiled as she spoke, but Thomas saw the fear in her eyes, and in the blank stare of *Katse'e*, too.

"I have good news," Marsh said, after he and the reverend had ordered food.

"About what?" Prudence asked.

"Your initiative." Marsh took his time shaking out his napkin and spreading it over his knees. After smoothing it flat with his soft hands, he looked up with that false smile. "I spoke with several people attending the fund-raiser tomorrow, and they're quite interested in your idea of having the federal government oversee the schooling of ex-slaves."

Prudence smiled at the reverend. "That is good news, isn't it, Brother?"

"Certainly is."

"There's more." With a smug expression, Marsh glanced at Brother Sampson. "Shall I tell her now? Or wait until after the gospel meeting tonight?"

"Tell me what?"

A prickle of alarm crept up Thomas's back. He felt a sudden and unreasoning urge to pull *Eho'nehevehohtse* from the room.

Lillian offered a spoonful of mashed potatoes to her doll, then shoved it into her own mouth instead. "What he talkin' 'bout, Miss Pru?"

"I suspect you had best tell her now." Brother Sampson's big, square teeth flashed in his dark face like a row of short tallow candles. "So she can make her plans."

Prudence stopped eating and looked at Marsh. Wary. Watchful.

"What plans?" *Katse'e* chased gravy smears on her chin with her tongue. "Nobody tell me nothing 'bout no plans."

For once, *Eho'nehevehohtse* did not correct her.

The woman came with the food. Marsh leaned back in his chair as she set it before him. "I hope you've practiced your presentation, Miss Lincoln," he said after the woman left. "Because if all goes well at the fund-raiser, you'll be asked to present it to the Committee on Education."

Prudence glanced from Marsh to the reverend, her uneasiness fading into a tentative smile. "Truly?"

Thomas felt something cold move through his chest.

Chuckling like a raven over a fresh kill, Marsh leaned forward, his pale eyes fixed on Prudence. "The committee meets in Washington."

"Washington?" The fork clattered to her plate. Prudence lifted a hand to her throat. And for a moment, before she masked it, Thomas saw the joy in her eyes.

It cut like a blade.

Marsh sat back. "We would have to leave the morning after the fund-raiser to be there before the committee adjourns for the Christmas season. I've already bought tickets for you and Brother Sampson and booked your hotel rooms." He glanced at Thomas. "I haven't booked yours or the girl's yet, Mr. Redstone, since I didn't know if you would be traveling with us or not."

Thomas looked at Prudence and saw the broken promise in her eyes, and his heart turned to stone.

"That's very kind of you, Mr. Marsh," Prudence cut in before Thomas could find his words. "But I haven't yet decided if I'm going."

"Isn't this what you've been working—"

"And if I do decide to go to Washington," she cut in, her gaze shifting to Thomas, "naturally, Thomas and Lillie would go with me."

Thomas sucked in air, not realizing until then that he had been holding his breath. "No," he said in a voice he did not recognize as his. "We will not go with you."

"But, Daddy—"

"Thomas—"

"No." He stood so fast the chair almost toppled to the floor behind him. "You do what you will, *Eho'nehevehohtse*. Lillian and I will go to Heartbreak Creek." Then, with the sound of their protests ringing in his ears, he left the room.

Seven

The peas stuck to the mound of mashed potatoes on Pru's plate looked like green warts on a white man's chin. The notion would have made her smile if she hadn't been struggling so hard not to vomit. She didn't want to cause a scene. She didn't want to draw attention to herself.

So, while dishes clattered on servers' trays, and voices rose and fell in a murmuring tide, and the sun slid steadily lower in the sky—she maintained her serenity by stabbing her fork into that mashed potato chin and wishing it were Marsh instead.

How could Thomas walk away from her? Why hadn't he at least given her a chance to explain?

Explain what? the traitorous voice in her head asked. *That for a moment—less than the time it took to draw a breath—you hesitated?*

How could she not? Taking her proposal to Washington was the dream of a lifetime.

Your dream. Not Thomas's.

"You're not eating. Are you unwell?"

Pru carefully set down her fork and met Marsh's question with a practiced smile. "Not at all. I'm simply too full to eat another bite."

Across the table, Brother blinked at her with his sad hound dog eyes. She hated that look. Hated his calm acceptance of Marsh's manipulations and the wrongs she fought so hard to right. Didn't he see what was happening?

Anger rose. Kept rising until something shattered inside. She heard it. Like glass breaking into tiny pieces. And with that thin barrier gone, fury seeped out. Boundless, hot, suffocating. Seeking a target. And like an arrow loosed from a bowstring, it found its mark in Reverend Brother Sampson.

How could he sit there and do nothing? Where was his anger? His outrage? How could he preach so eloquently from his pulpit, yet stand silent while others suffered? Was she to fight this battle alone?

Alone. Always and forever.

The breath went out of her. With her serenity in tatters, shards of the past rushed in to fill her mind. She clamped her eyes shut against the assault, but still, they came. A kaleidoscope gone wild, spinning images faster and faster until she couldn't separate one from another—water and searing pain—Black Sam rising above her—ebony eyes in mahogany faces watching impassively while Lone Tree laughed and kicked and laughed—Thomas walking away.

She almost wept in anguish. *How could you leave me?*

"Well then, if we're finished . . ."

With a jerk, Pru opened her eyes and saw Marsh setting his napkin beside his plate, and the chaos faded away. She looked down at the red crescents her nails had left in her trembling palms, and she welcomed the pain.

Marsh pushed back his chair and rose. "Perhaps we should get an early start. This being our last meeting, I've a feeling we'll have a full house tonight."

"That 'cause Miss Bessie lettin' me sing again." Grabbing Miss Minty, Lillie hopped down from her chair and waited for Pru to take her hand. "Peoples jist loves to hear me sing, ain't that right, Brother Sampson?"

"You do have a voice, Miss Lillian. Never heard the like."

"I hopes Daddy hear me. He come back to hear me sing, won't he, Miss Pru?"

"I'm sure he will," Pru lied.

He didn't.

By the time the meeting began, Thomas still hadn't arrived,

even though he must have known how important it was to Lillie that he be there when she sang.

Battling rising irritation, Pru sat stiffly in her chair behind Brother Sampson, hardly attending the reverend's fine sermon. She felt raw and ragged, her emotions bouncing between exasperation that Thomas would allow his anger to spill out onto Lillian and terror that she would never see him again.

Would he still meet Chester and Mose Solomon at the appointed time tonight? Or had he simply left, as he often did when frustration ruled him?

She'd have to go herself, she decided. As soon as the meeting ended, she would leave Lillian with Bessie Prescott and race over to the metal works, hoping to avoid Marsh and arrive in time. She would have to convince Chester to take Mose to Westfield on his own or risk a delay and ask her contact to find someone else to take him.

One more mess in her wake.

The sermon ended. Brother Sampson turned and said something to Bessie, who was sitting with Lillie and her doll and the other choir ladies on the opposite side of the small stage from Pru. The child was so proud to sit among them. A real gospel singer. But an impatient one. Pru had watched her fidget with Miss Minty and squirm throughout the long sermon. But now her time to sing had come.

Pru braced herself, not knowing what to expect.

Bessie led Lillie over to stand by the podium, then returned to her seat.

Resting a hand on the child's shoulder, the reverend smiled at the faces looking up from the crowded benches that filled the huge tent. "If you haven't heard this little angel sing, then you're in for a fine treat." He paused when Lillie jerked on his coat. She whispered something, then Brother straightened and looked out over the congregation.

From behind, Pru watched his head turn as he scanned the crowd, then felt a shock when she saw Thomas standing against the back wall beside the entrance flap. When had he arrived?

She smiled, hoping to draw his attention, but he never glanced her way, his attention fixed solely on Lillie. He looked carved in stone.

Brother said something to Lillie that made her bounce on her toes like she did when she was excited—probably because Thomas had arrived—then the reverend faced his congregation once more. "Tonight, our Lillian has chosen a song that has special meaning for all of us. And she sings it for her daddy."

A murmur rippled through the smiling congregation, although Pru noticed no change in Thomas's stony expression.

Leaving the blind child standing with one hand on the podium and Miss Minty tucked under her other arm, the reverend came to take his seat beside Pru.

"Prepare yourself," he whispered.

Lillie lifted her chin, took a deep breath, and let the music soar.

> *"Amazing grace! How sweet the sound*
> *That saved a wretch like me!*
> *I once was lost, but now am found;*
> *Was blind but now I see."*

Pru's mouth fell open. It was breathtaking. Like being transported to heaven and hearing an angel sing. Every note so sweet and clear it brought an ache to her chest. She felt uplifted. Reborn. Humbled. By the time Lillie began the third verse, there wasn't a dry eye in the house.

> *"Through many dangers, toils and snares*
> *I have already come;*
> *'Tis grace that brought me safe thus far*
> *and grace will lead me home."*

But when Lillie sang the final verse—the one not written by the original lyricist, Newton, but passed down from one slave to another until it was put on paper in Harriet Beecher Stowe's famous book, *Uncle Tom's Cabin*—sobs broke through the crowd.

> *"When we've been there ten thousand years,*
> *Bright shining as the sun,*
> *We've no less days to sing God's praise,*
> *Than when we first begun."*

Giddy with pride, Pru looked toward the back wall for Thomas's reaction, wondering if he was familiar with the hymn, or knew that it had been sung by the Cherokee as they had been marched along their Trail of Tears forty years ago.

But he was no longer there.

Thomas stood in the darkness outside the tent, his face wet with tears. As the last notes of Lillian's song faded into a hushed silence, he took a ragged breath, wiped his coat sleeve over his eyes, and started walking.

He got as far as the shadows behind the vendors' carts before Prudence ran up behind him.

"Thomas, wait! I need to talk to you."

He did not want to talk. But after hearing Lillian's sweet song, much of his anger had faded away, so he let her pull him to a stop. "I do not have time for this, Prudence. The black men wait."

"You still intend to take Mose Solomon to Westfield?"

"I said I would. And I always keep my promises, *Eho'nehevehohtse*."

His barb struck home. "That's not fair. I didn't break my promise. I never said I would go to Washington."

"*Nehetome.* You are right. You did not say the words, but in your heart you know the truth. You want to go."

"Of course I do. If the committee adopts my proposal, it will help thousands of Negroes all over the country."

Thomas remained silent.

"But I won't go if you don't go with me," she added firmly.

Yet when he looked into her eyes, Thomas saw the doubt. He sighed, his breath clouding in the air. "That is your decision, Prudence Lincoln. But *Katse'e* and I will not go with you. Nor will we wait here for you to return."

When she started to protest, he put his hand on her cheek. Her skin was warm and soft and as smooth as the shiny ribbons in her hair. Touching it made his heart kick in his chest. Afraid he would weaken, he took his hand away. "I have chased you as far as I can, *heme'oone*. I will chase you no more."

"But—"

"No. I will not fight with you about this, Prudence. But

while I take Mose Solomon to safety, think about what I have said and decide what it is you want. I will do the same. When I return, we will talk again. Now kiss me."

He waited, needing her to come to him. But when her soft lips touched his, pride deserted him. Wrapping his arms tightly around her, he pulled her slender body against his.

He tasted the salt of her tears and wondered if she had shed them because of the strife between them, or because of the beauty and sadness of the song Lillian sang. His desire for her grew. The warm softness of her body drew him in. Her scent lit a fire in his belly. He trembled, his resolve weakening, his mind urging him to do whatever he must to keep her in his arms.

A feeling came into his mind—not a thought, or an image, or even something he could put into words—but a feeling so strong it embraced the whole of his being. He needed this woman. Like air and water and food. And even if she left him tomorrow, she would still hold his heart in her hands until the day the Great Spirit called him home.

With a gasp, she broke the kiss. "We have to stop. People are staring."

But instead of pulling away from him, she rested her head in the hollow of his throat. He felt the rush of her breath against his skin and wanted to carry her into the darkness.

She let out a trembling breath. "You make me forget all the orderly lessons drilled into me."

"That is a good thing." He had to smile, despite his uncertainty. *Eho'nehevehohtse* and her rules. If he ever had the chance again, he would show her that order does not come from rules, but in finding harmony with all living things. If he could teach her that, she would be free of fear forever.

With a soft laugh, she gently pushed him away. "Go. They're waiting. And Lillie will be looking for me."

He struggled to calm his thundering pulse. It was a moment before he could make his hands let her go. "Tell *Katse'e* I am proud," he said, once he was sure of his voice. "And that I will return to her."

"I will. Be careful, Thomas."

"And you."

Then, while he still had the strength to leave her, he hurried into the night.

The man named Chester was waiting when he arrived a few minutes later at the abandoned metal works. With him were two sturdy horses and a tall, broad, hairless man who was even bigger than Declan Brodie, the largest man in Heartbreak Creek. His skin was so dark it was hard for Thomas to read his expression in the moonless night.

Chester danced like a new foal, probably nervous because Thomas had frightened him the previous night. He looked around, his feet shuffling from side to side. "It so dark. How you see where you going?"

"*Na'tsehe'stahe.* I am Cheyenne."

Thomas moved closer to study Mose Solomon, stepping to the side to draw the hulking man's face toward the faint torchlight coming from the area where the tent and food wagons stood.

He wore tattered overalls, the strap on one side held together by a shred of cloth that was the same color as his shirt. He had no coat and shivered when the breeze moaned through the broken windows of the metal works building. There was pride in his stance and a forward thrust to his chin. His hands were big, and made big fists at his side. Satisfied, Thomas nodded.

"Do what I say, Mose Solomon, and I will keep you safe. Do you understand?"

"Yessuh."

"Do not call me sir. My white name is Thomas Redstone. Will you fight if we are set upon?" Thomas needed to know if he could count on this man.

"Fight?" Chester looked fearfully around. "You 'spectin' trouble?"

"I'll fight," Mose Solomon said.

"*Epeva'e.* That is good." Thomas held out his hand in the white man way.

The big black man accepted it. His grip was firm and strong, his palm rough with calluses and broader than any Thomas had ever held.

"You have no coat?" Thomas asked him.

"I be fine."

Thomas knew he would not be fine. They would have to set a fast pace, and the cold would cut through his thin shirt and make him shiver until his strength ran out. Thomas wore two shirts under his coat, and even he felt the chill.

"They's blankets tied behind the saddle," Chester offered. "And food in the saddlebags. Maybe even gloves. Headin' north, are you?"

Thomas found not only food and gloves in the bags, but also two pistols and a box of bullets. Apparently, whoever had arranged for Mose's escape was not a Quaker. With his long knife, he cut a slit in the center of one of the blankets to make a poncho for the big black man.

"Good folks up north." Shoulders hunched against the cold, Chester watched Thomas cut off several long strips of latigo leather from one of the saddles. "Quakers, I hear."

After tying the leathers into one long strip, Thomas gave it to Mose Solomon to belt the poncho at his waist.

Chester stomped his feet and looked around. "'Specially around Westfield. Got a whole bunch of Quakers up there."

Deciding to leave the bigger, heavier sorrel for the black man, Thomas vaulted up onto the long-legged bay. He watched Mose Solomon speak quietly to the sorrel before gathering his reins and mounting, and was satisfied the man knew his way around horses.

"That where you're headed?" Chester asked. "Westfield?"

Thomas looked down at him. "Who told you to ask, Chester Hogan?"

"What? No. Nobody." The nervous man backed away, palms upraised. "I just wonderin' is all."

"This is good. Because if someone follows us, I will have to kill him. Then I will have to come back and kill you."

Chester made a garbled sound.

With a nod to Mose Solomon, Thomas reined his horse away from the rail yard and north toward Westfield.

"He not a very good daddy," Lillie complained as Pru led her past the vendor carts after the gospel meeting broke up. "Runnin' off like that."

"He stayed long enough to hear you sing. And he was as proud of you as I was." Pru slowed to guide the girl over the tracks behind the depot. "Told me so himself."

"Where he at, anyways?"

"Yes, where?" a voice said, startling Pru. She turned to see

Marsh less than a dozen feet behind them. Had he been following them all along?

"Where did your Mr. Redstone go?" he asked, coming up beside them. "Or is he still in a tiff about your going to Washington?"

"We haven't discussed Washington." Pru continued toward the hotel, Lillie's hand tight in hers. "Nor have I decided if I'll go or not."

"Haven't you?" Marsh fell into step beside them. "When you left the meeting early, I assumed it was to talk it over with him."

"You leave, too?" Lillie accused.

"Just for a moment," Pru assured her, then to Marsh, added, "Thomas was in a hurry. We only exchanged a few words." And a kiss that still left her weak.

"Gone where, do you suppose?"

"I don't know." It didn't bother Pru in the least to lie to this man. "He's very independent, and not given to explaining himself. He'll return when he's ready."

"Will he miss the fund-raiser, too, do you think?"

"I wouldn't know."

They walked in silence for a moment, then Marsh smiled down at Lillie. "Senator Brooks said very nice things about you, Lillie."

"Who he?"

"An important man. He helps run a special school for children like you."

"Po' little blind black orphan chilrin?"

"Among others."

"I not like school."

"You might like this one. And Senator Brooks said he would be happy to have you join the other students while Miss Lincoln is in Washington."

"I haven't yet decided to go," Pru reminded him.

That oily smile. "I really think you should, my dear. Your initiative is vital to our plans."

Our plans? Why was her being there so important that he would use a child to force her to go?

"I realize you're concerned about the girl, Miss Lincoln. But I assure you she'll be quite safe at the school until you return."

Pru kept her head down so he wouldn't see her rising panic. Senator Brooks was no better than Marsh was. She had instantly distrusted him when she'd met him before the service began. He oozed that self-righteous contempt that overbearing, self-important people wore like armor. And no matter what Marsh said, Brooks had not been "taken" with Lillie. Rather, he seemed to regard her as a new recruit for his lunatic asylum. He probably got a stipend from the government for every child at the school.

As if Thomas would ever be parted from Lillie.

"Tell the senator I appreciate his interest, but I will be taking Lillie to Colorado." She had said it on impulse, but as soon as the words left her mouth she knew it was the right decision. She and Thomas could make Lillie's life richer than the senator and his school ever could.

"Fo' true?" Lillie squeaked.

"I doubt that would be possible," Marsh cut in.

Pru's steps faltered. Stopping in the middle of the sidewalk, she turned to Marsh. "Why not?"

"Because she's not your child, Miss Lincoln. She's a ward of the state."

"Then I'll adopt her."

"What 'dopt mean?"

Marsh shook his head and resumed walking, forcing Pru to hurry to keep up. "An unmarried woman? No judge would allow it. But if it is something you want to pursue, we can discuss it more fully when you return from Washington. Well, I see we're here."

Pru only then realized they had reached the Beckworth Arms. Forcing her lips into a smile, she said, "Thank you for walking us back, Mr. Marsh. But we'll bid you good night now. Lillie is quite tired."

"Of course." Marsh tipped his hat. "Sleep well. Tomorrow will be a big day. For all of us, I suspect."

As soon as they walked into the lobby, Pru asked the desk clerk for a pad and pencil, then scribbled a note to Brother Sampson. As she pushed it across the counter, she told the clerk to see that the reverend got it the moment he returned. "It's terribly important that he get this as soon as possible."

She watched the clerk slip the note into the slot marked

206, then headed upstairs. If for some reason Brother didn't get the note tonight, she would go to his room herself. There was more than one way to stop Marsh and keep Lillie safe, and she had only a day to do it.

Knowing they could move faster in the dark on smooth land, Thomas stayed on the road, rather than risk damage to the horses on a less-traveled trail. He set a hard pace, varying their speed from walk to trot to lope, then back down again, so the horses would not get winded or tire too soon. And always, he stayed alert, eyes scanning the ground in front of his horse, ears cocked for riders coming up behind them.

He did not trust Chester. A man so easy to frighten would be quick to talk if pushed. "Did you see anyone follow you and Chester?" he asked Mose Solomon.

"I wasn't lookin'. But Chester, he seem mighty nervous."

Frowning, Thomas nudged his horse into a trot.

Since leaving behind the lights of the city, his vision had adjusted to the darkness. Even though there was no moon, the cloudless sky was not completely black. The stars sprinkled overhead gave enough light for him to see a darker outline against the deep blue of the night sky.

A line of trees. Pines, he guessed, since the shadows were tall and the branches short. Deciding this would be as good a place as any to rest the horses, Thomas reined off the road. As they moved silently across the frost-curled grass, the white trunks of aspens showed in the shadows beyond the pines, and his bay picked up his pace. Where there was aspen, there was water.

In a meadow bordered by trees on one side and a sluggish creek on the other, they dismounted and loosened the girths of their saddles. Thomas let the horses drink a small amount, then moved them away from the water to graze in the clearing. The breeze had strengthened, and it swept through the long pine needles with a sound like rushing water. Needing a quieter place to listen for followers, he left Mose Solomon to watch over the horses and went closer to the road.

Half hidden behind a stump, he waited for a long time, but saw and heard nothing. Finally, he rose on cold-stiffened legs and went back to the clearing.

The black man stood on the bank of the creek, giving the horses another drink. "See anything?"

Thomas shook his head.

After tightening the girths on their saddles, they mounted again and went back to the road. Thomas stopped often to look behind them and listen for followers, but other than a farmer taking a wagon of hay to town, no one else was out in the dark. Occasionally, a dog barked in the distance, warning them away from a lonely farmhouse. Once, a horse whinnied from a field nearby, but for most of the night, they rode without speaking, the *clomp* of the horses' hooves the only sounds to break the silence.

Thomas thought often of Prudence. He knew the chance for them to make a life together was slipping away, but he did not know how to stop it. Or even if he should. Perhaps he was holding on to her too hard, using her as a crutch for all he lacked. Maybe they were not meant to be together.

The thought settled like a stone in his chest.

They rode on. The ride seemed endless. Then the sky began to fade into a paler blue, and a faint smear of light kissed the horizon to the east.

Relieved to be nearing the end of this half of his journey, Thomas pushed the weary horses faster. It wasn't until he saw the lights of Westfield winking to life through the trees ahead that he heard the sound of horses behind them. Coming fast.

As soon as Lillie fell asleep, Pru tiptoed into the hall, locked the door behind her, then hurried to room 206. Luckily Brother was still dressed.

Ignoring his look of surprise, she slipped past him into the room. "Didn't you get the note I left with the clerk?"

"The clerk wasn't at the desk. Is something wrong, Miss Lincoln?"

"Can you perform marriage ceremonies?"

He blinked in surprise—then smiled. "You and Mr. Redstone?"

"Yes. How soon can you marry us?"

"Tomorrow, if the courthouse is open and I can get a license."

His smile faded into a look of concern. "Why the rush, if you don't mind me asking?"

She told him all that Marsh had said, and about her suspicion that he wanted to put Lillie into the senator's school to ensure that Pru would go with them to Washington to present her initiative. "I don't know why it's so important that I be there. You're going. Why can't you present it?"

"He'll have a better chance of success with you. I heard him tell Brooks that if the initiative succeeds and a committee on Negro education is formed, they'll need someone to run it. Why not him?"

Pru's knees almost buckled. A man as evil and corrupt as Marsh would bleed off all the funds needed to help the Negroes. Her hard work would have been for nothing. "We have to stop him."

She began to pace, thoughts bouncing through her mind. Without her, the initiative might fail. That was why Marsh was so determined that she be there. And the only way he could be sure she would cooperate . . . "He's using Lillie." *That bastard!*

Brother stared at her. "To what purpose? I don't understand."

"To make me behave." She whirled to face him. "When I told him I wanted to adopt her, he said no judge would allow an unmarried woman to do that."

"So you plan to marry Mr. Redstone and adopt her?"

She gave a shaky smile. "If they'll have me."

Eight

Early the next morning, Pru and Lillie went with Brother Sampson to the courthouse. Leaving Lillie on a bench just inside the Licensing and Records Office, Pru and Brother approached the man at the reception desk. It took some explaining—to both Brother and the harried clerk—about why the intended groom wasn't with them, but eventually Brother was able to convince the clerk to issue the license.

It wouldn't be the wedding Pru had envisioned—a hurried ceremony in a dismal hotel room with some hapless stranger as witness—but perhaps later she and Thomas could have a real ceremony in Heartbreak Creek. Edwina would probably insist on it, assuming they could get Thomas into the church.

"Don't tell Lillie about it yet," Pru whispered to Brother before they collected the girl chatting happily to Miss Minty. "I want to surprise her."

"When do you expect Mr. Redstone back?"

"Tonight. After the fund-raiser. Can you do the ceremony then?"

"I can. We'll need a witness, though. Perhaps the man at the hotel desk will agree to it."

"Let's hope adopting Lillie will go as smoothly."

The records clerk had given them a stack of papers to fill out and the name of a judge who might expedite matters. For the first time, Pru welcomed white indifference. It was obvious by the clerk's attitude that legal matters pertaining to coloreds weren't as strictly monitored as those involving whites.

Sending Lillie with Brother to oversee the dismantling of the meeting tent, Pru sat on the bench in the courthouse hallway and filled out the adoption papers. After leaving them with Judge Kohler's clerk, she promised to bring the marriage certificate tomorrow, then hurried back to the hotel.

At least now there was a record of her intention to adopt. And when she and Thomas brought proof of their marriage to Judge Kohler's clerk tomorrow, they would find out what else they could do to expedite the adoption.

Adoption. Marriage. It was a great deal to take in all at once.

She and Thomas had never discussed a proper, legal marriage. Pru wasn't sure Indians had formal marriage rites and had never pressed the matter. But if he knew this was the best way to protect Lillie, surely Thomas would go along with it.

An odd mix of emotions swirled in her head. Was this what she wanted? What Thomas wanted? All those obstacles still loomed before them. She knew they loved each other—there would never be any other man but Thomas in her life. And they both loved Lillie. Surely, they could overcome the hurdles ahead.

Just a few more hours.

If everything went as planned, before the night was over, she would be married and Lillie would be safe. Until then, all that remained was to get through the fund-raiser tonight, and the wedding ceremony after. Then they'd be free of Marsh forever.

It was dark when Brother Sampson escorted Pru and Lillie and Miss Minty into the lush home where the fund-raiser was being held. Pru saw immediately that other than the Negro servers in their white jackets and white gloves, the three of them were the only people of color at the crowded event. It made her nervous, all those white faces staring at them. Especially those announcing—with varying expressions of resentment, disdain, or forced amiability—that coloreds didn't belong here among them.

Pru tried not to take it personally. Having been emancipated by her white father on the day of her birth, she had never been a slave. As proof, she still carried the manumission papers everywhere she traveled—out of fear or pride, she wasn't sure which. In addition, and also because of her white father's generosity, she had an education equal to or better than that of any white woman in this room.

But she wasn't their equal. The inescapable truth was that even with her white blood and high learning, she would never belong among these wealthy, finely dressed white people, any more than her black blood made her acceptable to the Negroes she saw wandering the streets, lost and bewildered by sudden freedom and unsure what to do with it.

Raised to think, rather than fearfully submit, she was despised by whites for her presumption, and resented by blacks for being blessed with advantages they had never had. She could do little to change the former, but she could certainly use those advantages to help those who had suffered so much more than she.

But it hurt.

Too base for one, too disparate for the other. Neither black nor white, but the bastard product of an alliance that was an affront to God and the law, she was welcomed nowhere, and belonged nowhere. Except in Heartbreak Creek. There both she and Thomas were accepted and loved despite their skin colors. It would be the perfect place to raise Lillie.

But first, she had to get through this fundraiser.

The irony of it didn't escape her: wealthy white people assuaging their guilt over the mistreatment of blacks by promoting the Negro cause, while she used that same Negro cause to lessen her own guilt that she had never been one of those mistreated blacks. When had her life become this convoluted?

It was so laughable it made her want to weep.

Instead, with the humility and gratitude expected of her, she tucked Lillie's hand into her elbow and followed Brother Sampson and Marsh around the room, pretending it didn't matter that she would always be an outsider with either race.

It was a lavish gathering, with goblets of fine champagne and trays of delicate treats. The men all wore dark suits. The women were elegantly flounced, bustled, and bejeweled. Pru felt rather dowdy in her Sunday best linsey-woolsey. And itchy. Had she known this was a dress-up affair, she would have worn her less warm but more fashionable blue worsted linen. Fancy enough to show respect, but inferior enough to assure everyone she knew her place.

In an effort to bolster Lillie's hurt over Thomas's absence, Pru had given her the dress she had bought her for Christmas. The bright color of the worsted wool looked quite festive, and when Pru put matching ribbons in Lillie's pigtails, the child looked just the thing. It helped lighten Lillie's mood somewhat, but she still seemed downcast without Thomas nearby.

Pru understood. She felt it, too—that vague uneasiness that kept her looking restlessly about, as if some vital part of her was missing and her nerves could only settle once everything—and everyone—was back in the proper place.

Or maybe that fidgety feeling was due to the wool in her dress. She hated wool. It made her feel like tiny ants were crawling over her skin. And she especially hated linsey-woolsey, despite its durability, practicality, and warmth. It always reminded her of Pricilla Whitney and the combined expressions of smug superiority and barely concealed distaste her father's wife wore when she passed out the annual set of linsey-woolsey clothing to the slaves at Rose Hill.

But that was then, and this was now. And no matter the guilt that had brought them all here tonight, Pru was grateful for the opportunity to present her proposal to wealthy people who might be able to move it along. Then, once that was done, she and Lillie and Miss Minty could happily leave them to their champagne and go back to the hotel. It was of utmost importance that she be there when Thomas returned.

They both had a lot to talk about.

"Try this." Pru set a chocolate-dipped strawberry in Lillie's free hand.

"What it is?" The child wrinkled her nose. "It feel sticky. And sweaty."

"If you don't like it, put it in your napkin. Don't throw it on the floor like you did with the goose liver sandwiches."

"Miss Minty do that, not me." She gave a lick. "Mmm . . . Chocolate. I jist loves chocolate." Grinning, she stuffed the entire strawberry in her mouth. "Got more?" she asked, juice dripping down her chin.

"I see you're enjoying yourselves." Marsh sidled up beside

them, unsuccessfully masking his distaste as Pru mopped up Lillie's face. He motioned to the man beside him. "You remember Senator Brooks?"

Pru tucked the soiled napkin into her reticule. "Of course."

Which was apparently all the encouragement the officious man needed to drone on for ten minutes about his school and the great work being done there. "We could do wonders for Lillian."

"Perhaps," Pru allowed. "But I've been working with Lillie myself, teaching her to read by Braille." She decided not to tell them about her intent to adopt Lillie until the papers were on the judge's desk.

"Have you?" The senator stared down at the child licking chocolate off her palm, his bushy white brows arching above cold, gray eyes. "You find she's intelligent enough to comprehend the six-dot method?"

Pru almost struck him.

Luckily, Marsh stepped in to remind her it was time for her talk. "Brother Sampson is introducing you now."

"But Lillie—"

"I'll keep an eye on her." Marsh reached out to put his hand on Lillie's shoulder. Then, seeing Pru's hesitation, he took the sticky little hand instead. "I know where there's a whole tray of chocolate-covered strawberries, Lillian. Would you care for another?"

Lillie perked up. "I jist loves chocolate strawberries. Miss Minty do, too."

"Then let's go get them, shall we?"

With a nod to Pru, Marsh and the senator led the child away just as Brother Sampson concluded his introduction.

"So let's give a warm welcome to Miss Prudence Lincoln, the author of the fine education initiative you've been hearing about. Miss Lincoln?"

With a last glance toward the back corner where Lillie was happily gobbling more chocolate-covered strawberries, Pru reluctantly walked through the crowd to do what she had come to do.

The first bullet drilled through the high cantle of Mose Solomon's saddle, came out the other side, and lodged in his side.

Thomas saw him lurch sideways and grabbed the reins of the black man's sorrel before they slipped from his slack hand. "Hang on!" Bending low over the pommel of his saddle, Thomas turned his bay sharply toward a group of trees and kicked him into a run, pulling the sorrel behind him.

More bullets. A searing pain. Thomas glanced down and saw a long tear in his jacket where a bullet had creased his upper arm.

They reached the trees. Another bullet cracked against a branch overhead, sending down a shower of splinters. A fourth plowed into the trunk of a tree beside Thomas's head.

They rode hard until they came up against a wall of brush and brambles. Thomas jumped down, grabbed the revolver and box of bullets from his saddlebag, and ran back to Mose.

The black man had already dismounted and was clinging to the saddle with both hands. Blood darkened the left side of his poncho. Thomas waved toward the brush. "Run! Stay low!"

Holding his side, Mose Solomon staggered out of sight.

Thomas slapped the horses, sending them back the way they'd come, then crouched behind a tree trunk as their pursuers charged through the trees behind them. Shouts. Curses. Two horses. Two riders.

Thomas checked the cylinder of his Colt. Six rounds. Thumbing back the hammer, he braced his arm against the tree trunk and sighted down the barrel.

The front rider crashed through the brush.

Thomas fired.

The man flew backward, blood spurting from his neck.

The second man kept coming.

Deafened by the blast, his eyes burning from spent powder, Thomas cocked and fired again. His shot went wide.

The second rider continued toward him, firing as he came.

Thomas ducked behind the tree again, struggling to listen through the ringing in his ears. Four shots? Or was it five? When the firing stopped, Thomas rose up, the gun cocked and ready.

An unfamiliar horse stood twenty feet away. His saddle was empty.

Thomas scanned the trees, saw nothing. He slid behind the trunk again, shaking his head to clear the buzzing in his ears.

"You killed my partner, you bastard!" The voice came from the right.

Thomas inched to the left and waited, gun ready. A bird flitted by. Somewhere overhead, a squirrel scolded. When the noise in his head began to fade and he could hear again, Thomas stepped around the tree again, caught movement, and lurched back too late.

The heel of a boot slammed into his chest. "Got you, you red son of a bitch!" a voice cried as the butt of a gun cracked against his temple.

"You're a success," Brother Sampson murmured at Pru's shoulder as they moved through the guests, nodding to well-wishers congratulating her on her speech.

"Let's hope the initiative is as well received."

"It already is. Look at the crowd standing at the table where donations are being taken."

Not a crowd, perhaps, but enough to ensure she hadn't wasted her time coming here tonight. Rising on tiptoes, she strained to see past the people milling about. "Do you see Mr. Marsh and Lillie?" She had tried to keep an eye on them while she gave her talk, but without a raised dais, she hadn't been able to see over the heads of the taller listeners.

"I believe they stepped out."

Panic brought her to a stop. "Stepped out? When? Where did they go?"

His smile faded. "Toward the entry. You don't think—"

"Oh, God." She shoved her way through the crowd. But when she reached the foyer, there was only a single footman standing beside the front door.

"Did a man and a little black girl come through here?"

The footman blinked at her in surprise, then nodded. "About five minutes ago. They went outside with Senator Brooks."

Panic escalated into full-blown fear. Ignoring the befuddled footman's attempts to help, she threw open the front door.

Marsh and the senator stood at the street next to a boxy black carriage.

Pru raced down the steps. "What are you doing? Where's Lillie?"

"I here!" A dark, tear-streaked face appeared in the coach window. "Miss Pru!" Small fists banged on the glass before a hand jerked her back.

"Lillie!" Pru ran down the walk.

At a nod from the senator, the carriage pulled away. High-pitched shrieks sounded from inside.

"No! Stop!" Waving frantically, Pru ran toward the carriage, but the coachman flicked the whip and sent the horses faster. Panting, she turned to the two men by the curb. "What's happening? Where are they taking her?"

Marsh glanced at the house and the people crowding the open doorway. "Calm yourself, Miss Lincoln. You're making a scene."

"Why are you doing this?" she cried, her voice shrill with tears. "Where are you sending her?"

"To my school, Miss Lincoln," the senator said. "For her own good."

"Her own good? What's good for her is to be with me! You have no right!"

"I have every right." Face flushed with anger, the senator said to Marsh, "I was afraid this would happen. These people are so excitable."

"*These* people?" Pru charged toward him. "You stole my—"

Marsh moved forward to block her way. "Miss Lincoln!"

"Stole your what?" The senator's voice was mild, but ice crackled in those cold eyes. "She's not your daughter, Miss Lincoln. She's not kin to you at all. By her own admission, she's an orphan and, as such, is under the protection of the State of Indiana."

"You can't—"

Marsh gripped her shoulder. Hard. She twisted, trying to break his hold. "Let me go! You can't do this! You'll be sorry for this! Both of you!"

Marsh's fingers dug deeper. "Go back inside now, Senator. I'll handle this."

Unable to pull from Marsh's grip, Pru stood shaking, breath rasping in her throat, her mind in tatters.

As soon as the door closed behind the senator and the front porch gawkers, Marsh shoved Pru away with an expression of disgust. "Do be quiet, Miss Lincoln. All this weeping and wailing won't get the pickaninny back."

Teeth bared, Pru ran at him, hands curled like claws.

Marsh caught her wrists. Gave her a hard shake. "But I can. I can bring her back."

She stilled. "Y-You can?"

"I can and I will." Releasing her arms, he smoothed his waistcoat as though brushing away any filth her nearness might have left on the silk brocade. That predator's smile thinned his pink lips. "Just as soon as you board the train for Washington, I'll make sure she's released."

Thomas awoke on his back, a boot planted on his chest. He reached up to push it off, then froze when he heard the click of a hammer being cocked.

He slumped back, his head spinning, tasting blood from a cut on the inside of his cheek.

"Where's the other one?" the man holding the gun asked.

Thomas cursed him in Cheyenne.

The barrel of the revolver cracked against his cheekbone. More blood dripped down into his ear.

"In English. You do know how to speak English, don't you, redskin?"

When he did not answer, the man leaned down and rested his forearm across the knee of the leg propped on Thomas's chest. "Now I can start shooting off parts of you," he said in a friendly tone. "Or you can answer me."

"What do you want to know, *ve'ho'e?*"

The spinning had slowed. As his head cleared, strength flowed back into Thomas's arms and legs. Muscles flexed in readiness. Soon, he would kill this man. But first he would find out who had sent him after them.

The tip of the gun barrel poked his nose. "I'm asking for the last time, redskin. Where's the other one?"

"He ran off. Who sent you?"

The man smiled, showing stained teeth and a wad of tobacco between his cheek and gums. "Someone who didn't want you getting to Westfield, I'd guess."

"A man named Marsh?"

"Maybe." Another poke with the gun. "Ran off where?"

"Into the brush."

Muttering, the man looked around.

He was not a big man. He did not wear the clothes of one who worked outside for his money, and his hands looked soft. The hands of a banker. Or maybe a gambler.

"I don't see him. What's he doing? Just hiding in there?"

Thomas filled his lungs and readied his body for the fight to come. "He is hurt." He tipped his head toward the brambles. "He crawled over there."

When the man turned his head to look, Thomas grabbed the ankle of the foot on his chest and pulled hard in one direction, and at the same time, drove the heel of his other hand into the side of the man's knee from the other direction.

Something snapped. The gun fell. Screaming, the man grabbed at his leg and toppled sideways. By the time he hit the ground, Thomas was on top of him, his knife at his throat.

Silence, except for the rasp of their breathing.

Thomas watched blood from the cut on his temple drip onto the man's face, leaving ribbons of red across his cheek. Blue eyes, wide with shock and pain, stared back at him, tears pooling in the corners.

"Oh, Jesus . . ."

"*Ma'heo'o* cannot help you now. Who sent you?"

"L-Like you said. Marsh."

"He told you to kill us?"

"If we had to. Just so you didn't come back."

At a sound, Thomas looked back to see Mose Solomon crawling out of the brambles, his face marked by thorns, one hand clamped to the blood-soaked poncho over his side.

The man on the ground looked frantically over at him. "Help me! Don't let him kill me!"

Thomas jiggled the knife to regain his attention. "Will you go back and tell Marsh that we still live?"

"No! No, I swear it!"

Thomas studied him for the space of a heartbeat. Then two. "I do not believe you," he said, and drove the knife down.

When the twitching stopped, he wiped the blade clean on the man's shirt and slipped his knife into the sheath at his back. He turned to find Mose Solomon regarding him with wide, fearful eyes. "He dead?"

Thomas did not bother to answer. "How bad are you hurt?"

"N-Not too bad. Bullet go clean through. Why you kill him?"

"So he will not tell anyone where you are, or who the people are who helped you." As he spoke, Thomas ripped off pieces of the dead man's shirt, folded them into pads and pressed them against the holes in the black man's side.

"I ain't never seen so much blood. Ain't never killed a white man, neither."

"You did not kill this one. I did." To distract Mose while he tore more strips to wrap around the black man's belly, Thomas asked what he would do when he reached Canada.

"Blacksmith. Workin' the forge and poundin' iron all I knows how to do."

"Will there be people there to help you?"

Mose winced as Thomas tied off the bandage holding the pads in place. "Cousin and his wife."

"That is good." Thomas rose. "*To'estse*. Get up. Gather the guns while I find our horses. We must hurry to reach the Quakers before full light."

Once he'd collected all four horses, Thomas stripped those belonging to the dead men and drove them into the brush. As he helped Mose Solomon onto the sorrel, the black man stared down at the bodies sprawled on the ground.

"We just gonna leave them? Not even bury them?"

"Do you have a shovel?"

"No."

"Then we cannot bury them. The coyotes will find them soon enough."

They reached the barn on the outskirts of Westfield just as the town was awakening. Several plain-dressed men were there to meet them. When the Quakers saw their injuries, they sent for a healer and rushed Thomas and Mose inside the barn to a special room built beneath one of the stalls.

An old woman with a medicine basket came down the ladder. While she tended their wounds, the men muttered among themselves. After a moment, the leader of the group, an older man with a round belly, stepped forward, his hands on his hips. "Thee will explain to us how this happened."

Thomas told them about the ambush and the two dead men in the woods.

It upset them. Some wanted to put Mose out. Others argued against it. Thomas knew Quakers were what the whites called pacifists, which meant they would not kill or fight. He did not understand that, but he was glad when they finally agreed to let Mose stay until he was well enough to move on.

His own injuries were nothing. While the woman put salve on the bullet crease and the cuts on his cheekbone and temple, the men argued about what to do with the bodies in the woods. They were afraid if they were found, it would bring suspicion down on them and their work with the Underground Railroad.

"Do thee know who sent these men after thee?" a man asked.

Thomas nodded. "A man named Marsh. But I think he does not care as much about the railroad or Mose Solomon as he does about killing me."

"Yet thee bring this evil into our midst?"

Thomas did not respond. It was always a waste of his time to argue with white people.

"Then we have no choice," round belly decided. "Thee will show us where these bodies are and we will bury them as is proper."

"I cannot stay to help you," Thomas said. "I am already late getting back. And I will need a fresh horse."

An hour later, Thomas left the Quakers and their shovels in the woods and headed back to Indianapolis. As the miles passed beneath the drumming hooves of his horse, one thought kept circling in his mind.

If Marsh was desperate enough to send gunmen after him and Mose Solomon, what might he do to Prudence and Lillian?

Nine

Pru stared numbly at the wall beside the bed in her hotel room. She was too empty to cry anymore. Too weary to check her watch again, as she had so many times over the last hours. Too distraught to think of a way out of this mess.

Brother had sat with her while they waited for Thomas. But after midnight came and went with no sign of him, she sent the reverend to his own room, telling him they would do the ceremony in the morning before they took the signed license to the courthouse.

This is what my blind self-importance has done to all of us.

She thought she could change the world with a slate and a primer. Instead, she had endangered all she held dear. If something had happened to Thomas . . .

She trembled with despair.

He should have been back hours ago. She prayed he had simply wandered off as he often did when upset, or had stayed away to give them both time to think. But hope was beginning to fray.

Be alive . . . please be alive.

With a hitching sigh, she rolled onto her back. Every part of her body felt brittle and withered, drained of even the energy to rise from her bed and change out of her wrinkled dress.

The last words Marsh spoke to her before he sent her away

now echoed through her mind. *If you want to see the girl again, be at the depot at eleven o'clock. As soon as you step on the train, she'll be released.*

Released? Had they locked her in a cage?

Oh, Lillie . . .

How frightened she must be, trapped in blindness among strangers. Did she think everyone had abandoned her?

Feeling herself sinking into a downward spiral again, Pru made herself sit up, hoping that would pull her mind out of the dark desolation that gripped her. But all she could think about was how alone she felt.

Images of Heartbreak Creek—the only home she had now—flitted through her mind. In her rush to change the world, she felt like she'd left the better part of herself behind.

She had missed the arrival of Whitney, her sister's first child. And later, the triumphant rebirth of Heartbreak Creek when the railroad finally came through. She hadn't been there to see Ash and Maddie off to Scotland and their new roles as the earl and countess of Kirkwell, nor had she been there to welcome the newcomers who had chosen her town as their home.

Her town. Would she even recognize it anymore?

The schoolhouse she had helped build was probably open and running by now. The new depot, too. Edwina's letters said new houses were cropping up everywhere, and soon, construction of a grand new hotel would start in the canyon, not far from the hot spring where she had wept in Thomas's arms and told him she was leaving.

How could she have thought helping strangers was more important than all the dear friends she had left behind?

Realizing she was starting to cry again, she swiped a hand over her eyes and rose from the bed. It wasn't too late. She could go back and start over again . . . as long as she had Thomas and Lillie by her side.

But first she had to fix this mess she'd made. Find a way to thwart Marsh, but still keep Lillie and Thomas safe.

Energized by desperation, she began to pace, plans forming in her mind.

She would go to the depot as Marsh instructed. Assuming Thomas would return before the train left, she would have him wait out of sight by the platform for Lillie. The moment the child arrived, Pru would signal Thomas to get his daughter, and then she would go to them. Marsh wouldn't dare try to stop her with so many people watching. And if he did try, Thomas would be there to protect them until the train taking Marsh to Washington departed. Then they'd be free.

The promise of it brought a sob to her throat.

Free to return to Heartbreak Creek.

Free to live in a tipi if she must.

Free to build a new life with Lillie and the man she loved.

"Why do you weep, *Eho'nehevehohtse*?"

With a cry, she whirled, saw Thomas standing behind her, and threw herself against him. "You're back! Thank God! I've been so worried. I thought you weren't coming. Oh, Thomas, the most terrible thing has happened!"

"Ssh. I am here now. All is well."

She drew back. "No! No, it's not! They've taken Lillie—" Words deserted her when she saw the bloodstains on his jacket, the cut on his cheek, the bruise darkening the side of his face. "My God, Thomas, what happened to you?"

Thomas wanted to ask her the same thing. She looked broken, a shadow of his beautiful Prudence. Then her words reached past his shock. "*Katse'e* is gone?"

"Marsh took her. I tried to stop him, but . . ." Suddenly words tumbled out of her so fast he could hardly keep up. "We were at the fund-raiser. Everything was fine until it was time for me to give my speech. Marsh said he would watch Lillie. I know I shouldn't have let him, but Brother was introducing me and everyone was waiting and—"

Thomas gripped her shoulders. "Breathe, Prudence. Slow down so I can understand you." It was hard to keep his voice calm. Hard to keep from breaking something. Tearing something apart with his hands. But before he could go after Marsh, he needed to know what had happened and where Lillian was.

"They took her, Thomas. Marsh and Senator Brooks took her while I was giving my speech. I tried to keep an eye on her, but there were so many people, and it wasn't until my speech was over that I realized they had her. I ran after them, but the carriage was already pulling away." Her voice broke. "Thomas, they've locked her in that asylum."

He started for the door.

"No!" She grabbed his arm. "Marsh said he would bring her back."

He stopped. "When? And why did he take her at all?"

"To make me behave. If I get on the train with him tomorrow, he promises he'll have her brought back."

He felt sick. "And you agreed to this, *Eho'nehevehohtse*?"

"Temporarily. Sit." Still holding his arm, she pulled him down onto the edge of the bed. "I think we can save Lillie and outsmart Marsh at the same time. But first, we'll have to marry so we can adopt her."

Marry?

It was not a bad plan, he realized, once his mind stopped spinning and she had explained what they would do. Not as final as his plan would have been, but not as messy, either. And although it bothered him that her need to protect Lillian was what had finally convinced her to take him to husband, he did not want to argue with her about it tonight. Tonight, he only wanted to hold her in his arms and forget the fear that had chased him all the way from Westfield.

"So don't show yourself at the depot until Lillie arrives," she finished. "I'll be standing with Marsh beside the train. Once I see you have her, I'll just walk away. He won't try to stop me with a crowd of people around."

"If he was dead, he could not stop you, either." *And then you would not feel you were forced to be my wife.* But he did not have the courage to say that out loud. "What will stop him from stealing her again?" he asked instead.

"You." She gave a grim smile.

Thomas did not respond, his mind moving on to other plans.

She must have read his silence as reluctance. "We'll be free, Thomas. Lillie will be safe and Marsh won't have any hold over us. And as soon as the eastbound leaves, we'll get on the first train headed west and—"

"No." He held up a hand. "We will not speak of that now."

"But I—"

"No, Prudence. Not tonight." Before she could question him, he rose and walked to the bureau. He did not want to hear grand plans or listen to more promises. He did not want talk at all. Hoping to avoid it, he poured water into the bowl for washing, then shrugged out of his coat.

"Thomas, is that blood on your shirt? How badly are you hurt?"

"It is nothing."

He saw her face reflected in the mirror above the bureau and knew by her expression that the harshness of his tone had hurt her. But how could he tell her he did not want to talk because he was afraid of what she might say? If she made promises tonight, then changed her mind about marrying him and got on the train tomorrow . . . that would be the end of it, and he was not ready for that.

In silence, he pulled his shirt over his head. He felt her watching as he splashed cold water on his face and neck and chest then wiped it away with his shirt.

One more night. That was all he wanted. If there were to be no more tomorrows for them, he wanted at least this one last night with her.

But his pride would not let him say that, or admit his weakness for this woman who had walked away from him so many times.

Weary from his long ride, he stood at the bureau, head drooping, hands braced on the wooden top. He watched water drip from his hair and felt the silence press around him. *Oh, Prudence. How has it come to this?*

After a moment, he heard her rise from the bed.

Lifting his gaze, he watched in the mirror as she came up behind him and slid her arms around his waist. Her touch sent a shiver through him, and he closed his eyes so she would not see the need in his eyes.

"Thomas . . ."

His body tensed when he felt the warm smoothness of her cheek against his back, the soft press of her breasts against his damp skin. A hot trail of silent tears rolled down his spine, and something shifted inside.

"I've made such a muddle of things, haven't I, Thomas? Will you ever forgive me?"

The ice around his heart cracked. Resolve shattered at his feet. With a groan, he turned and pulled her into his arms. He couldn't stop shaking. Couldn't stop the burning behind his eyes.

"*Heme'oone,*" he whispered in a rough voice. "I will always forgive you. But tonight, we will not speak of the troubles between us. Tonight, I only want to hold you and show you how much I have missed you. Can we do that?"

She leaned back to look into his eyes. Tears shimmered in the lamplight. Her lips trembled. He could see that her earlier words still hurt her, yet the hand that cupped his unmarked cheek was gentle. "Will you at least tell me if Mose Solomon is all right?"

Pleased to speak of less emotional things, he began undoing the buttons down the front of her dress. "He was shot, too, but he will be safe with the Quakers until he recovers."

She stiffened. "Shot, *too*? You were shot? Why didn't you tell me? How bad—"

"I am fine," he cut in. Then, before she could ask more questions, he hurried on. "Marsh sent men to stop us. They will not return to tell him they failed. Why do you wear clothes with so many buttons?"

"But how did Marsh know where you were going?"

He undid the last button, then slid the dress over her shoulders and down her hips. "Chester Hogan told him, I think. Step out."

She stepped out. He could see her legs were shaking, and kept a hand on her hip to steady her. It felt warm and soft beneath his palm. Her scent rose up, inflaming his senses.

"Why would Chester do that?"

"Fear. He has the courage of a mouse." He finished loosening the tabs on her petticoats, let them fall, then began on the laces down the front of her corset, a foolish thing women wore to push their bodies into unnatural shapes. "I have thought about your plan, *Eho'nehevehohtse,* and I will do as you say. But Marsh must not know I still live until *Katse'e* is safe." He tossed the corset aside. "Then you will decide if you come to us or get on the train."

"But I've already de—"

"No. We will speak no more of it." Putting his hands on her shoulders, he leaned down to kiss the tear tracks from her cheeks. "The time for words is past." With suddenly clumsy hands, he fumbled with the buttons on his trousers. Another reason he preferred his Cheyenne clothes. They were much easier to get out of. "It is time for you to show me that you missed me, too."

He let the trousers fall. "And you will start by taking off your shift."

"Will I?"

"Yes, *Eho'nehevehohtse*. You will."

He stood before her, a proud, battered warrior whose strong, sleek body bore a patchwork of scars: twin ridges across his chest from the Sun Dance ceremony—a puckered line down his muscular thigh from the wound he'd taken when Lone Tree's men abducted her—the dent from a bullet here, a knife slash there. The first time she had seen them, she had been horrified.

"Scars are marks of courage," he had told her when she had finally allowed him to see her own scars. "They tell what we have endured. Only survivors wear them."

With those words, he had helped her accept the senseless act that had left her disfigured. But even now, she had a hard time accepting his scars and the brutality that had caused them. How hard his life must have been.

He misread her hesitancy. "Put your worries behind you, Prudence. Think only of me."

"I'm not worried. I'm enjoying the view." Her shift fluttered to her feet.

Laughing, he scooped her up into his arms and carried her to the bed, then stretched out beside her.

The feel of his lips across her face, her scars, her breasts, sent her mind into breathless turmoil. His magical hands awakened her body to a trembling need. How easily he called her to surrender.

"You are eager, *Eho'nehevehohtse*," he whispered against her quivering abdomen, his thick, dark hair framing his face.

"Yes."

"I will make you even more eager." And dipping his head, he did just that.

She twisted, mouth open, fingers tangling in his hair, until finally she could take no more. Pulling him up, she put her open mouth against his, putting into that one point of contact all the need and love and emotion she had locked away during the lonely months apart from him.

"Now, Thomas," she said, moving restlessly beneath him.

Laughing softly, he rose above her on thick, muscular arms.

With a single long stroke, he pushed inside her, then stilled, his belly against her belly, his gaze locked on hers.

A fierce look came into his eyes. Something primal and almost savage added sharp edges to the taut features poised above hers. "You are *nahe'e*. My woman. Feel that I am part of you." He pressed deeper. "All that separates us is the air we share."

"Yes."

"Say it."

"I'm yours, Thomas." With a trembling hand, she stroked his beloved face, tracing the ridge of his nose, his stern brow, the strong angle of his jaw. He was so beautiful. So utterly male. "And you're mine."

His chest expanded on a deep breath. A shiver ran through his big body. *"Nemehotatse, Eho'nehevehohtse."*

Something inside her contracted, then released. Doubt and fear fled her mind. She watched a drop of sweat roll down his face to drip from his chin onto her breast—a hot brand she felt all through her body. "I love you, too, Thomas."

Triumph flared in eyes still locked on hers. Then, with slow, controlled movements, he began to move within her.

And the real magic began.

Thomas awoke as morning light gave a warm glow to the soft skin of *Eho'nehevehohtse*'s back and turned the rough edges of the pale scars across her shoulder into gold-tipped lace.

Leaning up on his elbow, he drew his tongue down the dip of her spine. She tasted salty and warm and felt smooth as glass.

She stirred beneath him. "Thomas?"

"Yes, *Eho'nehevehohtse*."

Yawning, she rolled over and blinked up at him. "Is it time?"

"Soon."

"Then let's go over the plan one last time."

After making love the first time the previous night, they had decided that as soon as the wedding ceremony was over, she would go to the depot as instructed, while Thomas and Brother Sampson went to the courthouse to register the signed and witnessed license in the record clerk's book. Then they would take proof of the marriage to the office of the judge who held the adoption papers Pru had filled out earlier. Once the notice to adopt was recorded, he and Brother would go directly to the train station. Thomas would hang back, watching, and as soon as Lillie was delivered safe, he would make himself known. By then, it would be too late for Marsh to stop them. But Thomas hoped he would try.

"Soon, Thomas." Prudence stretched, her back arching, her hands clasped over her head. "Soon it will all be over and we'll be safe."

"That is my hope." He watched her, his body reacting as it always did when he was near her. He could awaken every morning to this woman and know his life was all he could ever wish it to be. She gave him the purpose he needed. A place of his own. He could not live like a caged animal on a reservation. Nor could he shed all of his Indian ways and become a white man. But with this woman, he could have a home. A place to belong. A reason to take the next breath.

He ran a fingertip over the curve of her breast. "Did you sleep well?"

She slumped back with a drowsy smile, moisture forming in her dark eyes. "You know I did."

"Then why do you cry?"

"That's perspiration. This room is too hot."

He grinned and thumbed her nipple. "Is it?"

"And because I'm happy."

Laughing, he leaned down and kissed her. "*Napevetano.* I am happy, too, Prudence. I do not like to be apart from you." Then, realizing he was drawing close to the subject he had vowed not to talk about, he rolled over and sat up on the edge of the bed. "It is late. Reverend Brother Sampson will be here soon."

He yawned, wincing at the sting in the cut on his cheekbone. Lifting a hand, he felt that it was not as tender as yesterday, and the swelling was almost gone. But a dull ache still pulsed in his temple where he had been kicked. He hoped his hair would hide most of the bruise. He did not want Marsh to think the men he sent had done him harm.

Her hand stroked his back. "You'll follow our plan, won't you, Thomas?"

He looked at her over his shoulder.

"I couldn't bear it if anything—"

"You are in more danger." He reached for the clean clothing

he had retrieved from his room during the night while Prudence slept. "You are the one who will be standing next to Marsh."

Her laugh was bitter. "He wouldn't hurt me. I'm much too valuable to him."

As he dressed, she watched him, a frown between her dark brows. "Remember to wait until Lillie arrives before you show yourself."

"I remember." She had told him at least six times.

"And don't forget to bring Lillie's bag." She nodded toward the pouch in the corner. "I've put her Christmas gifts inside."

"You worry too much."

"I know. But you are so dear to me, Thomas. If anything happened—"

"Nothing will happen," he said for at least the tenth time. He leaned down to give her a last kiss, then straightened, branding the sight of her in his mind.

She was so beautiful, bathed in sunlight, her eyes still showing the passion he had awakened in the night. It took all his strength to turn away and let her dress.

By the time the reverend and the man who watched over the lobby arrived, they were dressed, packed, and ready. Prudence looked nervous, but happy. The clerked looked sleepy. It saddened Thomas that *Katse'e* was not with them, but he was glad Prudence had not told her of their marriage. He wanted to be with her when they gave her the news. He smiled, thinking of her squeals of joy.

The ceremony was short, and meaningless to Thomas. In his heart, he and Prudence Lincoln were already joined. But civilized people had their laws and rules, and if Thomas wanted to be the man *Eho'nehevehohtse* needed him to be, he would say the words she wanted to hear and put his mark on their paper.

As soon as it was done, the clerk pocketed the coin Thomas gave him and left. Thomas picked up his and Lillian's clothes bags and threw them over his shoulder. "Reverend Brother Sampson will come to you as soon as the judge has the papers. I will wait until Lillian arrives."

And because the white rules said it was now okay for him to do so whenever he wanted with his wife, he gave his beautiful bride a long, thorough kiss.

"Be safe, *Eho'nehevehohtse*."

"And you, my love."

Ten

"Just like I promised," Marsh murmured in a voice that wouldn't carry to Brother Sampson and Bessie Prescott, who stood talking by the last passenger car. "There she is."

Pru almost wept with joy when she saw the familiar black carriage stop near the platform beside the depot. A woman in dark clothing stepped out, then reached back inside to help someone else climb down.

Lillie.

Relief hit so hard Pru had to clench her teeth to keep from crying out.

Safe. Thank you, God.

She started forward, then stumbled back when Marsh caught her arm.

"Where do you think you're going?"

Frowning, Brother and Bessie stopped talking and looked over at them.

Marsh shifted to block their view, then leaned in with bared teeth. "Don't give me any trouble, Miss Lincoln. You know what I can do."

She wanted to shout at him that she was Mrs. Redstone, not Miss Lincoln, and he couldn't do anything to her now, but she had decided not to reveal that until Lillie was safe. No use stirring up trouble until she had to.

Out by the carriage, the woman bent to say something to Lillie, then straightened, her gaze fixed on Marsh.

Pru tried to jerk her arm from his grip, but his fingers tightened, digging deep into her flesh. "What is she doing? Why is she just standing there?"

"You didn't think we would bring the girl along with us, did you?"

"What?" Pru twisted to look at him. "But you said you'd let her go."

"Keep your voice down! I intend to let her go. But to the Prescott woman, not you."

"But you never said—"

"Quiet! Or I'll send her back to the school. Is that what you want?"

When Pru didn't answer, he gave her arm a vicious twist that brought her up on her toes. "N-No."

Thomas will be here soon. He'll stop this madness. And once he gets Lillie away—

"What the hell?" Marsh had turned to wave to Bessie Prescott, but now stood motionless, his hand hanging in midair. "What's he doing here?"

Pru looked back, saw Thomas step onto the end of the platform, and almost collapsed. *Thank God.* Her legs shook with the need to run to him, but it was too soon—he had to get Lillie away from the woman first. *Hurry!*

She watched him study the people standing beside the railcars. When his gaze found hers, he started forward.

No! Not yet! Frantic, she shook her head, hoping he would see and go to Lillie instead.

He stopped. She could sense his impatience and confusion from thirty feet away. Then he saw Lillie and headed in her direction with long, purposeful strides.

"Don't think his arrival changes anything," Marsh warned. "In fact, it makes it easier." He waved to Brother and Bessie. "Get on board," he ordered Brother. "And you," he added to Bessie. "You're not needed anymore. Run along."

"But I thought—"

"Go!"

Bessie sniffed, affronted by his tone.

Rebellion flashed in Brother's eyes, then faded as he turned to the fuming black woman. "Good-bye Miss Bessie. Thank you for your help with the choir."

"My pleasure, Reverend. You have a nice trip, and God bless." Then, ignoring Marsh, she stomped toward the station where the other two choir ladies waited to wave them off.

With a worried glance at Pru, Brother went up the steps of the last car.

Thomas had reached the carriage. Shoving the woman aside, he scooped Lillie into his arms. Even from this far away, Pru could hear the girl's cries of joy.

Safe. Finally. Jerking her arm free, she glared at Marsh in triumph.

But he was smiling—that smug, I've-got-you-now smile. He nodded to the woman still standing beside the carriage.

She tossed Miss Minty onto the wooden decking, then climbed back into the carriage.

"See? Just like I promised. And to make sure you keep your end of the bargain . . ." Marsh pointed toward the depot. "See those two men watching us?"

When Pru looked over, a man with a thick mustache pushed his coat aside to show the gun holstered on his hip . . . and the badge pinned to his vest.

Her knees wobbled.

"A nod from me and they'll be on your redskin like hounds on a rabbit. So be warned, Miss Lincoln. If you don't get on this train without a fuss, I'll have the redskin arrested for kidnapping a ward of the state, and the pickaninny sent back to the home forever. Do you understand?"

"Why are you doing this? You said you'd let her go."

"And I have. I don't care who has the girl or what happens to her. As long as you get on the train. She and your Indian are simply insurance."

Pru gaped at him, the horror of what he'd done finally dawning. She was trapped.

"Come now," he said in a chiding voice. "Did you really think I'd trust you to get on the train once the girl was returned?"

No! She wanted to scream. Claw that smile from Marsh's eyes. Tear this pain from her body.

Marsh chuckled, and in a tone that was almost gentle, said,

"Please stop fighting me, Miss Lincoln. Don't try to run out on me or slip away at the next stop. We're going to Washington, and that's that. Now wave goodbye to your Indian."

Pru shook her head, unable to believe this was happening. How could she tell Thomas she was leaving him again? "You don't know him. He'll never let us leave. He'll hunt you until—'

"Then *make* him leave," Marsh growled in her face. "Send him back to his tipi with the girl, or watch them both get locked away for the rest of their lives."

As the carriage rolled away, Thomas set Lillie on her feet and handed her Miss Minty. Then, holding her hand, he straightened and looked at Pru.

Her throat constricted. He seemed so tall and strong and unstoppable, with his feet braced and his shoulders thrown back. But she knew he was only flesh and blood. He could die as easily as any man. And without him, Lillie would be doomed to live a horrid life in an asylum, and she . . . she couldn't live at all.

The conductor started down the line of passenger cars. "All aboard!"

Pru forced herself to look at the man beside her. With his pale skin and eyes, he looked like a bottom dweller, some bloodless creature that might have slithered out from beneath a rock. "Why are you doing this?"

He shrugged. "You know why. I need you to put your education proposal before the committee in Washington. And this is the best way to ensure your cooperation."

"Why is my initiative so important to you?"

"It isn't. Nor are you. But once you convince the powers in Washington to pay for it, I have people poised to see that I'm appointed to oversee all those funds. Hundreds of thousands of dollars at my fingertips."

"You vile, despicable—"

Fury flashed in his eyes. "Watch your mouth, girl. The war might be over, but in some places, there's still a bounty on niggers. And Indians."

Pru saw Brother Sampson frowning at them from his window inside the passenger car. She almost called out to him, then realized he was as vulnerable as she was. There was nothing anyone could do. Not even Thomas.

And now she knew too much. Having admitted to her that

he planned embezzlement, Marsh would probably kill her once she'd served his purposes. She was doomed.

But Thomas and Lillie could live. As long as she sent them away.

The pain of it pierced her heart. She could almost feel the blood leaking into her chest.

Marsh pushed her roughly forward. "Get it over with, Miss Lincoln. Tell them good-bye and make him believe it. And remember what I said." His gaze flicked to the men waiting for Marsh's signal. "We'll have our eyes on you."

Thomas watched her approach. Before she was halfway back to him, he could see by her expression that she was leaving him.

Helpless rage engulfed him, so sharp and painful his limbs went numb and tears pressed behind his eyes. He wanted to shout and break things. Shove his knife into Marsh. Peel the skin from his body.

But Marsh was not sending Prudence Lincoln away.

It was her decision to go.

The ache in his chest almost took his breath away.

It was over. Despite the words saying they were now man and wife, all that remained to him were memories of what he had let slip from his grasp. He let his gaze move over her as she drew closer, storing away for the long years ahead every shadow and sweet, soft curve. The proud line of her back, the brave smile, the intelligence in her dark, soulful eyes. He loved this woman—his wife. And she was leaving him. How was he to live with that?

"Where Miss Pru?" Lillian asked, yanking on his hand.

"She is coming. But you must be strong, *Katse'e*, and tell her good-bye without tears."

"She leavin'? Without us?"

Thomas could not answer.

"When she come back?"

"I do not know."

Her grip on his hand tightened. "You mean she maybe gone *fo'ever*?"

"Stop shouting, Lillian, and dry your tears."

"But she cain't leave! Not without me!"

"You are my daughter now, *Katse'e*. And I will not let anyone take you away ever again."

The crying stopped. Her eyes widened. "I you daughter?"

"Yes. And the daughters of Cheyenne Dog Soldiers do not wail and weep like *me'esevoto*—little babies. Now smile and be brave."

Thomas braced himself as Prudence stopped before them. But nothing had prepared him for the pain in her eyes. She did not want this, either, he realized. Yet she was still leaving him. "You have made your decision," he said.

"Thomas . . ." Her voice cracked.

You are my wife, he wanted to shout at her. *You promised to stay with me.*

But when he saw a tear roll down her cheek, anger left him. This had been coming for a long time. He should no longer be surprised. Reaching up, he brushed the tear away with his thumb. "Do not cry, *Eho'nehevehohtse*. I knew you would leave." He let his hand fall back to his side so she would not see it tremble.

"You wrong!" Lillian cried, her face twisting. "She cain't leave! She 'posed be my new mama."

"Oh, dearest . . ." Bending, Pru pulled the girl into her arms. "I love you so very much."

"Then don't leave me!"

"I must." Letting the girl go, Prudence straightened and looked at Thomas. "I'll be back as soon as I present my proposal to the committee. I promise—"

"No more promises." Thomas struggled to take the emotion from his voice. "I have known for many months that there is greatness within you, *Eho'nehevehohtse*. It is right that you follow the path put before you."

"Thomas . . . I-I'm so sorry."

"Do not be." Unable to keep from touching her, he framed her face with his hands. It was a moment before he could speak. "When I first saw you in Declan Brodie's wagon, Prudence Lincoln, with your shy smile and great, wounded eyes, I knew that I would love you. And later, when I held you in the sacred pool, and spirits trailed ribbons of light across the moonless sky, I knew that I would lose you. I accept that."

Shoulders shaking with silent sobs, she tipped her head against his chest.

Katse'e pressed against his leg, her tears wetting the cloth of his trousers. He felt like he carried the weight of the world's sorrow on his shoulders.

He waited for the emotion blocking his throat to ease, then said in a ragged voice, "But know this, *Eho'nehevehohtse.* Through all the days I have left . . . until the last sunset unfurls across the sky and the owl calls my name into the night . . . I will never forget you."

"Thomas . . ."

"Go now."

"No!" Lillian grabbed blindly at the air.

"Last call," the conductor shouted.

"Miss Lincoln." Marsh waved his hat. "It's time."

Thomas gently pushed her away. "Be well, *heme'oone.* And may the Great Spirit walk beside you."

Sobbing, Prudence stumbled away.

"Daddy, please!" *Katse'e* cried, jerking on his hand. "You cain't let her leave! You cain't!"

A single glance back, then Prudence stepped into the last car, leaving Marsh standing at the rail of the rear observation deck, smoking a cheroot and watching Thomas.

The conductor signaled to a brakeman near the front of the train, then went up the steps behind her. After locking the chain across the stair opening, he stepped past Marsh and went inside.

The parting whistle sounded.

"Please, Daddy," *Katse'e* wailed. "Don't let her go with him!"

"Lillian—"

"No! Marsh bad! He hurt her!"

Thomas frowned down at her. "You do not know that."

"I do! He hurt lots of folk. Hit and call names. Ev'rybody 'fraid of him."

Thomas watched the well-wishers back away from the billowing steam as the locomotive rolled forward. At a wave from Marsh, the two men who had been leaning against the wall, watching them, turned and walked away.

"Do somethin', Daddy! She don't want to go! Marsh makin' her."

Doubt rose in Thomas's mind. Lillian was right—it was plain that Prudence did not want to go. Then why did she get on the train? With *Katse'e* safe, what threat could Marsh use to force her to leave with him? And why would he let her live once she had served his purpose?

Marsh flicked his smoke onto the tracks. With a mocking grin, he tipped his hat at Thomas and went inside.

The insult fanned the fury still smoldering in Thomas. He felt the heat of it in his chest, his arms and legs. Felt the hot trail of rage burning through his mind. He breathed through his teeth as muscles tightened and senses sharpened and the fire that always came before battle ignited in his belly.

He might not be able to keep *Eho'nehevehohtse* with him, but he could still protect her from Marsh. He looked around, his mind searching, planning. When he saw the choir woman move through the door into the station, he hurried toward her, dragging *Katse'e* by the arm. "Bessie Prescott!"

The woman stopped halfway across the waiting area, saw Thomas, and smiled as he and Lillian crossed toward her. "Why, Mr. Redstone. Mr. Marsh decide he want me to keep Lillie after all?"

Unsure what that meant, Thomas brushed the question aside. "You live close to this place?"

"Just through those trees yonder." She pointed out the front window and past the field where Thomas and Lillian had shared a chicken dinner the night they had first arrived. "I do loves the sound of a moving train, I surely do."

He thrust the crying girl at her. "You will watch Lillian until I return."

One dark brow rose. "I will?"

He glanced back, saw the train pulling away. "Please!"

"Hurry!" Lillian pushed at him, her words garbled with panic.

"You must do this, Miss Prescott. It is important."

Chewing her bottom lip, the black woman looked down at the sobbing girl, then up at Thomas. "Well, I suppose . . ."

"*Nia'ish*—thank you. I will return, *Katse'e*," he called back as he dashed out the front doors and across the street in front of the depot.

He ran into the field. Past the stump where Lillian had perched with her box of chicken—past the men taking down the big white tipi—cutting north toward the curve in the tracks at the edge of town. He crashed through brush and trees along the tracks until the sound of the locomotive roared in his ears and he saw the last car ahead.

Lungs burning, he lengthened his stride. Breath rasped in his throat. His heart kicked against his ribs. A few more feet. He stretched out, his hand clutching at air. Then, using the last of his strength, he lunged.

His palm slapped against the handrail by the steps. Struggling to keep a handhold on the cold metal, he let himself be towed along until he could swing his foot up onto the steps. Gasping, he pulled himself up onto the rear deck, then slumped against the wall, chest heaving, his legs shaking beneath him.

As soon as he caught his breath, he crossed the rocking platform to peer through the glass in the top of the rear door.

The car was nearly full. All of the seats faced away from him and most of those along the aisle were taken. On the right inside wall, near where he stood, was a narrow door. From his earlier train trips, he knew it led into a storage space. A good place to hide. Several feet deeper into the car, behind the last seats, stood a small coal stove.

Thomas reached for the latch, then whipped away from the window when a black man in the white coat of a railroad steward stepped out from the other side of the stove and walked toward the rear of the car.

Pru couldn't stop shaking. Couldn't keep the tears at bay. She knew Brother Sampson, on the bench facing her, was looking at her in concern, but with Marsh sitting on her right, she dare not speak.

What could she say, anyway? The reverend knew why she was doing this. He knew what Marsh was capable of, and if he hadn't tried to stop him before, why would he now? With every clack of the wheels over the joints in the track, her spirits sank lower. The only thing that consoled her was that at least now Thomas and Lillie were safe.

I'll go back. As soon as I present my proposal I'll board the first train to Colorado. If Marsh lets me. She might have made a pact with the devil, but she'd had no choice. Surely Thomas would understand that. Wouldn't he?

Unless Marsh killed her first.

Brother Sampson leaned forward. "Are you all right, Miss Lincoln?"

Pru forced a nod. "A chill, that's all."

"Hot tea might help," the demon beside her said in a jovial tone. "Sampson, go see if the steward has some."

Like the puppet he was, Brother left.

Marsh saw her disgust and chuckled. "Don't give me that look. The good reverend is simply a tool, just like you."

"I wonder that he puts up with it."

"He puts up with it for the same reason you do, Miss Lincoln. I help you achieve your goals, and you help me reach mine."

"Without a care to those you harm in the process?"

But was she any better? How many times had she put her goals first, making promises to Thomas she didn't keep? The idea that she might not be so different from Marsh sickened her.

"Ah. You're talking about Redstone now, aren't you? Upset that he got roughed up while abetting a wanted felon?" Marsh met her surprised look with an oily smile. "Blame yourself for that, my dear. I warned you what would happen if you persisted in that Underground Railroad foolishness."

How had she ever allowed this evil man into her life?

"Oh, don't take on so," Marsh said in a bored tone. "He's just an Indian."

Pru stared down at her clenched hands. "I hope you have the poor luck to meet that Indian in a dark alley someday."

"He may not live that long."

Her head flew up. "What do you mean?"

"The road to Colorado can be quite perilous, I hear. He and the pickaninny could have an accident along the way. One never knows."

Pru itched to slap him. Dig her nails into his eyes. Kick that smile off his face. "If you hurt Thomas or Lillie—"

"Hurt them?" Marsh spread his hands in a show of innocence. "How could I do that while I'm sitting here on the train with you?" When she didn't respond, he let his hands drop back to his lap and shrugged. "But then, accidents do happen."

Pru looked blindly out the window, almost breathless with terror. He was toying with her just for fun. She should have let Thomas kill him. Or jumped off the train and run back to them. She thought she was keeping them safe, but instead, she might be sending them into worse danger.

Thomas stepped again to the window in the rear door and looked inside.

The steward had his back to him, loading coal into the stove. The aisle between the bench seats was empty.

Knowing this was his best chance to get into the car unnoticed, Thomas slipped silently through the door, then froze when he saw Reverend Brother Sampson rise from his seat in the middle of the car and step into the aisle. As the reverend turned and started toward the steward, Thomas quickly opened the narrow door by his shoulder, saw coats swinging on hooks, and ducked inside.

Leaning against the outside wall, almost deafened by the clacking of the wheels beneath his feet, he pulled the knife from the sheath at his back and waited.

When Brother Sampson returned to his seat, Pru noticed he was frowning. With an air of distraction, he reported that the steward had no tea, but they could get some at the next stop.

"Thank you," she said through stiff lips.

He didn't respond, his face thoughtful as he gazed out his window.

Pru wasn't sure which made her more nauseated: the clove-scented pomade of the man beside her, her emotional state, or the rocking of the railcar. She comforted herself with the notion that if she did vomit, she would aim it at Marsh.

They sat in silence for a time, swaying to the motion of the railcar and trying to ignore the tension building between them.

Finally, with a sigh, Marsh rose. "Think I'll brave the cold and take a turn out back." Smiling, he pulled a cheroot from the inside pocket of his overcoat and strolled toward the rear observation deck.

Eleven

Thomas huddled in the cloak closet, impatience gnawing at his gut. He wondered if Reverend Brother Sampson had seen him.

After he had ducked inside, he had heard the black men talking about tea. After a minute or so, the reverend had left. Thomas was glad. He did not want to hurt him. He wished the steward would leave, as well, but could still hear him rustling around outside the closet door, whistling to himself.

Then the whistling stopped and a new man spoke. It was hard for Thomas to hear his words over the noise of the wheels, but he recognized the voice.

Marsh.

Excitement made his heart race. Holding the knife ready, he pressed his ear to the door and listened as the voices came closer.

"Yessuh, the observation deck open," the steward was saying. "But it right cold out there with the train moving. Best button that coat, lest you take a chill."

"How long until the next stop?"

"'Bout an hour or so. It's only a water stop, so we'll be on our way again pretty quick."

Thomas tightened his grip on the knife hilt as footsteps sounded in the hallway only inches away.

The outside door opened. Cold air rushed through the gap

between the closet door and the floor. For a moment, the clacking of the wheels sounded louder, then abruptly faded when the outside door clicked closed.

Thomas waited to see if the steward would leave. When he realized he wouldn't, he quietly opened the closet door and stepped out, staying flat against the wall so he would be harder to see from the observation deck.

"Jesus Lawd," the steward choked out when he saw Thomas standing there.

Thomas showed him the knife. "Do not speak."

The steward blinked at it, his mouth hanging open. "Yessuh." Then hearing that he had spoken aloud, he clapped a hand over his mouth.

Thomas opened the closet door and pointed with the knife. "Inside."

Without hesitation, the shaking man stepped into the closet. "Please don't hurt me," he whispered into the coats hanging in his face.

"I do not want to." Thomas leaned closer to whisper into his ear, "But if you ever tell anyone I was here, I will come in the night and put my knife in your throat."

"Oh, Lawd . . ."

"Sleep," Thomas said, and brought the hilt of his knife down on the back of the steward's head. Catching the unconscious man before he hit the floor, Thomas laid him against the wall, checked that he still breathed, then stepped into the hallway and closed the door behind him.

The aisle was empty. Through the glass window of the rear door, he saw his enemy standing at the back rail, feet braced for balance, hands clasped behind his back. A wisp of smoke curled around his head before the wind sucked it away.

Thomas drew in a deep breath and let it go. His hand was steady. His heart beat fast and strong, and vengeance sang through his veins.

He opened the door.

"What do you mean Thomas is on the train?"

Brother Sampson winced, then motioned for Pru to lower her voice.

She looked nervously around, but the passengers seated nearby continued to chat with their seatmates, stare out the windows, or doze, their heads bobbing to the motion of the train. "You saw him?"

He nodded. "When I went to ask the steward for the tea, he slipped into the cloak closet by the rear door."

Pru blinked in confusion. She had seen Thomas and Lillie on the platform when they'd pulled away from the station. How had he gotten onto the train? "Was Lillie with him?"

"I didn't see her. I think he was alone." When Pru started to bolt from her seat, Brother quickly motioned her back down. "I suggest you stay put, Miss Lincoln. When he's ready to contact you, he'll make himself known. No use drawing unwarranted attention."

Reluctantly, Pru sat.

"Why is he here?" Brother asked

"I'm not certain." It definitely wasn't part of their plan. "But I suspect he's come to save me. He's like that. Very protective. The Cheyenne in him, I suppose." A new fear sent her leaning forward. "Please . . . you won't tell anyone he's here, will you?"

"Not unless it's necessary. Protect you from what? Marsh?"

Pru nodded. But she was more concerned about Thomas. "Maybe we should do something."

"What do you suggest?"

A new thought struck terror. If Marsh found out that Thomas was on the train, he would—*No!* She couldn't finish the thought. "Marsh made me get on the train. He threatened to send Lillie back to the school and have Thomas arrested if I didn't. I don't know how Thomas figured it out, but—what if something happens to him?"

"Miss Lincoln."

She didn't realize she was gnawing her thumbnail until the reverend pulled her hand away.

"Do you believe in the wisdom and mercy of our Savior?"

She stared at him, taken aback and a little put out that he would start preaching at her when Thomas might be in danger. "Yes. Of course I do."

"Then have faith." Releasing her hand, he sat back. "He will provide."

"Perhaps. But maybe we should do something anyway. In case God or Thomas needs help."

When the door behind him clicked closed, Marsh turned and saw Thomas standing there. The cheroot dropped from his mouth, releasing a spray of hot sparks as it bounced down the front of his coat. "Redstone!"

Thomas stepped forward.

"What are you doing here?"

Another step.

Marsh leaned back against the railing, his gaze pinned to the knife in Thomas's hand. "Put that away before I have you thrown off the train, you goddamn Indian!"

Thomas took another step.

"What the hell do you think you're doing?"

"I have come to kill you."

Marsh sidled away, coming up against the chain at the top of the steps. He looked down at the brush rolling past, saw they were starting over a high trestle, and his breathing changed. "I-I'm not armed."

"I am." Another step.

"If you hurt me, they'll know it was you."

"How? I was at the station when the train left. Many saw me, including the two lawmen who watched us."

"The steward—"

"Sleeps." Thomas took one more step, then stopped. Only three feet separated them. A knife slice away.

Marsh pressed against the chain, shaking like an aspen leaf. "For God's sake, man, don't do this!"

"You threatened Prudence Lincoln. My *wife*. You sent men to kill me. You took my daughter away." Thomas tossed the knife from his right hand to his left, watching the fear build as Marsh's eyes followed the movement. "I am Cheyenne. Did you think I would do nothing?"

"I'll pay you!"

"I have not come for money."

"Then what? Anything you want! It's yours. Just ask!"

Thomas smiled. "I want to see you fly."

As understanding dawned in the pale fox eyes, Thomas

kicked out, driving the heel of his boot into the center of Marsh's chest.

With a choking sound, the man flipped over the chain, thudded once against the steps, then disappeared from view.

Holding a roof brace, Thomas leaned over to watch his enemy fall toward the canyon far below. When the man's head bounced off one of the braces and the screaming stopped, Thomas straightened.

A sense of triumph filled him, and a relief so strong, he shook with it. He wanted to give a war cry and raise his fist in the sky. Instead, he slid the knife into the sheath at his back and took a deep breath. When he let it go, some of the fury that pulsed within him went with it.

It was over. He had not failed her. *Eho'nehevehohtse* was safe.

Feeling weary and drained, he stepped through the door to check on the steward, then stiffened when he saw Brother Sampson standing in the narrow walkway, looking at him.

The black man did not seem surprised—or happy—to see him. "Where's Marsh?"

"He left."

"Left? The train?"

Thomas did not answer.

Brother Sampson thought for a moment, then nodded. "The Lord works in mysterious ways."

Thomas did not know how to respond to that, so he remained silent.

"Are you leaving, too?" the black man asked.

"I have done what I came to do."

"And Miss Lincoln—I mean, Mrs. Redstone? Will you take her with you?"

Thomas shook his head.

"You're letting her go on to Washington?"

"It is her purpose."

That seemed to confuse the black man. "What about you?"

"My purpose is done. *Eho'nehevehohtse* is free now to follow her path."

Which seemed to confuse Brother even more. "She knows you're on the train. I told her I saw you when I went to speak to the steward."

"Tell her you were wrong."

The reverend started to speak, then frowned and looked around. "Where is the steward? You didn't hurt him, did you?"

"He is resting." Thomas nodded toward the cloak closet. "When he wakes, you will help him. You will also remind him he did not see me. Nor did you."

Brother Sampson thought for a moment, then held out his hand. "I understand. And I wish you well, Mr. Redstone."

Relieved that he wouldn't have to hurt this man, Thomas accepted the handshake. "And I wish the same for you, Reverend Brother Sampson." He studied the twisted fingers in his grip, then lifted his gaze.

Seeing the question Thomas did not ask, the reverend explained. "I dared to touch a white woman. As punishment, my master had a wagon driven over my hands."

Hiding his disgust, Thomas released the crippled fingers.

"And because I dared to love her," the black man added with a bitter smile, "they took my manhood, as well."

Thomas recoiled, understanding now why the man seemed so soft . . . so sad. "Did you kill the ones who did this to you?"

"For a long time I wanted to. But the man who found me bleeding in the ditch taught me a better way."

The notion was strange to Thomas, so he said nothing.

"I'm telling you this," the reverend went on, "so you'll know your wife is safe with me."

"I think she would have been safe, even if you had not been cut."

Brakes squealed. They both swayed for balance as the train slowed and couplers between the cars banged against one another. Thomas felt the floor shift beneath his feet and sensed they were going into a curve. At the front of the train, the steam whistle shrieked.

The reverend braced a hand against the wall as the car jerked and bounced. "We must be slowing for another bridge."

"Good-bye, then, *nesene*—my friend. I will remember you." Turning, Thomas opened the door onto the observation deck.

"Is there anything you want me to tell your wife?"

Wife. Another promise broken. But Thomas had no more anger left. If *Eho'nehevehohtse* did not want to stay with him, he would not make her.

"Tell her I understand." And letting the door swing closed behind him, he vaulted over the railing and dropped into the brush beside the tracks.

By the time the car carrying *Eho'nehevehohtse* rolled over the bridge, he was jogging back the way they had come, the voices of his spirit guides echoing in his mind.

Hearing footsteps behind her, Pru twisted on the bench seat to see Brother Sampson coming from the rear of the car. "Did you see him?" she whispered as he sank into the seat across from her.

"I did." Pulling a wadded handkerchief from his pocket, he scrubbed at a stain on his hand. A red stain. Blood.

Panicked, she leaned forward. "Is he all right? Is he hurt?"

"Ssh. He's fine."

When Brother started to slip the kerchief back into his pocket, Pru grabbed his arm. "Why is there blood on your hand?"

"It's not his," Brother murmured. "It's the steward's."

The steward's? *Sweet heaven.* What had Thomas done?

Seeing her look of alarm, Brother leaned close to add, "The man fell and nicked his head. That's all. He's fine."

Speculation ran rampant. "Fell how?"

"He doesn't remember." With a warning look, Brother added, "And he assures me he never will."

Both relieved and confused, Pru sat back. "What about Marsh?"

"He's gone."

"Gone where?"

"Thomas said he left. That's all I know."

Left? The train? Did that mean . . . "Is he . . ." She couldn't say the word, not because the notion of Thomas throwing Cyrus Marsh off a train horrified her, but because it didn't. What a ghoul she had become.

"Dead? I assume so."

"How can you be sure? People fall from trains all the time and live to tell about it." Tait Rylander had. He bore scars from his fall, but he lived.

"We were going over a trestle at the time. A very high trestle."

It took a moment for the full meaning of his words to sink

in. When it did, relief almost caved in her chest. She began to tremble, buffeted by an onslaught of thoughts and images and emotions.

It's done. Over. Thomas and Lillie are safe. Marsh is gone. We're free.

Dropping her head into her hands, she struggled to catch her breath. It took a long while for her nerves to settle, and by then, they had reached the next station.

The train rolled to a stop. Around her, people rose from their seats and stretched. Others moved toward the observation deck at the rear of the car.

A giddy sense of euphoria blossomed in Pru's chest. Pulling out the valise stored under her seat, she rose. "I have to go back."

"You can't."

"I need to tell him—"

"He's gone."

"Gone?" She sank back into her seat, the valise in her lap. She saw pity in Brother's eyes. "Gone like Marsh?" *Or gone . . . from me?*

"He jumped off after we cleared the trestle."

Gone forever. She slumped back, her mind reeling.

The train car emptied except for a man snoring near the front, another man reading a newspaper, and a woman rocking a crying baby in her arms while an older child slept against her side.

Gone. Without a word. Not even a good-bye. Her fingers curled into fists atop her valise. She wanted to throw it through the window. They were safe now. Why had he left her?

Because you told him to go.

Brother's hand closed over hers. "I'm sorry."

No! A sense of desperation gripped her. With trembling fingers, Pru shoved the reverend's hand away and pulled her gloves from the pocket of her coat. "I'm going after him. I have to talk to him. Explain why I got on the train."

Why wouldn't her fingers go in the holes? In mounting frustration, she stuffed the gloves back into her pocket and clasped her shaking hands on top of the valise. In clear, precise tones, she said, "I need to tell him that Marsh would have had him arrested and sent Lillie back to the school. But now, without

Marsh's threats hanging over our heads, we're safe. I don't have to go on to Washington. I can go home with him and Lillie."

"No, you can't."

"You're wrong! I have to!" Or he would never forgive her.

"Think, Miss Lincoln. Wouldn't the authorities find it suspicious if you left the train right after Marsh disappeared? Especially after that scene last night at the fund-raiser?"

So what if people had seen her shouting at Marsh and the senator? Pru swiped dampness from her cheeks and wondered when she had started crying. It seemed she was always crying lately. "They were taking Lillie away."

"For her own good, they'll say."

The senator's exact words. But it wasn't true. The best place for Lillie was with her and Thomas. "No. She belongs with us. Besides, with Lillie safely returned, I'd have no reason to push Marsh from the train."

"Perhaps. But there's still the fact that you were arguing with Marsh last night, and again at the station this morning. When the authorities find out he's missing, and learn that you're involved with Redstone, a man who has made no secret of his animosity toward the missing man . . . who do you think they'll blame?"

Pru stared at him, icy hands of panic closing around her throat.

"The woman at the heart of it all, that's who. The *black* woman. The one who was sitting beside Marsh just before he disappeared."

"But I've done nothing," she cried.

"Ssh. I know that. I'm sure they will eventually realize you're innocent. But when they do, who do you think they'll suspect next?"

Thomas.

Pru closed her eyes, desperate to block Brother's words. But she couldn't ignore the truth behind them. This was her doing. She was the one who had brought this horror down on Thomas, on Lillie, on herself. It was all her doing.

Out by the depot, the conductor called the "all aboard." People entered the car and settled into their seats.

"So what do we do?" she whispered. "Just continue on to Washington as though nothing is wrong?"

"For now." Brother paused while two men moved past. "After a few more stops, I'll tell the conductor we haven't seen Marsh for a while. He'll probably think he got off at one of the earlier stops and didn't get back on. Maybe he'll get around to checking the other cars to see if he changed seats. But it probably won't be until we reach the big terminal in Philadelphia that anyone will take our worries seriously. By then, we'll have established our concern."

She studied him, surprised that behind those hound dog eyes lurked such a devious mind. It seemed uncharacteristic for such a godly man. Had she misjudged him, thinking he had turned a blind eye to Marsh's manipulations? "Why are you helping us?"

He opened his mouth, closed it, then sighed. "Even in Schuler, I saw how Marsh treated you, Miss—Mrs. Redstone. I know he was using both of us to further his own ends, yet I looked the other way because he made it possible for me to spread the Gospel to more people." A look of disgust crossed his sad face. "I thought the good would outweigh the bad. But after what he did to Lillian, I realized how wrong I was."

Pru looked out the window, digesting all the reverend had said. Was she any better? Hadn't she been just as guilty of being blinded by her own ambitions?

"Thank you for shielding Thomas."

"He's a good man. And God needs all the warriors He can get."

The locomotive whistle blew. With a jerk, the train began to move.

As the outskirts of the town slipped past the window, images of Lone Tree and the Indian camp flashed through Pru's mind. Dark eyes watching. Heads turning away. No voice rising in protest.

She remembered how utterly helpless she had felt. She had realized then how her black brothers and sisters must have suffered—doubly damned, first by their white owners, then by a world indifferent to their plight. A plight she had neither shared nor understood until Lone Tree's brutality had opened her eyes.

That was how evil flourished. When good people looked on, but did nothing. Well, she would no longer remain silent.

"Marsh sent men to kill Thomas and"—she caught herself—"another man."

"Mose Solomon."

Pru drew back in surprise. "You knew about him? That I was helping the Underground Railroad?"

He gave that sad smile. "Who do you think recruited you?"

Pru thought of the black woman who had stayed behind after her speech at a local church. "You sent her? Wisteria Price?"

He nodded.

"I'm glad you did."

"But it's troubling that Marsh found out," Brother went on. "Is Mr. Solomon safely away?"

"So far." Without revealing where Mose was now, Pru told him about the shooting and that Mose was recovering at one of the safe houses. "But you must warn others in the organization. Thomas thinks Chester Hogan alerted Marsh."

"If so, he was probably forced to do so. Doesn't matter now, I guess."

"Why do you say that?"

"With Marsh dead, the threat to all of us is gone. For a while anyway." He gave her a speculative look. "I'm assuming you'll go back to Colorado once we're finished in Washington."

Pru thought of the set look on Thomas's face as the train had pulled away. "If he'll have me."

"He killed for you, didn't he?"

Maybe. But that didn't mean he would take her back. Thomas had a strong sense of right and wrong and a strict code of honor. He had made it clear that if she walked away from him again, he would put her from his life.

And Thomas never lied.

"He said he understood," Brother told her. "When I asked him if he had a message for you, he said, 'Tell her I understand.'"

"Understand what?"

"The way he said it, sounded like he thought you would know."

What it sounded like to Pru was defeat. That he had given up on her—on them. That he understood why she had lied to him, *yet again*—and even though she was walking away from him, *yet again*—it was okay because he *understood* why and forgave her for it. Thank you, good-bye, it's over. The end.

What drivel.

This from a man who carried a grudge and a spent bullet around for years, nursing his need for vengeance. Understanding? Forgiving? She didn't believe it for a moment. And the more she thought about it, the angrier she became.

It wasn't okay. And this certainly wasn't the end of it. She wasn't about to let him get away with such a pathetic good-bye.

She and Thomas Redstone were far from over.

Part Two

A Native American grandfather talking to his
    young grandson tells the boy he has two wolves
    inside of him struggling with each other.
The first is the wolf of peace, love, and kindness.
    The other wolf is fear, greed, and hatred.
"Which wolf will win, grandfather?" asks the
    young boy.
"Whichever one I feed," is the reply.

Twelve

The soul would have no rainbows if the eyes had no tears.

—Native American proverb

HEARTBREAK CREEK,
COLORADO TERRITORY, JANUARY 1872

As the *chuffing* of the locomotive faded, other sounds penetrated the gentle drift of snow falling silently down from clouds that hovered just above the tops of the trees.

Thomas closed his eyes and listened. The *plop* of snow sliding off a drooping limb. A lone chickadee calling his mate. The rattle of wheels over frozen ruts. And, barely heard, like the whisper of wind through summer aspens, the sound of rushing water.

It was good to be home.

Lillian moved restlessly beside him, interrupting his quiet thoughts. "This it, Daddy? Fo' true?"

He looked down and saw frizzy black hair already poking out from under the woolen scarf he had wound tightly around her small head. Maybe Prudence Lincoln's sister, Edwina, would know how to make braids. Or how to deal with the girl's moods. Or could teach *Katse'e* to speak so people could understand her.

He had not realized how troublesome a girl-child could be until they started this long journey.

Katse'e let out a deep sigh that fogged the air. Did she feel the mist of it on her face, or remember watching clouds form from her own breath?

"Miss Minty say this place quiet as a church on Monday."

"Then she is not paying attention, *Katse'e*. Close your eyes and listen."

"Hope you not tellin' *us* close our eyes. I blind, 'member? And Miss Minty only gots buttons fo' eyes. We cain't even see the things hittin' our face. They better not be bugs."

"They are snowflakes."

Maybe he could get Edwina to take Lillian as her own. She was raising Declan Brodie's children. Why not his? The girl needed a mother, and he was tired of being fussed at for allowing *Eho'nehevehohtse* to leave them.

"Miss Minty wonderin' why we standin' here gettin' snowed on. She cold."

"We must wait for the wagon that will take us to town."

"I thought we already in town."

"We are at the depot. The town is nearby."

"Hope that wagon get here 'fore Miss Minty pee her pants."

"Redstone? That you?" A grinning man wearing a snow-dusted slouch hat stuck his head out the depot door. Thomas recognized him. A drinker, but harmless. When Thomas had been Declan Brodie's deputy, he had locked him up several times. It was good he carried no grudge for that. "Ho, Kincaid."

"Welcome home, you damn wagon burner. Clerk said you needed a ride?" When Thomas nodded, Kincaid waved them inside. "Come on, then. I got womenfolk waiting at home."

Thomas guessed he meant his milk cows. Kincaid supplied most of the milk for Heartbreak Creek. Maybe he needed help. Thomas smiled, picturing the look on Lillian's face if he set her on a stool and put a teat in her hand.

"Here to stay this time?" Kincaid asked as they crossed through the depot and out front to where his wagon waited.

"Maybe."

"Take a seat." Kincaid hooked a thumb toward the back of the wagon, where crates and boxes and a bulging mail pouch were already loaded.

Thomas lifted Lillian up, tossed their clothes bags over the back rail, and climbed in beside her. As soon as he settled, the girl pressed up against him.

"How far town?" she asked.

"Not far."

"It where you live, right?"

"Sometimes." Although now that he had a child to watch over, he would probably have to spend most of his time in town. He frowned, not liking that idea. Maybe he could leave her with the old couple who had come to Heartbreak Creek with the woman Ethan Hardesty married. Winnie and Curtis Abraham. They were black-skinned, too, and might understand the girl better than he did.

Lillian pressed closer. "You not run off an' leave me, will you, Daddy?"

Thomas looked down at her, ashamed of his unkind thoughts. She looked so small and defenseless huddled beside him. It must be hard for such a strong spirit to rely on others to show her the way. Thomas doubted he would have had the patience for it. Looping an arm around her shoulders, he pulled her tight against his side. "I will never abandon you, *Katse'e*. You are my daughter." Whether the judge in Indiana ever mailed the papers or not, Lillian was his. For better or worse.

She sat in silence for a moment, then tipped her face up to whisper, "You know I make that up, right? You not my daddy fo' true."

He picked up the hand not holding her doll and put it to his chest. "In here, you will always be my daughter. And as your father, I will watch over you, and take care of you, and do what is best for you. You know this."

"That why you let Mama run off?"

Thomas released her hand. He thought about tossing her off the back of the wagon, but restrained himself. "I told you we will not speak of that." He was glad she did not know he and Prudence were married, or she would never shut up.

Several minutes later, they stopped in front of the Heartbreak Creek Hotel. Many horses stood at the rail out front, and several wagons sheltered against the side of the building. "What is this day called?" Thomas asked Kincaid as he unloaded Lillian and their clothes pouches from the back of the wagon.

"Sunday."

Sunday was the day a number of local families gathered for dinner at the hotel after they left the Come All You Sinners Church of Heartbreak Creek. But there were too many wagons and horses here for that small a group.

Kincaid leaned over and spit into the snow. "Lucky you missed the service this morning. Heard the reverend was in top form. Gave a fine, arm-waving, Bible-thumping, come-to-Jesus welcome to the New Year, bless his heart."

Days ago, Thomas had given *Katse'e* the gifts Prudence had packed to mark the birth of the Christian god. But he did not know the New Year had come, too.

"Nobody was about to go to church twice in the same week," Kincaid went on, "so the reverend gave his welcome today, rather than last Monday." He squinted through the front windows. "Looks like you're still in time for dinner. Big doings. Whole town's invited, but I got my ladies to tend. Step clear."

As the wagon pulled away, Thomas looked through the window at the people eating inside. He did not want to go in there. He was not ready to answer questions about Lillian and Prudence Lincoln. But until he found a place for them to stay, the hotel was his only choice.

"Miss Minty smell food. She say she hungry."

"Miss Minty talks too much."

"We not eat?"

"Yes, we will eat. But first there are people who will want to meet you." He rested a hand on her shoulder to make sure he had her attention. "You will remember your manners, *Katse'e*. Can you do that?"

"I sweet as pecan pie with molasses and a chunk of sugar cane on top. Ev'rybody love me. You see."

Dreading what was to come, Thomas led her into the hotel.

He was glad Lillian could not announce to everybody in Heartbreak Creek that he and Prudence were now man and wife. He did not want to answer questions about that, or about why his wife did not come, or who the child was he had brought back with him. He could hardly make sense of it himself.

Yancey, the brown-toothed old white man Lucinda Rylander paid to watch over the lobby, dozed in his chair.

Thomas did not wake him, but moved toward the room where food was served.

In the doorway, he stopped, amazed at the number of new white faces. Some he recognized, including those who had come from England—Rayford Jessup's new wife, Josephine, and her son, Jamie, as well as the two workers from her English home, Gordon and Henny Stevens. But there were others he had never seen before.

When had so many people come to Heartbreak Creek? They were like ants, overrunning everything in their path.

For a moment, no one noticed them, then Edwina Brodie bounded from her chair. "Thomas! You're back!"

Faces turned. Voices called out. Edwina rushed forward, arms out-flung. "Did you bring Pru? Rafe and his bride, Josie, arrived with the horses over a week ago." Abruptly she stopped, her look of surprise giving way to a wide smile that crinkled the corners of her blue eyes. "And who is this precious little thing?"

"She talkin' 'bout me?" the girl whispered.

"Say hello, *Katse'e.*"

"Hi, ev'rybody!" Lillian shouted. "It me, Lillie Redstone. Some calls me Lillian. Daddy mostly call me Cat-see, but he a Cheyenne Dog Soldier and talk funny so I think he mean Can't-see on account I cain't see, being a po' blind black child and all." She held up her doll. "This here Miss Minty. She hungry 'nuff eat worms. But first, she need to pee. You gots a necessary room 'round here?"

It was late. *Katse'e* and the two youngest Brodie children, Brin and Whit, along with Rayford Jessup's new son, Jamie, were all sleeping in one of the hotel rooms under the watchful eye of Mrs. Bradshaw, the hotel housekeeper. Their parents sat with the Rylanders and Hardestys in the empty dining room, plying Thomas with questions over coffee and tea for the women and whisky for the men—except Thomas, who shunned alcohol. Even Ida Throckmorton was there, the old woman who had followed Lucinda Rylander from New York. A cantankerous *mahatamaahe.* The Cheyenne would have left her in the woods long ago.

Thomas tried to remain patient. This was his Heartbreak Creek family. His only family now, except for Lillian. They would want their questions answered.

Once they made their jokes about his white clothes and short hair, they started in about *Katse'e*.

"They simply let you walk off with her?" Edwina Brodie asked.

"She said I was her father."

"And they believed her? Heavens, you look nothing alike. You're not even the same color."

"Edwina Whitney Ladoux Brodie!" From her slouched position, Lucinda Rylander pointed at the far wall. "Go sit in the corner and think about what you just said." Then, ignoring the shock on the Southern woman's face, Lucinda turned to her husband. "Too much, do you think?"

Tait smiled. "It was very good, sweetheart. Maybe less pointing."

When she saw the confused looks turned her way, Lucinda patted her enormous belly. "I'm practicing." Cocking a wheat-colored eyebrow at Declan Brodie, she added, "None of *my* children are going to run around like wild Indians. No offense, Thomas."

"Your daughter needs to be taken in hand," old lady Throckmorton told Thomas. "Taught manners and proper speech. I did an excellent job with my ward, here, who was deplorably Irish. If pressed, I could try my hand with Lillian."

No one pressed. Thomas glanced from the stern-faced old lady to Lucinda Rylander, a hard-eyed beauty who bossed the whole town. He would be afraid to count coup on either one of them. "Maybe the old black couple will take her."

"*Take* her?" Edwina Brodie whipped toward him. "You better not be thinking to give that child away, Thomas Redstone. It's plain as pudding she adores you, and when Pru comes back—"

"*Nehetaa'e!*" Thomas slapped his hand onto the tabletop. "Does no one hear my words? Prudence may not come back. We will speak no more of it."

The old lady sniffed. Lucinda Rylander narrowed her eyes at him. The men frowned in watchful silence, knowing better than to speak.

Thomas let out a deep breath. "I would not give *Katse'e* away. But I must find work and a place to stay if I am to take care of her. And someone will have to watch over her while I earn money to do that."

"Work?" Declan Brodie gave him a skeptical look. "Does that mean no more wandering off when the mood strikes you?"

"I have a daughter now. I will do what I must."

Edwina frowned. "You've changed. Not just the clothes or hair. I've never heard you talk so much. Or smile so little. Our old Thomas is still there, isn't he?"

Thomas shrugged. Sometimes he wondered, too.

Across the table, Rayford Jessup regarded him with troubled eyes. Rayford and Thomas had spent much time together in England and in the land where the Scotsman lived. Rayford had helped Thomas write his book, and had also helped him write a letter to Prudence Lincoln. They had fought, and fished, and spent long days in a cold English jail. Like Declan Brodie—who had helped Thomas through his darkest days and had later trusted him to be his deputy—the quiet Texan was almost a brother to Thomas and knew him well. Well enough to say nothing now.

His pretty English wife remained silent, too, a look of bewilderment in her two-colored eyes as she glanced from one person to another. Thomas did not blame her. The white people in Heartbreak Creek were a strange tribe.

"Perhaps the Abrahams might help," Edwina Brodie said. "They've been helping with our baby Whit, but he's almost one now, and as busy as a one-handed sheep shearer. They'd probably appreciate an older, quieter child to look after."

Lillian—quiet? Thomas almost laughed. "Until I find work, I cannot pay them much."

Edwina waved a hand in dismissal. "Just give Winnie room for a garden and Curtis a rocker in the sun. They'd be fine grandparents for that sweet baby."

Sweet? Thomas did laugh at that one.

Declan Brodie, his big frame sprawled in the chair, hands the size of dinner plates clasped over his belt buckle, asked Rayford Jessup if he needed help with the thoroughbreds he had brought back from England. "Thomas is pretty good with horses."

"I am better with horses than you, cow chaser."

"Not until spring," Rayford Jessup answered. "It's chaos out there now with all the construction and trying to get the place ready for Ash and Maddie's return in a couple of months."

Tait asked the man picking his teeth at the end of the table how construction was coming along.

"Stable's done," Ethan Hardesty said. "The house is behind schedule because of the nursery modifications, but it should be ready when the Wallaces arrive this spring." Beside him, his wife scribbled furiously in a small tablet.

"Oh, I forgot to tell you, Thomas!" Edwina's big smile reminded him of *Katse'e*, except Prudence's sister had all her teeth. "Maddie had her baby! We received a telegram from Ash's Boston bankers yesterday. A little baby earl."

"Actually," Josephine Jessup cut in, her clipped English accent an odd contrast to the lilting, southern tones of Edwina Brodie, "Donnan will be a viscount until his father passes and he inherits the title of Earl of Kirkwell."

"Wait! Say that again." Audra Hardesty flipped a page in her tablet. "I want to be sure to get it right for tomorrow's edition."

While Josephine Jessup repeated her words for the newspaper lady, Lucinda crossed her arms over her bulging belly. "Well, I don't think it's at all fair. Her baby wasn't due until next week. And my Uthred is already eight days late."

"Rothschild," her husband corrected.

"Harold," Ida Throckmorton snapped. "And it's highly improper to discuss such things in mixed company. They're men, for heaven's sake."

It seemed no one considered the possibility that the babe would be a girl.

"I'll talk to Chick," Declan Brodie said to Thomas. "He told me he's ready to come back to work at the ranch. With his peg leg, he was never that suited to the sheriff job, anyway. You interested in being the full-time sheriff, Thomas?"

Although he hated the idea of being trapped in town so much, Thomas had not minded his time as deputy. At least as sheriff, he would have no one ordering him around except *Katse'e*. "Will we be able to stay in the sheriff's house?"

Edwina shook her head. "We bought it from the bank for a

Sunday house so we'd have a place to stay when we came to town for shopping and visiting and church services. And it's good for Brin to be around other girls."

"That hellion could use some mannering, too," Ida Throckmorton muttered.

"You know," Rayford Jessup cut in, "not that I don't think Thomas would make a suitable sheriff, but from what I remember from my days as a marshal, they're usually elected officials."

"Not here," Declan told him. "No one wants the job, so we have to appoint."

"Take the Arlan place," Ethan Hardesty suggested to Thomas. "Since Audra's father passed on, there's just the two of us." He glanced at his wife, who quit scribbling to give him a sad smile. "We've been talking about moving to the new house we're building on the flats near the Wallace place. All the structural work is done. Only a matter of finishing up. We could move tomorrow."

"Then it's settled." Tait Rylander raised his whisky glass high. "A toast to old friends returned"—he nodded toward Thomas and Rayford Jessup—"and to friends newly arrived"—a smile for Josephine Jessup—"and to those yet to come"—a gentle pat on the belly of his wife. "May eighteen hundred seventy-two bring us all health, wealth, and happiness."

A chorus of "cheers" went around the table. Thomas forced a smile. But they all knew what Tait Rylander had not mentioned in his toast. Those who were absent and not coming back.

WASHINGTON, D.C., JANUARY 1872

Pru was met by thunderous applause as she stepped away from the podium and back to Brother's side. Her proposal was a success. Even before her speech, there had been talk of forming a committee to further Negro education. Her work was done.

Yet it felt like a hollow victory. The weeks away from Thomas and Lillie had caused a rift in her heart and a shift in her mind. The dreams that had driven her for so long had faded.

Her priorities had changed. Now her every thought focused on getting back home to her family and friends. Thomas needed her. Lillie needed her. And she needed them even more. She felt as if she were missing a vital part of herself. The best part.

"Now for home," she murmured to Brother as they left the meeting room through a side door.

Brother chuckled. "Me, too. My flock is liable to have flown without me there to keep them penned. If you'll be traveling through Indiana, we can go together."

When they stepped into the hall, two men in dark suits by the exit door turned to watch them.

"I'd feel safer if we did." Pru had never traveled alone before, and being a woman of color presented its own problems. "I need to stop in Indianapolis to see the judge and make sure the adoption was finalized."

The men started toward them, their faces set in firm lines.

Instantly alert, Pru glanced about for another doorway out of the building. Her proposal might have gained followers, but there were still those resentful of Negroes upsetting the applecart with radical ideas. Significant change, she had realized, would be slow and arduous.

The men lengthened their strides. Wariness tightened Pru's chest.

She glanced at Brother to see him tracking their movements, too, a worried look on his face. She pointed to a side door. "Perhaps we should go out that way."

He nodded and started to turn when one of the men called out, "Reverend Sampson? Mrs. Redstone?"

"Yes?" Brother stopped, his hand on her elbow pulling Pru close to his side. "I'm Reverend Sampson. And this is Mrs. Redstone. How can we help you?"

"You can turn around." The closest man reached under his coat to retrieve something at his back. Pru saw what looked like a badge on his shirt, and her throat constricted.

"Stay behind me," Brother muttered as the men continued toward them with determined strides. "Who are you?" he demanded, his voice rising on a current of fear.

"U.S. Marshals." The second man pulled a pair of handcuffs from his pocket, spun Brother around, and snapped the manacles on his wrists.

"What are you doing?" Pru cried as the other man jerked her arms behind her. Cold metal closed around her wrists.

"You're both under arrest."

"Why? What for?" Pru's legs threatened to give out as she and Brother were shoved roughly toward the exit.

"For the murder of Cyrus Marsh of Indiana."

COLORADO TERRITORY

The morning after his and Lillian's arrival in Heartbreak Creek, Thomas ate breakfast with Declan Brodie at the hotel, while *Katse'e* knocked around the empty dining room hunting the hotel cat.

"Talked to Ethan Hardesty this morning," Brodie said, jiggling his large baby on his knee while he fed him bites from his plate. "Said he and Audra would be out of the Arlan house by noon. Place is all yours."

Before Thomas could respond, Edwina Brodie swept in and plunked a big basket on a table near theirs. "Where's Luce and Tait?"

"Lucinda's battling the heaves," her husband said. "Tait's hiding from Mrs. Throckmorton. What's in the basket?"

"Nothing for you. Thomas, Audra said they were leaving behind the furniture Lucinda had donated after the hotel renovation. Apparently, Ethan's ordering all new. Has Whit eaten anything, Declan?"

"Most of my breakfast," her husband complained.

"He's not getting that appetite from me. I'm Southern."

"Southern people do not eat food?" Thomas asked.

"Not like that child does. I swear he's going to be a giant someday."

He already was a giant.

"I spoke with the Abrahams." Settling into the chair beside her husband, she took over the feeding of the baby giant. "They'd love to help with Lillie. In fact, they're already carrying things over to their old room at the Arlan place."

Thomas knew Ethan Hardesty and Curtis Abraham well, but not their women. He could hardly keep up with all the people who had moved into Heartbreak Creek since he had first come to the canyon. He did not know what brought them. Or understand why white people could not stay in one place but felt driven to move on, gobbling up whatever land they wanted, no matter who already lived there. They seemed to have no sense of tribe.

Yet he had noticed that once they came here to this little mountain town, they stayed. He had, too. Perhaps they were building a new tribe.

The Abrahams had come to Heartbreak Creek with Audra Pearsall and her sick father last year. But after the old man died and Ethan Hardesty took the Pearsall woman to wife, the black couple had moved into the carriage house behind the Brodies' Sunday house so they could help with the children when the family came to town. He hoped Declan Brodie was paying them well.

"It was a bit disconcerting, really," Edwina Brodie went on, trying to wrest the spoon from her son's grip, "how the Abrahams dropped everything and ran to get their belongings. Almost as if they were glad to be leaving us."

Thomas was not surprised. With Declan Brodie's three unruly sons and one daughter from his first marriage, and now this giant baby he had gotten on this new wife, they must have felt like a haunch of fresh venison in a cage of starving dogs. "I am glad for their help."

They all flinched when a chair toppled. "Gotcha, kitty!" Lillian crowed.

Brodie reached for the last piece of toast. "Talked to Chick and the mayor about the sheriff job. Chick says he's tired of city living and wants to go back to chasing cows. Mayor Gebbers will meet you at the sheriff's office at three to give you the oath. You do know how to tell time, don't you, Thomas?"

"Three o'clock. The sun one hand-width past the tallest peak. I will be there."

Brodie smirked. "That how you Indians tell time? What about cloudy days?"

"On cloudy days we kill rich white men and steal their watches."

"Good luck finding an Indian smart enough to read a dial."

"Or a white man rich enough to own one."

"Hush, you two. You'll give Lillie the wrong idea."

Thomas and Brodie looked at her.

"Law's sake. Everyone knows you men love each other like brothers. Give me the spoon, Whit."

Brodie flushed. Thomas looked down at his plate. Real men did not admit to such feelings, even if it was true. Thomas rose. "*Katse'e*, get your coat."

"What 'bout kitty?"

"The cat belongs here. Come."

"Don't forget that." Edwina pointed a jelly-smeared finger at the basket she had brought in earlier. "Just a few things to get you through the next few days. Let me know if you need anything else."

Thomas needed little, but he was glad his friends were trying to make it easier for *Katse'e*. He hoped it would help her to put aside her anger. Then maybe he could put aside his.

"We'll come by tomorrow before we head back to the ranch," Brodie said.

"I'll bring a kitten," Edwina added. "The carriage house cat recently had a whole mess of them. Would you like that, Lillie?" she called over to *Katse'e*.

"I jist loves kitties."

As Thomas recalled, she thought cats were sneaky. But he said nothing. Picking up the basket, he nodded to the Brodies. "I am glad for your help."

"What?" Brodie grinned at his wife. "Did he just thank us, Ed?"

Edwina Brodie laughed. "He did. England must have tamed him."

Ignoring them, Thomas took *Katse'e*'s hand and led her outside.

The day was clear and cold. A new layer of snow bowed the limbs of the firs along the creek and icicles hung from the edges of the roofs along the boardwalk. As soon as the sunshine touched his face, Thomas's spirits rose.

"I ain't no baby," Lillian complained, before they had walked twenty steps. "I ain't deaf, neither. And I sure don't need no watchers."

"You will stay in that big house all by yourself?"

"How big it is?"

"You will see."

"How? I blind, 'member?"

His spirits fell. Thomas had hoped after the fuss everyone had made over her, *Katse'e* would have softened her heart toward him. But ever since he had come back without Prudence Lincoln she had clung to her grudge like a stone fly to a river rock—which fueled his own anger. He needed silence. Solitude. A place away from all the voices and questions and *Katse'e*'s barbed words. Since they had left Indianapolis, he had not had a moment to think, or plan, or decide what to do.

It was an effort to keep his voice mild. "Because there are many rooms in this house, two other people will live there with us."

"My watchers."

"The Abrahams. They are old and kind and will keep you company while I earn money to take care of us. Their names are Winnie Abraham and Curtis Abraham, and they are black-skinned like you."

She thought for a moment. "Miss Winnie cook good?"

He hoped so. "She will also plant a garden. You will help her with that." Thomas guided her off the boardwalk and they continued along the road toward the edge of town.

"What the house like?"

Thomas saw it through the trees ahead. Already he felt the walls closing in.

"It is tall. Two floors. And it has a porch in front that will shade us from the summer sun. On the side of the house is an open place for a garden. Behind it is a creek, lined with tall cottonwood trees. When the snow melts, the creek will run high and fast below your window and sing you to sleep."

"I gots my very own window?"

"And your own sleeping room on the top floor."

For a moment she was too surprised to speak. Thomas enjoyed the quiet.

"What if Miss Minty scared?"

"I will get her a toy dog. Here are the stairs. Four steps up to the porch."

She counted each step as he had taught her, and at the top, probed with her foot to make sure there were no more. "Maybe she want a real dog instead."

"If she behaves, and stops talking about Miss Prudence, and learns to braid her own hair, I will think about it."

"Big bother fo' jist one dog."

Thomas opened the front door and led *Katse'e* inside. High wooden walls. Tiny windows. Tables, chairs, and all the clutter white people thought they needed.

Lillie sniffed the air. "I smell muffins."

"Oh," Winnie Abraham said with a start, coming through a doorway on the other side of the big rock fireplace. "Didn't hear you come in. Curtis! They're here!"

"Hold your water," Curtis yelled back. A moment later he came through the door with a load of firewood. "Hidey," he called, stomping snow off his boots.

"They nice," Lillian whispered.

"You will be nice, as well," Thomas whispered back.

"Hi," Lillian said in a loud voice. "It me, Lillie Redstone. Who you?"

Wiping her hands on her apron, the black woman came forward. "Pleased to meet you, Lillie. I'm Winnie, and that man you heard is my husband, Curtis."

Katse'e held up her doll. "This here Miss Minty. She not allowed to say nothin' 'bout Miss Pru, so she don't talk much. But she sho' 'nuff like muffins."

Thomas wondered if anyone would notice if he pitched a tipi under the trees.

Thirteen

The next morning, Thomas was helping *Katse'e* count the steps down to the first floor when someone pounded on the front door. Several voices muttered to one another, then one called out, "Thomas, you in there?"

Katse'e froze halfway down the stairs, one hand splayed on the wall, the other clutching her doll. "Who that?"

"Sounds like Joe Bill. You met him last night. Curtis, see what he wants."

By the time Curtis crossed to open the door, Thomas and Lillian had reached the bottom of the stairs. "Fifteen," Thomas said. "Can you remember that, *Katse'e*?" He needed to put up a sturdy railing so she would have something to hold on to when he was not there.

Children rushed into the room. Joe Bill, the troublemaker; his younger, quieter brother, Lucas; Rayford Jessup's English son, Jamie; R.D., the oldest Brodie boy; and Brin, the smallest and youngest of the tribe, and the only girl.

"Oh, Lawd," Winnie muttered, over by the stove. "They found us."

"Guess what, Thomas?" Brin shouted, trailing after her brothers. "Mrs. Rylander's having her baby. I wanted to see but Ma said it was a lady thing and made us come here. But I'm a lady, ain't I? So why can't I see?"

"You're not a lady yet," Joe Bill told her. "Ladies wear dresses."

"Dresses are stupid."

"Got anything to eat?" At fourteen, almost as tall as his father and with an appetite to match, R.D. headed straight for the kitchen end of the large open room.

"How long you children gonna be here?" Curtis asked.

"Till the baby comes. Here, Ma said to bring you this." Joe Bill thrust something furry into Lillian's face.

Katse'e let out a high-pitched scream, tried to bat it away with her doll, and stumbled back into the stairs.

Joe Bill blinked at her in surprise. "What's wrong with her? It's only a kitten."

"And how would she know that, Joe Bill?" Thomas shoved him and his kitten aside, so he could make certain Lillian had not hurt herself when she fell into the stairs.

"If someone put a hairy, squirmy thing in my face in the dark," Jamie Jessup said in his crisp English accent, "I would scream like a banshee as well."

"What's a banshee?" Joe Bill asked.

"A wailing spirit that warns when someone is about to die."

"We don't have those around here. You take it." Handing the kitten to Jamie, he followed his brothers and sister into the cooking area. "Winnie, you got any muffins?"

"You are safe, *Katse'e*," Thomas told his daughter. "He forgot you could not see the cat."

"He still here?"

"The cat or Joe Bill?"

"Joe Bill. I wanna kick his fanny."

"I'm sorry he frightened you, Lillie." Jamie sat beside her on the bottom step. "I don't think he meant to. And it's a lovely kitten."

"Fo' true? What it look like?"

"It's orangey-yellow for the most part, with three white paws and a little white stripe down the middle of its head. And it's ever so soft. Would you like to hold it?"

Lillian took the kitten. After feeling it from head to thin, twitching tail, she held it to her cheek. "It a boy or girl?"

"I'm not sure."

"Then how we know what to name it?"

"How about Harriet? You could shorten it to Harry if it turns out to be a boy."

"It hairy, sho 'nuff. But soft."

Taking that as a signal that all was well, Thomas went over to the table to grab at least one muffin before the Brodies finished them off. "Where is your father?" he asked R.D.

"Having breakfast with Mr. Rylander and Rafe Jessup."

"You do not go to the ranch today?"

"Me and Pa and my brothers are going tomorrow. Ma and Brin and Whit are staying to help Mrs. Rylander."

"I still don't think it's fair!" Brin spoke with such force, bits of muffin flew from her mouth. "I'm not a little kid anymore. I'm almost nine. And I seen calves and foals and puppies and kitties being born. So why not a real baby?"

With a look of sympathy to Curtis and Winnie, Thomas left.

But when he reached the hotel, the dining room was empty. Yancey, at a desk in the lobby, told him the men had gone into the Red Eye Saloon next door. "Too much hooting and hollering."

Thomas knew many women died bringing their *me'esevoto* into the world. He hoped that would not be so with Lucinda Rylander. Despite her managing ways, he admired her spirit. She had endured much in her short life, but had not let it harden her heart. "The birth does not go well?"

"Hell if I know." The old man dropped his voice to a whisper. "It's that old biddy, Mrs. Throckmorton. Been ordering everybody around like she was General Ulysses hisself. I was you, I'd make a run for it before she sees you."

Sound advice. Thomas had started for the door when Edwina Brodie stuck her head out of the Rylander rooms in the long hall behind Yancey.

"Get Tait!"

"She dead?" Yancey called back.

"Lord, no, you nitwit! He has a daughter. Go get him!" She disappeared back into the birthing room.

"I will tell him." Thomas thought for a moment, then said to the old man, "If he does not come soon, stick your head in and tell him his daughter is here." Smiling, Thomas went through the door behind the desk that led into the saloon.

The Red Eye usually did not open until the middle of the day. But it shared a door with the hotel lobby, and although Lucinda Ryland had put a stout lock on it, her husband knew where she kept the key. Whenever he and his friends felt the need to escape their wives or families, they ducked into the deserted saloon and pulled out the bottle of whisky the Scotsman had brought from his homeland. After his dark time of drunkenness, Thomas shunned alcohol, although he had once tasted the brew the other men seemed to enjoy. It smelled like buffalo piss and kerosene, and tasted at least that bad, although he had never tried either.

Tait Rylander, Declan Brodie, Rayford Jessup, and Ethan Hardesty were all sitting around their usual table in a back corner.

"Grab a ginger beer and pull up a chair," Declan Brodie called.

"I cannot stay long." Thomas went over and rested his hand on Tait Rylander's shoulder. "Your woman is strong. She will bear you a strong daughter."

"Daughter?" The new father reared back to stare at him through red-shot eyes. "How do you know it will be a daughter?"

Thomas shrugged. "I am Cheyenne. I know these things."

Brodie laughed. "Bunkum. You're as full of crap as a spring heifer."

"You doubt me?" Thomas pulled a coin from his pocket and slapped it on the table. "I say it is a girl. I am also sure you will hear of her coming very soon, but I will not bet on that."

"Hell you say!" Brodie dropped a coin on the table. "It's a boy and won't arrive until tonight."

"I'm in." Rayford Jessup put down his money, followed by Ethan Hardesty.

Tait Rylander shook his head. "Doesn't seem right to bet on my own child."

"That is wise, even for a white man."

The door swung open. "You better come quick, boss," Yancey called to Rylander. "Your daughter's here."

Tait Rylander shot from his chair. "And my wife?"

"Doing fine, from what I hear."

With a shaking hand, Rylander tossed the door key onto the table, told them to lock up when they left, then fled into the lobby.

Thomas scooped up his winnings.

"You knew," Brodie accused.

"Yes. And when I told you I knew, you called it bunkum."

"He's got you there," Rayford Jessup said.

"Still cheating."

"Maybe. But you make it so easy."

Several coins richer, Thomas left the saloon and went down to the sheriff's office. A man stood outside, one foot on the bench as he studied the wanted posters stuck to the wall above it. Thomas recognized him as Buster Quinn, the ex–Pinkerton detective who had come to Heartbreak Creek last spring. He had since gone to work as chief of security for the Denver & Santa Fe Railroad, as well as the Rylanders' Pueblo Pacific Bridge Line that ran through the canyon.

Thomas stopped beside him to unlock the office door.

"Morning, Redstone. Heard you were the new sheriff. Good choice. Not that Chick didn't do the job as best he could, but with that leg he didn't ride out much."

Once inside, Thomas motioned Quinn to the chair in front of the desk, hung the key on a hook, then set a fire in the small coal stove. "What did Chick miss?"

"Probably not much."

While Thomas dumped water and ground beans into the blackened coffeepot, Quinn settled in, one ankle on the opposite thigh, his hat perched atop his bent knee. "The usual derelict miners, a few wanderers passing through, and a reclusive fellow folks get glimpses of now and then. Nothing troublesome yet, but it might help if you made your presence known. I helped Chick out when I could, but I'll be busy for a while."

Leaving the coffee to boil, Thomas settled in the chair behind the desk. His desk now. Seemed odd, owning furniture. Another rope that tied him down. "Busy with what?"

"Railroad problems. I may need your help."

Buster Quinn was a quiet man of middle years who listened more than he talked. Rylander had told them that Quinn had left the New York Pinkertons when the thievery of the government under Boss Tweed had soured him. Incorruptible, Tait had called him. Not long after, Rylander had hired him to bring his wife's guardian, Mrs. Throckmorton, and her housekeeper, Mrs. Bradshaw, to Heartbreak Creek. Soon after he arrived, Quinn had taken the job of watching over the railroad, the same way Thomas would now be watching over the town. If a man with such experience asked for help, it must be serious. "What do you need?"

"Mostly keep an eye on the line running through the canyon."

The coffee came to a boil. Thomas grabbed a handful of eggshells from a jar on the shelf beside the cups and dropped them in to settle the grounds, then moved the pot to the cooler side of the stove. "You expect trouble?"

"Maybe. Heard about that train robbery in Kansas a while back? Two bandits killed the express man when he wouldn't open the till, then roped the safe and dragged it off. Found it later shot to hell, but unopened. Nothing much worth stealing anyway. But now that we're moving payroll, I expect more attempts."

Thomas poured coffee into one of the cups, set it on the desk before Quinn, then returned to his chair. He did not drink coffee, because it tasted like burned buffalo chips. But when he was Brodie's deputy he had learned to make it. And not very well, judging by the face Quinn made after he took a sip.

"You expect trouble in our canyon?" Thomas asked.

Quinn shoved the cup aside. "It would be the perfect place to ambush or derail a train." When Thomas started to protest, Quinn raised a hand. "I'm aware that it's not part of your duties to watch over the railroad. But no one knows this country like you do. It would be a big help if you kept an eye on folks traveling through and took note of anybody up to no good. You'd do that anyway as sheriff, wouldn't you?"

"I would." After the fire and murders last year, he would keep a close watch on his mountains, especially when workers came to begin work on the new hotel up in the canyon.

"All I want is for you to report what you find. I'll take it from there."

"I will do as you ask."

They spoke a while longer about changes in the town, strangers who had moved in, and the new daughter born to the Rylanders. As a detective, Buster Quinn had learned to study things with more than his eyes. For a white man, he was smart, and Thomas valued the older man's words.

"Overall, Heartbreak Creek is a pretty quiet town now that the mines have played out," Quinn said. "If we watch each other's backs, we can keep it that way." He rose and settled the hat on his head. "Hope you're planning to stay awhile."

"I have a daughter now. She needs people around her."

"Heard she was blind."

Thomas nodded. "A fever when she was eight. She holds no bitterness about it, but I worry about her." He walked Quinn toward the door.

"Had a blind uncle once. Used a stick and a dog," Seeing Thomas's confusion, Quinn motioned with an imaginary stick. "Ran it back and forth along the ground in front of him so he'd know what was ahead. Got around pretty good. Might try it with your daughter."

Thomas liked the idea. The more independent *Katse'e* could become, the easier it would be on both of them.

Quinn opened the door, then stopped when he saw a woman standing on the other side, fist raised to knock.

With a look of surprise, she stepped back, almost dropping the napkin-draped tray balanced on her hip.

"Let me help you with that, Mrs. Bradshaw." Quinn stepped forward to take the tray from her hands. "Smells good."

"It's just lunch." The middle-aged woman swept a hand over her tightly pinned, gray-streaked hair. "Mrs. Rylander has the hotel send lunch to the sheriff's office each day."

Quinn set the tray carefully onto the desk. "That's mighty nice of her."

"Thank you—I mean, it wasn't my idea, but I'll tell her . . ." Her words trailed off. Her cheeks turned red.

Quinn shifted from one foot to the other and stared at the floor.

Ho, Thomas thought, watching them.

"Did you hear about the new baby?" When she smiled, Mrs. Bradshaw was a fine-looking woman. It seemed Buster

Quinn agreed, because he smiled back . . . something he had not done with Thomas.

"I did. The sheriff here told me. She's hale and hearty?"

"Very much so."

"Mrs. Rylander, too?"

"Yes. Tired, of course, but Doctor Boyce said they are both doing well. Troopers, he called them. Said she looks like her father. The baby, that is."

"That's nice. Real nice."

A long pause. Thomas rested a hip against his desk, crossed his arms over his chest, and watched them. Had he and Prudence Lincoln been so uneasy with each other those first few meetings?

"Well, then." Mrs. Bradshaw wiped her palms down her skirts. "I should go. As you can imagine, things are in a bit of an uproar."

"I'll walk you back."

"That's not necessary."

"It is to me."

"Oh. Well, then." A flash of a smile. Another red rush over her cheeks. "Thank you, Mr. Quinn."

"My pleasure, Mrs. Bradshaw."

Thomas stared at the closed door for a long while after they left. Then, with a sigh, he pushed thoughts of *Eho'nehevehohtse* from his mind and settled at his desk to eat his lunch. He would have to get a stick. And a dog. But first, he would walk through the canyon and find the peace that eluded him.

"I need a dog," Thomas announced that afternoon when he joined Jessup, Hardesty, Brodie, and Quinn in the Red Eye to congratulate Tait Rylander on his new daughter. The saloon was open now, and many men came by the table to offer good wishes. The Rylanders had much money and spread it freely about the town. For that and their fine characters, they were held in high esteem.

"Phoenix had pups a while back," Hardesty said. "Only one left is the runt. A male. You're welcome to him."

"Who is this Phoenix?"

"The dog Audra took in. We think she ran off from Weems."

Thomas frowned.

"The murderer you killed last summer?" Ethan prodded.

"Did I kill someone last summer?"

"Actually, it was the fall that killed him," Declan Brodie said. "You haven't killed anyone since you knifed the man who tried to take Brin. Been a slow year for you."

"Not anymore."

"Aw, hell. Who was it this time?"

Thomas sipped from his ginger beer.

"More than one?"

"What does it matter? They were all white."

"Well, that's just perfect. We hired a murderer for our new sheriff."

"Who said I murdered them?" Thomas studied the man beside him. Declan Brodie walked such a straight line, sometimes he tripped over his own righteousness. But he had made a good sheriff, and Thomas respected him for that. "No body, no proof of murder. Is that not what you told me last summer, *ve'ho'e*?"

"At least tell us you had reason, or were defending yourself."

Because he saw true concern in his friend's eyes, Thomas decided to explain his actions, something he rarely did. "Two of them tried to ambush me, and the other sent them to do it. He also threatened Prudence Lincoln, and put Lillian in a place called an asylum. Is that reason enough?"

"Damn," Hardesty muttered.

"Reason enough for me," Rayford Jessup said. "Sounds like they needed killing."

Tait Rylander studied him, the fingers of his right hand absently stroking the scar at his temple. Buster Quinn stared into his glass. Brodie said nothing. All three men were bound by laws that seldom made sense to Thomas.

"What do you need a dog for?" Hardesty asked, breaking the long silence.

"To help *Katse'e* find her way."

"Find her way where?"

Buster Quinn explained how his blind uncle's dog had warned him of approaching dangers, like creeks, or drop-offs, or obstacles in his path. "Damned good guard dog, too."

"I should get Rosie a dog," Tait said.

Declan Brodie frowned. "Who's Rosie?"

"My daughter. Who'd you think?"

"I thought her name was Rosaleen."

"It is. I shortened it to Rosie. Sounds more . . . baby-like."

"Then why didn't you name her Rosie in the first place?"

"Because Luce's mother was named Rosaleen, and she wanted—hell, never mind." Grabbing the bottle of the Scotsman's whisky, he poured into his glass. "Sometimes talking to you is like pissing up a rope."

Ethan Hardesty looked from one to the other. "I thought her mother's name was Ida."

"Ida Throckmorton is her guardian, not her mother."

"Even I knew that," Rayford Jessup said. "And I'm new." He topped off his own glass, then slid the bottle on to Buster Quinn. "As long as the pup isn't a sight or scent hound, it might work for Lillie. Those hounds are too easily distracted for nursemaid work."

"He looks a bit like Ash's wolfhound, Tricks. Same rough coat, but I doubt he'll get near as big."

"Rosaleen," Brodie mused. "Sounds Irish."

"For God's sake," Tait burst out. "It *is* Irish. My wife is Irish. Her mother was Irish. Why is that so hard to figure out?" Tossing back the last swallow, he plunked the glass onto the table and rose. "I'm going to see how she's doing."

After Rylander slammed out the door, Brodie stoppered the bottle and frowned thoughtfully. "Seems cranky."

"Not surprising," Quinn said. "Helen told me he was up most of the night."

Brodie studied him then swirled the whisky in his glass. "Girls are hard. Brin came out crying and didn't shut up for six months. And then there's that whole after-the-baby thing. Tait's in for a hard time."

Nods all around. Like Thomas, they probably remembered how Edwina Brodie had made everyone suffer after Whit was born. But her spirits seemed recovered now, so there was hope for Tait Rylander.

Thomas asked Brodie when he was going back to the ranch. "R.D. said you and the boys were leaving tomorrow?"

"First light. Chick's loading the wagon now. By the way, when Jessup came, we brought your horse back from the ranch. He's got it out at the Wallace stables."

"I will come for him."

Jessup nodded.

A long pause, then Brodie swiveled in his chair to pin Quinn with a smirky smile. "So, Buster. You going to tell us who Helen is, or not?"

Thomas watched color stain the older man's cheeks. "Helen Bradshaw. The housekeeper."

"Oh. *That* Helen."

"I knew that, too," Jessup said and belched. "Don't you ever talk to your wife, Declan?"

"Not if I can help it."

The other men laughed. Thomas didn't. When Brodie caught his glare, he said, "I was joking, Thomas. You know I meant no disrespect to Ed. I just don't talk much, and when I do, I seem to get into trouble."

"This is true." Thomas rose. "Now I must go get my horse and see what damage your children did to the house while I was gone."

Fourteen

One week stretched into two. Then three. By the end of the first month, Thomas's life had taken on a sameness that calmed the turmoil in his mind, even as it numbed his spirit.

Every morning, he walked *Katse'e* to the new two-room schoolhouse built on the ashes of the Chinese camp that had burned last year when fire swept down the canyon. He had made her a walking stick from a length of ash, and she was learning to use it. On Joe Bill, if she had the chance. The pup Ethan Hardesty gave her was too young to be much help—and might never be. As the weeks passed, he looked more and more like the Scotsman's Irish wolfhound, a dog bred to hunt. But *Katse'e* loved him, and someday he would make a good guard dog like his sire, despite being named Bitsy.

After leaving her off at the school—and in the care of Jamie Jessup, who watched over her even though he had three years less than she did—Thomas would walk through the town that he was paid to watch over, stopping at different shops and stores along the way to answer questions or listen to complaints. But rarely to visit. The townspeople seemed to prefer that he keep his distance, which was fine with him.

The rest of the morning he spent in his office, looking over paperwork, updating the wanted lists, and waiting for his lunch to arrive. Afternoons, he did his work from horseback, riding along Mulberry Creek, or up to the old mine, or along canyon trails. Then, if Curtis had not gone to get her from school, it was time for Thomas to walk *Katse'e* back to the Arlan house—he still could not think of it as home, and doubted he ever would.

Every evening, he sat before the fire and read aloud from a book Rayford Jessup had given him about a Scots hero named Rob Roy. It was slow going with all the Scottish words, but *Katse'e* seemed to enjoy it—as did Miss Minty, Harriet, Bitsy, and the Abrahams. He also read from the braille book Prudence Lincoln had bought for her, while *Katse'e* followed along, her small fingers moving over the raised dots that made up the letters and words. It was a halting process, but Thomas felt a father's pride when Lillian was able to read a few of the words on her own.

Nights were long and restless.

Then dawn would come, and the cycle would begin again.

It was hardly the warrior's life he had once envisioned, but at least he had a purpose, even if it was not one of his choosing.

He thought things were going well, but then not long after *Katse'e* started school, he came home to find her hiding under the back stoop with Bitsy. Neither of the Abrahams had been able to coax her out. Curtis had walked her home from school that day, and he said everything was fine until she heard Thomas come through the front door.

Wondering what he had done this time, Thomas went out to talk to her.

"What are you doing under there, *Katse'e*?"

"Hidin' from you."

"Why? Did you do something wrong?"

"No! *You* the bad one! You stay away from my dog!"

Baffled, Thomas bent to peer under the step. "What did I do?"

"You a Dog Soldier!"

He glanced at Curtis, but the black man shrugged, looking as confused as Thomas was. "Yes, I was a Dog Soldier. But you knew that, *Katse'e*. Why does it upset you now?"

"'Cause you eat dogs, that why! But you ain't eating mine!"

Thomas jerked back when the stick poked from beneath the step to ward him off. He heard whining, but did not know if it came from the dog or his daughter. Both seemed upset. "Who told you I eat dogs?"

"Joe Bill. He say that why you called a Dog Soldier, 'cause you eat dogs." She was crying now, the pup whimpering with her.

Thomas sighed. "Joe Bill was wrong, *Katse'e*. That is not why we are called Dog Soldiers. I do not eat dogs." Not lately, anyway. They were not that tasty.

"Fo' true?"

"For true. You will come out now before the spiders find you."

"Spiders?"

People rarely stopped to visit. Tait Rylander spent most of his days with his wife and new daughter. Declan Brodie and his oldest son had returned to the ranch. Edwina Brodie and the younger children had stayed at the Sunday house so the ones old enough to attend could go to school. Every morning, he nodded to Audra Hardesty through the window of the *Heartbreak Creek Herald* office, but Ethan was trying to finish their new house, so he only came into town for building supplies. He saw Rayford Jessup more often, but as the weeks passed, he grew busy at the Wallace stables, readying them for the foals that would arrive next fall.

And little by little, as the turmoil eased and the numbness faded, Thomas's anger grew.

At first, he had no focus for it. But it was there when he awoke, and there when he lay tossing at night, festering under his skin like a mesquite thorn. Then one morning, he awoke so filled with rage his jaw ached, and one face filled his mind. *Eho'nehevehohtse*. His wife.

Three times he had gone to her and three times she had sent him away. Yet she still haunted his thoughts. He was weary of it. After this long with no word, he accepted that she would not come back to him. It was time to cut her from his life and his mind, or he would never find peace. So he blocked her in every way he could, until finally, he could pass an entire day without thinking of her more than a few times. And slowly, as Mother Earth gave birth to spring, he began to heal.

The days lengthened. Snow on the south-facing slopes melted away, and the creeks that spilled out of the mountains rose against their banks. On his rides through the canyon, he welcomed the first early buds pushing up through the damp soil—dewberry, bitterroot, blue flax. Before long, aspen would leaf and arrowroot blossoms would cast a yellow blanket over the sunny slopes. Already birdsong filled the air, and overhead, squirrels leaped from limb to limb.

But down below, in the soft, damp ground where the snow had melted, and in the ice-crusted patches that never saw the sun, tracks showed. Human tracks.

Most of the miners had left with the first snow and few trappers stayed now that the game had dwindled with the arrival of so many people. But these tracks were new. And familiar. Thomas had seen them earlier in snow—wide, slightly toed-in, separated by a long, dragging stride.

Several times on his rides, he had smelled wood smoke, but had not been able to make out the source. And twice, he had seen a dark form move through the trees. Tall. Upright. Wearing the pelt of a bear, but moving like a man. A big man.

The last time he had seen him, Thomas had called out. But the figure had scurried higher onto icy slopes where Thomas's horse could not go. When he talked to Quinn about it, they decided he was the recluse that several townspeople had seen, but none had spoken to. Crazy, maybe, but harmless. So far.

As time passed, *Katse'e* grew less fearful that he would leave her. She had taken well to the Abrahams, and their gentle patience gained her trust. She spoke of Prudence Lincoln less and less. Thomas was grateful for that.

The cat turned out to be male, and his name changed from Harriet to Harry. As the days warmed, the cat spent much of his time prowling the creek and leaving fresh kills on the doorstep. But Bitsy rarely left Lillian's side, even sleeping in her room on an old blanket. Each day, Thomas worked to train him, but the dog had a sharp nose and preferred to chase after every scent the breeze brought his way. Once, the pup was lured away by coyotes. An hour later, he limped home with several bites and blood on his muzzle. A good lesson for both the dog and the girl.

"Them bad coyotes," *Katse'e* had scolded as Thomas smeared Winnie's salve on the pup's bites and cuts. "They play too rough."

"*Okom* does not play. *Okom* is always hungry and will hunt where he must."

"Hungry? You mean he eat Bitsy?"

"If he can." Seeing her shock, he tried to explain. "It is the way of things, *Katse'e*. Food is life. And in the forest, an animal is either the hunter or the hunted. Until your dog is bigger, he will be hunted. That is why we must keep him on a rope when he is outside, and guard him well until he is big enough to guard you."

"You mean coyotes eat me, too?"

"I think you would be too stringy. But you should never go into the woods alone. It would be easy to lose your way. Even with your dog and your stick."

She grinned. "That stick a good whacker. Give that stinker Joe Bill a good crack yesterday. Sent him runnin', sho' 'nuff."

"No, Lillian." Thomas tried to sound stern, but he knew what a trial Joe Bill could be. "Your stick is not a weapon. It is to help you find your way, not hit other people."

"He say I blind like a mole."

"He is right. You are blind. But he is also wrong to tease you about it. Tell him you do not like it. If he does not listen, we will try another way."

"He also tease me about the way I talk. Can I whack him for that?"

"No. But maybe if you spoke more like the others, you would not be teased as much."

Tears rose in her eyes. "You think I talk funny, too?"

He brushed a finger along her cheek. "Not funny, little one. But sometimes it is hard to understand your words."

Tears gave way to belligerence. "You want me to be more white."

Thomas sighed and struggled to find the right words. "I want you to be *you*, my clever, funny, spirited daughter. But how will others see the best of you if they cannot understand your words?"

She thought long and hard, then let out a deep breath. "All right. I try to do better. But you try, too. Sometimes you ain't—*aren't*—so easy to understand, either."

Despite her troubles with Joe Bill, she seemed to enjoy school, and although she could not read or write, she had a good memory and a quick mind and was able to keep up with most of the lessons.

She was settling in. She had friends now, and a family, and animals to tend. But what most helped her find her place in Heartbreak Creek was her singing.

Thomas knew music was important to her, so the Saturday after they arrived, he had gone to speak to Pastor and Biddy Rickman.

"I will bring her to your church," he had told them, after explaining about his new daughter and that she liked music. "And you will let her sing."

"Of course. I'm sure the choir ladies will happily welcome—"

"No. Alone. She will sing alone." He glanced at Biddy Rickman, who pounded on the church piano like she was killing ants. "No piano. No other voices. Only her. You will nod to me when it is time, and I will lead her to the front."

They blinked at him.

"Good. I will bring her to services tomorrow," he said, and left.

The next morning over breakfast, he asked *Katse'e* if she would like to sing at the church.

"Sho' 'nuff! I jist loves to sing. Ev'rybody love to hear me, too. Ain't—*isn't*—that so, Miss Winnie? You asks me to sing all the time."

"You have a gift, child, and that's God's own truth. What will you sing?"

"'Mazin' Grace' my favorite. That a good one?"

"It certainly is."

"You come hear me sing?"

"Of course we will." Winnie gave Thomas a look. "And your daddy will come, too." The Abrahams knew Thomas rarely went inside the church.

After breakfast, Thomas had dutifully gone upstairs to put on his fancy suit and help *Katse'e* into the dress Prudence Lincoln had bought her in Indianapolis. Then the four of them had walked down to the Come All You Sinners Church of Heartbreak Creek.

He had been inside the church only a few times—mostly for weddings and christenings. All that hellfire and damnation made his head hurt. So when he led Lillian and the Abrahams to a bench that second Sunday morning after they had arrived in Heartbreak Creek, many surprised faces turned his way.

He ignored them. And he ignored most of what the pastor said, until the wild-haired man nodded to Thomas, then spoke to the people sitting on the benches.

"And now, folks, I'd like to introduce a new member of our congregation, and ask her if she would like to sing for us."

Thomas led *Katse'e* forward. Standing beside her, he faced the gathered townspeople. "This is my new daughter, Lillian Redstone. The Great Spirit took her sight three years ago. But he gave her the gift she will now share with you." A last pat on her thin shoulder, then he walked back to his seat.

As soon as she sent the first note bouncing against the rafters, she won the hearts of all those within hearing. Crossing his arms over his chest, Thomas had sat back, filled with pride and the same awe he had felt the first time he had heard her sing. He suspected *Katse'e* would always find her place in this world, no matter the trials put before her. Her spirit was very strong.

By the time the month called March arrived, they were settling in as a family and Thomas was beginning to find his balance. This might not be the life he had expected to lead, but with *Katse'e* to take care of and the town to watch over, he was beginning to feel part of a tribe again.

Then, early the following week, everything came tumbling down around him when Curtis ran into the sheriff's office and told him *Katse'e* was gone.

WASHINGTON, D.C.

Pru watched the man shuffle through papers strewn across the scarred tabletop in the stark interrogation room at the jail where she had been held for well over a month. This was the first time she had dealt with this questioner. His suit was rumpled. His muttonchops needed trimming, as did his thin brown hair. He looked tired and bored, and hadn't even bothered to introduce himself when he'd come in a few minutes earlier.

She was so weary of all this . . . the endless interrogations, being frightened all the time, wondering if Brother was faring any better than she was. And she worried constantly about Thomas and Lillie. Were they being detained, too? She dared not ask and draw attention to them. But not knowing how they fared was eating a hole in her stomach.

She prayed each night that they had made it safely to Heartbreak Creek. And she also prayed that they had forgiven her for leaving them. She missed them with an ache that left her weeping through the long nights and moving numbly through the days.

"When did you last see Cyrus Marsh?"

Startled from her thoughts, she glanced up to find the questioner studying her through gray eyes as flat and hard as two chips of flint. Hearing the hint of Mississippi in his voice made her spirits sink. Even though the vast majority of Southerners hadn't owned slaves, many blamed blacks for the many changes and difficulties that still plagued the South almost six years after the war had ended. She would have to tread carefully with this man. "When he left to smoke a cheroot on the rear platform of our rail car."

"When was that?"

"Not long after we boarded the train in Indianapolis. I'm not sure of the exact time."

He made a note on a crumpled sheet of paper. "When he didn't return, what did you do?"

"Brother Sampson reported his absence to the conductor."

"And what did the conductor do?"

"He told us he would check the other cars, but it wasn't until we arrived at the Philadelphia station that the railroad seemed concerned. I told all this to the other men who came to question me."

He flipped through his papers again.

Pru watched his hands. They were broad and short-fingered, with chipped nails and scarred knuckles. A brawler's hands. They would cause damage if used against her. In jail, she had heard stories of beatings and threats directed at the black prisoners. So far, other than these interrogations, she had been largely ignored. But in this man, she sensed a brutality that could easily turn to violence.

"Says here you were crying on the train. Why?"

"I was distraught about leaving my family."

His head came up. "Marsh forced you to go?"

She and Brother had agreed to minimize any conflict with Marsh, but as Pru looked into the steely eyes of the man across the table, she feared she might falter. Keeping her gaze locked on his, she tried to keep the lie out of her voice. "It was my decision to go to Washington to present my education initiative. Mr. Marsh, as trustee of the school where I was employed, was always very supportive. He even arranged for our travel."

"Did you go out on the rear platform with him?"

"No."

Folding his thick arms atop the papers, he stared at her for several moments. "Maybe you wanted some fresh air, too. Maybe you went out there hoping to get more from him than train tickets."

Under the table, Pru clasped her hands so tightly her fingers went numb. "I never went out onto the platform. Nor did the reverend."

"Maybe when he made his move, you shoved him away so hard he fell over the railing."

Perspiration slicked her palms. "Mr. Marsh is a moral man. He would never make improper advances. Especially to a black woman." Anger rippled through her. "I assume by your questions you haven't found Mr. Marsh, so you have no idea what—if anything—happened to him."

"What do you think happened to him?"

"I don't know. Perhaps he stepped off at one of the water stops, had an accident, or was assaulted, and was unable to return to the train before it left. Perhaps he changed his mind about going to Washington. Perhaps he came on a later train and is now here in Washington. There are many reasons why he might be absent. You assume foul play, but without a body, how can you be so certain that a crime has even been committed?"

"We've looked hard, Mrs. Redstone. He's not here, or in Indiana, or anywhere in between."

"So you've decided that somehow I was able to do away with a man much larger than I am, while traveling on a moving train in full view of dozens of passengers? Does that make sense?"

Anger flashed. "Maybe you had help."

"From whom?"

"The reverend."

She allowed her disgust and disbelief to show. "Have you seen his hands? Do you actually think it possible that he could overpower a younger, larger man with those hands?"

"Then maybe your husband did it. He's an Indian, isn't he? Redskins are known for their savagery. Maybe he didn't want you to go and decided to do something about it."

Pru shot to her feet. "This is ridiculous! Either charge me and allow me to face my judgment in a court of law, or let me go." She saw fury darken his face, but didn't care. As long as she could deflect attention away from Thomas and Brother, it would be worth the beating that was surely headed her way.

He rose and gathered his papers. "We'll talk again, Mrs. Redstone, after you've had a chance to calm down." He sauntered toward the door, then paused and looked back at her. "I hear you've been teaching some of the other prisoners to read and write. I'd be careful with that, if I was you. Some folks might not appreciate your interference." His smile dripped venom. "You stay safe now, y'hear? Prison can be a dangerous place."

COLORADO TERRITORY

Above the chattering of her teeth, Lillie thought she heard Winnie calling, but it was so far away, she wasn't sure. Or maybe it was Bitsy whining.

"You Bitsy! That you?"

Silence.

"You better git you fanny here right now. I means it."

Nothing. *Damn that dog.* With one hand against the tree trunk, she crouched down and felt the ground. No snow. Not dry, either, but she sat down anyway. Her shoes were wet from tromping through snow. Sticks and pinecones poked through her dress and cold wetness soaked into her underpants. Pulling her knees up against her chest, she wrapped her arms around her legs and tried not to shiver.

Why had no one come looking for her? Did they even care she was lost?

She didn't want to be a baby, but she was starting to get scared.

Her eyes burned. Something warm trickled down her cheek. Tears or blood? She lifted a hand to the knot on the side of her head. No blood. The last time she fell, she hit her head hard. And after crashing through the brush, she had so many stinging, itchy, burning places, she could be bleeding to death and not even know it.

Not that anyone cared. "'Specially that damn dog. Daddy be mad, sho' 'nuff," she yelled. "He feed you to *okom*, you run off like this."

It helped to hear her own voice. Made her think she wasn't all alone, and helped to block other sounds. Like crackling sounds. And crunching. Unfamiliar, sneaky noises. But when she yelled too loud, it scared her worse, because she could hear the fear in her voice.

"I not afraid," she said, in case anyone was listening. "Daddy find me."

How long had she been gone? It seemed forever since Bitsy had dragged her across the yard, barking at something. She'd held on as long as she could, but then something tripped her, and when she fell, the rope had slipped through her hands. She'd almost lost her stick, too.

She'd called so much, her throat hurt, but Bitsy hadn't come back. Then she'd heard him barking not too far away. She'd gone toward the sound, raking the ground with her stick like Daddy had taught her. When the barking faded into high-pitched whining, she had tried to go faster, beating at the bushes and calling.

"You leave my dog alone, *okom*! I fight you with my stick! Whack you good!"

But she must have gone the wrong way, because after a while, she couldn't hear the whining anymore. She stood for a minute, not sure what to do. Finally, thinking she should get Winnie and Curtis to help her, she had turned back.

But it didn't feel right. Too brushy. Too many trees. Something was wrong.

She stopped to listen. Off to the right, she heard the creek. She headed toward it, then stopped when her stick hit something hard and hollow-sounding on the ground. Bending down, she felt it with her hand. Wooden planks. Then she straightened and traced it as far as her stick could reach. After a few careful steps, she decided it was a skinny wooden bridge stretching across the water.

Bridges meant people. Maybe there was a road or a house nearby. Certain she was headed in the right direction, she crossed over and kept going up what felt like a rocky trail. But it still hadn't felt right. Like the trail was getting steeper and steeper. And the farther she walked, the more snow she stepped in. It scared her that she couldn't hear the creek anymore. Had she turned into the canyon instead of toward town? She decided to go back, but when she turned, the trail was gone.

Panicked, she beat at the ground with her stick, but kept hitting trees and brush. The harder she worked to get back to the trail, the more lost she felt. She kept stumbling into things and falling over sticks and rocks, until finally she had tripped over a fat log, hitting her head hard and sending her stick flying. Rising on wobbly legs, she had kept going, hands stretched before her.

Finally, too cold and scared and weary to take another step, she had slumped down beside the tree where she sat now, thinking maybe if she stayed in one place, Daddy would find her.

That was a long time ago. Or maybe just a few minutes. She was so turned around and scared she didn't know where she was, or how much time had passed. So here she sat in her wet skirt and shoes, getting poked in the fanny by pinecones and probably catching a mess of ticks from this scratchy tree. No dog. No stick. No way to find her way home.

Was anybody even looking for her?

"Daddy!" she shouted. "Daddy, it me, Lillie! Come git me!"

Something chattered above her head. She shrank against the tree. A squirrel?

Probably a squirrel. She remembered squirrels. She had liked watching their tails twitch back and forth like little furry flags.

But what if it wasn't a squirrel? What if it was something big?

"Damn dog!" she shouted. "I spank you fur plum off you fanny you don't come right this minute!"

Silence. Even the squirrel—if that's what it was—shut up.

Dropping her cheek to her knees, she let the fear take over. "Daddy find me," she whispered into the darkness. "He a Cheyenne Dog Soldier. He find anything."

Thomas bolted from his chair. "What do you mean she is gone? Gone where?" Shoving past Curtis, he ran out the door.

Curtis followed him onto the boardwalk. "I don't know

where. I checked along the creek but didn't see nothing of her or the dog."

Thomas jerked his pony's reins free of the hitching rail. "How long?"

"Long as it take me to run here. Last I saw of her, she standing in the side yard, holding Bitsy's rope while the dog do his business. Next thing I know, I hear barking. It was so far away, I don't think much about it, but when I go back to see what was taking so long, she and the dog both gone. Winnie and me, we call and call, but we don't hear nothing. You think she crossed the creek? She had her stick with her. Maybe she'll find her way back."

Thomas vaulted into the saddle. "Get help. Send them to the house." Wheeling the pinto, he kicked him into a gallop.

When he reached the Arlan place, he saw Winnie standing in the yard. Jumping to the ground, he ran toward her. He could tell by her expression that *Katse'e* had not returned, but he asked, anyway.

"Not a thing." The black woman pressed her apron to her eyes. "I been yelling and yelling. Lawd, that poor child. Mr. Thomas, you got to find her."

"Curtis brings help. Tell them to spread out along the creek."

Thomas ran toward the trees at the back of the house. He coursed back and forth until he saw a dog track in the soft ground along the bank. He crossed over and studied the other side. More dog tracks, heading west along the creek. But no small human print. He came back over, and followed the bank behind the house toward town.

At the turn where the creek veered north, he searched beneath the trees until finally he saw a shoe print—small, not deep. *Katse'e*'s?

He had not been this afraid in a long time. As memories of past conversations and scolding words filled his mind, his regret grew. Had his harsh words sent her away? He told his spirit guides he would be a better father if they would lead him to his daughter. He made promises to *Ma'heo'o*. He sent pleas up to the Great Spirit.

But still, he did not find her.

He tracked deeper into the trees, found the narrow wagon trail that led up to the old mine, and followed it across the wooden bridge. Water swirled around the log braces that supported it, running fast and deep. He looked downstream, saw no small form in the water, then studied the banks on both sides, but saw no new tracks.

"Lillian!" he yelled.

Silence.

Had he gone the wrong way? Could she have fallen into the water?

His heart pounded so hard it deafened him to other sounds. He made himself breathe deep and bring the fear under control so he could hear if she answered.

He called again and again. Then listened.

Dimly, he heard voices calling from the direction he had come. But they called for Lillian, not him.

A new surge of fear blossomed in his chest. He forced it back and continued following the damp edges of the trail. At last, he saw a small footprint. Then another. A faint scrape that could have been made by her stick.

He started jogging, head bent to study the trail.

Katse'e was smart. She would know to sit and wait for him to find her. But already the sun had slipped behind the tall peaks. Light would fade fast and soon the air would grow cold. Too cold for a small girl lost in the dark.

He kept going, hope fading with the daylight. As the trail climbed, mud gave way to snow. When he found no more tracks, he decided she must have wandered off the trail. So he did, too, climbing north over rocky ground and through tangles of brush. Could she have made it this far over such rough ground? He doubted it. He was about to turn back when he saw something caught in a bush.

Her stick.

Relief gave him new strength. Cupping his mouth, he called out again and again until his voice grew hoarse.

Nothing.

It was almost dark now, but he kept going, trying to focus on the faint tracks in the dirt and not on the fear that built with every step, or the tiny snowflakes falling from the leaden sky.

Lillie couldn't stop shivering. She felt hot and cold at the same time, and now tiny snowflakes were hitting her face. How long was she supposed to sit here before somebody came looking for her? She would call out again, but her throat was so sore from all her yelling she could hardly swallow and her head hurt something awful. Muttering a word she wasn't supposed to know, she slumped back against the tree.

Daddy, where are you?

Was it night? The air seemed much colder than before. And quieter. No birds. No squirrels. And a faraway sound that might have been rushing water in the creek. Or wind through the trees.

And sometimes, a crunching noise, like footsteps on snow or icy ground. Sneaky footsteps. Starting and stopping, like whoever or whatever it was, was creeping along slow and careful, maybe listening to see where she was.

She heard a wheezy sound, realized it came from her own self, and clapped a hand over her mouth. She felt prickly and sweaty-cold. Maybe she should go back toward the sound of the creek—if what she'd heard was really the creek. If she followed it, wouldn't it lead her home, or to town?

Unless the water she heard was from a different creek. Daddy had told her that when the snow melted, water ran in lots of places down the canyon.

Maybe she should go anyway. She was thirsty. It might make her throat feel better. And she didn't like whatever was sneaking around out there.

But didn't animals get thirsty, too? Big, hungry animals? Like coyotes? And mountain lions, and bears?

The crunching stopped.

Lillie waited, hardly daring to breathe.

Then it started again. Closer, louder, heading her way.

She began to rock, arms wrapped tightly around her raised knees. Tears spilled down her cheeks. "Daddy . . . where are you?" she whimpered, too cold and frightened to yell anymore.

The crunching got so loud she couldn't hear anything else. Then it suddenly stopped right beside her. She heard breathing—up high—from something big. And smelled something stinky—worse than a dog or a pig or a cow.

"Well, well," a man's voice said. "Looky what I found."

Fifteen

Thomas was about to go back and get a torch, then he realized it was snowing harder now—not the tiny flakes that had fallen earlier, but big, wet flakes that would quickly cover the ground. And Lillian's tracks. So he kept going, his head and shoulders growing damp with melting snow, his vision fading with the light. Then he saw more tracks headed in the same direction as *Katse'e*'s. Deep and big, with that familiar dragging, toed-in stride.

The recluse.

His tracks were easier to spot in snow and mud than a child's shallow print, so he followed them, a terrible fear building in his mind.

In the faint twilight, he almost missed where the bigger tracks crossed *Katse'e*'s. Thomas knelt to study the ground. It looked like the man had stopped and milled around for a moment, then followed the small footprints that led deeper into the brush. Where was she going?

Or was she being chased?

If the man was tracking her, he made no secret of it . . . and he also had to know it was a child he followed.

"*Katse'e!*"

Silence.

He stumbled on, fear pounding through him so hard it made him light-headed and dizzy. He kept imagining what

Katse'e was going through. Her fear. The blackness. Wondering where she was and if he was looking for her.

If he lost another child . . .

Bile surged into his throat. Bending over, he braced his shaking hands on his knees and struggled to settle his nerves. Then he straightened and called again.

This time, he heard something. A single, short sound that was not a birdcall, or an animal. It did not sound like a voice, either. But he turned toward it because it was all he had.

And the snow kept falling.

Lillie flattened against the trunk of the tree as the man stomped around her, mumbling to himself. Finally, he stopped. She heard rustling, then he spoke, so close she could feel his stinky breath on her face.

"What you doing out here all by yourself, little girl?"

She cringed away, not just from fear, but from the stink. "Huntin' my dog. But now I lost. Who you?"

"Tombo." More rustling and muttering. "Most call me Moose on account I'm so big." He must have straightened, because she couldn't feel his breath anymore, but the stink was still bad. "The mean ones call me Dummy. I don't like that. It makes me mad. So mad I just wanna . . . wanna . . . break things."

He sounded mad. Crazy-mad. And he talked funny. Like he wasn't sure of the words. Lillie didn't remember hearing anyone in town talk that way. She wanted to tell him she wouldn't call him Dummy, and ask him if he would take her home, but she started coughing so hard it was a minute before she could catch her breath. "You take me home?" she finally managed.

"Home? Where's that?"

"Town."

"Nope. Can't."

"Why not?"

"I don't go to town." He moved around, mumbling to himself. "Town folks don't much like me."

"Why? You bad?"

"No! I'm not bad!"

Lillie ducked her head, but the blow never came.

Then in a strange, high, woman-sounding voice, he said, "Accidents happen, Tombo. It's not always your fault, even though mean people might think so." His voice changed back to a man's voice. "That's what Ma always said. She said 'cause I'm big and clumsy and funny-looking, accidents happen. But if I stay away from people, accidents won't happen. See? That's why I live in the woods."

Lillie didn't know what to say to that. But she was feeling too bad to be afraid anymore. He didn't sound mean, although he sure did stink. "You hunting me?"

"Yep. Heard you yelling and wondered what you was doing. It's starting to snow. What you doing out in the snow?"

"Huntin' my dog, like I said."

"I ain't got a dog. Used to. Not anymore."

Lillie licked at the snowflakes on her chin and lips, trying to cool her mouth. How could she be so cold and hot at the same time? She was so tired of shivering, but it got worse the longer she sat here in her wet drawers. "I wanna go home. You gonna take me?"

"Nope. Can't." Mumbling.

She caught a few words this time. "Trouble . . . hurt . . . mean." None of it made sense. "Please. Mrs. Winnie give you muffins."

"Too dark. Can't hardly see nothing, and the snow's coming down hard. I better go."

Lillie threw out an arm. "No, wait!" she cried, then started coughing again. "Don't leave me. Take me home. Please . . ."

"Why don't you go your own self?"

"I cain't see."

"It's not that dark yet. Just head down that a ways."

"No!" She started coughing so hard she nearly threw up. "I not know which way to go," she said in a raspy voice once she caught her breath. "I blind."

A long pause. "You mean you can't see nothing? Nothing at all?"

Suddenly the stink got worse. She felt a light breeze over her lashes and wondered if he was waving a hand in her face to test her.

"Then what you doing out here, if you can't see where you going?"

Lillie struggled for patience. "My dog run off. I afraid coyotes get him so I go after him. Now I lost. Why you stink so much?"

"I stink?" He sounded surprised.

Tears welled up again, and she dropped her head on her folded arms. "I not feel so good." In fact, she thought she might puke for true. "You help me or not?"

"I dunno."

"Daddy pay you." Unless he was too mad at her for going into the woods.

More mumbling and pacing. "I better not."

Anger surged through her. "You in big trouble you don't. He the new sheriff and he put you in jail you don't help me."

"Jail? No, no. No jail."

"Please . . ." She could hardly hear her own voice over the drumming in her head. "I think I sick."

"Don't want no trouble. No, no."

"You let me die out here, they come for you, Tombo. You knows they will."

"No, no, no." He started stomping around beside her, muttering and sniffling. Was he crying? "I didn't mean to. Sorry, sorry, sorry."

In the distance, a voice called.

Daddy! With one hand braced on the tree, Lillie struggled to stand. She was so dizzy she almost fell, but managed to stay on her feet. She took a wheezing breath. "Da—"

A hand clamped over her nose and mouth. "No, no, little girl, you can't do that! You gots to be quiet."

In panic, she shoved at the hand, but it didn't budge. She fought to drag in air. Couldn't. Then an arm grabbed her around the waist and jerked her from the ground against something hairy. In a frenzy of terror she kicked, bucked, clawed at the hand.

She couldn't breathe!

Daddy!

Thomas followed the tracks to a tall fir. It was snowing harder now, and was so dark he could hardly see, but the heavy branches overhead kept most of the new snow from covering the ground around the trunk. Bending down, he ran his finger-tips lightly over the dirt and found a small, smooth depression where Lillie had sat.

Heart drumming, he circled the tree, tracking as much by feel as by sight in the fading light. Then he found them—the big tracks he had been following. Like *Katse'e*'s small prints, they came toward the tree. But then they led away again, kicking up clods of mud and fresh snow, like he was running.

Katse'e's tracks had disappeared.

He had her.

Rage exploded. Throwing back his head, Thomas gave a bellow of fear and frustration—a war cry that echoed along the rocky walls. Then he began to run, following the deeper tracks into the canyon, praying the snow wouldn't cover the prints until he found his daughter.

When he made it back to the wagon trail that went up to the mine, he saw three horsemen coming toward him. Two carried torches. The third led Thomas's pinto. Breathing hard, he stopped, grateful to see Jessup, Hardesty, and Rylander.

"Any luck?" Jessup asked, tossing him the reins of his painted pony.

Thomas untied the poncho behind his saddle and pulled it on. "The man who hides in the woods has her."

"The hermit?"

"I do not know what he is called, but he tracked Lillian into the brush, then carried her off that way." He pointed up toward the abandoned mine, then swung up into the saddle. "Many trails lead from there higher into the canyon."

"How do you know he has Lillie?" Rylander asked.

"I tracked them both." Tired of wasting time with words, Thomas kicked his horse into a gallop. The others followed.

Lillie huddled against a plank wall. If it was in a house, it hadn't been lived in for a long time. Smelled like mouse pee. And something else—something she'd never smelled before. The floor was wood, too, and gritty, but dry. Wherever the man had taken her, it at least had a roof.

But she still couldn't stop shaking. Her wet clothes itched her skin, and her bones hurt almost as bad as her head.

He was muttering and pacing again. She thought he might be crying, but what grown man cried?

She was still mad at him for grabbing her that way. She thought he was trying to kill her. Then he started running and she almost puked up her innards until he banged in here and dumped her on the floor like a sack of potatoes. When Daddy came, Tombo would be in big trouble.

"You okay?" he asked. "You sound funny."

"No, I not okay!" Lillie tried to sound mad, but it came out more like a frog croak. "What you thinkin', draggin' around a po' blind black girl like that? If I could see you, I puke all over you shoes." A fit of coughing grabbed her and she curled tight over her aching stomach. Even breathing hurt her throat.

"You cold?"

Lillie was shivering too hard to think of an answer. He really was a dummy.

"I ain't got no blankets. I could let you use this, I guess."

A minute later, Lillie was engulfed in stink. Furry stink. "What this?" she choked out, trying to shove it off.

"My bearskin coat. Nice, ain't it?"

More like heavy and stinky. And prickly, rather than soft. But so warm, Lillie felt like she'd slipped into a hot bath. She pulled it closer and breathed through her mouth so she wouldn't have to smell it. Maybe if she slept, Daddy would be there when she woke up. He would take her home, and Bitsy would be there, and she wouldn't mind hardly at all if they both got whippings for running off.

Thomas burst through the door of the overseer's shack at the old mine, his knife up and ready.

But the shack was empty.

He looked around, his mind still gripped in a red haze and unable to accept that *Katse'e* was not there.

Tait Rylander charged through behind him, followed by Jessup and Hardesty. "She's not here?"

Whirling, Thomas shoved past them and studied the ground outside. He cursed in Cheyenne. With their arrival, they had disturbed any tracks that might have shown in the fresh snow. He saw several that might have been the big tracks he had been following, but none as small as a little girl would have made.

He stood, his body shaking with frustration and fear, unable to decide what to do next. He had been so sure the hermit had brought her here. The tracks led this way. So where was he?

A big hand gripped his shoulder. "Isn't there a mine shaft somewhere nearby?" Rayford Jessup said. "Might he have taken her there?"

Thomas shook off the fog in his head. "There are several." He started toward the rocky wall beneath the abandoned scaffolding that clung to the side of the bluff. There were many shallow, jagged depressions where the water cannon had dug away earth and stone to get to the veins of silver that had once striped the rocky hillside. All were empty.

Disheartened, they gathered around the faint light of a lantern they had found inside the entrance of the biggest cut and discussed where to go next.

"Anyone see any tracks leading away from the shack?" Rylander asked, his voice bouncing back at them from the rocky walls.

"Could he have gone on past the mine and deeper into the canyon?" Ethan Hardesty suggested.

"On the way here, I checked the water tower above town," Jessup said. "No fresh tracks anywhere around it."

Thomas did not respond. He barely heard them. Motioning them to silence, he closed his eyes and concentrated all his being on any sound moving along the damp, rocky walls.

Nothing but the men breathing around him and the slow drip of water off the icicles clinging to tiny seams in the stones overhead.

And yet . . .

He drew in a slow, deep breath, letting the air flow gently through his nose, down his throat and into his lungs. There. Beneath the smell of burning kerosene from the lamp, and the damp wool of their jackets . . . so faint it was barely noticeable . . . a rank animal smell.

"Do you smell that?" he whispered to the others.

Deep breaths. Sniffs. "Bear?" Jessup guessed. "Maybe this is a winter den."

Drawing his knife, Thomas went deeper into the darkness at

the back of the cut. The others followed, Jessup holding the lantern high so that Thomas's shadow crept ahead of them along the walls. They reached the back of the depression, which was so far into the hillside it felt more like a shallow tunnel.

Thomas stopped and tested the air. Urine. Pungent. Fresh. Someone or something had been in here recently. Yet there was nothing left now but rocks piled along the back wall, a pickax with a broken handle, a dented bucket . . . and that strange, rank animal smell.

Jessup stepped closer, holding the lantern high. "See anything?"

Thomas scanned the floor, the walls. Nothing but shadows. One seemed especially deep. Stepping forward, he stuck his hand into the shadow, but instead of touching more wall, he felt only air. He grabbed the lantern from Jessup, thrust it into the shadow, and was shocked to see that behind the rocks piled up at his feet, the tunnel turned and continued.

Hope building, he handed the lantern back to Rayford Jessup, gripped his knife tightly, and stepped over the rocks and into the darkness beyond.

Jessup followed, the light of the lantern stretching ahead of Thomas.

This back tunnel was not very long, or high, or wide. The animal stink was so strong Thomas expected to see a bear charging toward him.

Instead, crouched against the back wall was a small, rough, wooden shack. On the sagging door, a crude skull and crossbones was painted above the words *Danger Black Powder.*

With a snarl of rage, Thomas raised his knife and flung open the door.

Someone cried out—a man, not a child.

Thomas squinted into the dimness, but could see nothing until Jessup pushed in behind him, holding the lantern as high as the sloping roof would allow.

A bearded, terrified man cowered in the corner, an arm flung up to shield his eyes from the light. A leather pack sat on the floor beside him. A mound of bear hide lay against the far wall . . . the same hide Thomas had seen the man wear the one time he had gotten a good look at him stumbling through the trees.

"Where is she?" he shouted. "Where is the girl?"

"Don't hurt me!" The man slid down the wall, both arms folded over his head, knees drawn up to shield his body. "I didn't hurt her, I swear. Didn't do nothing but get her out of the snow."

Thomas stepped closer, teeth clenched. "Where is she? Tell me now, or I—"

"Thomas!"

He glanced over, saw Rafe lifting the edge of the bearskin coat.

"She's here, but I think something's wrong."

Forgetting the cringing man, Thomas rushed over to the tiny form shivering on the ground. He put a hand on her cheek and a new fear thundered through him. She was hot with fever. "*Katse'e?*"

The dark brown eyes fluttered open, stared blankly past his shoulder. "Daddy?" It was little more than a sigh and ended in a hoarse cough.

With shaking hands, Thomas dropped the stinking pelt back over her and scooped both her and the bearskin into his arms.

"What about him?" Tait Rylander nodded toward the cowering man.

"I didn't do nothing!" Tears slid down the man's cold-reddened cheeks and disappeared into his beard. "Just wanted to get her out of the snow. Didn't even know she was sick until I got her here. I never hurt her, I swear!"

Thomas barely spared him a glance. "Put him in a cell. The key ring is on a nail."

Then he rushed out the door, his precious burden clasped to his chest.

Sixteen

Thomas would have preferred a Cheyenne medicine man, but since there was none within a two-day ride, he had to take *Katse'e* to the white doctor. The old man did well healing the wounds of the body, but did little for the spirit.

He was familiar with the medicine rooms at the back of Doctor Boyce's house, so he took *Katse'e* through the side door, yelling for the doctor as he hurried down the hall.

A doorway opened behind him. "What the hell?"

"She has fever," Thomas called back over his shoulder. "Where should I put her?"

"In the exam room. On the right."

Thomas gently laid *Katse'e* on the high table, then folded back the fur. Her breathing was raspy, and even though they had just been out in the snow, her skin still felt hot, and she trembled like a reed in the wind.

Doctor Boyce hurried into the room. "Lord, what's that smell?"

"Bear." Thomas pulled the pelt from beneath *Katse'e*'s shivering body and slung it into the hall.

The white-haired man bent over the frail form on the table. Gently prying open *Katse'e*'s chattering teeth, he peered into her throat.

"You will heal her," Thomas said.

"Or what?"

"Or I will put my knife in your neck."

"Some sheriff you've turned out to be." Grabbing a listening thing from a peg beside the table, the doctor stuck the ends into his ears. "Now stop yammering so I can hear."

Thomas watched him move the metal disc on the end of the ear tubes all around her chest. He even rolled *Katse'e* onto her side and listened to her back.

"Well?" he asked, when the doctor had pulled the tubes from his ears.

"Influenza. Maybe pneumonia."

"What does that mean?"

"Means she's sick. Hopefully not mortally. I'll give her something to bring her fever down. Cold sponge baths, if necessary. Other than that, most we can do is give her plenty of water and let her rest. This the one who was lost? Your blind daughter?" The doctor rummaged in a cabinet beside the table.

"Yes. Her name is Lillian. She has ten years."

"Been blind all her life?"

"Three years. Fever."

"Hear she's a helluva singer."

"She is." A stinging spread behind Thomas's eyes at the thought of never hearing that sweet voice again. Or her mean, complaining voice, either. Or seeing another gap-toothed grin. "Will she die?"

"Not if I can help it." The doctor opened a brown bottle and stuck in a glass tube with a round, soft top. After sucking some of the liquid into the tube, he opened *Katse'e*'s mouth and squirted it against her cheek.

"What can I do?" Thomas asked.

"Get her some dry clothes. Her doll if she has one. And a book to read to her."

Thomas gave him a questioning look.

"She may not be as asleep as she looks. If not, she'd probably take comfort in hearing your voice and knowing she's not alone. You can read, can't you?"

Thomas turned toward the door.

"Best get dry clothes for yourself, too. I don't need two sick patients. And find someone to take over your sheriff duties temporarily. She's liable to be sick for a while, and I can't watch her all the time."

WASHINGTON, D.C.

"How did you get that cut? And those bruises?"

Pru leaned gingerly back in her chair, trying not to jar her sore ribs. She smiled weakly at the young bespectacled solicitor seated across from her at the same interrogation table she had sat at several days ago. This man was friendlier, and had even smiled and extended his hand when he'd introduced himself as Peter Faraday. "I fell."

His worried look said he didn't believe her.

"I have had fewer falls lately," she assured him with a wry smile. After she had started teaching the other prisoners to read and write, she had gained quite a few protectors. "Who sent you?" Pru didn't think for a moment that the man who had questioned her last time had sent him.

"Reverend Brother Sampson."

Wincing, she sat up. "He's well? Is he still in jail?"

"He was released yesterday. The first thing he did was contact the legal aid group where I work."

Tears threatened, but Pru blinked them back. "Thank the Lord he's safe."

"Now let's do the same for you." He plopped a case bulging with papers and folders atop the desk, then began rifling through it.

Hope surged. "You can help me? You can get me out of here?"

"Hopefully." He shoved the spectacles higher up his nose. "Just waiting on the inquest."

Seeing her look of confusion, he explained. "They found Mr. Marsh's remains at the bottom of a gorge under a high railroad trestle not far from Indianapolis. The inquest is to determine if his death was accidental or the result of foul play. If the judge rules his death was an accident, you will no longer be a suspect and should be released forthwith."

"And if they suspect foul play?"

His smile faded. "Then they'll probably charge you with his murder, and hold you over for trial."

"Trial? But I'm innocent!"

He lifted a staying hand. "Remain calm, Mrs. Redstone. Just hear what I have to say."

Pru struggled to slow her breathing, but her mind kept spinning.

"We have three things in our favor," Faraday explained. "One"—he held up a long, ink-stained finger—"I've seen the coroner's report. All of Mr. Marsh's injuries appear to be the result of his fall, not foul play. Two"—he held up a second finger—"you're innocent. And three"—this time a sly smile along with the third finger—"the presiding judge is a staunch abolitionist." He let his hand fall back to the desk. "We'll get through this, Mrs. Redstone. Before you know it, you'll be heading back to your family in Colorado. Just have faith." He grinned. "And that's a direct order from Reverend Sampson."

COLORADO TERRITORY

Lillie awoke to the sound of a voice droning nearby, and a sharp smell like kerosene, only different. She ached all over, as if her joints had turned to rust. It even hurt to bend her fingers. Her head pounded terrible bad, and every time she sucked air in or out, it made a wet, rattling sound.

"Who there?" she croaked, then fell into a coughing fit that set fire in her throat.

She felt a warm presence beside her. "You are awake, *Katse'e.*"

Daddy. She smiled, then winced at the pull on her chapped lips. He didn't sound mad at her. She hoped he wasn't. It seemed that for a long time, her head had been filled with all sorts of strange voices and pictures and sounds that kept weaving around behind her eyes. But at least now, everything seemed better.

"Where am I? It smell funny." This time, she didn't cough so much after she spoke.

"You are at the house where the white doctor works. You have been sick, but now you will get better."

Sick? All at once, as if gates had opened in her mind,

everything came rushing back—Bitsy, the man, the stink, being lost and cold. She felt the warm tickle of tears run past her temples and into her hair. "Bitsy run off."

"We found him. He is well. Like you, he went into the woods even though I told him—and you—not to." He took a deep breath. When he spoke again, his voice was nicer. "Here." He put something soft into her hands. "Even Miss Minty was worried about you. We all were."

Smiling, she hugged the doll close. "You not mad at me?"

"No, *Katse'e*."

"Then how come you not come find me?"

"I tried, but when the man carried you to the mine, it took longer."

"He stinky."

"That was his bearskin coat." There was a pause, then, "Did he hurt you, *Katse'e*?"

Lillie tried to remember, but mostly all that came to mind was the smell. "Only once. I hear you call out, but he put a hand over my mouth so I not able to answer. Then he grab me and carry me to a shack somewheres."

"He did not hurt you?"

"He not mean. Only afraid. And not very smart. When I tell him you put him in jail, he started crying like a baby. I'm hungry. Feel like my po' belly stuck to my backbones. Got anything to eat?"

"Yes, *Katse'e*." She heard the smile in his voice. "Miss Winnie sent you soup."

"No muffins? Even fo' a po' sick blind girl?"

"Later."

"Later" stretched into a week. Then another two days in bed in her room at the Arlan house. *Katse'e* was not an easy child to tend when she was sick. But Thomas was grateful to do it. At least she was healing.

Once assured of that, he headed back to the sheriff's office to relieve Rayford Jessup of his temporary duties.

The ex-marshal looked up from his book when Thomas walked in. The Texan read more than any man Thomas had ever known. "How's she doing?" Jessup asked, closing the book.

"Complaining. How is Tombo Welks?"

"Complaining. You should either charge him with something or let him go. It's been ten days."

"Have you questioned him?"

"His story matches Lillie's. He didn't hurt her. But I did find this." Reaching into a slot under the desk, Jessup pulled out a wanted poster. "Might be Tombo Welks. Might not."

Thomas studied the drawing and the words printed beneath it. *"Wanted for assault."* The paper had come from a town in Kansas.

"What are you going to do?" Jessup asked.

Thomas thought of all that Lillian had told him about the man, what he had said and done. During the time *Katse'e* was at the doctor's house, Thomas had talked to Tombo Welks several times. A part of him wanted to punish the trapper for daring to touch his daughter, even though he did not harm her. But another part of him hesitated to add more burdens to a man hardly able to manage those he already carried. "He is not right." Thomas motioned to his head.

"You mean he's slow?" Jessup nodded. "But I think he acts more out of fear than meanness. People aren't all that kind or forgiving when it comes to folks like him. Or anyone different."

Like Indians. Jessup did not have to say that aloud. All his life, Thomas had seen the angry and frightened looks pointed his way.

But *forgiving* was something Thomas was less familiar with, even though he had heard Reverend Brother Sampson speak of it in his big white tipi. It was a hard thing for Thomas to accept or understand. But it was also hard for him to carry around so much anger. It seemed he had spent most of his life being angry about something. He was weary of it.

He frowned at the far wall and thought about what to do with Tombo Welks. *Katse'e* had suffered no harm at his hands. And in a way, Welks had helped him—if Thomas had not spotted the man's big tracks, he might have missed Lillian's small ones. Worse, if Tombo Welks had left *Katse'e* under that tree, she might not have survived until Thomas found her.

"I will not jail him."

Jessup held up the wanted poster. "What about this? You going to turn him over to them? There's a reward. Not a big one, but still . . ."

Thomas gave him a look that made Jessup grin. "Sorry. I forgot it's about honor, not money, with you Cheyenne."

Lifting the ring of keys from the peg behind the desk, Thomas went to the cells in back of the office.

Tombo Welks sat slumped on his cot, picking at his fingernail. When he saw Thomas unlock the cell door, he flattened against the wall, his eyes as wary as those of a kicked dog.

Thomas swung the door wide, then stepped back. "You are free, Tombo Welks."

It took a moment for the words to sink in. "You mean I can go?"

"You can go."

"What about my coat?"

"It hangs outside. It stank too much to bring indoors. What did you cure it with?"

"Cure it?"

"Never mind. You will go now."

"Go where?"

"Wherever you want, as long as you do not cause trouble."

Tombo glanced from Thomas to Jessup, who watched from the doorway behind Thomas. "But I like it here. It has good food, and it's warm. I don't wanna go."

"This place is for lawbreakers. You have broken no laws, so you cannot stay."

The prisoner tugged at his beard and thought for a moment. "What if I broke a law? Just a little one. Could I stay then?"

Thomas looked at Jessup, but the Texan raised his hands and backed away.

"Can you sweep?" Thomas asked Tombo.

"Sweep what?"

"Floors. The boardwalk outside. Whatever I tell you to sweep."

"Yeah. I'm a good sweeper. I used to sweep at a store back home in Kansas till I knocked over a shelf on accident and broke some bottles. The man who owned the store started hitting me, so I got mad and hit him back, then ran away."

Thomas shared a look with Jessup, then turned back to Tombo. "You will not hit anyone here. If someone hits you, you will come and tell me and I will take care of it. Do you understand?"

"Okay."

"If people say mean things, you will not get mad. You will come tell me that, too."

"Okay."

Thomas hesitated, wondering if he was doing the right thing. With the Cheyenne, the entire tribe watched over those touched by the Great Spirit. But whites seemed to toss them aside or fear them. "Then I will give you one nickel a day to sweep," he finally said. "You will also bring in firewood for the stove, run errands as I need them, and do other chores when I tell you. You can sleep in your cell unless I need it for a real lawbreaker, and the hotel will bring you two meals a day."

"A nickel? Every day?"

Thomas nodded. "The broom is inside the front door. The firewood is behind the building. Go do your work."

Grinning, Tombo Welks clumped out the front door.

"Ought to teach him to make coffee, too," Jessup suggested. "Yours tastes like gunpowder laced with pine tar."

"You teach him. I do not drink buffalo piss."

"That must account for your cranky mornings."

Tombo Welks was a hard worker, as long as he understood exactly what he was to do. The townspeople lost their wariness once Thomas convinced the man to shave off his beard and bathe occasionally. Several merchants even hired him to keep the boardwalks in front of their stores swept or free of snow, and when Thomas asked Cal Bagley, the owner of the mercantile, to donate a new set of clothes for Welks, he happily agreed. Not because he was a good man, which he was not, but because he was afraid of Thomas. Which was as it should be. Bagley had once insulted Prudence Lincoln, but after a talk with Declan Brodie—sheriff at the time—and a later visit from Thomas, he had quickly become the most agreeable store owner in town.

Katse'e continued to improve, and Bitsy and Harry continued to grow. Welks caused no trouble, spring bloomed across

Mother Earth, and Thomas's life slowly settled back into a routine that left him with too much time to think.

Then, just as the first robins hopped across the thawing ground, heralding the arrival of the late March Worm Moon, a letter arrived for Edwina Brodie and everything changed.

It was Sunday. From the church steps, where he usually sat during services, Thomas had watched the train pull into the depot at the edge of town. No one got off. After it had continued on through the canyon, he saw Kincaid load his wagon with crates, and packages, and the mail pouch, stop to give something to R.D. Brodie, who was riding by on horseback, then head back into town.

This Sunday, the usual families were to meet for dinner at the new Hardesty house. The Abrahams were helping, since Audra Hardesty was an even worse cook than Edwina Brodie. Or Josephine Jessup. Or Lucinda Rylander. Thomas often wondered how white men survived since their women did not cook or prepare their food. It was lucky for all of them that Winnie Abraham loved to cook and was good at it.

She rotated houses each week, which meant they could all enjoy a good Sunday meal. Today, *Katse'e* and the Abrahams would ride from the church in the Rylanders' big four-wheeled carriage. Thomas would walk, as he usually did. No Dog Soldier would ride in a carriage.

That early spring Sunday was a good day. A light breeze from the west might push rain clouds over the mountains later, melting away the last of winter except for the snow on the highest peaks, but for now, it was sunny. He enjoyed having earth beneath his feet and silence in his ears.

He arrived late because he had stopped to watch a herd of *wapiti*—or elk, as the whites called them—drift out of the trees to graze the new grass sprouting across the flats between the church and the new houses built by the Scotsman and Hardesty. When he walked in, every head turned his way.

But not in welcome.

He stopped in the doorway, looking from one troubled face to another. "What is wrong?" he asked when no one spoke.

"Nothing," Edwina Brodie blurted out, then fled into the kitchen.

"I'd better go help." Lucinda Rylander thrust her squirming daughter at her husband and hurried after her.

Audra Hardesty and Josephine Jessup looked at each other, then left, too.

Thomas turned to Declan Brodie and waited.

"A letter for Ed came in the mail pouch today. R.D. brought it from the depot. It's from Pru."

"She in jail!" *Katse'e* shouted.

Brodie rounded on her. "No, Lillie, she's not in jail. She was. But she's out now." He turned back to Thomas, a thin smile on his face. "Seems the judge was a staunch abolitionist with a kindness for Negroes."

Jail?

"She comin' back home, Daddy! She on her way."

Thomas did not react. Could not. The words made no sense. *Eho'nehevehohtse* in jail? Why? Then *Katse'e*'s other words echoed through his mind.

She was coming back home.

The air went out of him.

Brodie came forward, an envelope in his hand. "Here. Read it for yourself."

"No." Thomas stepped back. "I do not want to read it. It does not matter." He shook his head, not knowing what to say or do. Finally he found his words. "When the meal is over, send Lillian home with the Abrahams." Spinning on his heel, he walked back out the door.

And kept walking. Retracing his steps past the church. Then the depot. Then turning left through town and following the trail up into the canyon. One step in front of the other, a calm steady drumbeat to the turmoil in his mind.

Home. His wife was coming home.

But not back to *him*. The letter had been written to her sister, Edwina Brodie. Not to him.

It did not matter. He had put her from his life. She no longer had the power to hurt him.

He hoped that by the time she arrived, that would be true.

It was late when he stopped in front of the Brodie Sunday house on Mulberry Creek, but there was still a light on inside. He walked up the front steps and sank down into one of the two chairs on the porch. A minute later, the light went out, then

Declan came onto the porch. Without speaking, he settled his long form into the chair beside Thomas's.

The late-rising moon cast bright splotches of pale light through the budding cottonwoods along the creek. Thomas watched the moon edge higher, dimming the stars as it rose into the night sky, and thought of the last time he had stood on this porch with Prudence Lincoln.

They had been watching over the Brodie children while their parents went with the Wallaces and Lucinda—Hathaway, then—to the meeting in Denver, where they would cast Heartbreak Creek's vote for statehood. It was not long after Thomas had rescued Prudence from the Arapaho, and although she knew she was safe with him, he could still see her fear, and feel the tremble of it in her body when he touched her. He had hated to leave her, but needed to go after the others to warn them about evil men who tracked them.

He remembered what he had told her that night before he had left.

When I return, Prudence Lincoln, you will accept me as your heart-mate. You will join with me and become my woman. If you cannot do this, we will part our ways.

She had called him arrogant and laughed softly—a breathless, timid sound like the whisper of wind through the first green leaves in the spring. But despite her fear, she had let him kiss her, and touch her in the moonlight, and feel the beat of her heart beneath his palm.

When he returned two weeks later, it was in the back of a wagon, his body burning with fever from a bullet wound. She had tended him. Kept him alive. And when he was whole again, she had taken him into her body and her heart. But, a month later, in the sacred pool in the canyon, while fire danced above them in the night sky, she had told him good-bye.

That was almost a year ago.

Since then, there had been three other good-byes, and each one had left him bleeding in her wake. It had weakened him. Left him reeling. Their partings had taken so much from him he had little feeling left. He welcomed that numbness.

"Why was she in jail?" he asked Declan Brodie after a long silence.

"A man she knew disappeared. They thought she might

have had something to do with it. Her, and a preacher named Sampson."

Marsh. I did this to them by killing Marsh. Tension moved through Thomas's arms and legs, tightened the muscles across his chest. He breathed deep and forced emotion from his mind. "Why did they let her out?"

"Found the man's body at the bottom of a gorge. No marks of foul play. Figured he fell off the train when they passed over a trestle. Unlucky timing."

Thomas felt his friend studying him, but did not look his way.

"You do that? He one of the men you killed in Indiana?"

Instead of answering, Thomas asked, "It is over, then?"

Brodie nodded. "Case closed. They let the preacher go, too. Asked them both a lot of questions about an Indian hanging around at the time of the disappearance, but she told them the last she heard, he had gone back to Oklahoma Territory. That's why she wrote to Ed instead of you. To draw them away from Heartbreak Creek. To keep you safe."

Pain moved through Thomas's chest, as if a hand had reached in to squeeze his heart. Keep him safe? Or to pretend he no longer existed. "When does she come?"

"End of the month. Maybe later. Letter said she had some things to clear up at the courthouse in Indianapolis first."

With Prudence Lincoln, something always came first. As Thomas rose from his chair, it felt as if the earth were shifting beneath his feet. He felt unsettled, his mind more troubled than ever. Did she want him to be here when she returned? Was she coming back to him, as well as the town? Or was she hinting she wanted him gone to Oklahoma by the time she arrived? Did he even have a wife anymore?

He did not know what to think. He did not know what to feel. Or if he should stay, or go. There was that hole she had left inside him, and he doubted even her return could fill it.

He started down the steps.

"What are you going to do?" Declan called after him.

Thomas did not know how to answer, so he kept walking.

Seventeen

"What you mean, you leavin'?"

"I will be gone for only a short time, *Katse'e*."

Thomas had already asked Rayford Jessup to take over his sheriff duties while he was gone, and had arranged for Fred Driscoll, who ran the livery, to let Tombo Welks stay in his barn. He had also filled the larder at the Arlan house and asked Curtis to take Lillian to and from school. Now, all he had left to do was convince *Katse'e* that she would be fine without him.

"Why cain't I go with you?"

Hearing the wobble in her voice, Thomas pushed his chair away from the eating table and pulled her onto his lap. "You told me poor blind black girls did not sleep outside."

"You sleepin' outside?"

"Until I set up my *xamaa-vee'e*, yes."

"You tipi?"

"Yes. But this one will be larger and will take longer to make."

"How you build one of them things?" Curtis asked from his seat across the table. "Looks like it'd fly off in a stiff breeze."

"It is tied to the ground."

"What kind of skins you planning to use?" Winnie asked.

Lillian wrinkled her nose. "Skins stinky."

"If not cured right, they can be." Thomas explained that since there were more *wapiti* than buffalo in the area, he would use elk hides and tan them with the brains of the animals he killed. While the hides dried, he would cut and skin many long, slim poles to form a framework. After smoking the hides so they would shed rain and snow, he would stitch them together in a pattern that would cover the poles from top to bottom.

"Sounds like a lot of work," Curtis said.

"It is. But a good tipi will last many years."

"How you get it to stand up on its own?"

"You fo'get *do*, Mr. Curtis," Lillian reminded him. "How *do* you gets it stand up." She gave a prim smile. "Old Lady Throckmorton teaching me to talk right. She say ev'ry time I do it wrong, she'll poke me with her cane. But my blind stick longer. Next time she poke me, I whack her good. She a mean ol' bitch."

"Oh, Lawd," Winnie muttered.

"Where did you hear that word?" Thomas asked her, even though he could guess.

"Joe Bill. He's not a Quaker, so it's okay."

"It is not okay, Lillian. It shows dishonor to your elder. You will not say it again. And you will not hit people with your blind stick. Did we not talk about that?"

"Maybe. But I didn't promise, so it doesn't count."

Ignoring the couple grinning at him from across the table, Thomas said sternly, "Then you will promise me now."

"If I do, you promise not to leave?"

"I cannot do that."

"Then I won't promise, neither."

Curtis must have seen that Thomas had reached the end of his tether. "You were saying how you get the tipi to stand up on its own?"

Accepting his latest defeat as a father, Thomas sighed. "Start with three poles. Plant one end in the ground and tie the crossed tops together. Stand up the other poles until they form a circle on the ground." He went on to explain that before placing the last pole, he would tie one end of the sewn hide to it, then walk the sewn-together skins around the wooden frame, leaving two smoke flaps at the top, and an opening for a doorway. "The entrance must face east to welcome the rising sun, which will bring wealth and good fortune. I will also add a small fire pit inside for warmth."

"Sounds complicated," Curtis said.

Thomas shrugged. "Once the hides and poles are prepared, it is easy to set up. Even our women can do it." At Winnie's look, he quickly added, "They are better at it than the men and take pride in painting symbols on the sides." That seemed to ease her anger. Thomas knew better than to offend the woman who cooked his food and kept his house.

Lillian made a snorting noise. "I don't understand why you do all that when you got this nice, warm house right here."

Thomas wondered how to answer. "I am Cheyenne, *Katse'e*," he finally said. "Sometimes living in this nice, warm house and walking in my grandfather's shoes makes me forget that. But I do not want to forget. So I am making a place where I can go to find peace and harmony with the earth and sky."

"You cain't find that here?"

"Not always." Glancing over Lillian's head at the two black people sitting across the table, Thomas gave a crooked smile. Three months ago, he had been a man with few ties to hold him down. Now he had two old people, a horse, a dog, a cat, and a whole town looking to him for protection. He also had a wife who did not want him, a big wooden house he did not build, and a girl-child who confounded him. The Abrahams understood his burdens.

"You promise to come back, Daddy?"

"I will always come back to you, daughter. You know this."

She grinned at his shoulder, showing the latest gap of another lost tooth. "You bring me a present when you do?"

He tipped his head to see her face. "A necklace of bear claws?"

She rewarded him with a grimace. "I'm thinkin' maybe a new blind stick." Leaning forward in his lap, she groped until she found her stick leaning against the table. Waving it like a war lance, she knocked over his cup of water, sent the lid to the butter crock crashing to the floor, and almost poked out Curtis's eye. "That stinker Joe Bill crack this one with his head."

Two days later, Thomas traded his white man clothing for Cheyenne leggings, moccasins, and war shirt, strapped his rifle, tools, and supplies on a spare horse borrowed from Rayford Jessup, and rode into the canyon, singing as he went.

"Such a precious little jewel," Edwina Brodie crooned, her heels clicking on the floor as she rocked Rosaleen in the Rylander suite of rooms at the hotel. "Don't you just love cuddling babies?"

Lucinda Rylander yawned. "Not at midnight. Then three in the morning, and again at six." One uninterrupted night's sleep. That's all she wanted. Maybe two. She hardly recognized the haggard face that stared back at her from her bureau mirror, and this morning she had found three white hairs tucked in among the blond. She'd be a crone by the time the *precious jewel* hit her fifth birthday. And Tait had the gall to ask her if maybe next time they might have a boy. *Next time?* Was the man demented?

"It'll get better, Luce, I promise."

Lucinda ardently hoped so. She remembered how overwrought Edwina had been after baby Whit was born. The prospect of finding herself in such a deep depression would have made her shudder if she'd had the energy.

God must be a man. Why else would He give women childbirth, and breasts, too? It seemed entirely unfair.

"Thomas has wandered off," Edwina said.

"Where to?"

"Who knows?"

Lucinda heard the peevishness in Ed's voice and hoped the volatile Southerner wasn't getting herself worked up. "He's an Indian. They do that."

"Well, I don't like it. First, he won't talk about Pru, then Pru doesn't even mention him in her letter—other than that odd reference to an Indian and Oklahoma Territory—and now, just when Pru's about to come back, Thomas rides off into the mountains to do God knows what. And he never smiles anymore. It's as if he's walled himself off from the rest of us and gone back to being the stoic Indian. Something's not right. Even Declan thinks so."

Lucinda was too exhausted to dredge up much interest. "They'll work it out," she said around another yawn. "They always do."

"If he actually wants to. What if this time he doesn't come back? What if he's done with her?"

"She did send him away every time he went to visit her," Lucinda reminded her. "No matter what her reasons were, I wouldn't blame him if he washed his hands of her."

"Lucinda!" Ed's heels hit the floor with jarring thump. Lucinda held her breath as the jewel's eyes popped open, rolled for a moment, then slowly slid shut again. "This is my sister we're talking about. She adores Thomas. He adores her. We have to do something."

Lucinda relaxed back into her chair. "I thought we were doing something about Helen and Buster Quinn."

"Well. There's that. When will those two realize they're in love?" Ed resumed rocking, her face thoughtful.

Which didn't bode well. For all her Southern charm and sweetness of nature, Edwina Brodie could stir up a hornet's nest faster than anyone Lucinda knew. She was the essence of busybodiness.

"Do you think they've . . . you know . . . consummated?" Edwina had lowered her voice, even though the door was closed and no one could have heard her.

The woman was a catalog of contradictions and had the strangest sensibilities and ideas of propriety. But what would one expect from a woman who married a man, sight unseen, then insisted on a three-month courtship *after* the marriage? "I do not know, nor do I care to know if Buster Quinn and Helen Bradshaw have consummated." Tipping her head against the back of the chair, Lucinda closed her eyes. "But I think not. Quinn is much too proper."

"I wonder if Thomas and Pru have."

"I wouldn't doubt it. What else would send a man chasing after a woman the way he has?"

"Is that why Tait chased after you all the way from New York?"

"Give me my daughter. Your thoughts are entirely too nasty to be holding an innocent child."

Lucinda said it without rancor, but she definitely didn't want to discuss what she and Tait may or may not have done on that train after she'd fled her own wedding . . . back before she'd started sprouting white hairs and her hips had spread with childbearing and her once-perky breasts had become giant leaking teats.

"What if that's why Pru won't come back? What if she found herself in a family way and has snuck off to have her baby and leave it on the steps of an orphanage? It happened to one of the McCardle twins. What a scandal that was."

"Don't, Edwina. Please . . . just don't." Lucinda hadn't the strength for dramatics, either.

"I could never give away my baby."

Lucinda had once thought that, too. But over the last two months, she had considered it. Several times. Then Rosie would fall into a milk-sated sleep, and Lucinda would think she was the most wonderful child in the world.

"What's that?"

Cracking open one eye, Lucinda saw Edwina peering at the crate in the corner. "Something for Thomas."

"What is it?"

"I don't know. I don't open other people's mail."

"It isn't from Pru, is it?"

"It's from Maddie's London publisher."

"How strange. Here, go change Rosie. She smells like poop."

Odd, how quickly babies brought those around them down to their level. Within just a few short weeks, hers and Tait's lives had come to revolve around the three *P*s—poop, pee, puke—words that before motherhood, Lucinda would never have allowed into her mind, much less her vocabulary.

It was disheartening how far she had fallen. From astute businesswoman to wet nurse. Where was the romance in that? She and Tait had hardly made love at all since the birth. Initially, because the doctor told them to wait at least six weeks—*thank you, Doctor Boyce*. But even after that restriction had been lifted, Tait seemed more interested in courting smiles from his daughter than in coaxing his wife into amorous activities. Probably because her breasts leaked all the time, she constantly smelled like one of the three *P*s, and most nights she was so worn out that if Tait even attempted such a thing, she would have used her double Derringer on him. Besides, it seemed that every time the mood struck, Rosaleen was crying for her next feeding. Still . . . he might not have given up so easily.

God. She was starting to sound like Edwina.

With a sigh, she pushed out of the chair and took her daughter. "What are you doing?" she asked when she saw Edwina bend over the crate.

"Testing the weight. It's heavy. I wonder what it is." She tugged at a loose corner.

"Books, I presume, since it came from a publisher."

"Why would a publisher be sending books to Thomas? Do you have something I can pry this up with? I'm getting splinters."

"It's not addressed to you," Lucinda reminded her.

"A shoehorn, maybe. There, those scissors would work."

"You're a bad influence on my daughter." Lucinda swept from the room, knowing that when she returned, the box would be open. At least she'd tried.

As she gently laid her sleeping daughter on an old blanket atop what had once been her desk, she had to smile. Rosie was so cute when she slept, her little hands curled into fists, her tiny mouth parted like an unfurling blossom. Unable to resist, Lucinda kissed her daughter's downy head. Despite her preference for food over sleep, Rosaleen truly was adorable. And she must be as exhausted as her mother—she scarcely moved while Lucinda changed her napkin.

"Well?" she asked when she returned a few minutes later and found Edwina sitting on the floor, staring at an open book in her lap.

"It's a book."

"I can see that."

Edwina lifted her head, a look of amazement on her face. "It's a book that Thomas wrote."

"Our Thomas?"

Edwina held up the volume so Lucinda could see *By Thomas Redstone, Cheyenne Dog Soldier* emblazoned across the front below the title *Tracks in Blood: A True Account of the Sand Creek Massacre*. "It's about some Indian chief named Black Kettle. Did you know about this?"

"Not a thing." Shaking her head in bemusement, Lucinda sank into the rocker. "Do you think he actually wrote it?"

Edwina didn't answer, her head bent over the book as she scanned the first page. "Laws amighty." She gave Lucinda a stunned look. "It's good. Listen to this: 'Our land is sacred to us. It is soaked with the blood of our People and marked with the tracks of those who died defending it.' Isn't that beautiful? And sad. From what I've read so far, this is really good."

"It sounds like Thomas. He has a rather violent outlook on life."

A knock on the door sent them both jumping with guilt. "Quick. Put it back in the box," Lucinda whispered. "Who is it?" she called in a louder voice.

"Yancey. You might oughta come."

"Probably Joe Bill," Edwina muttered. "He's always getting into mischief."

"Is something wrong?" Lucinda waved for Edwina to put the lid back on and shove the crate into the corner.

"It's Mrs. Bradshaw," Yancey whispered through the gap between the door and the frame. "She's crying again."

Again? Lucinda and Edwina looked at each other.

At Lucinda's nod, Edwina went over and opened the door. "Is she hurt?"

Yancey shrugged. "I ain't about to go see. Her and Quinn was talking in the closed dining room, then he leaves, and I hear her crying in there. Think I should get the sheriff?"

"The sheriff is out beating a tom-tom somewhere," Edwina snapped. "Is she still in there?"

"I ain't going to see. Crying women give me the shivers."

Lucinda came up behind Edwina. "Attend your duties, Yancey. And say no more about this. Do you understand?"

"Yes, boss. I gotta restock the coal bin in the washroom anyway."

As soon as the old man clumped out of earshot, Edwina turned to Lucinda, her blue eyes tearing. Ever emotional, the pretty Southerner was. Lucinda envied her that openness. "We should go to her, Luce."

"Of course we will. But we mustn't dally too long. The jewel will be hungry again in a few minutes."

They were crossing the lobby when Tait came through the front doors with a package under his arm. When he saw them, his face reddened and he shifted the package to his other arm, as though trying to hide it. Not very subtle.

Naturally, Lucinda stopped to find out what he was hiding. The parcel had postal stamps all over it, but she didn't remember ordering anything. "What's that?"

"Nothing. Some equipment I sent for."

Tait was usually scrupulously honest—especially with her. But her female nose for male misbehavior told her he was hedging. She narrowed her eyes at him. "What sort of equipment?"

He opened his mouth—to lead her off the scent, no doubt— then closed it and gave a crooked smile. "It's a surprise."

She instantly perked up. "For me?"

"In a way. But the whole family will benefit. Good morning,

Edwina," he added with a smile to the woman he'd hadn't yet acknowledged, even though she stood less than a yard away. "Where are you ladies off to in such a hurry?"

"To talk to Mrs. Bradshaw." Lowering her voice, Edwina nodded toward the closed dining room doors and added, "She's in there crying."

Taking that as her cue to do the same, the jewel opened her eyes and took a deep breath. But before she let loose the first squawk, her gaze found her father, and she immediately broke into a toothless grin.

"About Quinn," Tait said to Edwina, even though he was making kissy noises at his daughter. "I was wondering when he would break it off with her."

"Break it off?" Both Lucinda and Edwina crowded closer to Tait. The jewel waved a pudgy arm.

"You mean he's not going to court her anymore?" Lucinda asked in a whisper.

"He was never courting her." He cooed at his daughter.

She cooed back.

It disgusted Lucinda how taken with the man the child was when it was her mother who did all the work. "You're trying to change the subject," she accused.

"Of course I am, sweetheart. It's none of your business why Quinn won't court her, or why Mrs. Bradshaw is in the dining room crying. I suggest you let it go." He punctuated that with a kiss on Rosie's tiny nose, which sent the child into thrashing pleasure. Then he straightened and looked at Lucinda with piercing intensity.

She saw laughter and a flicker of something else in his dark gray eyes. Mischief? Arousal? Surely not.

Footsteps sounded on the stairs. Lucinda recognized the halting tread of Mrs. Throckmorton.

But before she could greet her guardian, Tait put his arm around her shoulders and turned her back toward the hallway. "If you'll excuse us?" With a nod to Edwina, he quickly ushered Lucinda out of the lobby. "May I see you in our rooms for a moment, Luce? It's important," he added with that devastating smile.

Flustered, she jiggled the baby to ward off a crying fit. "Rose is hungry."

"Excellent timing. Hurry, sweetheart. You know how cranky Rosie gets when she doesn't eat on time."

But before they reached their room, an imperious voice rose behind them. "Where are you going with my granddaughter?"

Rosie let loose a chorus of delighted squeaks and coos. The infant had deplorable taste.

"It's time for a feeding," Lucinda called back as her husband relentlessly steered her down the hall.

"I'll bring her up to your room as soon as she's finished," Tait promised, without slowing his stride.

"But I could help."

"You do too much as it is, Mrs. T.," he lied. "Please allow us to indulge you every now and then." Opening the door into their room, he shoved Lucinda inside, then turned back to give his best smile to the old woman leaning on her cane at the end of the hallway. "An hour. Maybe less." Then before Lucinda's guardian could offer further protest, Tait closed the door and locked it. "That was close." Ignoring Lucinda's look of astonishment, he tore into the wrapping on the parcel. "Hurry. Take off your dress."

She couldn't even summon a response.

Rosie could, and it rose in a lusty cry, her tiny fists waving in impatience.

"Trust me, Luce." He winced as their daughter's cries escalated into furious wails. "Get your dress off. Now."

The last time she had heard that was just before Rosie was conceived. Had it been almost a year? It seemed like the little tyrant had been with them forever.

Knowing the shrieks wouldn't stop until the baby was fed, Lucinda set her outraged daughter on the couch, unbuttoned the front of her dress, and slipped it down her arms. "I don't know what you have in mind," she said over her shoulder as she undid the tabs on her chemise, "but Rosie won't brook delay in her feeding schedule. For any reason. Not even for you."

"I'm not asking her to. You undressed yet?"

Ignoring him, Lucinda let the chemise fall to expose her breast. Picking up her irate baby, she sank onto the couch just as Tait pulled his "surprise" from the box.

"Use this." Beaming, he held up a device that must have come straight from an Inquisition dungeon. "It's called a breast pump."

Lucinda was aghast. "Like a milking machine?" She had

heard about milking machines and the terrible things they did to cows. "I will not put a catheter in my breast."

"It's not a catheter." Tait dug in the box for a small pamphlet that explained how to use the mechanism. He held it toward her. "Read this. You'll see."

With a sniff, she settled Rosie at her breast. To be attached to some farm implement was unthinkable. And highly insulting. "I can't believe you would suggest such a thing," she said, struggling not to cry. Was that how he saw her now? Little more than a milk-swollen bovine?

Her husband—the cad—sat beside her on the couch. "It's not a machine, sweetheart. Just a little pump. See? You put this over your nipple, then push up and down on this little lever. Just like a hand pump on a water well."

God. This got worse and worse.

Blithely unaware of her growing distress, Tait wiggled the lever, studying it with that rapt expression he wore when confronted with some new and innovative locomotive part.

"How could you ask me to use that thing?"

The quaver in her voice must have finally pierced his fascination with his new toy. "It's perfectly safe, Luce. I read about it in *Scientific American Magazine.* They've been around since the first patent was issued almost a decade ago."

Tears spilled over. "I'm not a cow, Tait."

"Sweetheart." With a look of chagrin, he tossed the pump aside and put his arms around both her and Rosie. "I didn't get this to insult you, Luce, but to free you. You said you wouldn't use a wet nurse, so I thought this might work."

Confused, she drew back to look at him.

"If you pump enough milk for a feeding and save it, I could put it in a bottle and feed Rosie at night, so you could sleep."

Sleep? Lucinda stared from him to the pump on the couch, then at Rosie, happily nursing in her arms.

Sleep.

"Wash it first."

Eighteen

A few days later, Rayford Jessup's stepson, Jamie, burst into the sheriff's office, a look of panic on his face. "You must come, Father! Straight away! There's trouble at the saloon by the hotel!"

Rafe set his book aside, glad to have something to do. Things had been so quiet in Thomas's absence that he had been spending the better part of his days reading.

Grabbing his gun belt off the desk—it was too uncomfortable to wear a holstered weapon while he sat and read—he buckled it on and bustled Jamie out the door. "Is anyone hurt?"

"I'm not certain. It sounded like there might have been some hitting, but it's hard for us to see over the adults."

"Us?"

"Me and the other children."

Rafe almost stumbled. "There are children involved? What are you doing out of school?"

"Miss Adkins quit."

"She did? When?"

"This morning. She told us she was leaving to get married, but I think it was because of Joe Bill and Lillie. They're quite disruptive."

The whole town knew of the animosity between the blind girl and the Brodie boy. Since Jamie was often caught in the middle of it, Rafe and Josie got a daily report over supper.

Down the boardwalk, a crowd gathered outside the Red Eye. Even from this distance, Rafe could hear the blind girl's shrill cries and the voices of the other children milling through the crowd.

He quickened his pace. "What did she and Joe Bill do this time?"

Jamie ran to keep up. "Nothing. They didn't start it."

"Who did?"

"A man outside the saloon."

Up ahead, Tait came out of the hotel and pushed his way through the crowd, shouting and shoving onlookers aside. By the time Rafe and Jamie arrived, he had managed to clear a circle around the combatants.

"Stay back," Rafe told Jamie and the other children, then elbowed his way past the gawking saloon patrons.

Lillie Redstone stood in the center, swinging her blind stick around like a sword. Her father would have been proud. Joe Bill stood beside her, his slingshot loaded and ready to fire. But neither child was menacing the other. Instead, all their anger seemed directed at a man at the front of the crowd.

Rafe stepped forward. "Put the stick down, Lillie. Joe Bill, drop the slingshot." He spoke in the same calm voice he used with restless or frightened horses.

It didn't seem to work on the little colored girl.

She rounded on him with what sounded like a snarl, and jabbed the end of her stick uncomfortably close to his groin. "Who that?" she cried.

With an expression of relief, Joe Bill eased the tension off the rubberized bands on his slingshot. "The sheriff."

Lillie's scowl gave way to a hopeful grin. "Daddy?"

"No, Mr. Jessup."

"What's going on here?" Rafe shoved the onlookers back.

Immediately, as if reminded of her purpose, the blind girl assumed her battle stance. "He hittin' Tombo."

Only then did Rafe see the man crouched against the front wall of the Red Eye, blood streaming from his nose and a cut in his lip. One eye was almost swollen shut, and he held an arm around his stomach.

"I didn't do nothing," Tombo Welks protested weakly. "I swear."

The object of the children's ire—a man Rafe didn't recognize—pointed to a half-starved, bleeding horse tied to the hitching rail in front of the boardwalk. "Goddamn dummy was trying to steal my horse. You ought to arrest him."

"He savin' him!" Lillie cried, jabbing in his direction with her stick. "You the dummy, hit a horse that way."

"How could you see me hit him, you blind-assed nigger?"

That's when Rafe hit him. He shouldn't have. He knew he was setting a poor example for the children, but the impulse came over him so fast he acted before he could control it. A man shouldn't talk to a child that way. Plus, the bully had abused a horse. Rafe couldn't allow either.

"Everybody clear out!" Rafe ordered.

Children scattered. The crowd thinned, except for Tait and another fellow new to town—obviously a cohort of the stranger groaning at Rafe's feet.

"You had no call to hit Frank," he accused. "Sheriff or not."

Rafe looked at him until the man edged back. Then, with quiet emphasis, he said, "I'm only the temporary sheriff. The regular sheriff is a Cheyenne Dog Soldier. He's away right now—probably sharpening his war axe and skinning things— but if you'd care to wait in jail until he gets back, he'd probably like to hear your reasons for defending the coward who called his ten-year-old daughter a blind-assed nigger."

"Daughter?" The man's gaze swung to Lillie. His face paled. He took another step back.

"You're ten?" Joe Bill looked at Lillie in surprise. "But you're so small."

"I nearly 'leven, same as you. But I sho' 'nuff smarter."

The boy wisely didn't argue the point. Lillie Redstone was smarter than most kids in town—except maybe his Jamie and Lucas Brodie. Smarter than a lot of adults, too.

Rafe waited to see if the man had anything else to say. When he didn't, he nodded. "Then unless you want to share a cell with your friend here, I suggest you step out of the way." Bending, Rafe roughly yanked the woozy man to his feet.

"You're locking him up? Isn't a man allowed to defend his own property?"

"Sure. But abusing horses and children is a whole different matter."

"Abusing? He never touched the brats, and he only gave the horse a kick for trying to bite him. There's no law against disciplining a horse, is there?"

"I'll have to check." Rafe studied the broken animal shivering at the rail. The scars showing through his matted coat bore testament to a lifetime of cruel treatment. "But if not, I'm sure by the end of the day there will be."

He started to lead the prisoner away, then stopped and turned back. "Unless you want to join your friend in jail, I suggest you ride out"—he glanced at Lillie—"before her daddy gets back. He's real protective of his little girl."

Muttering under his breath, the man stomped toward the horse tied beside the beaten one. As he swung into the saddle, Rafe waved the last stragglers back into the saloon. "Thanks for backing me, Tait. Come along, children."

"You puttin' us in jail, too?" Lillie asked in a quavering voice.

"It wasn't her that started it," Joe Bill argued, which surprised Rafe, considering their history. "She was just sticking up for Tombo."

"He my friend." Lillie groped until she found the cowering man's shoulder. "He took care of me when I was lost in the woods. Now I take care of him. Git up, Tombo, and stop that cryin'. You sound like a titty baby. Joe Bill, help me. He's your friend, now, too."

Strange, how things work out. Before the fracas, Joe Bill and Lillie had been on a course headed for mutual destruction. But by the time they dutifully gave Rafe their accounts of what had happened, then suffered through a stern lecture about taking matters into their own hands rather than summoning the proper authorities, they seemed to have reached an accord. Not a particularly friendly one—yet—but it was a start.

"Do we still have to go to school now that Miss Adkins left?" Joe Bill asked.

"I hope so. I jist love school."

"You would. You're a girl."

"I like it, too," Jamie said, backing Lillie.

"We'll find someone else to teach you." Rafe wondered if he could convince Josie to take on the task. She seemed at loose ends, rattling around in Ash and Maddie's big house, especially with Henny and Gordon Stevens—the English couple who had come from England with her—doing most of the heavy work. A woman needed a place of her own. Maybe now that Ethan Hardesty had finished his home, Rafe would ask him to build one for him. Something close to the Wallace house so Rafe could oversee Ash's breeding and training program, but far enough away to give them some privacy. Henny could continue to run the big house, and her husband could take over the stable chores. It would be a while before Ash and Maddie arrived in Heartbreak Creek with the baby earl, and Josie needed something to occupy her time until then. She was smart and patient. She would make a good teacher.

"Doesn't seem fair," Joe Bill complained. "If your teacher runs off, you shouldn't oughta have to get stuck with another one."

Apparently Joe Bill wasn't an enthusiastic student.

"Can Tombo go with us?" Lillie asked. "He needs schoolin' bad."

It seemed the children had taken up a cause: watching out for Tombo Welks. Which, judging by the pleased grin on the man's bruised face, meant Tombo Welks would be watching out for them, too. Feeling pretty good about the way he'd handled it, Rafe rewarded the three children and Tombo for their courage and loyalty by buying them each a string of rock candy. Sadly, Joe Bill and Lillie ruined his gesture by getting into a shouting match about whose string was longer. Luckily, Curtis came to collect Lillie before it came to blows, and he offered to have Winnie patch up Tombo while he delivered Joe Bill and Jamie to their homes.

After they left, Rafe grabbed a deck of playing cards from the desk and went to the cells in back, hoping Frank, the horse beater, was as stupid as he looked.

He was. It took Rafe less than an hour to divest the fool of his money and his horse.

A while later, Fred Driscoll arrived for the night shift. Rafe explained about the prisoner, adding, "If he gives you any trouble, come get me or send word. I'd rather you not shoot him. That requires a mess of paperwork. And keep an eye on Tombo. He got pretty banged up today."

The next morning, a few minutes before the westbound pulled into the depot, Rafe went to Frank's cell again. The prisoner had just finished his breakfast.

Leaning his shoulder against the barred cell door, Rafe put

on a regretful expression. "I'm sorry about winning your horse last night."

"You should be." Frank gave him a sour look. "You're the one forced me to play cards even though you knew I was feeling poorly. Now I got nothing."

"No, I'm sorry about winning. The horse died overnight." That was a lie. The animal was happily eating his way through a mound of hay at the livery. But Rafe had no intention of letting Frank leave with the animal, and Tombo seemed to have taken a shine to the poor beast.

The prisoner grinned, showing the missing and broken teeth of a lifelong brawler. "Damn horse was useless anyway."

Hiding his disgust, Rafe pulled a voucher from his pocket. "Here's a ticket for the train at the depot. It's scheduled to leave in about fifteen minutes. I suggest you get on it before the real sheriff comes back. He's not as nice as me."

Frank took the voucher.

That evening at supper, such as it was—apparently, Henny had the day off—Rafe brought up the subject of the decamped Miss Adkins.

"She was a wretched teacher," Josie said. "Deplorable. Even though he's only just eight, our Jamie is far ahead of the majority of the other students."

"She mostly just read us stuff," Jamie put in.

Josie's brows rose. "Read us stuff?"

"Books," her son corrected. "She read books to us. Ones that were quite boring, actually."

"Just so." His mother sent Rafe a see-what-I-mean look.

Rafe cut into a burned piece of chicken. Being raised in privilege, Josie had planned many menus, but never prepared one, yet she wouldn't stop trying, God love her. "Prudence Lincoln should arrive soon. She taught when the school first opened. Maybe she'll do it again. Tait said she was very good."

"What will we do in the meantime?"

He slipped an undercooked bean into his mouth and smiled as he crunched it into swallowable chunks. "I was thinking maybe you might take on the job."

"Me?"

"You're a natural, honey. The smartest lady I know. Look what a great job you've done with Jamie."

"He had tutors." She set down her fork, took a sip from her glass, then pressed her napkin to her lips. Always proper, his Josie. With the manners of a true lady. No one looking at her would ever guess the wondrous things that prim mouth could do to a man in the dark.

Realizing he was on the verge of embarrassing himself, Rafe spread his napkin over his lap. She caught the movement and smiled in a way that made him shift in his chair.

"Perhaps I'll talk to Lucinda about it in the morning," she said, picking up her fork again. "It's gossip day."

Her easy agreement reinforced what Rafe had been thinking. She was lonely. Other than Henny, the nearest female was Audra Hardesty, and she was away all day at the newspaper office. But Josie had nothing—other than trying out new recipes on him and Jamie—to keep her busy.

Did she have regrets about leaving England? He knew that because of her father's situation and the circumstances surrounding Jamie's birth, she had lived a lonely life before he came. He had hoped the lively society in Heartbreak Creek would have made her feel less isolated here. But now he realized it was probably worse. She was a vibrant woman. She needed people around her. Women. Friends.

His concerns must have shown on his face. Even though they had been married only a few months, he was never able to hide his thoughts from his sharp-witted wife.

Leaning over, she took his hand. A simple touch, yet he felt it through every inch of his body.

He needed this woman. Needed her laughter, her touch, and her smile. Needed the warmth of her body against his in the night. If she wasn't happy here—even if it meant he grew webbed feet and never saw the sun again—he would buy tickets on the eastbound tomorrow and take her back to rainy England.

"Jamie," he said, tearing his gaze from Josie's, but keeping a firm grip on her hand, "have you fed your horse yet?"

"I usually feed Blaze after I finish with supper."

"You're finished."

"What about dessert?"

"It can wait."

The boy's gaze moved from Rafe to his mother and back

again. "You're not going to kiss, are you? Kissing is disgusting and terribly unsanitary."

"Tell me that when you're older."

"Joe Bill says kissing is just trading spit."

"For Joe Bill, that will probably be true. But for you, it'll be different."

"Why?"

Luckily, Josie jumped in to save him. "Because you're kind and polite and quite handsome," she told her son. "I daresay the girls will be chasing after you all the time."

"I pray not." The boy looked at his plate, the tips of his ears turning red.

"Wait and see. Now do as your father asked you."

"Yes, ma'am."

Your father. Rafe liked the sound of that, even though he still wasn't used to hearing it.

As soon as the door closed, he pulled Josie into his lap and traded spit with her. "That's not disgusting at all," he murmured a few minutes later when he came up for air. "Is this, I wonder?" He ran a hand over her breast.

Her breathy laugh sent heat pulsing through him.

But before he could carry her upstairs, she slipped away and back into her chair. "Now tell me what's wrong, dearest. I can see something is troubling you."

He looked into her mismatched eyes, trying to read the answer to the question he hadn't yet found the courage to ask. A beam of late afternoon sunlight cut across her beautiful face and made the splash of blue in her right eye shimmer like the clear water in a cool crystal pool.

"Do you have regrets, Josie?" he finally asked. Then, afraid of what she might say, he hurried on before she could answer. "I don't want you to be lonely here, honey. Or to feel lost, or homesick for England. If you want to go back, we can leave this week. Just say the word."

It was a long time before she spoke. So long, Rafe started to sweat.

"Rubbish," she finally said. "That's the word. That, and no. No, I am not lonely. No, I have no regrets. And no, I do not want to go back."

Relief left him weak. He grinned at her, his eyes burning. "Good heavens. You're not going to cry, are you?"

"I think I might. Perhaps if you took off your clothes and sat on my lap, I'd feel better."

"What good would that do, if you don't take off yours, as well?"

The smartest lady he knew.

"So it's settled then. We have a teacher." Lucinda smiled in satisfaction at the three other ladies gathered around the corner table in the deserted hotel dining room. "We owe Josephine our complete support."

Audra Hardesty wrote furiously in her small tablet. She paused to study the pretty Englishwoman, now the town's new teacher, and wondered if it would be forward to ask why she had one brown eye and one that was half blue and half brown. Probably. The longer she worked at the newspaper—*her* newspaper now, a wedding gift from Ethan—the better she came to know the people of Heartbreak Creek, and the more blurred the lines between reportable news and outright gossip became. Especially with these women.

Edwina reached past her to squeeze Josephine's arm. "Bless you, Josephine. You have no idea how grateful I am. The idea of having Joe Bill underfoot all day—" She stammered to a stop as if realizing what she had said. Then, with a flustered smile, she tried to explain. "That's not to say he's actually *bad*. Or troublesome, or . . ."

"Give it up, Edwina." Lucinda waved away the Southerner's fumbling excuses. "Everyone knows Joe Bill is a handful. But I suspect all that frightful energy will make him famous one day."

Audra thought it generous of her to say "famous" rather than "notorious."

"I shan't worry about it," Josephine said in her proper British accent. "I shall have Joe Bill reciting sonnets by summer."

That boast made all of them, Josephine included, laugh out loud.

"I just hope you can teach Lillie to speak so we can understand her," Lucinda said. "Mrs. T. has failed dismally. A few days ago, I found them going at each other with their sticks. Apparently, my guardian tried to poke the child with her cane, and Lillie retaliated. Not that I blame her."

Edwina sighed. "She's no better than Joe Bill. Probably because they're near the same age, despite the size difference. Best prepare yourself, Josephine."

"They're only children. How much trouble can they be?"

Which prompted another burst of laughter.

Audra studied these women who gathered weekly to share tea, scones, and gossip. She was so grateful to have them as friends, and although she had only arrived in town a few days before Prudence left, she felt she knew her, too. Sometimes, Helen Bradshaw or Mrs. Throckmorton joined them. But today Helen was busy with her housekeeping duties at the hotel, and Mrs. Throckmorton was in the Rylander suite, watching over baby Whit while he napped and feeding Rosie.

Audra was still amazed about that. The feeding part.

Last week, Lucinda Rylander had shown them how such a thing was possible. Without even a blush of embarrassment, she had marched up to the table and plunked down next to the marmalade a device that sucked milk right out of a woman's breast.

Imagine that!

Josephine's mismatched eyes had almost popped loose, and Audra still smiled when she thought of how far Edwina's jaw had dropped. Audra had been shocked, too, but intrigued. The reporter in her, she suspected.

According to Lucinda, the torture device was well worth the humiliation of being pumped like a cow, since it freed her to enjoy her first full night's sleep in almost three months. Freed her to enjoy other things, as well, Audra surmised, noting the beard rash on the blond beauty's neck.

Audra chided herself for noticing such a thing, but being the owner, operator, lead reporter, and editor of the *Heartbreak Creek Herald*, she was obliged to keep abreast of everything around her.

Abreast.

An unfortunate—and amusing—choice of words. *I should be writing a humor column,* she mused. Rather than listing train schedules, calling for volunteers for the garden below the leaky sluice, or writing death and birth notices. She should be announcing to the world that her own child was on the way.

But not yet. It was too soon. What if she lost this one, too?

The thought bounced through her head, ripping open scars barely healed.

She was only now recovering from . . . what was she to call it? A death? An aborted life? A child that would never be? There were no words for what she felt. Her baby had never taken a breath. Audra had never held it, or even known if it was a boy or a girl. But the grief of losing that tiny life haunted her still.

Physically, she was fine. But emotionally . . .

She longed to tell someone, to share her pain and the irrational fear that gripped her each morning when she awoke, wondering if she was still pregnant . . . or if today would be the day she lost this baby, too.

Dr. Boyce said it happens—to give it time. Her longtime friend and onetime housekeeper, Winnie Abraham, said to put it in the Lord's hands. Ethan said it was okay, they could keep trying.

But it wasn't okay. Her baby had died. That would never be okay.

"Audra? Are you well?"

She looked up to find three faces staring curiously at her. Pulling herself together, she forced a smile. "Woolgathering. What did I miss?"

"We were discussing whether we should tell Helen that Buster Quinn has left."

"He left? When?"

"On the eastbound, yesterday morning."

Audra liked Helen. The woman was efficient, friendly, and quite attractive for a lady in her middle years. But reserved. Audra always sensed a touch of sadness beneath her pleasant smile.

Buster Quinn was even harder to get to know. She knew something of his background—he had fought for the North, later worked in New York as a Pinkerton detective, and several years ago went into private security. Tait Rylander had met both Quinn and Mrs. Bradshaw through a business associate— the man Lucinda had almost married. A rather tangled mess. Audra wasn't sure how it was resolved, but when Lucinda's guardian, Mrs. Throckmorton, moved to Heartbreak Creek last summer, she had brought Buster Quinn and Mrs. Bradshaw with her. Over the ensuing months, Helen had been all smiles whenever Buster was around. Buster had seemed happy, too. So what had gone wrong? "How is Helen taking it?"

"Not well," Edwina answered. "A few days ago, I found her in here crying. When I asked her what was wrong, she wouldn't talk about it."

"Tait says Quinn never courted Helen." Lucinda exchanged a knowing look with Edwina. "But there was something going on between them. You could tell."

"We should do something," Edwina said.

Josephine lifted her brows. "Like what? Drag him back by his heels?"

"I don't know yet. But I'm thinking on it."

"Oh, dear." Lucinda rolled her eyes. "Poor Quinn."

Which made them all laugh again.

Audra felt better than she had in days . . . other than that persistent queasiness she refused to think about.

Nineteen

A few days later, Declan Brodie sat in the dark on the porch of his Sunday house, listening to the frogs by the creek and contemplating the mess he'd have on his hands if Thomas never came back. Not that he would blame him, if what Ed said was true. No man liked being turned away time and again.

It had been almost two weeks since Thomas had left: not much time in male terms, but for a female as prone to worry as Ed was, it was a week and a half too long. Pru was her half sister, after all, and Thomas was family. Southerners doted on their families, and Ed fussed over hers like a mother hen.

Declan was worried, too. The town wouldn't be the same without Thomas. The Cheyenne added a sense of stability to the landscape, like a boulder in the middle of a slope—too big to move, and forcing you to go around it, but so solidly grounded it kept the rest of the slope from sliding away. In a similar fashion, his friends all made allowances for the Dog Soldier—staying clear when he was in a mood, or altering plans to accommodate his Indian ways. But you always knew he was there, rock-solid and immovable, watching your back.

Being his friend had made Declan's life richer. In fact, without Thomas, he might not have gotten through that hard time after his first wife had run off with her gambler and gotten attacked by an Arapaho war party. He trusted the Cheyenne with his life, his wife, and his children. But he needed him to get his ass back home so Ed would calm down. As soon as Pru returned, Declan wanted to get back to the ranch. Calves would be dropping any day, and he should be there to see that all went well. But if Ed got herself worked up about her sister and Thomas, he might never get home.

"Pa?"

Declan looked over to see his ten-year-old son, Lucas, standing in the doorway. "What are you doing still up?"

"I couldn't sleep."

Declan wasn't surprised. Lucas had a mind that never stopped. He nodded toward the chair beside his. "Come on, then. But only until Ed catches you."

The boy let the door close and came forward, looking frail and thin in the faint light of the crescent moon. He wasn't big like fourteen-year-old R.D., or as robust as eleven-year-old Joe Bill. But he made up for it by having such a strong mind it sometimes felt like he could see straight into a person's head.

"Something worrying you, son?"

A shrug.

Declan didn't push him. The boy would talk when he was ready.

Lucas was the easiest of his sons. Never caused trouble, never goaded Ed into a temper like Joe Bill did, and hardly ever raised his voice, especially after his ma left them five years ago. Ed's coming had loosened him up somewhat, but Declan still worried that he was too withdrawn.

"You cold?" he asked, seeing the boy shiver in his nightshirt—something Ed had insisted on right off—"I don't need a passel of naked boys running around like plucked chickens!" She'd also insisted they take baths most nights before they put them on.

"A little."

"Come here." Declan patted his knee.

Lucas probably considered himself too old to sit in his father's lap, but Declan was glad he climbed up anyway. The time for holding his sons was passing fast, and he welcomed the chance to do it before it was too late. "Pretty evening," he said, pulling the boy back against his chest.

Lucas nodded. "The last of the Worm Moon."

"Worm Moon?"

"That's what Indians call the full moon in March."

"Why?"

"Because that's when the ground thaws." Lucas swiveled to face him, his face showing the excitement it always did when he talked about his bugs and reptiles and anything else that crawled, slithered, hopped, or flew. "Worms come up from where they've been sleeping all winter and leave casings on the ground. Some people think casings are poop, but they're mostly dirt."

"You don't say."

A vigorous nod. "That's when robins come, too. They see the casings on the ground and start looking for a worm to show up. I saw two of them today."

"I'll have to watch for them."

"Look by the creek," he advised, and settled back against Declan's chest. "They like water. Most birds do."

Declan smiled, amazed by all the facts the boy carried around in his head. He might not be as sturdy as his brothers, but Lucas had the gift of a curious brain and a fascination with how things worked. He was happiest when he was buried in a book, or drawing up plans for some invention he'd thought up, or tracking the smallest bug across the grass. Declan was never quite sure what was going on in his head, but he loved this quiet, sensitive boy with a fierceness that went beyond what he felt for his other sons.

"The frogs are noisy tonight," he ventured, hoping to keep him talking.

"They're waking up, too. They freeze over the winter, then thaw out when the dirt does."

Declan looked at him in surprise. "Freeze? Solid?"

Lucas nodded. "That's what Thomas told me." He fidgeted for a minute, then asked in a worried tone, "When is he coming back?"

"I'm not sure."

"What if he never does?"

And there it was—the worry that had kept the boy up so late. After losing his ma at an early age, he fretted when people left, fearing that they wouldn't come back. Plus, Lucas near-worshiped the Cheyenne, mainly because the Indian took the time to teach the curious boy all manner of things that couldn't be found in the pages of his books. Declan's wouldn't be the only life diminished by the Indian's absence. "He'll come back if I have to drag him home by his topknot."

"He doesn't have a topknot anymore."

"Then by his temple braids."

A snicker told Declan the boy was feeling better. "They'd probably break off. Human hair isn't as tough as horse hair. Although an Indian's hair is—"

"That's it. No more lessons. Go to bed."

As if on cue, Edwina appeared at the door. "There you are, Lucas. I thought your collection of beetles had carried you off."

"I'm not dung. But if we had enough ants, they might be able to carry me off. Or eat me. Did you know there are ants in Africa that eat everything in their path?"

"Like R.D.?" Ed asked.

"Worse. They could eat him down to bones in only a few minutes."

"No wonder you can't sleep." Declan lifted the boy off his numb thighs. "Go dream of pretty girls, instead of ants."

"Girls are stupid."

"And dung beetles aren't?" Ed steered the boy into the kitchen, then glanced back with a grin. "I'll be back for you later."

"I'll be waiting."

A few minutes later, the house went dark. When she came back out, she wore a gown and robe, her hair falling around her shoulders in a tumble of light brown curls. She looked wild and mysterious in the glow of the moon, and so beautiful she didn't seem real. Declan thought again about how lacking his life would have been if he hadn't posted that ad in *The Matrimonial News*.

He patted thighs that were just beginning to wake up. "Have a seat."

Smiling, she settled crosswise in his lap with the familiarity of many a night spent in his arms. With a sigh of contentment, she tipped her head back to kiss his chin, then squirmed until she got comfortable.

Which made him less comfortable. Pulling her closer, he rested his cheek on hair that smelled like lemons and was so fine it caught in the stubble on his chin.

After a while, his thighs went numb again, but he didn't

mind. He liked holding her. Liked knowing this emotional, courageous, and loving woman was his to hold whenever he wanted. Or whenever she would let him. "You cold?" he asked, sliding a hand along her hip.

"Not really."

"You feel cold."

She snuggled closer, twisting to face him, which had the lucky benefit of making her more accessible to his roving hands. "Do I? Where?"

"Here, for one." He slipped his hand under her robe to stroke her belly through her gown. "And here." He moved his hand higher. "But especially here." His fingers grazed the tip of her breast.

"Oh," she breathed, arching into his hand.

He loved the way she responded to him, loved the sounds she made and how open she was to him. She never made him feel too big, or clumsy, or rough for gentle play. She had once even called him beautiful. But more often, she called him a big lump and punched his shoulder. He loved both.

"You haven't put on a peep show for me in months," she complained, wiggling her bottom in a way that woke his thighs up fast.

"It's too cold." He moved his hand to her other breast.

"I'll manage."

"I meant it's too cold for *me*."

"Oh, I doubt that." Lowering her hand between her hip and his belt buckle, she tested the ridge in his trousers. "You feel quite warm to me. But maybe I should check, just to be sure." She began loosening the buttons on his Levi denims.

His lungs stopped working. "Ed," he warned when he could breathe again.

"What?" Pushing the fabric aside, she reached into his drawers to give his John Thomas a squeeze that almost brought him out of the chair. And not only because her hand was cold.

"The children are just inside," he said through clenched teeth.

She kissed his neck, then stretched to whisper in his ear, "I'd like for you to be inside, too."

The little hussy. His pulse hammered. His mind started to spiral. "You really want to do this . . . now . . . out here?"

"Do what?"

Before he could summon an answer, she gently raked her fingernails up his length, sending John Thomas into bobbing delight. "I'm about ten seconds," he said hoarsely, "from tossing that gown over your head."

She gave a squeeze.

Lights flashed behind Declan's closed eyes.

"I want my peep show first." A gentle stroke. "And one teensy, weensy other little thing."

"You trying to manipulate me, wife?" Not that he minded her attempts. But he wanted her to know that he knew what she was up to, so that when he gave in, which he always did, she'd know it was because he wanted to, and not because she'd manipulated him into doing it. Mostly.

"I might have been softening you up to ask a favor, but it seems to have had the opposite effect."

"As you knew it would."

She pulled her hand out of his trousers. Her saucy smile crumpled, and tears glistened in the moonlight. "I know you're anxious to get back to the ranch." She swiped a hand over her eyes and tilted her head back to see him better. "But could you do one thing before you go?"

When she looked at him like that, he would do anything for her, whether her hand was in his trousers or not. This woman had brought such joy, and laughter, and love back into his and his children's lives, he would give her the moon if he could reach it. Dipping his head down, he kissed her forehead. "Sure, Ed. What do you need me to do?"

"Find Thomas and bring him home."

"Done." Gathering her in his arms, he headed for the door, grateful he didn't have to agree to anything he hadn't already decided to do. Other than putting on a peep show. Which he didn't mind at all.

Thomas was sitting on a scrap of elk hide in front of his tipi, carving a length of antler into a flute for *Katse'e*, when Declan Brodie finished the long climb up from the sacred pool.

"What took you so long?" he asked, without looking up.

"Jesus." The big rancher plopped onto the ground beside him, his chest heaving. "You could have at least hidden out somewhere my horse could go."

"I do not hide."

"Like hell." Muttering under his breath, Declan shrugged off his duster and tossed it aside. "I'm sweating like a butcher pig."

"Sweating is good for you. It draws bad spirits from the body."

"Bunkum. You got any water around here that doesn't smell like rotten eggs?" Brodie had such an aversion to the smell of the water in the sacred pool, he had never even waded in.

Thomas nodded toward a swollen elk bladder hanging on a peg. "That holds water."

Brodie eyed it in disgust. "Never mind. But I wouldn't mind a bite of that elk jerky." Without waiting for Thomas to offer it, he pulled a strip of dried meat from the drying rack and bit off a chunk. "What have you been doing up here all this time?" he mumbled while he chewed.

"Building this fine tipi."

"That took you two weeks?"

Thomas held up the piece of antler. "I am also carving this flute for my daughter."

"You ought not leave her so long. She could get herself into trouble."

Thomas shrugged. He knew Declan would come get him if *Katse'e* needed him. Setting aside his knife and the flute, he rested his hands on his folded knees and looked at his friend. "Why are you here, Declan Brodie?"

"Ed is worried."

"Ho. So it is your wife who sends you up here. Not your concern for my daughter."

"Your daughter can take care of herself. She proved that last week."

Thomas felt tension rise in his chest. "What did she do?"

"You mean after she and Joe Bill threatened a man for hitting Tombo Welks? Or after she went at Mrs. Throckmorton with her blind stick?"

Thomas waited.

"Nothing real bad so far," Declan finally admitted. "But she's due. You need to come home."

Home. Was there such a thing for him? Was Heartbreak Creek truly where he belonged? Sometimes it felt like it. But still, there was something missing. And he knew what it was.

"So when are you coming down off your mountain here?"

"Soon." Thomas let the tension bleed away. He picked up the knife and flute again. "I am glad you came, *nesene*."

While Brodie worked on his strip of jerky, Thomas scraped the rough edges off the knife cuts on the antler. The sun dipped toward the western peaks, casting an orange wash over the high, snow-covered slopes and turning the wispy clouds above them into bands of red and gold and purple.

Declan Brodie was right. It was time for Thomas to go back into town, where the sunsets would be hidden from him by the walls of his wooden house. He would put on his white clothes, and pin his sheriff's badge on his shirt, and return to his duties as a father. He could do that. What he did not think he could do was open his heart again to Prudence Lincoln.

A cool wind rushed up the slope as it did in the evenings, making the elk hides on the tipi shiver and the flap over the entrance snap against the leather tie.

Brodie reached for his duster. "Why didn't you put your tipi behind those boulders so you'd have a wind break?"

Thomas said nothing.

As Brodie pulled on his duster, he studied the boulders, his frown giving way to a look of astonishment. "There's nothing behind those boulders, is there? That's a sheer drop-off." With each word his face had grown paler.

Thomas had forgotten the big man feared high places.

Brodie slowly stood, arms out for balance, panic showing in his eyes. "You put your tipi on this tiny little strip of bare rock?"

"There are trees over there." Thomas nodded toward a line of stunted spruce on a ridge to the north. Granted, below that ridge was a bluff that would have been impossible to climb without lengths of stout rope. But Thomas doubted Brodie could see it from where he stood.

"Holy hell."

Seeing the fear on his friend's face, Thomas tossed the knife and flute into a leather pouch, then rose. "I will help you down."

"I don't need any help."

"I will go with you anyway."

They started down the slope, sliding where snow had turned to slush and sinking into mud where it had melted. It took a long time, because Brodie moved with great care, but they finally made it down to the brush corral Thomas had built for his pony. Brodie's big sorrel stood tied nearby.

"I'm never going up there again," Brodie announced, color returning to his face. "And you're a damn fool to build camp in such a dangerous place."

"It is easy to defend."

"Against what? Eagles?"

Knowing his friend was only reacting to his fear, Thomas did not argue. "How did you find me?"

"Followed elk bones and coyote scat. Lucky you didn't draw a griz up there instead of me."

"I feel lucky."

"Go to hell."

"I think I will go home instead." As he saddled his pinto, Thomas heard the distant shriek of a locomotive whistle. The westbound. The one that would bring Prudence Lincoln back to Heartbreak Creek.

He looked at Brodie.

The rancher shook his head. "Pru's not on that one. Ed got a wire this morning saying she'll be on the Friday westbound. That's the day after tomorrow, in case you've lost all sense of time, hiding out up here like a damn hermit."

Friday.

Stay or leave?

He had two days to decide.

When Declan walked into the kitchen of his Sunday house, his older children were off doing their after-dinner chores, Whit was down for the night, and Ed was sitting at the table making a list.

His wife loved making her lists. She had shopping lists for the necessities to keep the house going and the children clothed and fed, lists of things she wanted to get done if she ever found the time, and lists she called her worry lists. By her expression, he guessed she was working on one of the latter.

"I brought him back," he said, hooking his Stetson on a peg inside the door.

She looked up, a sad smile on her face. "I almost wish you hadn't." She thumped a piece of paper beside her list. "This came while you were gone."

He recognized it as a telegram. "She back in jail?"

"Delayed. Apparently, whatever she had to clear up in Indianapolis has taken longer than she anticipated. She's not sure when she'll arrive."

"Thomas won't like it."

"I know. But at least she hasn't changed her mind about coming home."

Yet. "Any supper left?"

Brushing a tear from her cheek, she rose, pulled a cook pot off the stove, set it on the table, then returned to her seat. "I don't understand her, Declan," she said in a tearful voice. "I know Pru cares about Thomas, but it seems every time they have a chance of getting together, she has something else to do first. Lucinda says that after the way Pru has treated him, she wouldn't be surprised if Thomas washed his hands of her."

Declan wouldn't be surprised, either.

He lifted the lid on the pot. Venison stew. Realizing she wasn't going to get them, he got a plate, utensils, butter crock, and the end of a loaf of bread and carried them to the table.

As he ate, Ed went on about what they should do, and why was Pru acting this way, and did she really think Thomas would wait for her forever?

Declan didn't bother to respond. He knew his wife wasn't looking for answers, just someone to listen. And he was better at that than talking, anyway. But he could see that worry over her sister was tearing apart his tenderhearted wife. Ed loved both Pru and Thomas and wanted them together and here with them in Heartbreak Creek. But it sounded like the chances of that happening grew slimmer with every excuse and delay. That made Declan sad, too. Mostly for Thomas. He'd never seen a man fall so hard, so fast.

Ed finally wound down with a deep sigh. "I guess I should go pack."

He looked up. "Going somewhere?"

"We need to get back to the ranch. Calving starts soon."

We. It pleased him to hear that. The woman was a blessing he'd never expected when he'd sent off for a mail-order bride. Sight unseen and with the signing of her name, she'd moved from plantation princess to rancher's wife and mother to four rowdy children. Declan doubted he would have had the fortitude to tackle the task with the good humor and patience she had shown. "There's no rush. Chick and Amos can handle anything that comes up."

"Why wait around if we don't even know when she's coming?"

"Because she's family. And that's what families do."

Fresh tears rolled down her cheeks. "I adore you, Robert Declan Brodie."

He felt himself blush and wondered if she knew how much those words meant to him. After a lifetime of feeling clumsy and awkward, to be loved by a woman like Ed was a wonderment.

Pushing his plate aside, he reached for his hat. "I'd best give Thomas the news." He hoped this latest delay didn't send the Cheyenne away for good.

Part Three

Hold on to what is good,
Even if it is a handful of earth.
Hold on to what you believe,
Even if it is a tree that stands by itself.
Hold on to what you must do,
Even if it is a long way from here.
Hold on to your life,
Even if it is easier to let go.
Hold on to my hand,
Even if someday I will be gone away from you . . .

—Pueblo Indian Prayer

Twenty

Our first teacher is our own heart.

—Native American proverb

The train began to slow.

In building excitement, Pru pressed closer to the soot-smeared window for her first glimpse of the new Heartbreak Creek Station.

When she'd left for Schuler a year ago to teach at the Hill-top Christian Academy for People of Color—before it became the Quaker school—the rails had reached only as far as Boot Creek, a small water stop several miles east of town. Where the Heartbreak Creek Station now stood had been a rail yard. Beside it, the once-bustling Chinese camp had been replaced by a heated water tower, fed by a sluice that brought clean—and drinkable—water from deep in the canyon.

Heartbreak Creek was no longer a dying mining camp with horrid water. By sheer force of will—and a suitcase full of money—Lucinda Rylander had brought the town back to life. And now a grand lodge was to be built beside the mineral spring where Thomas had taken her that snowy night over a year ago.

So many changes. She was sorry she had missed them.

When the passenger car rolled slowly up to the station, Pru

saw that the platform was empty. She was disappointed, but not surprised, since she'd sent no word of her arrival today. Besides, it was Sunday. Everyone would be in church.

The moment the conductor opened the door, she pulled her valise from beneath her seat and hurried toward the exit. A stiff breeze dissipated smoke from the locomotive stack, and as she stepped onto the wooden planks beside the tracks, she filled her lungs with the first cool, clean air she'd breathed since boarding in Schuler many days ago.

She was so grateful her ordeal was over and she was home at last.

"That you, Miss Lincoln?"

Pru turned and saw a smiling man leaning against the wheel of a buckboard while a railroad worker loaded boxes and crates from the baggage car into the bed of the wagon. It took a moment for her to place him. "Mr. Kincaid?"

"Yep. Surprised you remember. Welcome back."

She smiled at the town's milk supplier. "I'm glad to be back."

"Going up to the church to surprise them?" he asked, walking toward her. "I know that little blind girl would be tickled to know you're here. 'Fore the train came, I could hear her singing, even this far away. Girl's got a powerful voice."

"She certainly does." Pru glanced in the direction of the church, but the train stood in the way. Mr. Kincaid had addressed her as Miss Lincoln, so it seemed Thomas hadn't told anyone they were married.

"You want, I can drop your valise off at the hotel. Or the Arlan house, if you prefer. That's where the girl's staying. Her and the Abrahams and our new sheriff."

Thomas. Pru pressed a hand to her fluttering stomach. Although she longed to see him, she didn't want to put either of them in an awkward position by showing up at the house uninvited. But if she went to the church . . .

She handed him her valise. "The hotel for now. And thank you."

"If you don't mind waiting, I can give you a ride."

"I appreciate that, but after sitting for so long, I think I'd rather walk."

By the time she had freshened up in the Ladies' Retiring

Room inside the station, Mr. Kincaid was gone, the train was pulling away, and she could see the church up the road.

A man was sitting on the steps. From this distance, she couldn't be certain who it was, but something in the set of his shoulders and the fact that he didn't wear a hat over his dark hair made it suddenly harder for her to take a full breath.

Reticule clutched at her waist, she marched resolutely toward her husband.

For a thousand miles, she had rehearsed what she would say to him—how Marsh had used threats against him and Lillie to force her aboard the train in Indianapolis; why she hadn't turned back when she learned Marsh was dead and no longer a danger to them; what had delayed her return to Heartbreak Creek.

Good reasons, all. But after so many broken promises, she wondered if he would believe her. Or trust her again.

He must. There was more at stake now than just her happiness and his. Lillie needed them both.

As she drew closer, he slowly stood, his attention focused her way. She had no doubt that he recognized her now. She could feel it. That intense gaze seemed to reach beneath her skin, set her nerves humming, scatter her thoughts like puffs of white lint across a Louisiana cotton field. Would he welcome her? Or walk away?

Her steps faltered. Her legs started to shake.

From inside the church came the sound of voices. She recognized Lillie's. Hearing it gave her strength. The child had been so distraught when Pru had left. She had suffered so much in her short life. But Lillie was a survivor. Children were resilient. They would get through this, then all three of them could begin to heal.

She was close enough now to see his face. He wasn't smiling, but he often didn't. More telling were his crossed arms and the fact that he didn't come forward to greet her. She hadn't known what to expect, but this chilly silence cut deep.

"Thomas," she said by way of greeting when she stopped at the bottom of the steps. She was afraid if she said more, her voice would crack.

Without responding, he came down the stairs.

"You look well." In truth, he looked tired. Worn. The lines

bracketing his wide mouth seemed set in stone, and his eyes were more shuttered than ever.

He stopped in front of her—less than a yard away, yet it felt like an immense distance. "Why are you here?" he asked in a hard voice.

She tried for levity. "Here, at the church? Or here, in Heartbreak Creek?"

He didn't smile.

So that was how it would be. Not wanting him to see how his coldness distressed her, she hiked her chin. "We need to talk, Thomas. But not here."

"I am in the sheriff's office every morning."

"I'll see you there." She started to step around him, but he stopped her with a hand on her arm. It wasn't a tight grip, but it wasn't tender, either.

"You will not hurt *Katse'e*," he said in a tone he had never before used with her. "You will not fill her heart with hope, Prudence, then walk away from her. Do you understand?"

The words knocked the breath from her. For a moment, she couldn't draw in enough air to respond. "Thomas—"

The church doors opened.

He released her arm.

"I will talk to you about it tomorrow," she said in a shaky voice, then put on a bright smile as people began to file out of the church.

When those who came first through the doors saw Prudence at the bottom of the steps, their voices rose in happy cries and words of welcome.

Thomas ignored them. Vaulting over the railing at the top of the stairs, he pushed his way through the crowded doorway. When he saw *Katse'e* at the end of the narrow aisle, walking with Winnie Abraham, he stepped between two rows of benches to wait.

The Brodie family came by. "What's the ruckus?" Declan asked.

Thomas cut his gaze to Edwina Brodie. "Your sister is here."

Her squeal echoed to the rafters. Declan had to hold his

wife back to keep her from mowing down the people in front of her.

Thomas had to repeat the news for the Hardestys and Rylanders and Jessups.

"Wonderful!" Lucinda Rylander cried. "Now she can meet our little Rosie."

Rayford Jessup paused beside him. "You still coming for Sunday dinner?"

Thomas had forgotten it was at the Wallace home today. His first instinct was to send Lillian without him. He was so rattled, he could hardly think. He thought he had prepared himself for this moment. He thought he had put her from his heart. It seemed he had not. Seeing her walk toward him had cut as deep as a knife thrust.

But he would not let her, or his friends, see him bleed.

"I will be there."

"Good. I think I'll uncork a bottle of Ash's fine whisky."

"I do not drink whisky."

"You might want to today."

Thomas saw understanding in Jessup's dark blue eyes and realized the Texan was not goading him, but offering support. He forced a smile. "Perhaps I should bring *mataho*, so we can all be foolish."

Jessup shook his head. "After what happened to Brodie when you gave him peyote buttons? I pass." Chuckling, he moved on.

The crowd thinned until only the Abrahams and Lillian remained in the church. Winnie Abraham must have seen that something was wrong. "What is it, Thomas?" she asked, stopping beside him.

"You hear me sing, Daddy? I was especially good today, ain't—isn't—that so, Miss Winnie?"

But Winnie was staring past him toward the doorway. A smile spread across her kind face. "Praise the Lawd, child. Your prayers are answered."

"Which ones? I pray a lot."

Thomas did not have to look back to see what had drawn Winnie's attention. He bent before his daughter. "*Katse'e*, Prudence Lincoln is here."

Her blank eyes widened. "Fo' true?"

"For true." *And may the Great Spirit rain curses down on her head if his wife leaves this child again.* Thomas rose and gave his daughter's shoulder a gentle shove. "Walk forward. She is only a few steps away."

"Miss Pru! Miss Pru!" Dropping her blind stick, *Katse'e* stumbled down the aisle, arms raised high. "Mama, you came home!"

Thomas turned to watch, something twisting in his chest.

Tears running down her cheeks, Prudence scooped the girl into her arms. "Yes, dearest, I'm home." Her gaze found Thomas's. He saw pain in her eyes. And something else he could not define. "And I will never leave you again."

If only he could believe that.

An hour later, Gordon Stevens, the groom who had come from England with the Jessups, gave the men a tour of the huge stable the Scotsman had had Ethan Hardesty build for his English horses. Because he feared fire, Ash had instructed Ethan to use stone wherever he could. He had also insisted on a coal stove to warm the foals due in the fall. Thomas thought that was foolish. Even though they would be young when winter came, with so many horses in a closed space, they would stay warm enough.

"As a wedding present to me and Josie," Rayford Jessup said with a grin at Thomas, "Ash is giving our Cheyenne friend here first pick of the foals."

Thomas barely heard him, his attention more focused on the house on the other side of a wide drive. He wondered how *Katse'e* was doing. His daughter had been chattering like a magpie when she and Prudence had climbed into the Rylander buggy in front of the church, and she was probably still chattering now. He hoped not about him.

"That's an odd wedding present," Tait Rylander said.

Jessup chuckled. "Then call it a bribe to induce Thomas to bunk with Jamie aboard ship and on the train as far as Indiana. The privacy was welcome."

"Privacy? What's that?" Tait gave a rueful smile. "No such thing if you live in a hotel with your wife's guardian and have a newborn in the next room."

"Speaking of foals," Declan said as they followed Gordon down the long, open aisle. "These are all fine-looking animals.

Which did you pick to breed, Thomas? Warmblood or thoroughbred?"

Thomas dragged his thoughts away from what might be happening in the house. "Both. Pembroke's Pride and a big bay warmblood mare."

"Good choices." Jessup explained the merits of both horses, his pride evident in the stallion he had won in the race in England. Thomas thought he was the finest horse in the stable.

Jessup gave a low whistle. All along the stone walkway, horse heads poked out of the open top doors of their stalls. "That's the mare." He pointed to a tall, sturdily built bay with kind eyes. "And down there"—he nodded toward the end of the aisle, where several stalls were separated from the others by an office and the tack, feed, and bunk rooms—"is Pembroke's Pride."

As if recognizing his name, the dark stallion looked out of the end stall, tossed his mane, and gave an impatient whinny.

"He's late for his morning run," Gordon said, stopping outside his stall. "Fastest horse you ever saw. Almost died proving it, too."

Thomas had not seen the thoroughbred since he'd returned to Heartbreak Creek. He was glad to see the animal's wounds had healed well. Other than the white hairs marking where the blade had cut into his neck and chest, he showed no sign of lasting injury.

A clang sounded over by the house. "Come eat!" Henny Stevens called.

"About bloody time." Gordon motioned toward the house. "Shall we?"

Letting the others go ahead, Declan turned to Thomas. "You okay?"

"Why would I not be?"

"Then smile. You look like a damned undertaker. Ed's worried."

Edwina Brodie worried about so many things Thomas had stopped noticing long ago.

"Have you had a chance to talk to Pru yet?" the rancher asked.

Thomas pretended indifference. "About what?"

Brodie made an impatient sound. "Everything. Anything.

Why she was in jail. How long she plans to stay. Christ, Thomas. The whole town's wondering what's going on between you two."

"There is nothing going on." Seeing more questions on the way, he held up a hand. "I will talk to her tomorrow. This is all I will say. Now we will eat."

As soon as they were gathered around the table, Lucinda announced that something had come in the post for Thomas. At her nod, Rylander rose. Picking up a crate in the corner, he brought it to the table and plunked it down beside Thomas's plate. "Just so you know, I wasn't the one who opened it."

Seeing the grins on Edwina's and Lucinda's faces, Thomas could guess who had. Lifting off the lid, he saw books inside. His book.

He stared. Until this moment, his book had not seemed real to him. But that was his name on the front, so it must be true. He lifted one out, studied the front and back, then opened it to the first page.

"*For my friends in Heartbreak Creek,*" he read silently, "*so they will know the man who walks among them.*" Then, below it, "*Thomas Redstone, Author.*"

He looked at Rayford Jessup. "You wrote these words."

Jessup nodded. "I was paraphrasing what you said to me when we began. I hope you don't mind."

Thomas wasn't sure. He had wanted to tell the story of his old chief, not see his own name in print. It stole a part of him. Put another label on him he was not sure he wanted. *Author.*

"Well, what is it?" Mrs. Throckmorton demanded, thumping her cane on the floor. "Get on with it, boy, so we can eat."

Before Thomas could answer, Edwina blurted out, "It's a book. Thomas wrote it! It's about Chief Black Kettle, and it's wonderful!" Then realizing what she had said, she put on a face of apology. "I'm sorry. I know I shouldn't have opened it, but I couldn't help myself. That poor man. Thomas, I cried. I actually cried."

She looked like she was about to again.

So did Prudence, despite the pride in her smile.

That confused Thomas. To cover it, he shoved the box across the table toward Rayford Jessup. "Your name should be on this, too."

"Next time."

"What do you mean, next time?"

"It's that good, Thomas. People who read this are going to want more. So you better start thinking. And practicing your signature. You'll be famous now."

Thomas blinked at him, feeling a mild sense of panic. He did not want to be famous. He did not want to write another book. It was hard work.

"Pass them around," Audra Hardesty suggested. "I want to see."

Soon children left the table set up for them and crowded Jessup as he handed books around the table.

"I want one!" *Katse'e* cried, arms outstretched.

"Here you go." Jessup put one in her hands, then smiled at Thomas when she clutched it to her chest like precious treasure. "Maybe your daddy will read it to you later."

"I daresay, you should come to school and read it to all the children," his wife, Josephine, suggested. "It is part of their history, too."

Thomas resisted the urge to flee the house. "It is only a book."

"A book written by someone we know and love." Edwina dabbed at her eyes. "I'm so proud of you, Thomas, I could just cry."

She was already crying. He snuck a glance at Prudence. She had her head down as she leafed through the pages. But he saw the smile playing around her lips and felt a shift in his resolve. Irritated by his weakness for this woman—his *wife*— he brought the flat of his hand down on the tabletop. "We will eat now."

Which, for some reason, made the others laugh.

Thomas remained silent for the rest of the meal. As soon as it was over, he rose. "I must go relieve Tombo Welks now. He cannot stay alone in the sheriff's office for long without getting nervous. *Katse'e*, the Abrahams will take you home."

"What about Mama?"

He looked at Prudence, then away again. "That is for her to decide."

"You want a horse?" Jessup asked him.

"I will walk."

"It's raining."

"Then I will walk fast." As soon as he stepped outside, the feeling of suffocation left him. He set out through a thick mist that only a dry-land Texan like Jessup would call rain. It softened the tree line along the creek and put wispy crowns on the tall firs. By morning those crowns would have turned to ice, and by noon, they would begin to thaw. But for now, he liked the solitude of being the only person on the road.

Several minutes later, he stopped under the overhang outside the sheriff's office, shook the dampness off his hair, then stepped inside. No sign of his temporary deputy. "Tombo Welks," he called.

"Back here."

Thomas went through the door behind his desk and found Tombo stretched out on the cot in the cell he called home. "What are you doing?"

"Hidin'."

"From what?"

Tombo leaned forward to peer past Thomas toward the front office. "He here yet?"

"Who?"

"That man what come by earlier. I didn't like him. Said he was from Indian-something." Tombo sat back, his fingers worrying a hole in his blanket.

"Indianapolis?"

"That's it. Said he was lookin' for Thomas Redstone. That's you, right?"

Thomas nodded. "What did you tell him?"

"That you were over to the church, but you'd be back later. And here you are. Can I go now?" He sat up, his eyes shifting from Thomas to the office door, as if expecting the man to burst through at any moment.

"Go where?"

"The livery. Mr. Driscoll said he'd pay me to work for two days."

"You can go after you tell me if this man threatened you."

"Nope, but he scared me some. I didn't like him."

"Why?"

"He had mean eyes. I don't like people with mean eyes. They not nice to me." Abruptly his face broke into a wide grin.

"And he had a black mustache that curled out past his ears. Looked like he was wearing little bitty longhorns on his top lip. He got mad when I laughed."

Thomas frowned. That might have described one of the men watching Prudence at the depot in Indianapolis. Thomas had not studied him well, but he remembered one of the men had hair on his face. If he was a friend of Marsh's, he had come a long way for a dead man. Was it chance that brought him to town the same day that Prudence arrived? Was he tracking her?

Or him?

Twenty-one

Pru braced herself as she went down the hotel stairs the following morning, fearing her friends would be waiting to pounce on her with questions they hadn't had a chance to ask at Sunday dinner.

Except for Yancey, dozing on his stool behind the front desk, the lobby was empty. She let out a relieved breath and tiptoed toward the double front doors.

"Not so fast, missy."

Drat. She had hoped to talk to Thomas first.

Showing his few teeth in a wide yawn, the old man pointed a gnarled finger at the closed dining room doors. "They're waitin'." With a look of sympathy, he added, "Good luck."

Waiting, indeed.

In addition to the usual inquisitors—her sister and Lucinda—Audra Hardesty sat at the corner table, pad and pencil at hand to take down every salient detail for the Wednesday edition. The only ones missing were the English-woman with the amazing mismatched eyes, Mrs. Throckmorton, and dear Maddie Wallace. Pru missed her dearly.

"Waiting for me?" she asked with mock innocence as she wove her way through the empty tables.

"I think *most* of us"—Lucinda paused to shoot a knowing glance at Edwina—"have been remarkably patient, considering."

Pru leaned down to kiss her sister's cheek, then settled into the empty chair beside her. "Considering what?"

"Jail, Pru?" Edwina slapped her muffin onto her plate, sending crumbs in all directions. "Even Mama, as horrid as she was, never went to jail! Daddy must be tossing in his grave. He always had such high hopes for you."

Although her stomach was a bit unsettled, Pru accepted a cup of tea and a muffin from Lucinda. "Father had expectations for both of us."

"Don't be silly. I only had to marry well. But you carried the weight of an entire race on your shoulders. Did they beat you?"

Pru blinked at her sister. Edwina's conversations were often hard to follow. "Did who beat me?"

"Your jailers!" Edwina waved a hand for emphasis, almost upending the teapot. "I've had such nightmares, Pru. Was it awful?"

"Not as awful as it could have been, if Reverend Brother Sampson hadn't spoken on my behalf." Other than that one beating—retaliation, she suspected, for her uncooperative attitude toward that one vile interrogator. It hadn't hurt, either, that she had gained the protection of other inmates in exchange for lessons. "I was housed in the female section of a newer facility, built after the war. And although my accommodations were Spartan, they were clean, and the food was passable."

Tears glittering, Edwina put her hands over Pru's. "So you weren't starved? Or set upon by the other prisoners?"

"I was not." Only the guards were a danger.

"Who was this man you were supposed to have killed?"

"Cyrus Marsh." Pru explained about Marsh's association with the Quaker school and his interest in sending her and her initiative to Washington. She left out any mention of his threats, seeing no need to add to Edwina's fears now that the danger was past. "He wasn't a very pleasant man, but I certainly didn't want to kill him." Not really.

"Then you're free of all suspicion now?" Lucinda pressed.

"So it would seem." Thomas and Brother, too, thank heavens. Pressing a hand to her stomach, Pru pushed her cup and saucer aside. "It was all a misunderstanding. Once they found

Mr. Marsh's body and determined his death was accidental, the matter was dropped."

"Accidental, how?" Audra asked.

"He fell from the train."

"Like Tait." Edwina gave a shudder. "I heard about a man who fell from a train. The wheels quartered him like a chicken. What a mess that must have been."

Pru swallowed. "When Mr. Marsh fell, we were crossing a trestle."

"Lucky for him."

"Indeed." Pru saw Lucinda studying her over the rim of her cup and wondered what she was thinking. Hard experience had left the sharp-witted New Yorker slow to trust. Considering what the woman had suffered as a child, Pru didn't blame her.

"Hold long were you incarcerated?" Audra asked.

"Less than two months, although it seemed much longer." Seeing the woman write that down, Pru put a hand over her tablet. "Please. Is there any way we can keep this just between ourselves? I had hoped the children—especially Lillie—wouldn't have to find out."

Audra paused, then set down her pencil. "Of course."

Pru smiled her gratitude. Anxious to switch topics, she asked where Josephine Jessup was. Even though they had spent little time together the previous day, Pru hoped to become better friends with the pretty Englishwoman.

"At the school," her sister said. "The other teacher escaped, and she's taken over the task until you're ready to return."

This was the first Pru had heard of plans for her to teach again. "I'm so grateful Lillie is allowed to attend. She needs something to occupy her mind."

"Her and Joe Bill, both," Edwina muttered. "At least *she* seems to be doing well."

Lucinda patted Ed's shoulder in sympathy. "I think it helps that Thomas reads to Lillian every night from that special primer for blind people."

Surprised and pleased, Pru smiled as she swirled the leaves in the bottom of her cup. "Thomas is very good with children. He's a wonderful father."

"He also made her that blind stick she carries everywhere . . . as both an aid and a weapon, I fear." Laughing, Lucinda told them about Lillie's run-ins with her guardian. "Mrs. T. is convinced she can teach the child manners and proper diction. And it seems to be working. Between Mrs. T., Josie, and Thomas, the child is making remarkable progress. You'll be impressed with how hard she's worked."

Pru looked around. "Where is little Rosaleen?" She ached to hold her again. It had been so long since she'd cuddled a baby.

"Napping with Mrs. T."

"That's enough chitchat." Folding her arms on the tabletop, Edwina fixed her blue eyes on Pru with alarming intensity. "What exactly is going on between you and Thomas? He never smiles anymore and whenever we mention your name, he refuses to talk. Sometimes he gets downright nasty about it, doesn't he, Luce? And then as soon as word comes that you're heading home, he runs off into the mountains to do God knows what. Did something happen in Indiana? Are you together or not? And how does Lillie play into all of this? I almost tripped on my chin when he walked in with his 'daughter.' When did he get a daughter?"

"All right if I come in?"

Saved, praise the Lord.

Yancey peered around the dining room door. "Got a wire for Miss Pru."

Lucinda motioned for him to bring it in.

"Who's it from?" Edwina asked as Pru opened the envelope.

"The reverend in Indianapolis." Further words deserted her when she read the message. *"Man headed to HC about our friend. Be careful. Brother."*

Pru's stomach rose into her throat. She pressed a hand over her mouth.

"Sister, what's wrong?"

Stuffing the telegram into her pocket, Pru rose on trembling legs. "Lucinda, have any strangers taken rooms over the last several days?"

"A Bible salesman, two men who work for the railroad, and a gentleman from Indiana who looks like an undertaker. Ghastly mustache."

Panic left Pru breathless. "Where's Tait?" Lucinda's husband was a lawyer. If anyone could get Thomas out of this mess, he could.

"In his office, going over plans for the new lodge with Ethan. Why?"

"I need him. Now."

As Lucinda hurried from the room, the other two women rose in alarm, both talking at once.

Pru held up her hands. "All I know is that a man is coming to question Thomas. I don't know why or about what. But I have to warn him." She rushed to the door, almost plowing into Tait Rylander as he walked in, followed closely by Ethan Hardesty.

Tait put out a hand to steady her. "What's wrong?"

"Thomas may be in trouble. Hurry. I'll explain on the way to the sheriff's office."

Edwina grabbed her wrap from the back of her chair. "Declan's at the mercantile, loading supplies for the ranch. I'll get him, too."

"And I'll bring my double Derringer," Lucinda called after her.

Tait swung toward her. "You will not!"

But his wife was already rushing out the door.

Thomas was putting the finishing touches on Lillian's flute when the door to the sheriff's office burst open and the Rylanders rushed in, followed by Prudence and then the Hardestys.

Seeing their alarm alarmed him. He rose, knife ready. "What is wrong?"

Tait stepped forward, Prudence on his heels. "Quick, Thomas. Give me your badge."

"Why?"

Prudence grabbed his arm. "A man is here looking for you. Maybe one of the men watching us at the station in Indianapolis. You have to leave." She tried to pull him toward the door.

He did not move. "What are you afraid of?"

"He wants to question you."

"I know."

She stopped tugging. "You do?"

"He came yesterday. I was gone. I expect he will come again today."

"Then you have to hide!" She looked around, panic in her eyes.

Behind her, Ethan Hardesty peered out the window, his

hand on the butt of the gun in his holster. Tait Rylander checked the rifles in the rack on the wall while his wife peeked into the cells in back, a useless pocket pistol in her hand. Audra Hardesty sat on a stool in the corner, scribbling in her tablet.

"What are you white people doing?"

"Trying to protect you."

Prudence let go of his arm and fumbled with his badge. "Give this to Tait. We'll pretend he's the sheriff. If this man is one of those who was at the station in Indiana, he'll be looking for an Indian, not a white man."

"No." He pushed her trembling hands away before she ripped his shirt.

"Thomas, you have to!" Her face twisted. Tears rose in her eyes.

Which alarmed him even more. Prudence rarely lost her composure.

The door burst open again. This time it was the Brodies. Declan had a gun in his belt and Edwina looked frantic. But she often did. The office was so crowded now, he would not be able to throw his knife without nicking one of them.

"Do you expect a war?" he asked.

Brodie scowled at him. "That's it? A knife? That's all you've got?"

"It is all I need."

"You can't be a sheriff without a gun. It's . . ." He searched for a word.

"Unseemly?" Audra Hardesty supplied, without looking up.

"More like stupid."

Thomas did not understand what they were talking about, nor did he care. He sat down again. "I do not need to hide. Or for you to protect me. You will all go away. Except for you, Prudence. I will talk to you now."

The others milled around for a moment, then Rylander herded them out the door. "We'll watch for him outside."

"That is not nece—" The door slammed closed on his words.

Prudence sank into the chair across the desk, one hand pressed to her stomach. "Yes, it is necessary, Thomas. You don't want to go to jail."

He watched her struggle to calm her shaking hands. Her fear

was a real thing that hung in the air between them. A fear he had brought to her. Instead of protecting her by killing Marsh, he had put her in more danger. Guilt clawed at him when he thought of Prudence in a cage. "Did they hurt you, *Eho'nehevehohtse*?"

She looked up.

"Your jailers. Did they hurt you?"

She shook her head. "It was more frightening than painful. And humiliating."

"Do not be afraid. I will not let him take you back."

She waved his words away. "It's not me I'm worried about. He's coming to question you, not me. Brother sent a telegram, warning me. Apparently, someone has been asking about you in Indianapolis. Do you know why?"

Perhaps the steward told them Thomas was on board when Marsh died. Or Bessie Prescott admitted that he had left as soon as the train pulled away. If so, he might have a war on his hands after all. He would not let this man take Prudence away. And he would not go, either. He would die before he let anyone lock him in a jail cell again. But he did not tell her all that. "Do not worry so much."

"But he could be here soon, Thomas. What are we going to do?"

We. Did that mean she had finally accepted him, now that it might be too late? With that thought, the anger he had stored for so long drained away. Resentment faded. All that remained was the raw emotion he always felt when he was with this woman.

"Why did you leave us, Prudence?"

She frowned at him. "Now? You want to talk about that now?"

"Yes."

She brushed a hand over her brow and sighed. "Marsh said if I didn't go with him to Washington, he would put you in jail for taking Lillie and send her back in the asylum forever. I didn't know what else to do."

"You could have trusted me to protect you."

"And watch you die or go to jail if you failed? No. I couldn't take that risk."

"It was my risk to take. Not yours. And I would gladly have taken it."

"I know. That's why I did what Marsh told me to do. Losing you would have . . ." Words failed her. With the hem of her skirt, she dabbed at her eyes. Then, smoothing the cloth back over her knees, she gave him a small, nervous smile. "Now I have a question for you. Why haven't you told anyone we're married?"

He shrugged. "I was not sure we still were."

"Why wouldn't we be?" A stricken look came over her face. "Does that mean you don't want to stay married to me?"

"It was you who walked away, Prudence, not me."

She seemed to shrink back into the chair.

He almost went to her then. The need to hold her burned inside him. But doubt remained, and there were still questions she needed to answer. "Once you knew Marsh was dead, why did you not come to us then?"

"Because Brother convinced me not to." She sounded weary. Defeated. "He thought if I left the train the same time Marsh disappeared, it would arouse suspicion. He convinced me we should continue on to Washington and I should make my presentation." A frown drew her dark brows together. "Which is why I don't understand why this man has come here now. Once they found Marsh's body and decided his death was accidental, all charges against Brother and me were dropped. So why is he here?"

"I will ask him."

"Please, Thomas." Her voice trembled as more tears gathered. "If you let Tait wear your badge and pretend to be you, this man will think he has the wrong Thomas Redstone and leave you alone. Then we can talk through all of this."

"I will not bring dishonor on myself by hiding behind my friends."

"How can you be so stubborn?!" Lurching to her feet, she loomed over the desk, tears and fury glistening in her eyes. "This isn't just about you and me anymore, Thomas. There's Lillie, too. She's our daughter now. She needs both of us. She *chose* both of us. And it's our duty to be the parents she needs to be."

He shot from the chair. "Do not tell me my duty, Prudence! Who has watched over her these last months? Me! Her *only* parent for too long!"

She glared at him, her expression as fierce as any warrior's, her beauty shining like a light from within. "I would have been here if I could."

How many times had he heard that excuse.

Voices rose outside. In a lightning move, Thomas leaped from behind the desk and positioned himself between her and the door. "Go into the back," he ordered, giving her a gentle push with the hand not gripping his knife.

"No."

"Prudence—"

The door opened.

Brodie stepped in, a confused look on his face. When he saw the knife in Thomas's hand, he silently motioned for him to put it away. When Thomas reluctantly put it back into his belt, Declan allowed a man with a bulging documents case to enter. As others came in behind him, Tait Rylander moved to Thomas's side.

"Let me do the talking," he said in a low voice.

"This fellow"—Declan hooked a thumb at the stranger—"was sent by an Indiana senator named Brooks, asking about a blind girl named Lillian."

Thomas studied the small man with the pointed mustache. He let out the breath he had been holding. This was not one of the men he had seen at the Indianapolis train station. "Lillian Redstone. My daughter."

With a hiss of irritation, Pru stepped out from behind Thomas. "*Our* daughter," she corrected, with a glare at her husband.

Audra wrote furiously.

Small eyes that were less brown than muddy moved over Pru in an intrusive way. His lips pursed and unpursed, making the lacquered ends of his absurd mustache—obviously dyed with henna, since the hair of his sideburns was gray—bob up and down like the wings of tiny black bird.

Not a lawman, she guessed. More like a courthouse bureaucrat.

"And who might you be?" he asked Pru in an officious tone.

She glanced at Thomas, wondering if he would admit to their marriage, but he said nothing. "Her mother. And you are . . . ?"

"Virgil Squibb, solicitor." He gave a nod so slight it verged on insult. "It was my understanding . . . ma'am . . . that it was Mr. Redstone, here, who took the child from the Riverbend

School for the Disabled in Indianapolis. Are you now admitting you took part in that abduction?"

"Abduction?" Edwina gave a trilling laugh that sounded close to hysteria.

Audra flipped to a clean page. "Is that 'Squibb' with two *B*s?"

Ignoring them both, Pru stepped forward. "Lillian was *delivered* to Mr. Redstone. By the school. As ordered by the late Cyrus Marsh, who—"

"Please," Tait interrupted. "I'll handle this." He turned to the solicitor. Hard gray eyes clashed with muddy brown. "May I ask what your interest in the child might be, Mr. Squibb?"

"Who are you?"

"Tait Rylander. I represent the Redstone family, which, of course, includes the child in question. Their daughter." He gave a smile that had doubtless struck fear into many an opponent— in either a boardroom or a courtroom. "And whom do you represent?"

Squibb drew himself up, although he still fell far short of Rylander's tall frame, and looked almost childlike beside Declan Brodie, who loomed behind him. "I am here at the behest of Leonard Brooks, Indiana state senator and sitting member on the Board of Trustees of the Riverbend School for the Disabled."

Tait didn't appear impressed. "And *his* interest in this matter is . . . what?"

"The child's welfare, of course." Squibb dug through his documents, pulled out a letter, and read, "'*In regards to Mr. Redstone's illegal removal of the disabled child in question—Lillian, last name unknown—from the protection of the State of Indiana and the Riverbend School for the Disabled, please instruct him to release the child into the custody of Virgil Squibb, representative of the aforementioned school.*'" With a flourish, he shoved the paper back into his case. "I also have a Statement of Special Education Needs issued by the administrator."

"May I see that, sir?" Audra asked.

He ignored her.

"The only things I would like to see," Tait said in a cold voice, "are any *legal* documents issued by the court. Subpoenas, summons, warrants, orders, jurisdiction and enforcement notices—whatever you have in that bag of yours that is material to this case."

Color flooded Squibb's face. "There is no case, per se. Not yet. And there will be none, if Mr. Redstone returns the child to the proper authorities."

Ethan straightened from his slouched position beside the door. Lucinda drew her pistol from her pocket. Brodie narrowed his eyes. "Is that a threat, Squid?"

The man's cheeks lost their rosy hue. "Of course not. And it's *Squibb*."

Tait waved Declan and Ethan away. "Then I ask again, Mr. *Squibb*. On what legal grounds do you ask Mr. Redstone to give up his daughter?"

Thomas's patience snapped. "I will not do it! Ever! Leave now!"

Pru put a hand on his arm. Being a man of action rather than words, Thomas had lasted longer than she'd thought he would.

Tait sent the Cheyenne a silent warning.

Pru added her own by squeezing his arm.

Muttering words she didn't know—which was probably best—Thomas jerked free of her grip, stomped around his desk, and plopped into his chair. "White people." With an air of disgusted indifference, he pulled out his knife and began cleaning his nails.

Declan relaxed. Ethan leaned back against the wall beside the door. Audra shook out a cramp in her hand.

But Pru wasn't fooled. She knew Thomas was acutely aware of all that went on around him. He probably just wanted a reason to get out his knife.

"Well, Mr. Squibb?" Rylander pressed. "Why should he give her up?"

The solicitor tore his gaze from the ten-inch blade in Thomas's hand. "Because he took custody of the girl under false pretenses. He is not the child's father, no matter what he or the child says. And it is illegal for unmarried persons, especially males"—he punctuated this with a glare at Thomas—"to adopt orphans. If he gives her up—"

"No!" Thomas shouted, leaping to his feet. His arm shot out. A *thunk* as the knife struck. "She is my daughter!"

Silence. They all gaped at the blade quivering in the front wall. Then with a cry, the solicitor dropped his case. Papers flew everywhere. "My God! He tried to kill me! Did you see? That savage attacked me!"

Declan snorted. "If he'd attacked you, you'd be dead by now."

"And good riddance," his wife seconded.

With a huff, Lucinda waved the hand still holding her double Derringer. "This is complete and utter nonsense. Tait, tell him."

"Only if you put that away, sweetheart."

Mumbling to herself, she complied.

With shaking hands, Squibb bent to gather his papers. By the time he had stuffed them back into his case, Tait had restored order.

"No one will be killing anyone, Mr. Squibb," he said with a strained smile. "But perhaps it would be best if we continued this discussion in the privacy of my office at the hotel."

"Oh, for heaven's sake," Pru burst out. "There is no discussion to be had!" Hands on hips, she rounded on Thomas. "Are you going to tell them, or shall I?"

He crossed his arms.

"Fine!" She faced the others. "Lillie's adoption is entirely legal, and was signed by Judge Kohler in the Indianapolis courthouse. I have the papers to prove it."

"Then the judge was misinformed, ma'am," Squibb snapped. "Or defrauded. As I stated earlier, unmarried persons are not allowed to adopt—"

"We are married, you cretin! And I have the certificate to prove that, as well!"

Gasps, cries, expressions of shock. Even Audra stopped writing to gape at her. And her sister, bless her heart, broke into sobs—not happy ones, either.

"Good Lord!" Pru raised her hands in exasperation, then let them fall back to her sides. "Truly? You're that surprised that we married?"

"It's not that," Edwina wailed. "It's that you did it without us!"

Twenty-two

To avoid further hysterics, Tait left the others in the sheriff's office and marched Pru, Thomas, and Mr. Squibb down to the hotel. There, behind the locked door of his office, they discussed the matter calmly and rationally. Even so, and despite having documents proving she and Thomas were married and Lillie's adoption was legal—Pru had spent three days sitting outside Judge Kohler's office to make certain of that—it still took hours for Mr. Squibb to agree in writing to relinquish all interest in Lillie. Tait's legal expertise aside, the deciding factor was when Thomas—who had remained sullenly silent throughout—leaned over and whispered in the solicitor's ear that he would put his knife in his throat if he did not put his mark on Tait's paper and leave. Now.

Pru was utterly exhausted. With Thomas contributing little to the debate beyond scowls and snorts, she felt she was fighting this battle alone. She had sensed him watching her throughout the long discussion, but his stony face revealed nothing of what he was thinking. Was he upset that she had blurted out that they were married? Was he sorry he was now permanently burdened with a wife and child?

She had reservations herself—the same ones that had plagued her from the beginning. After all they had been through together, they were still so far apart in culture, religion, expectations, she wondered if they would ever find a common ground, other than Lillie.

"Are you well, Pru?"

She looked up to see Tait eyeing her with concern.

"You didn't eat much of the lunch I had sent in."

Aware of Thomas studying her, she put on a smile. "I'm just tired. It's been a very exciting, troubling, emotional few days."

"Perhaps you should go rest. I'll tell Mrs. Bradshaw to send up a tray later, so you don't even have to come down for supper. How does that sound?"

"Wonderful." She hadn't the energy to be interrogated by Thomas again, or answer Lillie's questions, or put on a happy face for her concerned friends. She just wanted to sleep. "Thomas, please reassure Lillie and tell her I'll talk to her tomorrow. And Tait," she added with a weary smile as she pushed herself out of her chair, "you're a brilliant lawyer, and we couldn't be more grateful. We must owe you a fortune."

"You're family. But a signed copy of Thomas's book would be nice."

Pru looked at Thomas.

He nodded.

"Then you shall have it. Good day, gentlemen."

Luck was with her, and she made it all the way to her room without her inquisitors finding her. As soon as the door closed behind her, she collapsed face-first on the bed, clothes and all. But she barely had a chance to close her eyes before the door opened again. Rising onto her elbows, she looked over to see Thomas standing in the doorway.

He held up her reticule. "You left this in Tait's office."

"Thank you," she said weakly and dropped her cheek to the pillow again. "Put it on the bureau."

She heard the door close, then rustling, then felt hands fumbling with the buttons up the side of her high-top walking shoes. She reared up. "What—"

"Be still," Thomas murmured.

A minute later, the boots and stockings were off and warm, strong hands began massaging her tired feet. She floated in bliss.

"Roll over."

He had to help her, and soon those talented hands had undressed her down to her chemise and had moved up to pull the pins from her hair. After he slipped the counterpane from beneath her and covered her to her chin, he sat on the edge of the bed.

"Prudence. Listen to me."

She forced open her eyes.

"I will tell *Katse'e* we are man and wife now, and that by the white man's law, she is our daughter forever. Tomorrow, you will move to the Arlan house, and there we will live as a family. But until you decide if we can make a life together, I will not ask you to live with me as my wife." His rough hand cupped her cheek. Sadness clouded his eyes. "We still have much to talk about, *Eho'nehevehohtse*. But for now, sleep. *Nestaevaho-sevoomatse*. I will see you again."

A light kiss on her mouth, and he was gone.

Pru slept like the dead, rousing only to eat a light supper from the tray Mrs. Bradshaw brought up, then sleeping again. At dawn, she awoke feeling like a new woman, and other than a headache and a slight queasiness from not eating enough the day before, she felt ready to take on the day. After a cold wash in the bowl atop the bureau, she dressed and quickly packed her valise for her move to the Arlan house. The sun was just peeking over the ridges when she hurried downstairs to go meet Thomas at his office.

She tiptoed past the dozing desk clerk and had almost reached the front doors when a familiar voice rang out, stopping Pru dead in her tracks and bringing Yancey awake with a start that almost toppled him from his stool.

"And where do you think you're going?" Her sister stood in the doorway of the dining room, hands on hips, Lucinda and Rosie at her shoulder.

Pru let out the breath she had been holding. "Did you stay awake all night, watching for me?"

Lucinda sniffed. "New mothers don't sleep."

"You have some explaining to do, Sister." Edwina waved her toward the dreaded corner table.

Leaving her valise under Yancey's watchful eye, which was only slightly safer than flinging it directly into the street, Pru dutifully followed her interrogators to the dining room. "Doesn't anyone in town eat breakfast anymore?" she asked, eyeing the empty tables. Before she'd left for Indiana, the dining room had been busy every morning.

Lucinda took her usual place by the window and gently settled her sleeping daughter into a wheeled bassinet by her chair. "Since the railroad workers left, we're only open for breakfast on the weekends. And don't try to change the subject."

Pru took the chair across from her. "What was the subject?"

"And don't be coy." With a swish of her skirts, Edwina plopped into the chair beside her. "Start talking."

"Can I at least have something to eat first? I'm starving."

"I've already alerted Cook," Lucinda told her. "It should be out soon."

Edwina plunked her half-finished muffin in front of her. "Start on this. Declan wants to leave for the ranch today, so I don't have much time." She sat back, arms crossed. "Everything. From the beginning."

Not surprisingly, they were less interested in Marsh and his threats, her work in Schuler, or even her education initiative, than in what was going on between her and Thomas and Lillie. Pru told them all she felt comfortable revealing—sisters didn't need to know *everything*, no matter how nosy they were. Most of it they had already heard from Thomas or guessed on their own.

Her food arrived. While Pru dug in to the delicious breakfast Cook had prepared, Edwina continued the questioning.

"So why did you keep sending him away?"

"No man deserves to be rejected so summarily," Lucinda added with a scolding look. "I don't blame him for being angry with you."

"You don't love him," Edwina accused. "That's why you wouldn't come back with him, isn't it?"

"Of course I love him!" Pru slapped jelly on her toast, wishing she were slapping her sister instead. "Thomas is the finest man I know. But I explained about my work and how important—"

"Nonsense! It's because of Lone Tree, isn't it?"

The toast fell to her plate. "What?"

"It's because of what happened to you in the Indian camp and what that vile Arapaho did to you. You can't bear to have Thomas touch you." Her sister's indignation gave way to rising tears. "Oh, Pru. I wish you could forget. I wish I could kill him for you all over again."

"You didn't kill him the first time," Lucinda reminded her. "It was the seventy-foot fall that did him in."

"*After* I hit him with the shovel." Edwina paused, a distant look in her blue eyes. "It made the most amazing sound— almost musical—when it struck his head. Like a bell, only twangier. I remember it so clearly."

Lucinda gave the Southerner a wary look.

Pru, being more accustomed to her sister's strange drifts off subject, let it pass. "Lone Tree didn't rape me, if that's what you're insinuating." Lifting her cup, she took a sip, pleased by the matter-of-fact tone in her voice. In the past, simply speaking his name would have sent her into panic, but now, she scarcely felt a thing. "The rape happened years earlier."

She blinked, shocked by her own words. Where had that come from? She hadn't thought of Black Sam in years. Realizing her hand was shaking, she set her cup back into the saucer. Seeing the faces gaping at her from across the table, she looked away and tried to calm the pounding of her heart.

Edwina found her voice first. "You were raped earlier? How much earlier? And by whom?"

Pru pressed both hands against her stomach, sorry she had eaten so much. "It was a long time ago."

"Answer me, Pru!"

Pru closed her eyes, saw that sweating, leering, snarling face above hers, and snapped them open again.

"Who?"

"Black Sam."

"But . . . the slave who ran the smithy? He raped you?" When Pru nodded, Edwina slumped back in her chair, one hand at her throat. "I remember the way he looked at us. He scared me. I knew he hated us, but . . . he *raped* you?"

"He did. His way of showing me that I was no better than him, even if I had white blood."

"Oh, Pru . . ." Tears brimmed again. "Why didn't you tell anyone?"

Pru pushed away her plate, appetite gone. "I was afraid of what Father might do. To me and to him. He probably would have hanged Black Sam. Or worse. Father was mostly a fair man, but I'd seen the whippings. Heard the cries and pleas when the overseer uncoiled his rope. I hear them, still."

"Father only punished them if they deserved it."

"Deserved it how? By being Negro?" A lifetime of bitterness left a vile taste in Pru's throat. "I was barely twelve when it happened. But even then, I knew I was treated better than the other coloreds. Educated, fed, clothed like a white. But whenever they looked at me, I knew it was a lie. I hate what Black Sam did to me. I still wake up with night terrors. But they had all suffered so much. Even him. Every day as a slave was a misery for them. I couldn't add to it."

Edwina dashed the tears from her eyes. "That's not fair! How were they miserable? Daddy wasn't cruel to his people. And he did everything he could for you. I don't understand why you're saying such mean things about him."

Pru put her hand over her sister's. "I loved Father, too. And I'm eternally grateful for all he gave me. But the world isn't always a fair place, Sister. People look at you and see a beautiful woman with a smile that lights up a room. They look at me and see an uppity colored stepping above her station. Same father. Same advantages. Same hopes and dreams. But viewed totally differently because of the color of our skin." She shrugged. "Maybe that'll change someday. I hope so."

Pru doubted Edwina would ever completely understand what it meant to be Negro. Or a slave. Where she loved, she loved completely. It truly didn't matter to her that her sister was mulatto. And Pru cherished her for that.

But Lucinda was Irish. She had seen much of the same ugliness Pru had. And although she might have clawed her way out of the foulest Irish hellhole and brothel district in New York, remnants of that cruel treatment still showed in her lovely green eyes.

"I understand all you've said here, Pru," Lucinda said now. "And I'm deeply saddened that you had to suffer. But there's one thing I'm confused about. If Lone Tree didn't force you, why were you so upset when you came back?"

Edwina nodded in agreement. "You were a mess. Wouldn't talk to anyone. Not even me. If you weren't raped, why were you so devastated?"

Pru wished Maddie were here. Maddie never judged, never criticized, and always found a better way to look at things. "It's complicated. I don't know if I can explain it so it would make sense."

"Try."

She thought for a moment. "As I said, Lone Tree didn't rape me, although he did make the attempt. Repeatedly. I think because he drank alcohol all day, he was incapable. And every time he tried and failed, it was my fault. He beat me. Kicked me. Treated me worse than the lowest dog." She looked down at the hand over her stomach and felt that empty ache that never seemed to go away. "I think he damaged something inside that prevents me from conceiving."

"No!" Edwina cried. "I don't believe it. You can't know that for certain until you and Thomas . . ."

Her voice trailed off when she saw Pru shake her head. "We have. Several times. And nothing has happened. I bled for a long time after I left the camp. Then I had terribly irregular courses. Now, I have none at all."

"Oh, dearest." Edwina leaned over to give her a hard hug, then sat back and wiped her face. "That bastard! I hated him before, but now I'm so glad I killed him."

"I'm glad he's dead, too. He was vermin. Less than human. But in some ways, what he did to me wasn't as bad as what the rest of his tribe did."

"What did they do?"

"Nothing."

Edwina blinked round blue eyes. "Nothing? No one tried to help you or stop Lone Tree?"

Pru shook her head. "They went about their lives as if my suffering was inconsequential. Beneath their notice." She gave a broken laugh. "Oh, a few of them jeered. One or two even sat and watched for a while. But most went by without even looking my way."

Long-buried anger rose, erupting from her body in the

shaking of her hands and the rawness of her voice. "I know whites and Indians have done terrible things to each other. I understand hatred and resentment. I saw it in Black Sam, and on the faces of whites who wanted to blame me for all that they lacked. But to be treated as if I didn't exist? As if my life and suffering were meaningless?"

Unclenching her fingers, she pressed her hands flat against her thighs. "That hurt. Worse than you can know. And at that moment, I finally realized what had driven Black Sam to do what he did. And what being a slave truly meant—the help-lessness, the humiliation, the degradation. And I resolved to do something about it."

Edwina looked at her in confusion.

But Pru could see that Lucinda understood. "That's when you decided to teach freed slaves," she guessed. "And what has prevented you from making a life with Thomas. You felt your work was more important."

Pru gave her a grateful smile. She felt she had been swim-ming upstream for so long, but finally, someone understood.

"*Is* your work more important?" Edwina asked.

"For a time, it was. But I've done all I can do. I brought my proposal to Washington. If it's worthy, someone else can take it and fly."

"And Thomas?"

Pru shrugged. "I don't know. He's a remarkable man. I don't think I could ever love anyone but him. But we're different on so many levels. How do we bridge the divide between us?"

"If you love him enough, you can."

Pru waved that away. "The question isn't whether we love each other enough. It's how much of ourselves we're willing to give up to close the gap."

"Seems like he's come farther over that bridge than you," Lucinda observed as she refilled her cup.

Pru frowned. "What do you mean?"

Lucinda took a sip, then returned the cup to its saucer. "What have you done for Thomas, except finally return to Heartbreak Creek?"

The barb struck deep. Did they truly expect her to live in a tipi and chew buffalo hides? "You think I'm being unfair to him?"

"Don't you?" Edwina burst out. "He's hardly Indian anymore. He's cut his hair, taken a job, given up most of his Cheyenne ways. He's even written a book! How much farther does Thomas have to go to close that gap before you'll even take the first step?"

Pru was so shocked she couldn't respond.

In her bassinet, Rosie began to fuss.

Seeing Pru's distress, Edwina made a dismissive motion. "I don't mean to sound harsh, Sister. But think about it. Thomas did everything he could to make himself worthy of you. Yet you sent him away. Now he's struggling to build a life—a *civilized* life—for him and Lillie, even though that means giving up most of who he is. And you still say that's not good enough."

"I never said that."

"You don't have to. Your actions speak for you."

"Now who's being unfair?"

"Stop it, you two!" Lucinda glared at them, tears streaming as she bounced her fussing daughter. "Now you've got me crying and you've upset Rosie. Forget everything I said. I was wrong. All of it. I can't bear it when you fight."

"Oh, Luce." Edwina bounded from her chair to give her and Rosie a hug. "We're sisters. We don't mean any of it, do we, Pru?"

"Of course not." Keeping her head down, Pru blinked tears from her eyes so she could see the dial of the watch pinned in her skirt pocket. "Mercy," she said with false gaiety to cover the hurt. "It's after ten. I must go. I told Thomas we would talk more today." As she pushed back her chair, she sensed movement behind her and turned.

Then froze.

Thomas stood in the dining room doorway.

His eyes met hers, dark and impenetrable. Then, without a sound, he turned and left the hotel.

Thomas was sorting through the day's mail and trying to come to terms with what he had heard when Prudence burst through the door. She stopped, one hand still on the knob, her eyes wide with panic, her lashes still damp with tears.

"What is wrong?" he asked.

She studied him, as if trying to read his thoughts, then let out a deep breath and closed the door. "How much did you hear?"

He went back to his mail. "Enough to know they should not have said those things to you." *And to finally know what happened to you in the Arapaho camp.*

"And if they were right?"

"One right thing does not make a whole truth." He set the papers aside. Poor Prudence. She wanted everything neat and tidy like the tintypes Maddie Wallace made—stark and colorless, bound by a clean, defined border. There was a reason many of the People thought photographs stole their spirits: in a single moment, everything that had gone before, and everything that was yet to come, was reduced to a single, flat, unchangeable image.

But life was messy and confusing. It required a person to change in many ways if he was to survive. And some had to change more than others.

He motioned to the chair in front of his desk. "Sit, Prudence."

With a look of defeat, she sank into the chair.

Not wanting barriers between them, he pulled his chair from behind the desk and put it near hers, then sat. Leaning forward with his elbows on his knees, he took her hands in his. He had much to say, and it took him a moment to gather his thoughts.

"*Eho'nehevehohtse*, I will not ask you to live in a tipi . . . although it would not upset me if you spent a night or two in one. With me. Alone."

She rewarded him with a small smile. It gave him hope.

"And I did not put aside my eagle feathers only to please you. Nor have I put them aside forever. It is not my hair, or my clothing, or the redness of my skin that makes me who I am. It is what is in my heart."

He brought a hand to his chest. "*Na'tsehe'stahe*—I am Cheyenne. I am also part white, a sheriff, a warrior, a father, maybe still a husband, and a man who has made mistakes." He let his hand fall back over hers. "But I know I must change—not *who* I am, but the way I live—if I am to understand this new world around me. I can do that."

A tear rolled from her eye. He reached out and brushed it away, then took her hands in his again. They felt cold, and soft, and fragile. Yet the pulse beneath his fingertips at her wrists was strong and steady . . . just as this woman was.

"Your friends tell you I have worked harder than you to cross the space between us. They are right. Perhaps I have had farther to go. Or, because I am stronger, I must take the harder path. I do not know. It is not important, anyway. As long as you take a single step toward me, then I will know someday we will come to a meeting point. One step. That is all I need from you."

Her lips quivered on a smile, even as another tear left a trail down her cheek. "Please tell me I won't have to chew buffalo hides."

"I will not ask you to do that. Nor will I ask you to join with me on a horse."

Her eyes widened. "What?"

"It is uncomfortable. And the horse does not like it."

"You're jesting."

He looked at her and smiled.

Some of the stiffness eased from her shoulders. "What is this one step you do ask of me?"

His amusement faded. "It is a big one, Prudence. And it will be hard for you to take. You must think well before you make your decision."

Thomas worried that he was expecting too much of her too soon. But better they face it now than later, when it would be harder to break away.

"I do not believe in your Christ, *Eho'nehevehohtse*. To the People, all life comes from the same Creator, and all things share the same breath, whether it is man or beast or the grass beneath our feet. And no one man stands for us before the Great Spirit. Can you accept that I am not Christian?"

She looked at him for a long time. "But you do believe in a power higher than yourself?"

"Yes. We call it by many names—Great Spirit, Creator, *Ma'heo'o*. We regard Heaven as our father, and Earth as our mother, and all things in between as our brothers and sisters. As I told Reverend Brother Sampson, we are all one child spinning through Mother Sky."

Another long pause, then a sigh. "I'll consider all that you've said, Thomas. But I'm beginning to think we're not that different, after all."

"That is my hope." He released her and sat back, hands tucked beneath his crossed arms so she would not see them shaking. "I also heard you tell them what happened to you in the Arapaho camp. I wish you had told me, Prudence. I wish I could take those memories from your mind and heal the scars in your heart. But I cannot. I can only love you. And hold you when the terrors rise in the night. And try to keep you safe from any harm yet to come."

She was weeping like a child now, her breath coming in hoarse, hitching sobs. Yet she was not pulling away from him and he took heart in that.

He waited for her to calm her tears, then spoke again. "It is also my hope, Prudence, that you will stop crying so much. I do not like it and it will upset our daughter. She becomes upset enough as it is."

"That's two things. But okay." Another tear dropped, even as her lips spread in a smile. "Now I have something to ask of you."

He nodded and braced himself. He would do much—give up much—to have this woman in his life. But still, he had to remain true to himself.

"If we decide to stay together, will you marry me again? In the church? So all our friends can be there?"

He closed his eyes and pictured it. The people—the crying and singing—*Katse'e* bouncing on her toes and waving her stick—that preacher, spewing damnation and tearing at his hair. He would almost rather go through the Sun Dance ceremony again.

Almost.

He opened his eyes and looked on her beautiful, tear-stained face. How could he deny this woman anything when she looked at him like that?

"Yes, *Eho'nehevehohtse*," he conceded, although it wasn't much of a concession at all. "But that will be the last time we marry."

Twenty-three

"You got married without me?" Lillie accused when Thomas brought Prudence to the house later that afternoon. "If you my mama, I 'posed be there, ain't I?"

"Aren't I."

"She is upset," Thomas murmured, setting down Pru's valise. "Usually she speaks better."

"And who's this?" Pru struggled to fend off a gangly puppy pawing at her skirt. "If we marry again, Lillie, I promise you will be there."

"And I can sing? I always want to sing at a wedding."

"Of course. I would have no other. Down, boy! And you'll have a new Sunday dress and white bows in your hair and flowers in your hands. Will somebody call off this dog?"

"Bitsy," Thomas said in a low, firm voice.

The dog immediately dropped to his haunches and stared up at him with tongue-flopping devotion. As well he should.

"You named him Bitsy?" Pru laughed. "Ash will be so proud."

"That reminds me." Thomas pulled an envelope from his shirt pocket. "This came today. I told the Western Union man I would give it to you, but then . . . I forgot." No need to mention his shock when he heard the women talking about him and heard what Pru had endured. He still couldn't come to terms with all of it.

"Is it from Ash? What does it say?"

He handed it to her. "You open it."

She read Rayford Jessup's name on the envelope and tried to hand it back. "It's not addressed to me."

"That did not stop your sister and Lucinda Rylander from opening my box of books."

She opened the envelope. Pulling out the note, she read, then grinned. "They're coming home!" She read the words aloud. *"'Will arrive by month's end. House better be ready. Kirkwell.'"* Laughing, she hugged Thomas, then Lillian, then raced toward the door. "I have to tell Luce and Ed!"

"You leavin' already!"

"I'll be back soon, Lillie. I promise."

"What Daddy do this time?"

Thomas ignored her. "Should you not tell Jessup first, since the telegram was sent to him?"

But she was already rushing down the porch steps. "I'll return soon."

"Miss Pru not a very nice mama to go runnin' off like that."

"She will be back."

"She gonna stay here now?"

"Yes."

"We'll be like a real family?"

"Yes." Eventually, he hoped.

"Who Ash?"

"Who *is* Ash," he corrected. "He is a man who wears a skirt, carries too many names, and speaks in a strange way." Thomas scooped up his daughter and walked toward the kitchen where Winnie stood at the stove, basting a roasting chicken. "His dog is father to Bitsy."

"So he my stepdaddy?"

"Exactly."

Winnie snorted. "You'll get in trouble, Mr. Thomas, saying things like that."

"I hope so. I have not fought anyone in a long time." He set Lillian back on her feet. "Look in my coat pocket, *Katse'e*. I made something for you."

Rising on her toes, she reached in and rooted around until she pulled out the flute Thomas had carved from the elk antler. "A stick? You gots me a stick?"

"A flute." He showed her where to blow and where to put her fingers over the holes. Soon the house echoed with high-pitched screeches and whistles. He must have done something wrong. He had never made a flute before.

Winnie told *Katse'e* to go take her flute to the porch, then sent Thomas a sour look.

He shrugged. "I would have made her rhythm sticks, but I thought she might hurt someone."

"So you let her make us deaf, instead. Good thinkin'."

When Pru rushed into the hotel, Yancey was crossing the lobby. Before she could ask, he pointed a finger at the closed dining room door. She veered toward it.

Since Lucinda had turned her office into a nursery, she often did her paperwork in the dining room before the staff set it up for the evening meal. Perhaps Edwina was still with her.

She wasn't. But Mrs. Bradshaw and Mrs. Throckmorton were.

Lucinda must have seen the excitement on her face when Pru rushed in. "What's happened?"

"Wonderful news!" Waving the telegram, Pru hurried toward them, then slowed when she saw the serious expressions on the women's faces and the way Mrs. Bradshaw hurriedly wiped her eyes. "Am I interrupting?" Pru made a half turn toward the door. "Perhaps I should come back later."

"Nonsense." Lucinda waved her to an empty chair. "Join us. We could use some happy news."

Reluctantly, Pru did. It was obvious she had walked in on a serious discussion. With an embarrassed nod to Mrs. Bradshaw— who was still fighting tears—Pru turned to Mrs. Throckmorton, who held the sleeping Rosaleen. "Aren't you the lucky one. She looks quite content in your arms, Mrs. Throckmorton. You must have a calming touch."

"So I've been told." The elderly lady sniffed in that haughty way she had, but Pru saw the smile teasing her lips. "I have a way with children. I always have. Ask Lucinda. I shudder to think what would have become of her if I hadn't taken her to my bosom."

Pru didn't dare look at Lucinda, fearing she might catch her in one of her sardonic eye rolls. Even though Luce and her guardian loved each other dearly, they did bring out the claws occasionally. Pru didn't want to get caught between them.

Lucinda poured a cup of tea and set it before Pru. "So what is this momentous news that sent you rushing in here?"

"A telegram from Ash." Unable to restrain her excitement, Pru thrust the envelope at her friend. "They're on their way and will arrive by month's end!"

Lucinda's face lit up as she read the wire. "At last! We shall have to plan a grand welcome."

"I wonder if he'll bring Pringle back with him?" Mrs. Throckmorton leaned toward Pru to add in a whisper, "He's been in love with me for years, you know. That's why I had to send him away with the Scotsman. It would never do to form an alliance with a servant, you see."

Abruptly, Mrs. Bradshaw rose. "I have to check with Cook about tonight's menu."

As the housekeeper disappeared through the door into the kitchen, Lucinda shot her guardian a severe look. "That was uncalled for, Mrs. T."

"I have no idea what you're talking about. Helen Bradshaw is a friend and erstwhile employee. I never thought of her as a servant. As for Buster Quinn, I had no idea he had a wife in a mental institution, or that he and Mrs. Bradshaw had developed feelings for each other. Had I known, I certainly never would have allowed him to accompany us from New York."

Pru blinked. *Wife in a mental institution?*

Lucinda stood, hands clenched at her side. "I think you judge him too harshly. And too soon. He'll be returning to town shortly. Until then, if you can manage it, please refrain from condemning the man until we hear his side of it. Now, if you will excuse me, I'll ask Yancey to fetch Edwina. Hopefully they haven't left for the ranch yet."

As Lucinda swept from the room, Mrs. Throckmorton sighed. "The child always was a woefully poor judge of character. That's why I had to save her from a disastrous marriage to that Irishman. I don't care how wealthy the man was, he was still a thug."

Pru wasn't sure how that related to Quinn or Mrs. Bradshaw. "Do you think she's misjudged Buster Quinn?" Pru scarcely knew the man. He and Mrs. Bradshaw had moved permanently to Heartbreak Creek with Mrs. Throckmorton after Pru had left for Indiana. But from what little she knew, he seemed honorable.

"Quinn?" The old woman reared back to glare at her. "Were you not listening? It was *my* character she was impugning. Insinuating I was a snob and looked down on Mrs. Bradshaw. Poppycock. As for Buster Quinn, he is above reproach, although he could certainly have been more forthright with dear Mrs. Bradshaw."

Pru was thoroughly confused now. "What did Mr. Quinn do?"

"I shouldn't say. I abhor gossip. But I assure you it was nothing illegal. Not yet, anyway. Luckily, he absconded before any real harm was done. There you are." She held Rosie out to Lucinda as she came back into the room. "You daughter has a definite odor."

Over the next days, Pru settled into the Arlan house, grew to love the Abrahams, and learned what a challenge it was to mother a blind ten-year-old who was smarter than she was. Her respect for Thomas and the Abrahams grew daily.

Having been passed around like unwanted baggage for most of her short life, Lillie had grown accustomed to scrabbling out her own place in this world, and was fearless in defending it. No matter that she had once been a slave, or that she was blind, and only a child, she refused to be ignored.

Pru adored her, and saw great promise in her future . . . once she learned to curb her demanding ways. She also suspected the child's often indecipherable speech was a form of self-protection. If she sounded ignorant, she would be discounted, which would leave her free to do things her own way, how and when she wished.

Pru wasn't fooled. But rather than browbeating the child into speaking properly—which Lillie's pride wouldn't allow—she gently corrected her without making an issue of it, then quietly moved on. At some point, Lillie would understand that Pru wasn't out to change her, but to help her find other ways of expressing herself. Words—well-spoken and understandable—would be more effective than broken speech and flailing the air with her blind stick.

She continued the lessons in the Braille primer and was astounded by the progress Thomas had already made with her. The evening readings continued, except—at his listener's insistence—Thomas read from his own book. It was an amazing story, and Pru understood why Rafe Jessup predicted Thomas would be famous someday. Not only were the words powerful and compelling, but when spoken in Thomas's low, musical voice, it touched something deep inside her.

As for her and Thomas, it felt almost as if they were courting. Glances, touches, smiles when no one else was looking, and evening walks along the creek that ended with long, breathless kisses. She often awoke from dreams of him to find small, simple gifts left beside her pillow. An eagle feather. A button carved from a shiny black stone. A rock that glittered with gold dust. And once a lethal-looking knife that fit into a beaded scabbard she was to tie around her waist under her skirt. There were other, less welcome gifts, too, but she guessed it was Harry, the cat, and not Thomas, who left the half-eaten mice by her bed.

The days warmed. The nights grew shorter. As Pru lay in her lonely bed, listening to him move around downstairs, washing and preparing for another night on the couch, she wondered why she was denying herself the closeness with Thomas she craved. Many times, she thought about going down there and telling him to stop this foolishness and come upstairs to bed like a normal husband.

But then the thought would come that maybe she wasn't the only one who had concerns about a future together. Maybe he had reservations, too.

Or, perhaps, he was waiting for her to court him.

So she tried that, cooking sumptuous meals, taking special care with her appearance, and waiting on the porch to welcome him home at the end of the day. She washed and mended his clothing, replaced missing buttons and turned the cuffs on his shirts. He accepted her offerings with a smile and a nod. Sometimes, she saw gentle laughter in his eyes. But still, at the end of the evening, he would follow her up the stairs to check on Lillie, give Pru one last kiss outside her bedroom door, then head back downstairs.

She was starting to unravel.

*   *   *

The month that whites called April came, and the first pink blossoms of wild phlox heralded the coming of the full Pink Moon. But still, Prudence did not come to him as he hoped.

Late one afternoon, he was in the side yard, putting Bitsy through his paces, when Prudence came through the front gate. Seeing him, she raised a hand in greeting and turned in his direction.

Motioning the dog to sit, he studied her. Even from this distance, he could see her steps dragged. Her hand was over her stomach again, and that nagging sense that something was wrong began to hum along his nerves.

He had heard what she had told Lucinda and Edwina about what the Arapaho had done. He remembered those days in the sweat lodge he had built for her, and his prayers that Mother Earth would take away her pain and fear. And he had seen how she had tried to hide from him the blood that stained her clothing.

Even now, it enraged and sickened him. Not only because of what she had endured, or that she might never bear his child, but because she suffered, still, over a year later.

Something was wrong.

The realization that he might lose her again—this time forever—opened a dark, empty place in his mind. A sense of urgency heightened that fear. And as he watched her walk toward him, he knew he could wait no longer.

"What's Lillie doing?" she asked, stopping beside him. In answer, a high squeak erupted from the house, making her wince and the pup whine. Even birds fled the trees. "I thought you were going to accidentally step on that flute."

"Are you in pain, Prudence?"

She startled, then frowned. "Why would you ask that?"

He nodded toward the hand over her stomach.

She quickly took it away. "Hungry, that's all. I didn't miss supper, did I?"

Before he could answer, she hurried on, words coming in a rush.

"I didn't mean to be away so long, but Lucinda is in a dither over Mrs. Bradshaw. Apparently, she received a letter yesterday that upset her, then this morning, with only a hurried apology, she ups and leaves. Just like that. Lucinda thinks it has to do with Buster Quinn, but we don't know what."

"They are both trapped in rules and have not found the courage to take what they want." Why was she trying to distract him?

"Perhaps." Linking her arm through his, she steered him toward the house, the puppy following behind. "I'll miss her, though. She was a lovely lady."

"Your friends are happy that Maddie Wallace returns in a few days?"

"Ecstatic. Although with Helen Bradshaw gone, Luce will be shorthanded for the big welcome-home celebration. And anyway"—she smiled and bumped her shoulder against his—"they're your friends, too."

He nodded absently, an idea forming.

"I can't believe it's been almost two years since the four of us came to Heartbreak Creek," Prudence went on. "Now all of us are married, and Edwina, and Lucinda, and Maddie all have babies, and . . ." Her voice trailed off. She blinked hard, then put on a false smile that did not hide the sorrow in her eyes. "It will be so nice to be together again."

He stopped and turned to her. "Go with me to the sacred pool, *Eho'nehevehohtse.*"

"The mineral spring? Now?"

"Tonight. Soon the workers will begin on the big hotel Tait and Ethan Hardesty are building. They will cut down the trees, and clear the slopes and shatter the silence with their hammers and saws. But for now, it is still a place of healing. Come with me tonight." And maybe the waters would heal whatever damage the Arapaho had done.

He saw her wavering . . . remembering that earlier night he had taken her there. Reaching out, he cupped her cheek, needing to touch her in some way. "Eat well, then rest. I will come for you after the house sleeps. Bring extra clothing. We will be away for three nights."

"Three nights? Where will we stay?"

"I have a tipi not far from there."

"Lillie will want to go."

"It is not a safe place for her. If she wants, I will put up a small tipi for her in the side yard, although she does not seem to have an interest in sleeping outside." Seeing her brow pucker, he laughed. "Do not worry, *Eho'nehevehohtse*. I will keep you warm and safe."

Interest sparked in her eyes. And a hunger that answered his own.

"I'll let you tell her we'll be gone," she said with a saucy smile. "I'm already in enough trouble for not letting Bitsy sleep in her bed."

The night was clear and cold. The moon had risen early and was already slipping down past the highest mountain peaks by the time they rode into the canyon. As before, Prudence wore the fur-lined coat and moccasins he had brought for her the first time they had come to this place, although this time he could see she wore no gown beneath it.

He held her in front of him, cradling her body against his as the horse worked his way up the steep trail. All around them the sounds and scents of the awakening season hung in the still air.

"The People have a saying," he whispered against her hair. "'Walk lightly in the spring; Mother Earth is pregnant.'"

Instead of speaking, she turned her head and pressed a kiss to his neck.

His body instantly reacted. As it always did. As it always would. This woman was part of him now, lodged so deep that every beat of his heart, every breath, every thought circled back to her.

As they climbed higher, the sharp, strong smell of the heated waters drifted through the trees. He heard the sound of fleeing hooves striking the earth and guessed they had disturbed a small herd of deer that had gathered to rest in the warm mist rising off the water's surface. "We are almost there."

She held a hand over her nose. "I can tell. It's lucky the sulfur smell doesn't carry too far, or Tait and Ethan would have to put their building miles away."

He laughed softly. "That is the breath of Mother Earth and is part of her healing powers. You will not notice it after a while."

She looked up through the trees overhead, her soft hair brushing against his chin. "Do you think the lights will move across the sky again as they did when you brought me here last winter?"

"I do not know. The dance of the spirits is a rare thing. If we see them tonight, it will be after the moon leaves the sky."

Thomas reined his pony toward the brush corral he had built below his camp. After helping her down, he untied the pouches of clothing and food he had brought, unsaddled, and turned the horse into the enclosure. "Come," he said, and held out the hand not gripping the pouches.

There was enough moon left for him to see the wide trail cut by the many animals that visited this sacred place. As they wove through the tall firs and pines, the smell grew stronger. He drew it in and called silently on Mother Earth to put her blessing on the woman beside him.

This time, he did not have to ask her to remove her fur-lined coat. As soon as she reached the water's edge, she pulled off her moccasins, tossed the coat over the boulders ringing the pool, then stepped down onto the shelf below the surface. "It feels heavenly." With a deep sigh, she moved deeper until the water reached to her shoulders.

Thomas joined her. Remembering she could not swim, he wrapped his arms around her from behind and pulled her back against his chest. Her body was slick and soft against his, but he could feel the sudden tension in her back and shoulders when he walked deeper and her feet no longer touched the bottom. Her hands came up to grip his forearms crossed over her chest, her fingers digging into his skin.

"I will not let you go, Prudence. You know this."

He waited for her fear to fade, then began to chant softly into her ear. "Let your arms and legs relax, *Eho'nehevehohtse*. Rest your head against my shoulder and let your body float. I will not let you sink. I will not let you go. Breathe deep and slow. Look up into the sky and watch the stars grow bright as the moon dims. We are safe in the arms of Mother Earth, so rest, *Eho'nehevehohtse*, and think only peaceful thoughts. Sleep. Sleep, and let your sorrow and pain drift away."

He felt her slowly go limp in his arms. Her eyes drifted closed. Resting his cheek against hers, he opened his mind to the stillness around them.

* * *

Pru wasn't sure if she slept—or, if she had, for how long—but gradually she became aware of cool air wafting over her wet body and Thomas carrying her from of the pool. Seeking warmth, she snuggled closer to his chest. "What happened?" she murmured drowsily. "Did I fall asleep?" In truth, she felt almost drugged, her limbs lethargic and her mind sluggish, as if she were floating in that blissful place between sleep and dreaming.

Smiling, he dipped his head and kissed her forehead. "Yes. But now you must wake. I cannot carry you all the way up to the camp."

"We're staying here?"

"Up higher, on a ridge." He let her legs slide until her feet touched the cold ground. "Keep your hand on my shoulder until you find your legs." He helped her into her coat and moccasins, then slung the pouches over his shoulder and took her hand. "I will lead the way."

Pru was panting by the time they climbed above the tallest trees and onto a high, flat shelf bathed in starlight. She stopped to catch her breath and look around.

It was a stark and beautiful place. She felt as if she were standing on the highest point of the earth, with nothing between her and heaven but an endless array of stars. Off to the west, a tiny sliver of moon was sinking below distant peaks, and to the east, the howl of a single wolf marked its passing. The only thing that broke the endless view was the tipi in the middle of the rocky shelf.

Releasing her hand, Thomas untied the entrance flap and tossed the pouches inside. After positioning long poles to hold open two flaps at the top of the hide-covered structure, he grabbed an armload of firewood from the stack outside. Smiling, he motioned her inside. "Come."

It was surprisingly cozy, but so dark she was only able to make out low shapes in the dim light coming through the opening overhead. Telling her to wait near the entrance, Thomas dumped his load of firewood on the ground beside what appeared to be a stack of rocks. A moment later, light flared, and soon burning moss ignited a crackling fire that lit up the tipi's interior and sent smoke coiling up and out of the open flaps overhead.

She saw a mound of fir boughs covered with several blankets and furs and assumed that was the bed. Other than the pouches he had brought, and a few tools and implements stacked to one side, there was little else in the tipi.

"Are you hungry?" he asked.

She bit back a yawn. "Sleepy."

"Then rest." He motioned to the blankets.

She let the heavy fur cloak drop from her shoulders and slid, nude, under the blankets and furs. She tried to stay awake. But the relaxing effects of the pool and the gentle crackle of the fire soon lulled her into a deep sleep.

Twenty-four

Hours later, Thomas sat in the dawn light coming through the open door flap and watched her come awake.

First, her lashes fluttered like the wings of a tiny wren. Her mouth parted on a half sigh. Then she stretched, arching her back, fists unfurling at the ends of arms thrown back against the furs.

Looking on her beauty filled him with such longing he regretted not joining with her during the night.

But it was not time for that yet.

Finally, her eyes opened. For a moment, her gaze circled the tipi walls, then came to rest on him. "Thomas," she said with a sleepy smile.

"*Pevevoona'o'*. Good morning, Prudence. Did you sleep well?"

"Better than I have in months." Rising up on one elbow, she tucked the blanket over her nakedness, then propped her head against one hand and studied him. "You're dressed. Are we leaving?"

"I am. For a while."

"Where are you going?"

Instead of answering, he began pulling items from the bag of food and setting them on a flat stone. "Here is dried meat. Cheese and bread from the hotel. Two apples. They are soft but still good." He pointed to a smaller leather pouch that hung from a nail in one of the poles. "That holds fresh water. I will bring more when I return."

She sat up, the blanket clutched to her chin, worry in her eyes. "You're leaving me? Here? Alone?"

"Do not worry, *heme'oone*. You will be safe. I will not be far away. But while I am gone, I ask you to think about what you want. I will do the same. When I return, we will talk about those things, and decide what to do with the years that lie ahead of us."

"I don't understand."

He rose and smiled down at her, painting her face on his memory. "*Nemehotatse, Eho'nehevehohtse. Nestaevahos-evoomatse*—I love you, Prudence Lincoln, and I will return."

Then he stepped through the entrance and headed down the long slope.

Pru stared at the flap over the entrance, half expecting Thomas to come back through it. When he didn't, she scrambled from the bed. With the blanket clutched over her nakedness, she ducked outside.

Sky. Distant peaks. Rocks. And more sky.

But no Thomas.

Panicked, she rushed in one direction, then stumbled back from the hundred-foot drop. In another direction were boulders and another lethal drop, and behind her was a sheer bluff rising to snow-dusted slopes hundreds of feet above her. Fighting a wave of dizziness, she crept to the top of the trail they had come up the previous night. It seemed too steep to have climbed in the dark.

Still, no Thomas.

Her mind reeling, she fled to the tipi. With shaking hands she put on the coat and moccasins, then sat on the blanket, eyes pinned to the flap, a hatchet in her hand. Not even a mouse came in.

By afternoon she was nauseated from lack of food and the stuffy air in the tipi. Grabbing the cheese and bread Thomas had left, she went to sit outside the entrance on a piece of hide.

While she ate, she watched wide-winged birds and clouds drift past, and she had to admit that Thomas had picked a stunning place to build his camp. Bordered as it was on three sides by natural deterrents, and on the fourth by a dizzying climb, she was probably safer in these mountains than in the snake and alligator infested swamps of Louisiana. Even the bugs here seemed benign—hardly the nuisance the huge roaches and water bugs were back home, or the mosquitos around New Orleans that gathered in such bloodsucking frenzies they killed cattle.

In fact, if she ever became accustomed to the cold, she could grow to love this country.

Hours passed as she contemplated this lofty view of the world and her place within it. The sun sank lower, but before it dipped behind the mountains, a pale quarter moon rose in the east, almost translucent at first, but gaining substance as the day died in fiery protest.

Darkness crept in on a gentle breeze. The temperature dropped. Soon the wind rose into gusts that made the sides of the tipi slap against the pole frame. Ducking back inside, Pru fumbled around in the dim light until she found the water pouch and dried meat, threw several blankets over her arm, and went outside again. She spread her meager dinner on a blanket, determined that if Thomas wanted her to think about their future, then this is where she would do it. Not hiding within the shelter of the tipi, but out here, under the moonlit dome of God's own church.

As she chewed the tough meat strips, she gathered her thoughts. She wanted to be logical, rather than emotional, but it was difficult to separate the two when thinking of Thomas. She loved him. Wanted him. Needed him, in ways she was only now beginning to understand.

But he also disturbed her. Thomas was an unmanageable and elemental force. He had the capacity to destroy the carefully established order of her life. But he could also trigger emotions she had buried for so long she had forgotten they were there. He made her laugh, and cry, and want. Only with him could she forget all the expectations and lessons drilled into her. Only with him could she forget the injustices of the past and the color of her skin.

With Thomas, she could let go and simply . . . be.

That frightened her. It was chaotic and unpredictable and left her vulnerable to hurt. But it also drew her.

Her friends were right. Thomas had changed. Grown. Over the last two years, he had become more than he had been when she'd first met him. Yet he was still and always her Thomas.

She had changed, too. She had learned hard lessons in their time apart. Not everyone wanted help. Not everyone had the ambition to do the hard work needed to improve their situations. Not everyone needed a savior. The meal finished, she stretched out on her back and stared up into the endless night sky. Instead of feeling diminished by the vastness of it, she took comfort in knowing she was a part of it and belonged to something bigger and grander than her mind could comprehend. When viewed from that perspective, the past seemed insignificant. The future, limitless.

She smiled. Then chuckled, feeling more carefree and unburdened than she had in a long time. Even the brush of the soft fur against her naked body made her feel new and uninhibited. She wanted to fly, to soar free and unencumbered and escape the fetters that had held her fast for so long.

Free.

Filled with a burst of unbridled delight, she threw her arms wide and laughed aloud into the night sky.

If she needed someone to teach, she could teach Lillie. If she needed someone to save, she could save Thomas by steering him away from making the same mistakes she had. Neither of them could rescue the world or right all the wrongs of the past. But they could still find fulfillment in each other.

Words he had once spoken to her echoed in her memory: *Do not let the past take up too much of today.*

The past was over. Today was new and perfect and unscarred by old wounds. But the future, and all the tomorrows stretching ahead of her, belonged to her and Thomas and Lillie.

A feeling of peace came over her. A sense of rightness, as if finally everything that mattered had settled into place, and all the rest had fallen away.

She must have slept. When next she opened her eyes, it was to blinding sunlight and the sight of Thomas standing at the edge of the drop-off, arms upraised, face lifted to the sky. He was power and strength. Unequivocally male. A mystical figure silhouetted against the distant mountains. She could almost envision him stepping off that ledge and soaring like an eagle into the sky.

Instead, he dropped his arms to his sides and turned to face her.

A stab of fear drove her to her feet. Something was different. "Thomas?"

He walked toward her, every motion fluid grace, from the swing of his glossy black hair to the sway in his powerful shoulders to his long, sure strides.

She wanted to go to him, but something in his face held her back.

He stopped before her. Taking her face in his broad hands, he dipped his head and kissed her. "*Nemehotatse, Eho'nehevehohtse,*" he whispered against her mouth, then kissed her again. "I love you. And I would have no other but you as *nahe'e*, my woman. Will you accept me, Prudence Lincoln?"

Tears brimmed. Knowing he didn't like them, she tried to blink them away, but more kept coming. "Yes, Thomas."

He smiled and took his hands away. "Good. *Napevetano.* I am happy."

But still, something had changed. "You're different. What happened?"

His smile broadened, spreading to eyes that were usually guarded, but now glowed with happiness. She had a sense that she was seeing him as few others had.

"Did you not know?" Pushing aside the opening of her coat, he put his hand on her belly. It was cold against her bare skin. "Can you not feel it, *Eho'nehevehohtse*? The babe that grows within you?"

"Wh-What?" She stared at him, her mouth falling open, her heart stuttering in her chest. "A babe?" She looked down at her body and the strong hand resting there. "But how . . . I thought . . ." All that pain. The bleeding. The fear.

"Do not worry. He is safe within you. All will be well."

"But I don't understand. How do you know this?"

"I see it in your eyes, *Eho'nehevehohtse*. I hear the whisper of it on the wind. I feel it here." He gently pressed his palm against her. "And here." He put his free hand over his heart. "He will be a fine man. Strong like me. Clever like you."

"He?"

He smiled. "Our son."

Her legs began to shake. Tears rolled down her face. "You're s-sure?"

He nodded, his own eyes filling. "My spirit guides tell me he will be a great warrior. He will see things we will never see, and go to places we can only imagine. But he will fight with words, not knives, and his voice will be heard."

Her knees gave out. Sobbing, she collapsed against him, bathed in a joy so intense if felt almost like pain.

"Ssh. Do not weep." Scooping her up in his arms, he carried her into the tipi. "Let me love you, *heme'oone*, and take your tears away."

Thomas gently laid her on the fur-draped boughs, then pulled the coat and moccasins from her trembling body. "Are you cold, Prudence? Should I light a fire for you?"

"You already have."

Pleased, he stretched out beside her. He kissed her beautiful face, licked the salty tears from her cheeks, and welcomed the need building inside him.

"You truly did not know?" he asked, gently stroking her belly.

"I thought something was wrong. That I was barren."

"I am glad."

"That I thought I was barren?"

"That you did not know."

She rolled toward him and rested her hand on his chest. "Why?"

"Because it tells me you came back because you wanted to, and not because of our child."

"I would have come back either way, Thomas." Leaning forward, she kissed the scar over his heart. "This is where I belong."

Emotion clogged his throat. Words would not come. Instead, he skimmed his hands over her, learning the feel of her all over again—tracing with his fingertips the changes in the sleek body carrying his child. Where her belly had once been flat and soft to his touch, now there was a new firmness, a gentle rounding that fit into his palm. As he stroked her breasts and hips and between her legs, he remembered another woman with a different child growing within her, and vowed silently that he would not fail this time.

Leaning over her on one elbow, he pressed his lips against her belly, her breasts, the scars across her shoulder. Then he straightened and looked into her eyes. "I cannot right the injustices of the past, *Eho'nehevehohtse*. But I will protect you from any that come in the future. That is my vow to you and our son."

Seeing the tear slide down his cheek brought new ones to Pru's eyes. Pulling him down, she rocked him in her arms, filled with such love it burned like a flame within her. "And my vow to you is that I will never leave you again."

He let out a deep breath. Muscles quivered beneath her hands, and she felt the warm wetness of tears on her shoulder.

"I love you, Thomas."

He rested against her for a moment longer, then rose on his arms above her, his legs hot and trembling against hers. "*Nemé-hotatse*," he said, and pushed inside.

And everything changed. The air in the tipi. The sound of the wind whispering along the hides outside. Her breathing. Again and again, their bodies came together, then slid apart, and came together again in a rhythm as old as the earth on which they lay.

This wasn't simply making love. This was a joining. A coming together in an elemental way beyond words or thought. This was soul-deep wanting put in physical form.

Pru lost herself to pure sensation. She wept. She clawed at his muscular arms. She urged him on with pleas and moans. As tension built, she pressed her open mouth against his neck, tasted the salty tang of his skin, and felt the pulse of his heart against her tongue. She felt filled. Complete. Exultant. And when bliss engulfed her, she cried out with the joy of it.

It was dark when they finally emerged from the tipi, sated and clinging to each other like new lovers, laughing over inconsequential things. Pru felt weightless and carefree, like a soap bubble rising in languid circles to meet the stars overhead.

Everything felt new. Sharper. Clearer. The sky seemed vaster, the stars brighter.

"Sit," Thomas said. Pulling her down between his knees, he wrapped his arms around her and settled her back against his chest. They sat in silence for a time, then he said, "You were different tonight. You held nothing back from me."

"I held nothing back from myself."

"That is good. It will only make us stronger for what lies ahead."

She felt a shiver of foreboding. "What do you mean?"

He kissed her cheek. "I hear worry in your voice, *Eho'nehevehohtse*. But all will be well."

Beneath the fur coat, she pressed a hand over the belly, as if to protect the life within. "I wish I could be as sure as you."

"We have traveled long to get here, and much has changed. But this"—he swung a hand to encompass the endless view—"remains the same. And what we feel here"—he cupped her breast over her heart—"is unchanged. From these things we will draw the strength to help our son find his true path."

"How?"

He was silent for so long she thought he wouldn't answer. "I have been thinking on that, Prudence. And I have decided that the best way to help him is to show him what lies beyond this canyon."

She straightened to look over her shoulder at him. "You mean leave Heartbreak Creek?"

"Not for a while, and never for long." He pulled her back against his chest. "There was a letter inside the box with my books. The man in England who printed my story wants me to write more stories. He also wants me to travel to other places to talk about them. If you came with me, you could talk to schools and churches about teaching black people to read and write, and our son could see that the world is more than these mountains, and will not be afraid to seek his purpose there."

She sat for a moment, letting the idea take hold. The world could be a cruel place. But would cosseting their son here in this canyon prepare him for the life he might want?

"Tell me what you see, Prudence."

Tipping her head back against his shoulder, she looked out

at the dark silhouette of the distant mountains. "More stars than I ever knew were there. Even the Milky Way is brighter."

"Now close your eyes and tell me what you hear and feel."

At first, nothing. Then, as her breathing slowed, little sounds stood out. "I feel your heartbeat against my back. I hear wind moving over the tufts of grass. An owl far off to the right."

"Those things will always be with you, *Eho'nehevehohtse*. They are part of you now, whether you are here on this mountaintop or in another place far away. All that you see and feel and hear—every animal and bird and blade of grass—is connected back to you. Accept that. Put away your fear, and harmony and peace will come into your heart. The child within you will feel that, too, and grow strong and unafraid."

With Thomas beside her, it might be possible. "I'll try."

"That is my hope."

His lips brushed against her temple. "Look, *heme'oone*." He pointed up at the sky. "The spirits have come to dance for us."

Arrows of light shot up from behind the mountains to the north, then faded, only to rise in another place. Then suddenly they streaked high overhead and burst into ribbons of color. It was magical, otherworldly, a soul-lifting display.

"Oh, Thomas. Isn't it beautiful?"

His lips brushed against her temple again. "The spirits are happy tonight. Their dance is a blessing upon our son."

The lights began to pulse with slow, undulating movements, as if mirroring the heartbeat of heaven itself. Blues, greens, streaks of red—fading, then growing brighter, moving to the music of the universe.

Pru watched in silent awe, unable to find words to express the wonder of it, but knowing that this moment, with the lights dancing overhead, and Thomas's arms strong around her, would be a memory she would hold in her heart forever.

Twenty-five

Maddie and Ash Wallace and baby Donnan arrived on the following Thursday, bringing with them an entourage befitting a Scottish earl and his countess and the Kirkwell heir. In addition to Donnan's nursemaid and Maddie's personal maid, there was also a tall, skinny young man named Roger, who supervised the unloading of Maddie's photography equipment, and Pringle, who was dragged off the train by Ash's huge wolfhound, Tricks. Apparently, he was glad to be home again—the dog, not Pringle.

Since Tait had been keeping track of the Wallaces' progress through his myriad railroad contacts and had alerted the town about their arrival, a large crowd had gathered on the station platform to welcome them home.

Thomas hung back with Lillie while Prudence rushed forward, tears streaming. Soon a knot of women formed around Maddie and baby Donnan, while men clustered around Ash, congratulating him with claps on his back.

The baby earl was a beautiful baby, and although his eyes were blue now, Pru hoped they would turn green to match his father's. He was quite large, too, and with a fierce intensity in his expression that marked him a child to reckon with. Pru hoped her own son would have as strong a friendship with Donnan as Thomas had with Ash Wallace.

When the big Scot saw Thomas standing with Lillie, he stepped over to greet them. Prudence and Maddie followed. "So this is the wee bairn, Lillie," he said in his musical brogue. "'Tis nice to meet you, lass. I've heard much about you, so I have." Bending, he stuck out his hand.

At Thomas's prompting, Lillie did, too. But she missed her mark, and instead of putting her small hand in the Scotsman's large one, her fingers brushed his leg.

Pru tensed for her reaction, and was surprised when the girl giggled and began to pat Ash's shin. "This Tricks?"

"Ah, no." Ash exchanged a look with Thomas. "'Tis my leg."

She yanked her hand back. "Your leg? You nekkid?"

"I told you, *Katse'e*," Thomas said before Ash answered. "He wears a skirt."

The Scot stiffened. "'Tis no' a skirt, ye bluidy heathen. 'Tis a kilt."

"Why is Daddy bleeding? And what's a kilt?"

"A skirt," Thomas promptly answered.

"Oh, dear." Pru took Lillie's hand in hers, hoping to stop further discussions of the Scotsman's attire, or lack of it.

But Lillie seemed more concerned about the dog. "If your dog is daddy to my dog, then you're my stepdaddy, right?"

Maddie stifled a giggle while Pru explained to the confused Scotsman that Lillie's dog was the offspring of Tricks.

"Bitsy is the best dog in the whole world," Lillie added with a big grin.   ·

"He? Ye named the lad Bitsy?"

"As is fitting," Thomas said with a smirk. "Since the owner of the pup's sire wears a skirt."

Luckily Lucinda stepped in. "I know you're anxious to get out to the new house," she said, urging the newcomers toward the wagons being loaded with the Wallaces' luggage. "The Jessups will take you in my carriage. Ethan is anxious to give you the full tour, and I know Rafe wants to show Ash how well the horses are doing. We'll give you a couple of hours to settle in, then we'll descend."

Ash's green eyes widened. "Descend?"

"Henny and Josie and Winnie have planned a lovely supper to welcome you home, so be sure to rest. And Maddie, as our birthday gift to Donnan, the ladies have furnished the nursery, since your last letter said you haven't had time to order anything yet. I hope it suits."

"I'm sure it will be perfect."

Once the nanny was settled in the carriage, Maddie passed in her sleeping son. "I doubt Donnan well have any problem adjusting to his new quarters. He's quite a sound sleeper."

Lucinda gave her a disgruntled look. "Aren't you the lucky one."

"I hope there's room in the nursery for the lad's wee sword," Ash said.

Thomas perked up. "A sword? How big?"

"Thankfully, it's wooden." Maddie allowed her husband to hand her into the carriage. "But the child-sized bagpipes are fully functional."

"Aye," Ash said, proudly. "I'll teach the lad myself, when the time is right."

Pru exchanged a look with Thomas. "Too bad Lillie won't be able to accompany him on her flute."

Lillie patted Pru's arm. "It's okay, Mama. Daddy's sorry he stepped on it. He says he'll make me a new one. I hope it's ready in time for the weddin'."

Maddie poked her head out of the carriage window. "Wedding?"

Ash rounded on Thomas. "Yours?"

Thomas grinned.

"Aboot time."

Maddie clapped her hands. "Oh, how wonderful!"

Pru lowered her voice so the Rylanders, who were supervising the loading of the other wagons, couldn't hear. "We haven't told anyone else yet. We hope to announce it soon."

"A wedding! Oh, Pru, I'm so happy you waited for us!"

"You will say nothing about this." Thomas scowled at Jessup in the driver's box. "Drive on."

"Yes, sir." A flick of the reins and the coach rolled forward.

The crowd began to disperse.

With Lillie holding their hands between them, Pru and Thomas headed back toward town. When the people walking nearby moved on around them, leaving the three of them alone on the path, Pru looked at Thomas. She wanted to tell Lillie about the baby before they told anyone else.

With a nod, he stopped and hunkered down in front of their daughter so their faces were on the same level. "*Katse'e*, we have other news. You will have a brother soon."

Her face lit up. "For true? When is he comin'? Is he from the school like me? I hope it's not that mean Bubba Harris. He always pulled my hair."

"No, it is not Bubba Harris. Or anyone you have ever met. When he comes to us next fall, he will be new to the world."

Lillie's eyes widened. "You mean he ain't—isn't—even borned yet? It's gonna be a baby?"

"Yes. Our baby." Lifting her small hand, Thomas pressed it to Pru's stomach. "He is here, inside your mother, growing strong."

"How'd he get in there?"

"I put him there, and your mother will keep him safe until he is ready to come into the world."

"So you'll be his daddy, too?"

"Yes. And you will be his big sister."

For a moment, Lillie stared past Thomas's shoulder. Then, grinning, she put her mouth close to Pru's stomach and shouted, "Hey, you in there! It me! Lillie Redstone. You one lucky baby, 'cause you gonna have the best big sister in the whole world!"

Pru wiped a tear from her cheek.

Thomas rose, his own eyes suspiciously bright.

Lillie gave Pru a pat. "And don't you worry none, Mama. Eve'ythin' be jist fine. I helped birth lots of puppies and kitties, and I know jist what to do."

"I'll alert Doctor Boyce."

That evening over the wonderful supper Josie and Henny and Winnie had prepared, Pru reluctantly divulged the plans for her second wedding to Thomas. She hadn't intended to make any announcements yet, not wanting to take away from the celebration of the Wallaces' return, but in her usual impulsive way, Lillie had broken the news.

"Guess what, ev'rybody!" she had shouted, banging on the table with her fork. "Mama and Daddy gettin' married jist like regular folk. And I get to sing!" Then, before that tidbit was digested, she added, "And Mama growin' a baby in her belly, too. Daddy put it there and he says it my baby brother!"

Chaos erupted. Mostly from Pru's sister, who burst into tears and sent her chair toppling to the floor in her rush to give Pru a hug. "Just like me!" she cried, laughing and crying and hiccupping at the same time.

Pru pulled back from her strangling embrace. "You're in a family way, too?"

"Heavens, no! But I was when Declan and I married the second time. Don't you remember how awful I looked in that beautiful dress y'all made for me? And now you get to wear it! It's destiny! Oh, Maddie, thank heavens you're here. You have such an eye for style!"

"Have you set a date?" Audra asked, digging in her reticule for her pad and pencil. "I want to announce it as soon as you do. And where will it be held? At the church?"

"Of course not." Lucinda pushed Edwina aside to give Pru a hug. "Thomas is deathly afraid of the church."

"I am not afraid," Thomas said.

"You should be." Tait gave his friend a slap on the back, and in a lower voice added, "Don't fight it. The ladies always win."

"We'll have it outside," Lucinda went on, her lovely eyes bright with plans. "Declan, you're an excellent carpenter. We'll need an arch. Something we can weave flowers through. And an altar. Maddie, do you still have that lace cloth we used at Audra and Ethan's wedding?"

"Oh!" Edwina cried, waving her hands in excitement. "I have the most marvelous idea! Let's have a double ceremony! Josie and Rafe need to marry again, too, since their first wedding was on board a ship and that doesn't really count. A double wedding! Wouldn't that be grand!"

"It definitely counted." Rafe winked at his wife. "I made sure of that."

Josie pressed a hand to her cheek, as if that might stop the rush of color into her face. "Actually, it was a lovely ceremony. We certainly don't need another."

"If we hold the ceremony outside," Ash broke in over Edwina's attempts to talk Josie and Rafe into another wedding, "I can play my pipes. For some reason, Pastor Rickman doesna allow them in the church."

A prolonged pause, then Maddie stepped into the silence with a strained smile. "An excellent idea, dearest. We'll have Ethan play his fiddle, too."

"And I'll sing!" Lillie shouted.

"Henny and I will cook up a fabulous meal," Winnie offered. "How many you inviting?"

"Why, the whole town," Lucinda said grandly. "Tait and I will supply the meat, and the rest will be a potluck picnic."

Pru looked at Thomas, wondering when everything had slipped beyond their control.

"Perfect!" Henny smiled broadly at Josie, the woman she had once served as a maid, but now counted as a friend. "And as a special treat, I'll whip up some of that lemon syllabub you enjoy so much."

"And I'll bring a big pot of cullen skink," Maddie offered, with a smile to her husband. "Although we'll probably have to use trout instead of haddock."

"No haggis?"

Her smile faded. "No, dear. But I'm sure your friends would enjoy a wee dram of Northbridge's fine Scottish nectar."

Vigorous nods from the men. Narrow-eyed warnings from the women.

Edwina gave Pru another choking hug. "It'll be just like last year's Spring Social. Except it'll be your wedding instead. I'm so happy I could cry."

"You already are, dear. And making me cry, too."

"As am I." Maddie wiped at her eyes. "Thank heavens I brought all my photography equipment. I want to make certain this wonderful day is captured forever. With it being outside, the lighting will be so much more dramatic."

And just like that, plans for her wedding were taken out of Pru's hands. She glanced over at Thomas, wondering if he felt as overwhelmed as she.

He was surrounded by his smiling friends, accepting their ribbing and congratulations with hardly a change in expression. Then, as if feeling her gaze on him, he turned his head and looked directly into her eyes.

For a moment, the world stilled around them. Then a slow smile spread across his somber features, growing until it crinkled the corners of his deep-set eyes, showing his strong teeth and that elusive dimple in his cheek.

And she knew that he was happy, too, and only joy awaited them.

Luckily God wasn't angry about having the ceremony outside and gifted them with a perfect, windless, cloudless day.

At Lucinda's urging, Pastor Rickman kept the fire and brimstone to a minimum and maintained a serenity not often seen during his church sermons.

Being out in the open also helped to dissipate the more pitchy notes from Ash's bagpipe rendition of the Robert Burns song "Scots Wha Hae," which sounded less like wedding music than a marching song, yet seemed to fit the occasion.

But when Lillie stood before them to sing "All Creatures of Our God and King," tears came to Pru's eyes. Neither she nor Thomas had known what she had chosen to perform, but the Francis of Assisi hymn was the perfect choice. When her beautiful and powerful voice rose on the words, *"Be praised, my Lord, through Sister Moon and the stars; in the heavens You have made them bright, precious and beautiful,"* Pru saw in Thomas's tear-sheened eyes the memory of that mystical night when the spirits danced for them across the sky.

After the ceremony, Maddie took over, having her assistant, Roger, position the bride and groom for their wedding portrait while she studied the images through the lens of her camera. Pru had been worried that Thomas might not want to participate, but he seemed not to have the aversion many other Indians had toward having their photographs taken.

"Stand closer," Maddie directed, waving them in. "You look so beautiful framed by the flowered arch. Lillie, you, too. Squeeze in there in front of your parents."

After completing the wedding portrait, she backed up her tripod to get all her Heartbreak Creek friends, children included, in one panoramic shot. "I want one of these to hang at Northbridge, and another to grace the new lodge Tait and Ethan are building. Joe Bill, no fidgeting." Only after taking several provisional exposures did she release the children.

As they ran toward the food-laden tables in the shade beside the creek, she moved about, taking a variety of other photographs while the light was still good. She had Rafe pose with his stallion, Pembroke's Pride, then took another of him with Josie and their son, Jamie. She even managed to corral all the Brodies together in one place for a family portrait, and found the perfect spot to photograph Tait and Lucinda Rylander with their new baby, Rosaleen. Then she took one of Tait Rylander and Ethan Hardesty, the builders of the soon-to-be-constructed Grand Heartbreak Creek Lodge, and another of Ethan with his wife, Audra, marking the announcement they had made earlier of the child on the way. She hoped the lens was able to capture the glow of happiness in Audra's beaming smile. And finally, she asked Roger to take a family portrait of her and Donnan and Ash, her husband standing proudly in his clan regalia with his bagpipes tucked under his arm.

After the wedding feast, the tables were carried away to make room for dancing, and Ethan got out his fiddle. A man with a mouth harp joined him, and another, who beat an empty kettle like a drum. But before the music started, people gathered around for a wedding toast. After the cups were filled with lemonade for the women and a splash of Ash's Scotch whisky for the men, Rafe Jessup stepped forward.

"Since I drew the short stick, I have to give the toast."

Laughter greeted his announcement, since everyone in town knew Rafe Jessup talked even less than Declan Brodie.

"I haven't been acquainted with Thomas as long as Declan has," he began. "And I only met Prudence recently. But I know of no finer people, and I'm glad they've come home to stay." Turning to the groom, he said, "Thomas, we've crossed an ocean together, shared a jail cell, and beaten each other to a pulp in an English corral. I'm proud to call you my friend, and I promise next time I'll let you win."

Cheers and shouts. Thomas crossed his arms and scowled, despite the laughter in his eyes.

"And to the lovely bride," Rafe said, turning to Pru, "I pray you're as patient as you are beautiful—you'll need to be. I wish you joy and prosperity, and hope all your ups and downs with this man will be between the sheets."

After the laughter faded, he told Pru to hold out her hand.

"Thomas, put your hand on top of hers. Now I ask everyone to pay silent homage to this solemn moment, 'cause this is the last time in this marriage Thomas will have the upper hand." He waited for the cheers and shouts to die down, then raised his glass high. "In the words of our red brothers . . .

> "'May the warm winds of heaven blow softly on your home,
> And the Great Spirit bless all who enter there.
> May your moccasins make happy tracks in many snows,
> And may the rainbow always touch your shoulder.'

"To Thomas and Pru!"

And the party began.

Hours later, just before the sun slipped behind the high canyon walls, Maddie prepared her camera for the photograph dearest to her heart—the one of the three women who meant so much in her life—the beautiful ladies who had come with her to Heartbreak Creek two years ago.

Setting the tripod at the precise angle she wanted, she turned the camera over to Roger and hurried over to sit with the three ladies gathered around a small draped table.

"I'll make copies for each of us," she said, blinking furiously as she took her place. "So we'll always remember this moment, no matter where life takes us."

"I'm going to cry," Edwina said with a sniff. "I don't want us ever to be apart again."

"Don't you dare start," her sister warned in a wobbly voice.

"Stop it, all of you." Lucinda swiped a hand over her eyes. "We'll have years and years of these gatherings."

"But we'll never be as pretty as we are today," Edwina said.

"Or as young," Pru added.

"But we'll always be the first ladies of Heartbreak Creek," Maddie, the optimist, said. "Now smile."

Epilogue

The past is a blanket of many colors
And each thread will lead you home.

—Thomas Redstone, Cheyenne author

HEARTBREAK CREEK, COLORADO, MAY 1935

They must be newlyweds, the old woman thought, watching the young couple coming hand in hand down the wide staircase of the Grand Heartbreak Creek Lodge. She had noticed them several times over the last few days, and their happiness was almost painful to see.

Crossing the foyer, they sent a nodding smile toward the table where she sat, then paused to read the daily activities notice posted on the wall beside the tall carved doors that led into the dining room.

The day was fine for late May, and the breeze coming through the tall arched windows was cool and pine-scented with only a faint trace of sulfur from the pool. The old lady had enjoyed a lovely afternoon watching the lodge guests come and go. But these two were her favorites. So refreshingly American. And so young. Just hearing their laughter made her smile.

"Looks like the whole town is invited to the Spring Social." The young man checked the watch hanging from a chain on his belt. "We have plenty of time. Shall we go?"

"Why not? It's a beautiful day." His bride leaned in to study a photograph in one of the inset displays along the wall. "Isn't that a beautiful horse?"

"His name was Pembroke's Pride," the old lady said, unable to remain silent. She loved talking about the photographs.

The young woman flashed a surprised smile. "Did you know him?"

"I met him a time or two before his owners took him east. Sired many fine foals. Even had a great-great-grandson in the Derby several years back. If you're into thoroughbred racing, you might have heard of his owner, Rayford Jessup. The man had a magical touch with horses. He and his wife set up a big stable in California, but they've retired here in Heartbreak Creek. Their daughter runs the stable, now."

The young couple walked slowly along the wall, studying the line of old photographs. "Do you know all these people?" the man asked.

"I do. Some are gone now, but the younger ones try to make it back every year for the annual Spring Social. An amazing group."

"In what way?"

"There was a joke about it. 'What happens when a mail-order bride, her half-black sister, a thief, and a runaway wife ride into town? They marry a sheriff, an Indian, a lawyer, and a soldier.'"

The young couple blinked at her.

She gave a dismissive wave. "I guess you'd have to know them."

Pushing herself from her chair, she walked forward, happy to share what she knew. Not many people stopped to look at old photographs anymore. The past held little charm for the young. "That big photograph in the center says it all."

The young woman smiled in delight as she studied it. "An outdoor wedding?"

"A second-time-around wedding." The elderly woman pointed to the couple on the left of the bride and groom. "Those are the Jessups I just mentioned. Their daughter wasn't yet born when this photograph was taken, but that's their son beside them. He inherited a grand estate in England, although no title came with it. Their parents have passed on, but I expect he and his sister will be here for the gathering. They come almost every year. It's become as much a reunion as a spring social nowadays."

"And these people?" The bride pointed to the next couple in the photograph, a tall, slim man and a petite woman.

"Those are the Hardestys. Audra was the town's newspaper publisher and editor. Ethan was the architect and builder of this lodge. Those big smiles are because the same day this photograph was taken they announced they had a baby on the way. Nice folks. Passed on about a decade ago, but their daughter, Phyllis, married a local rancher and still lives here."

"What about the bride and groom?" The young man leaned in to study the faces in the photograph. "They seem rather unusual."

"They were." The old woman laughed, remembering the way strangers always stared at the handsome couple. "The groom, Thomas Redstone, was a Cheyenne Dog Soldier and later became a famous author for his time. His wife, Prudence, was the prettiest woman I ever saw. She became famous in her own right for advancing education among ex-slaves after the Civil War. That child standing in front of them is Lillian, their adopted daughter. She's still alive. You may have heard of her, too. She was a gospel singer who toured with the evangelist D.L. Moody. Poor thing was blind most of her life, but she never let it keep her down. She's seventy-three now, but still does charity work at the Fanny Crosby Memorial Home in Bridgeport, Connecticut. Never married, but was like a second mother to every child she met. Quite a character. Temper, too."

"What happened to her parents—the bride and groom? Are they still around?"

That tug of memories plucked at her again. She had been fascinated with Thomas Redstone. Especially when he'd donned his Indian attire, complete with eagle feathers and war axe. And he'd had the most startling smile. "The Redstones died within a day of each other in the 1918 Spanish Influenza outbreak. It was sad to lose them, but at least they were together."

The young man nodded in understanding. "My grandfather and uncle died in that. I was just a kid, but I remember the church bells never stopped ringing."

"A tragedy. A half a million people gone in no time at all."

"Did they have other children? Seems I've heard the name Redstone recently."

"A son, Lincoln Redstone. He's been in the news lately, stirring up Congress over his Indian rights proposal. A fine man. And quite handsome, like his parents. He would have made them proud."

They moved on past several more photographs—Tait Rylander and Ethan Hardesty standing in front of the half-built lodge, children playing, a panoramic view of the storefronts along the main street in Heartbreak Creek in 1872.

"These pictures are amazing." The young woman stopped before a portrait of a man in a kilt holding bagpipes, the woman beside him holding a baby. She studied the writing below the photograph and gave a laugh. "A Scottish earl? How exciting."

"A Highlander and proud of it. An unusual man. Born out of his time, I always thought. But he could charm the birds from the sky." She smiled, fondly. "His countess, Maddie, was the kindest woman I ever knew." Puffed with pride, she waved an arm toward the photographs along the wall. "She took all these pictures. Female photographers were quite unusual back then, but she was a true artist."

"Are the earl and countess still alive?"

"Sadly, no." Emotion put a wobble in the old lady's voice. "They were on the *Titanic* in 1912, traveling with Tait and Lucinda Rylander back from Scotland to Heartbreak Creek. A terrible loss, not only for their families, but for the whole town."

"And their son?"

She gave a low laugh. "He's very much alive and, like his father, can charm the birds from the trees."

They moved slowly down the line of photographs. "Are the Rylanders pictured here, too?" the young woman asked.

"Of course." The old woman pointed to the family portrait of a tall, handsome man with a scar down one side of his face and a beautiful blond woman holding an infant in her arms. "The town hasn't been the same since that ship went down. One of the survivors said the women wouldn't leave their men, no matter how hard they tried to get them into the lifeboats."

"This is a large family." The young man had moved farther down to stand before the Brodie family portrait.

Glad of the distraction, the old lady followed. "Declan and

Edwina Brodie." Smiling, she shook her head. "You wouldn't believe the stories their grandchildren tell. Declan was a rancher and sometime sheriff and the biggest man in town. Edwina was his second wife—a mail-order bride. It was rough going at first, but Ed managed to win them all over. She was a force of nature, that one."

Starting from the left, she pointed out the Brodie children. "This is the oldest, R.D., and the image of his father. He married young, but after his wife died in childbirth, he went off to join Teddy Roosevelt's Rough Riders. Had a distinguished military career and retired with a chest full of medals. Very likeable fellow, but doesn't talk much. Like his father in that respect. If you go to the social, you'll notice him straight away. He's even taller than his father was.

"The light-haired boy next to him is Joe Bill, a trouble-maker if there ever was one, but a charmer, nonetheless." She smiled, despite the sad memories flooding her mind. "Fell in love with a local girl, but she had her attention fixed elsewhere. When she married, he left Heartbreak Creek. We heard he caught gold fever and headed up to Alaska during the Yukon gold rush. Never married."

"Did he strike it rich?" the young man asked.

She shook her head. "Not in yellow gold, but he did spend the next twenty years hunting for black gold along the North Slope and around Cook Inlet. Had better luck with that. I don't know if he'll be at the social. Some years he just shows up, unannounced. Joe Bill was always a bit unpredictable."

She pointed to the next Brodie child, a dark-haired girl with a big grin. The camera had done a fine job of capturing the mischief in her startling gray eyes. "This pretty thing was their only sister, Brin. What a beauty. Ed convinced Declan to send her off to finishing school, hoping to curb her wildness, but just after her twenty-first birthday, she ran off to join Buffalo Bill Cody's Wild West Show. You should have heard the row that caused. But that was Brin. Headstrong and free-spirited. She toured for fifteen years, then eloped with an Italian count. They're living the high life in Paris now.

"And this is Lucas." She pointed to a slight boy with a shock of dark hair hanging over one eye. "A brilliant boy. Very quiet and studious. Became fascinated with airplanes, and later worked on internal combustion engines for aerodromes. Made enough of a name for himself that he was appointed to the National Advisory Committee for Aeronautics. He's in his seventies now, but they still call him in to consult now and then. Married a lovely woman. They'll be here for the social with some of their grandchildren."

"And the baby?" The woman nodded toward the toddler sitting on his father's shoulders.

The old lady chuckled. "That baby is a year older than me. Whit Brodie. He's the one who married the Hardesty girl, Phyllis. They took over the Brodie ranch when Declan retired. They're still there, although their children now handle the day-to-day operations. The senior Brodies are long dead and sorely missed."

She was almost sorry she'd started this conversation. Talking about friends she hadn't seen in so long, and others who had changed greatly over the years, brought an ache to her heart. These were her people. Her family. And time had left so many of them behind, except for these slowly fading black-and-white photographs.

"Do you live here?" the woman asked, walking with her toward her chair.

"Not for a long time. But I try to return for the annual social every few years."

The young woman paused, her attention drawn to a photograph of four women gathered around the same small, draped table where the old woman had been sitting. She read aloud the caption below the print: *The First Ladies of Heartbreak Creek*. "Who are they?"

"The ones who started it all." She smiled at the beautiful faces, so familiar to her even though they'd been gone for many years. "They arrived together when this town was little more than a dying mining town. Sixty-five years ago last month. As feisty a group as you'd ever want to meet. You've seen them in other portraits along this wall. Lucinda Rylander, Edwina Brodie, Maddie Wallace, and Prudence Lincoln. An Irish businesswoman, a Southern princess, an English photographer, and a Negro educator. Brilliant, beautiful women, and so full of life they lit up a room." She pressed trembling fingertips to the glass over the images. "I still miss them."

"Are you in any of these photographs?"

Taking her hand away, the old lady stiffened her back and blinked away her tears. Ladies didn't weep in public and make spectacles of themselves. Especially ladies in her position. "Only one. I was scarcely three months old when these photographs were taken."

"Oh? Which one are you in?"

She turned to point out the portrait of her family, then hesitated when a tall, white-haired gentleman stepped onto the porch, a rangy, gray wolfhound straining at the leash in his hand.

"There you are, love," he said in a lilting brogue.

She smiled, that breathless, jittery feeling rising in her throat as it always did whenever he walked into the room. She forgot her earlier sadness and the young newlyweds standing beside her. All of her attention focused on the man walking toward her, his back straight, that rakish gleam in his green eyes, and a smile that melted bones. Even after over forty years of marriage, she never tired of watching the man move.

Bending down, he kissed her cheek. "I dinna ken where ye'd disappeared to, Rosie, lass."

She gave him a chiding look. "I've been waiting right here, Donnan, as well you know." Taking his arm, she sent a gracious smile to the wide-eyed newlyweds. "The earl and I must be off now. The Spring Social wouldn't be a party without a piper, now would it? And I do hope you'll attend. Everyone is always welcome in Heartbreak Creek."

Author's Note

Being a writer of fiction, I try not to let facts stand in my way. However, in deference to the true historians out there, I humbly confess to taking a few liberties.

Although Mose Solomon is a fictional character, the massacre at Patenburg, New Jersey, was very real. It happened several months before this story takes place, but I included it to show that even seven years after the Civil War ended, the killing continued.

The Underground Railroad was the pathway to freedom for an estimated one hundred thousand American slaves, and it stands as one of the nineteenth century's greatest examples of whites and blacks coming together to right a grievous wrong. Although I found no evidence that the railroad was still in operation seven years after the war, I'm hoping it was. With Reconstruction, there were still wrongs to right and people to save, and in my imagination, Mose Solomon was one of them.

Kaki

Glossary of Common Cheyenne Words and Phrases

Eho'nehevehohtse—One Who Walks in Wolf Tracks
Epeva'e—it is good
Haaahe—hello
Hahoo—thank you
Hea'e—maybe so
He'e—woman
Hee hee'—Yes
Heavoheso—devil
Heme'oone—sweetheart
Hovaha or **Ma'hahe**—friend
Ka'eskone—child
Katse'e—little girl
Ma'ęhóóhe—fox
Mahatamaahe—old woman
Ma'heo'o—God
Ma'hahko'e or **Xamaa-vee'e**—dwelling
Mataho—peyote buttons
Me'esevoto—babies
Naehame—my husband
Nahe'e—my woman
Napevetano—I am happy
Na'tsehe'stahe—I am Cheyenne
Nehetaa'e—that's all; that's enough

Nehetome—you are right
Nemehotatse—I love you
Nesene—my friend
Nestaevahosevoomatse—I will see you again.
Nia'ish—thank you. **Nea'ese** (the more common Cheyenne
   word)
Notaxeo'o—warrior
Noxa'e—Wait!
Oeskeso—dog
Okom—coyote
Pevevoona'o—good morning.
To'estse—get up (said to one person)
Tosa'e—where?
Va'ohtama—welcome
Ve'ho'e—white man
Voaxaa'e—eagle
Xamaa-vee'e or **ma'hahko'e**—dwelling

Read on for a special excerpt of
the first Runaway Brides novel
by Kaki Warner . . .

HEARTBREAK CREEK

Now available from Berkley Sensation!

Twenty-seven days after signing over her childhood home to the Bayou Bank & Trust of Sycamore Parish, Edwina Ladoux stared bleakly out the soot-streaked window at her shoulder.

Just a few more miles. An hour, at most. And they would finally arrive in Heartbreak Creek and begin the exciting new life awaiting them.

The thought filled her with absolute terror.

Not that she wanted to put off this meeting forever. Or could. The signed proxy papers were in her carpetbag, all nice and tidy and legal. She had spent the man's money and had used the train tickets he had sent. She was obligated. Married. A wife again.

Thank heavens she had had the foresight to insist upon a two-month waiting period before actual consummation took place—God, how she dreaded going through that again—so for now, anyway, her husband couldn't force his attentions on her. *Her husband.*

It was madness. Ridiculous. The very idea that Edwina Whitney Ladoux, once the reigning belle of Sycamore Parish, should be reduced to marrying a complete stranger—a man who apparently was so hard-pressed he had to advertise for a wife in a newspaper—was ludicrous. Absurd.

Yet here she was, so terrified at the thought of having a husband again, her stomach felt like it was stuffed with hot nails.

Especially when the train began to slow. She clutched at Pru's arm. "Are we there? So soon?"

"Soon? It's been almost three weeks, Edwina. I, for one, am ready for this journey to end."

"Maybe something has happened." Edwina peered out the window toward the front of the slowing train, but saw nothing untoward. "We just stopped to put water in the tender, so it can't be that. Perhaps there's been a rockslide. Or a tree has fallen across the tracks."

She hoped so. She hoped it was something so catastrophic she could delay the meeting looming ahead of her for weeks. Months. Forever.

"Second thoughts, Edwina?"

Of course she had second thoughts. Hundreds of them. Thousands. What had seemed like a viable solution back when penury was panting in her face now seemed like the most foolish thing she had ever done. Not that she would ever admit such a thing to her sister after tearing her from the only home she had ever known and dragging her halfway across the country. It was too late, anyway. Edwina had given her word and had signed her name. There was no stopping it now.

Unless she died. Or the train fell into the ravine. But that seemed a bit drastic. "Maybe it's another herd of buffalo."

"Oh, I doubt that." Beside her, Pru fussed with the front of her traveling cloak, then checked the tilt of her black horsehair bonnet. "They rarely range this high into the mountains."

Ever neat, Pru was. Sometimes such excessive attention to detail drove the imp in Edwina to do or say something to mess up that perfect order. But not today.

Today—assuming a host of guardian angels didn't swoop down to rescue them—they would arrive at the small depot five miles south of Heartbreak Creek, where her husband would be waiting. With his four children. Arms outstretched to welcome his bride.

The thought almost made her vomit.

"I suppose it could be a herd of bighorn sheep," Pru mused. "Or elk. The book said both are common in mountainous terrain."

Oh, who cares? Biting back her mounting apprehension, Edwina stared stoically out the window. She wished she could be more like her sister, eagerly devouring each new tidbit of information, delighting in every long-winded description of the fauna and flora of the Rocky Mountains, as if this journey were some grand adventure rather than an act of pure desperation.

But then, Pru wasn't the one who would soon have a strange man coming at her with consummation in mind.

Edwina shuddered. In sudden panic, she reached over and gave her sister's hand a hard squeeze. "Thank you for coming with me, Pru. I couldn't have come without you."

"And I couldn't have stayed without you."

With a sigh, Edwina tipped her head against the cool glass and studied the small canyon below with its fast-moving stream and toppled boulders and deep, dark forests pushing right up to the edge of the churning water. Back home, the bayous and rivers were sluggish and warm and brown, shaded by sycamores, stately cypress, and moss-draped oaks. By now, the redbuds and dogwoods would be blooming and the magnolia buds would be fattening for their annual summer display of fragrant, showy blossoms.

A sudden, intense swell of homesickness almost choked her. Gone. All of it. Forever.

The *clackety-clack* of the slowing train wheels gave way to the *screech* of brakes. Finally the train shuddered to a full stop. Passengers twisted in their seats, trying to see past the vapor from the smokestack that coiled around the windows like lost clouds.

The door at the front of the passenger coach swung open, and the conductor stepped inside. Stopping in the aisle between the two long rows of bench seats, he hooked his thumbs into his vest pockets and studied the expectant faces turned his way, his lips pursed beneath a bushy gray mustache that looped around his red-veined cheeks to join equally bushy muttonchop sideburns. He didn't look happy.

"There's a problem, folks," he announced. "Three miles up, a washout took out the Damnation Creek trestle."

The passengers moved restively. "What does that mean?" one asked.

"Means we'll be stuck for a while."

Edwina perked up. A while? How long was "a while"?

Raising his hands to quiet the angry muttering, the conductor explained. "They're sending wagons to carry you around the washout to Heartbreak Creek. The railroad will put you up there until the trestle is repaired."

"How long?" a man called out.

"A week. Maybe two."

Immediately, more voices rose. The conductor had to shout to continue, but Edwina scarcely heard a word. With something akin to giddiness, she turned to Pru. "We're saved, praise the Lord."

"A reprieve only." When Edwina started to say something more, Pru shushed her and leaned forward to attend the conductor's words.

But Edwina was feeling too euphoric to heed more than a word or phrase here and there—"hotel . . . meals . . . don't drink the water." To her, it all meant the same thing. A delay. A blessed reprieve. She wouldn't be meeting her new husband in Heartbreak Creek today as expected.

Thank you, Lord.

The conductor concluded his announcements and left, promising the wagons would arrive within an hour or so.

Pru fidgeted and sighed. "At least they'll be covering the cost of our accommodations in Heartbreak Creek until the tracks are repaired." She shot Edwina a look. "Stop grinning. And what makes you think your new husband won't travel the extra distance around the washout and be there waiting?"

"Oh, Sister, pray he doesn't."

Pru's elbow poked her ribs. "Hush," she warned in a low voice. "You must stop referring to me as your sister."

Edwina almost snorted. Prudence was more than her sister. She was her lifelong best friend, her confidant, the one who gave her courage when everything seemed so bleak. "You *are* my sister," she argued, rubbing her bruised side.

"Half sister. And to call attention to that fact is unseemly and casts your father in a poor light."

"*Our* father."

Pru pressed her full lips in a tight line, a clear indication she was losing patience. "Must you be so obstinate? If you're trying to make a new start, Edwina, why carry old baggage along?"

"Old baggage?" Edwina gave her a look of haughty disbelief.

"Even though you're twenty-seven and an *entire* year older than me, *Sister*, I have never considered you '*baggage*.'"

Waving that aside, Pru went on in the same low voice. "There is no need to bandy it about that your father—"

"*Our* father. Who adored *your* mother. As well he should." Edwina was growing weary of this endless argument. Back home, Pru's parentage had been common knowledge. Everyone at Rose Hill had loved Ester, who had taken on the role of Edwina's mammy as soon as it had become apparent that Pricilla Whitney was incapable of caring for her own child. Had he been able, Charles Whitney would have gladly married Pru's mother; as it was, he had been utterly devoted to her until the night the Yankees had swept through Sycamore Parish, leaving death and destruction in their wake.

In truth, Edwina had loved Pru's mother more than her own.

Her gaze dropped to the fine, pale web of scars marring the brown skin that showed between the cuff and glove on Pru's right wrist. Other scars, hidden by the long sleeve of her gray bombazine, stretched up her right arm and halfway across her chest and back. Burn scars, given to her by Edwina's mother when Pru had tried to protect her little sister.

Edwina had scars, too, although other than a few pale stripes across her back, they were of a more subtle kind, the kind that festered in the soul and left behind invisible wounds of doubt and guilt and distrust.

She owed Pru her sanity, if not her life. And she loved her for it.

"Be that as it may," Pru went on, regaining Edwina's attention, "races don't mix. It's against the laws of man and God, and you know it."

"Here we go again." Edwina faked a yawn behind her gloved hand. "If reason fails, bring out the Scriptures."

"Edwina!"

"Well, really, Pru. If it's true that white and black shouldn't mix, you would be a drooling, cross-eyed hunchback with an extra ear. Instead you're beautiful."

Pru snorted. "Except for the hair and nose."

"Not as bad as the wart on my elbow," Edwina chimed in. "And my less-than-ample bosom and—"

A soft, feminine chuckle interrupted Edwina's self-deprecation. Looking past Pru, she saw the blond lady across the aisle was smiling at them. Edwina had seen the smartly dressed young woman several times over the last days, nearly always seated with another young, attractive lady toward the rear of the coach. But today, after the train had stopped in Santa Lucia to fill the tender with water, both women had moved to the vacant bench across the aisle from Pru.

"Are you truly arguing about which of you is less attractive?" the woman asked, her green eyes dancing with amusement. Beautiful eyes, with a slight upward tilt at the outside corners that might have hinted at wide-eyed innocence if not for the hard knowledge behind the knowing smile. A Yankee, by her accent. Poor thing. No wonder she seemed jaded.

Before Edwina could respond to the comment, the other woman, seated next to the window, looked over with a wide smile. Where the blond had shown a worldly-wise weariness beneath her cool green eyes, this auburn-haired lady seemed without artifice. An ingenuous, dimpled smile complemented intense chocolate brown eyes that sparkled with such life and intelligence Edwina couldn't help but smile back. "You are both too beautiful by half," the woman said in a clipped English accent. "Your bone structure is superb, both of you. And I assure you, I would know."

Edwina wasn't sure what to make of that. Usually, any compliments she received—mostly from men—involved her magnolia skin, which always sounded a bit sickly to her—or her glorious hair, which she thought was abysmally average, ranging from mouse brown to light brown, depending on how many lemons were available—and her soulful blue eyes, which were admittedly her best feature and the exact shade of the early spring forget-me-nots that had bloomed along the garden wall back home.

How sad that they, and the wall, and all the handsome young men with their pretty compliments were gone forever.

"Excuse me for intruding." The blond woman held out a hand encased in a finely sewn white kid glove. "I'm Lucinda Hathaway."

"Edwina Ladoux . . . Brodie." Leaning past Pru to take the proffered hand, she noted the gold ear bobs, the fine fabric of the blond's traveling cloak, the shiny button-top boots planted protectively against an expensive leather valise stowed under her seat. Even though Edwina had supported herself and Pru as a seamstress—barely—and was skilled at refitting made-over dresses to look stylish, she couldn't help but feel dowdy in comparison to this pretty woman. "And this is, Prudence, my—"

"Traveling companion," Pru cut in, ignoring Edwina's sharp look. "So pleased to meet you."

"Madeline Wallace, but I prefer Maddie," the auburn-haired woman chimed in with a wave in Edwina's and Pru's direction. She wore no gloves, and a thick signet ring was visible on her left hand.

"You're married?" Edwina was taken aback by the notion that a married woman would be traveling alone if she didn't have to. Then realizing how rude that sounded, she quickly added, "I saw your ring."

Maddie held up her hand, palm out. She studied the thick gold band for a moment, then shrugged. "I suppose I am married, although I haven't heard from Angus in over three years. Perhaps he's dead." A brief flash of distress at that startling announcement, then she let her hand fall back into her lap and smiled. "He's Scottish," she clarified, which clarified nothing. "A soldier. I couldn't bear to stay another day with his family—they have low regard for the English, you know, and little hesitation in showing it—so I left."

"Good girl," Lucinda murmured.

"Left?" Edwina parroted, shocked by the notion of a woman simply heading off on her own to a foreign country just because she didn't like living with her husband's family.

"I'm an expeditionary photographer. A tintypist, really, specializing in *cartes de visite*." Maddie smiled as if that explained everything, which it didn't. "The *Illustrated London News* is paying me to capture the American West from a woman's perspective. Isn't that grand?"

It was unbelievable. A female photographer? Edwina couldn't imagine such a thing. It had taken all her courage to travel a thousand miles, yet this tiny woman had taken on a man's occupation and crossed an ocean to an unknown country. How daring. And terrifying. And admirable.

"And you?" Lucinda inquired, jarring Edwina back to the conversation. "Do you live in this area?"

Edwina blinked at her, wondering how to answer. "Yes. I mean, I plan to. That is to say, I will. Soon."

"She's traveling to meet her husband," Pru piped up in an attempt to translate Edwina's garbled response.

"How nice." Lucinda's voice carried a noticeable lack of enthusiasm.

"Not really."

"Oh, dear," Pru murmured.

The two women across the aisle stared at her with brows raised and expectant expressions, so Edwina felt compelled to explain. "I've never met him, you see. We married in a proxy ceremony."

A moment of awkward, if not stunned, silence. A pitying look came into Lucinda's eyes, but Maddie clapped her hands in delight. "A mail-order bride! How perfect! How utterly western! You shall be my first subject! Won't that be delightful?"

Delightful in a ghoulish, horrifying way, Edwina thought, not sure she wanted her misery captured on tintype for all time.

That afternoon, when the wagon transporting the passengers rolled to a muddy stop outside the hotel, Edwina decided that if Heartbreak Creek was an example of divine intervention on her behalf, then God was either extremely angry with her or had a macabre sense of humor.

But she still offered up a grateful prayer of thanks that no tall, dark-haired, unsmiling man rushed forward to greet her.

"Oh, my," Maddie breathed, eyes sparkling with enthusiasm as she peered over the side rails. "I could take photographs here for a month."

"If we live that long," Lucinda muttered. Clutching her leather valise in one hand and raising her skirts with the other—much to the glee of three reprobates grinning from the doorway of the Red Eye Saloon next door to the hotel—she gingerly stepped out of the wagon, onto the mounting block, then up onto the boardwalk. With a look of distaste, she dropped her skirt and looked around. "Two weeks. Here. Surely they're jesting."

Edwina climbed up onto the boardwalk beside her, followed by Maddie, then Prudence. Moving aside to make room for the other passengers clambering out of the wagon, the four women studied the town.

It was a dismal place.

Situated at the bottom of a steep-sided canyon, the town was a rat's nest of unpainted plank-sided buildings, sagging tents, dilapidated sheds, and lean-tos, all sandwiched between a flooded creek and a single muddy dunghill of a street. And the crowning glory, perched on the rocky hillside north of the wretched town, was a sprawling, many-scaffolded edifice that looked more like a monstrous spider poised to strike than a working mine. The entire town had a haphazard, unfinished feel to it, like a collection of random afterthoughts thrown together by a confused mind.

And yet, Edwina realized, looking around a second time, if one looked beyond the eyesore of the mine, and the squalor and taint of decay that seemed to hang in the air like stale wood smoke, there was astounding beauty to be seen. Tall conifers rising a hundred feet. Stark cliffs sheened by cascading waterfalls winding down the rock face like frothy ribbons. High, white-capped peaks cutting a jagged edge against a cloudless blue sky. It was savage and mysterious . . . but it was also blessedly free of the ravages of war, and for that reason more than any other, Edwina liked it.

"I wonder what they mine?" Maddie asked, squinting up at the sprawling hillside monstrosity.

"Nothing lucrative," Lucinda murmured, eyeing the ill-kempt, wide-eyed gawkers now spilling out of the saloon to get a better look at the ladies. "This place is one step from being a ghost town."

"A ghost town!" Maddie fairly glowed with excitement. "Two weeks won't be long enough to do justice to this marvelous place. And look at those faces! Each one tells a story. I can't wait to get to work."

"Then you'd best start unpacking," Lucinda advised, eyeing the boxes of photography equipment crowding the boardwalk.

Prudence nudged Edwina's arm and nodded to where the conductor was crossing names off a list as the other passengers filed into the hotel. "Let's get settled."

The Heartbreak Creek Hotel might have been—for a month or two, anyway—a thriving place. But years of neglect had reduced it to a bedraggled, rickety old dowager, barely clinging to the threadbare remnants of her brief glory. Sun-faded drapes, scuffed wainscoting against peeling wallpaper, once-lovely oil sconces now caked with soot and dust. Even the air that met them when they stepped through the open double doors smelled musty, laced with the lingering scents of stale cooking odors, tobacco smoke, and moldy carpets.

As they waited their turn before the conductor, Edwina scanned the lobby. Directly across from the entry doors was a high paneled counter that showed remarkable, if grimy, workmanship, manned by a harried elderly clerk passing out brass keys as the passengers signed in. Beside the counter rose a steep staircase that led to a banistered mezzanine off which doors into the upstairs rooms opened. To the right of the entry, an archway opened into a dining area, now deserted in the midafternoon lull, while to the left stood a closed door that led, judging by the tinkling piano music and loud voices, directly into the reprobates' saloon.

"She with you?" a voice asked.

Turning, Edwina found the conductor frowning at her, his small, faded blue eyes flicking to Pru, who stood slightly behind her. Edwina read disapproval in his expression and felt her ire rise. "She is."

The conductor's lips thinned beneath his bushy gray mustache. "You'll have to share a room. That all right by you?"

"Of course it's all right." Edwina started to add, *and why wouldn't it be, you pinhead?* when a sharp tug on the back of her coat choked off the angry retort. Pru hated scenes.

The conductor licked the tip of his stubby pencil and squinted at his list. "Names?"

"Edwina Ladoux . . . Brodie. And this lovely lady with me"—ignoring her sister's warning glare, Edwina swept a hand in her direction—"is my—" Another jerk almost pulled her backward. Before she could recover, Pru stepped forward to say, "Maid. Prudence Lincoln, sir."

While Edwina coughed, Pru accepted their room assignment, nodded her thanks, and shoved Edwina on into the lobby, where the front desk clerk was directing passengers to their rooms.

"You almost choked me," Edwina accused, rubbing her throat.

"Hush. People are looking."

"At my vicious *maid*, no doubt."

"Welcome, ladies. I'm Yancey." Showing stained teeth—what few were left, anyway—in a broad smile, the hotel clerk, a grizzled old man with eyebrows as fat as white caterpillars, beckoned them forward. "Room number?"

Before Pru could answer, Lucinda stepped past them and up to the counter. "Room twenty." Setting her valise on the floor, she gave Pru and Edwina an apologetic smile. "I told the conductor we would share. I hope you don't mind. It'll be safer," she added in a whisper. Then without waiting for a response, she turned back to the slack-faced clerk, plucked the pen from its holder, dipped it in the inkwell, and smiled sweetly. "Where shall I sign?"

"Twenty?" The old man was clearly aghast. "But that—that's the Presidential Suite!"

"So I've been told."

"But you're not the president."

"Alas, no." Turning the full force of those dazzling green eyes on the befuddled Yancey, Lucinda leaned closer to whisper, "But Uncle insisted I take it if I ever came to Heartbreak Creek. Will that be a problem?"

"Goddamn."

Apparently, that meant it wasn't. After ordering a freckled boy to take fresh linens and water to "the big suite," he reverently placed the key in Lucinda's gloved hand and bowed them toward the stairs. "Last room at the end of the hall, ladies. The boy is setting it up now."

As they headed toward the staircase, Edwina gave Lucinda a wondering look. "Are you really Grant's niece?"

"Grant? Who said I was Grant's niece?"

"But, I thought . . . you mean, you're not?"

Lucinda laughed. "That old drunk?"

Not much of an answer, but apparently all Lucinda was willing to give. As they trooped up the stairs, Edwina mused that there were a lot of unanswered questions about Lucinda, not the least of which was what was in that valise that she guarded so protectively. Edwina sensed that like her, Lucinda had been through hard times and devastating loss. But Lucinda had chosen to fight back, while Edwina had chosen to run.

But, really, what choice had she? Raised in the lap of luxury without a care beyond what to wear to the next ball, Edwina barely knew how to survive. Oh, certainly she had skills—dancing, flirting, performing parlor tricks like finding water with willow sticks or playing the piano blindfolded—but that hardly put food on the table. Other than her meager sewing income—which Pru augmented with sales from their vegetable garden and the occasional household position that came her way—the only thing that had kept them going through the last hard years was hope. But after five years of the excesses of the Reconstruction, that was gone, too. Now all that remained of her past was a weed-choked cotton plantation sold for back taxes, her father's watch, and a graveyard full of new markers.

The South she loved was no more. She had realized that the day Pru had been spat upon by a white man just because of her dark skin, while she, a white woman, had been vilified for sharing blood with a woman of color.

No, she wasn't running away. She just had no reason to stay.

As they neared their room at the end of the landing, the door swung open and the freckled boy darted out. "All set up, ma'ams. You need anything, just yell over the banister to Yancey." Then he was off at a run down the hall.

"Set up" meant tattered linens were stacked on the unmade beds in each of the two bedrooms opening off the sitting area, and a pitcher of cold water sat on the bureau. Edwina peered down into its murky depths. "Is this the water we're not supposed to drink?"

"I'll stick with brandy," Lucinda muttered, carrying her valise into the bedroom on the left.

Maddie stopped beside the pitcher, took a look, and shuddered. "It looks used. How vexing."

"I wonder what's wrong with it?" This whole water thing confused Edwina. "With a creek running right through the middle of town and all those waterfalls streaming down the slopes, how could the water be so bad?"

"Probably the mine," Pru said as she hung her coat on a hook beside the door. "They often use harsh chemicals to leach gold or silver from the raw ore. If it seeps back into the ground, it can taint the entire water table."

Edwina turned to stare at her. "How do you know these things?"

"I read."

"About mining practices?" Edwina shouldn't have been surprised. Her sister took in information like a starving person gobbled up food. But mining practices? "Why would you read about mining practices?"

"Why wouldn't I?" As she spoke, Pru set herself to rights, straightening her sleeves, brushing her skirts, running a hand over her tightly pinned hair. "I'm only guessing, of course. But since the mine is upriver from the town, and I did see some sluices and a thick canvas pipe running down from one of those waterfalls to what I assume is a concentrator, I can only deduce the water is being used to leach out unwanted chemicals." She paused in thought, one long, graceful finger gently tapping her full lower lip. "Or maybe it's for a water cannon. I'll have to check."

"Oh, please do!" Shaking her head, Edwina walked into the bedroom she was to share with Pru.

An hour later, their valises were unpacked, their beds made, and they were as refreshed as four women could be, sharing one pitcher of cold water between them.

"We're famished," Lucinda announced, walking into the sitting room with her valise in her hand and Maddie on her heels. "Shall we brave the cooking in this wretched place and go down to the dining room?"

"Dare we?" Edwina asked.

Pru straightened her collar and checked her buttons. "I'm willing."

"Excellent." Swinging open the door, Lucinda motioned the other ladies into the hallway, stepped out after them, and locked the door. "And while we eat," she said, following them down the stairs, "Edwina can tell us all about her new husband, and Maddie can tell us about her errant husband, and Pru can tell us what she hopes to do with all that astounding book learning."

And perhaps while we're at it, Edwina added silently, *you'll tell us what you have in that valise you guard like stolen treasure.*

FROM AWARD-WINNING AUTHOR

KAKI WARNER

Where the Horses Run

The Heroes of Heartbreak Creek

Wounded in body and spirit after a shootout, Rayford
Jessup leaves his career as a lawman and uses his gift
with damaged horses to bring meaning to his solitary
life. Hired by a Scotsman in Heartbreak Creek to purchase thoroughbreds, he travels to England, unaware
that a traumatized horse and a beautiful Englishwoman
will change his life forever...

PRAISE FOR *WHERE THE HORSES RUN*

"A compelling, radiantly written romance."
—*Library Journal*

**"This beautifully rendered love story is tough and
tender—just what Warner's fans have come
to expect from this gifted storyteller."**
—*RT Book Reviews*

facebook.com/kakiwarner
facebook.com/LoveAlwaysBooks
penguin.com

**BERKLEY
SENSATION** | Penguin
Random
House

M1645T0215